A WIZARD'S WAR AND OTHER STORIES

TALES OF THE THREE WORLDS

IAN IRVINE

SANTHENAR PRESS

A Wizard's War and Other Stories

Tales of the Three Worlds

Santhenar Press

National Library of Australia Cataloguing in Publication data:

Irvine, Ian, 1950- A Wizard's War and Other Stories

ISBN 978-0-6482854-3-4

ISBN (Hardcover) 978-0-6482854-2-7

AUTHOR'S NOTE

These stories are set in my Three Worlds epic fantasy sequence, which has sold over a million copies. The sequence comprises 13 published novels from *The View from the Mirror* quartet, *The Well of Echoes* quartet, the *Song of the Tears* trilogy and the first two books of The Gates of Good and Evil quartet (the sequel to *The View from the Mirror*). All these titles are available in print, ebook and audiobook formats worldwide.

The remaining two books of *The Gates of Good and Evil* will be published in 2019-2020.

STORY I

THE PRICE OF FREEDOM

1

This short story is from the Distant Past, more than 3,900 years before the events told in The View from the Mirror *(see Timeline of the Three Worlds, on my website). It portrays one of the most important moments in the Histories of the Three Worlds – the first meeting of Rulke, the greatest of all the Charon, and the young, brilliant but troubled Tensor.*

The outcome of that meeting will echo down the ages.

Someone was pounding on the curved outer door of Tensor's tiny house. 'Layaley! Dreadful news!'

Beside him, Tensor heard Layaley's eyes flick open. It was midnight and as black as a Charon's heart.

'What does she want now?' she groaned.

He slid out of bed and conjured a glimmer from a fingertip. 'I'll go.'

'It's all right. Nuliam is *my* sister.'

Layaley rose, rubbing her eyes. Tensor had a few seconds to admire her full figure before she swathed it in a midnight-blue robe. He brightened his finger light and went with her.

Nuliam, a big, fleshy woman with pitch-dark eyes and a diagonal streak of white in her short hair, was panting as if she had run all the way up the hill. Her sweat had an acrid, offensive tang that matched her personality.

She looked him up and down, contemptuously. No man was good enough for her little sister, least of all Tensor. He was too poor, his family too insignificant and, worst of all, he was a common artisan, a worker in metal and stone. No one in her family worked with their hands.

Nuliam had done everything possible to separate him and Layaley, and when that had failed she had set out to undermine him in her eyes.

'What is it?' he said with frosty politeness.

She barged past. 'Layaley, there's word from Santhenar. Bad word! Rulke wants more.'

'More what?' said Layaley.

'More *thralls*. More of us to die uselessly in his service.'

'You'd better come through.'

Nuliam inspected Tensor's little house, which he had built himself in the shape of a cluster of three soap bubbles, and curled her lip. In the azure-tinted galley he filled a cubic pot with water, spread his remarkably long Aachim fingers around the sides and subvocalised, *Boil!* The water boiled. He tossed in a pinch of shredded red spice-bark, crushed four blue pepperberries, finely chopped a finger of black ginger root and stirred everything in, then indicated the oval chairs.

She sat, rubbing the faint crest on the top of her head. Layaley conjured three cups from their hooks, strained the deep purple tea into them and put a bowl of mushroom bread on the table. Tensor dressed swiftly.

Fifty years had passed since Rulke, the greatest of that superhuman species, the Charon, had made a portal from Aachan to the world of Santhenar, and passed through in furious pursuit of Shuthdar and the golden flute he had made for Rulke, then stolen. Kandor had gone with him, and they had also taken a hundred Aachim thralls.

Fifty years, and in all that time there had been no word; no hint that any of them had survived. The people of Santhenar, who called themselves *old humans*, had a pathetically short lifespan, averaging only seventy years, but they numbered millions and were very warlike. It had been assumed that Rulke, and everyone who had gone with him, had been dead for decades.

Tensor sat in the third chair, studying the two women. They were different in every way. His gentle Layaley had a sweet, oval face and large amber eyes; the anger that burned in Nuliam was absent in her.

'Yalkara has abducted another hundred and twenty of our people,' said Nuliam to her sister, 'and is gathering supplies.'

Tensor shivered. In some respects, Yalkara was worse than Rulke; she was hard, driven and implacable. 'You mentioned word from Rulke?'

Nuliam grimaced, as if the very question was impertinent. 'He hasn't found any trace of Shuthdar or the golden flute, and most of his thralls are dead from disease or conflict with the people of Santhenar.'

'And perhaps from desertion,' said Layaley.

'We can hope,' said Tensor.

'Apparently Rulke has been trying to send a message back for years,' said Nuliam, 'but has only now succeeded. And Yalkara has found a way to carry *objects* through a portal – this time everyone won't end up on Santhenar naked and unarmed.'

'If objects couldn't be carried through a portal,' said Layaley, 'how did Shuthdar escape with the golden flute?'

'Since it can create portals, it carries itself.'

'This is unbearable!' Tensor banged down his cup and rose, six feet six of frustration and bitterness. 'Before the Charon stole our world, we had a great civilisation.'

'We still do,' said Layaley.

'Yet they control our lives. There has to be a way to bring them down.'

'We've been searching for a way for six centuries,' said Nuliam, as if he was an idiot.

Tensor peered out a porthole into darkness. The Charon's sentinel devices were everywhere out there – watching, controlling, punishing. 'How can so few Charon hold a hundred thousand of us in thrall?'

'A mere hundred took our world from us,' said Layaley. '*The Hundred* – led by Rulke.'

'In a few hours Yalkara will have made a portal and she'll be gone. If only there were a way ...'

'What about your gift?'

He frowned at her. 'What gift?'

'The outgift Master Shaper Aoife gave you when you completed your metalsmith training.'

Nuliam curled her lip. Tensor suppressed the urge to order her out and forced his mind back sixty years, to the time when he had been a lad. Sixty years was the blink of an eye to an Aachim, who might live a thousand years and more; he was eighty-six now and still a very young man.

'The Mirror of Aachan, Aoife called it,' he said thoughtfully. 'I was young and proud, delighting in my mastery of my trade. I felt as though the world lay at my feet ...'

'But the Charon's shadow lay over us,' said Layaley.

'It *burns* me!'

'Yet you've done nothing about it,' Nuliam said waspishly. 'What is this mirror?'

'Aoife said it was an entirely new kind of *seeing* device,' said Tensor. 'One that could be used to look from place to place, and even find things that had been lost or hidden – if the user was strong and skilled enough.'

'I sometimes wondered if she had *crafted* you,' said Layaley, 'as carefully as she shaped the Mirror of Aachan.'

'To what purpose?'

'As a weapon against the enemy.'

Tensor snorted. And yet, the idea had a certain appeal. He was stronger than any Aachim he knew, and a better craftsman than most. And he would soon be a master of the Secret Art. 'She once said I could be the one to free us from the yoke of the Charon ...'

Their thraldom was unbearable and something had to be done. And if he could, it would prove his worth to Nuliam. Not that he cared what she thought, but for Layaley's sake –

'Where is this *marvellous* mirror?' said Nuliam with a knowing smile.

He went into his storeroom and, after a hunt through chests and boxes, found Aoife's outgift. At the table, he unfastened the white cords and folded back the pale yellow, silken wrappings. The faintest scent, like a musky rose, drifted up, and it took him back sixty years in an instant, to the insecure, over-eager youth he had been.

The Mirror of Aachan was made from polished black metal, with a narrow raised frame of the same material. Being corrosion-proof and immensely hard, it was as perfect as the day Master Shaper Aoife had made it.

'Doesn't look anything special,' said Nuliam.

Layaley frowned at her. 'Don't do the enemy's work for them.' She met Tensor's eyes, smiling dreamily. 'That day, it was as though Aoife had cut the bonds that bound you.'

'In that hour I felt that I could do anything I set my mind to,' said Tensor.

'Yet sixty years later your *brilliant* promise is unfulfilled,' sneered Nuliam. 'You must feel such a failure.'

It hurt but he was not going to give her the pleasure of showing it. He took the mirror in both hands and felt an overwhelming surge of self-confidence; he was almost drunk on it.

'It's ... as if the enemy's control has slipped,' he said wonderingly.

'Maybe you *do* have a destiny,' Nuliam said slyly. 'But dare you reach for it?'

If only the Aachim could be free again, and he could be the hero and architect of their renascence. He would give anything for that. 'To what purpose?' said Tensor.

She thrived on conflict and he wasn't giving her one. Disagreement and indecision were the Aachim's great weaknesses; it was why the Hundred had beaten them so easily.

'With the mirror you could find all the enemy's local sentinels,' said Nuliam, 'and destroy them.'

'That would bring the Charon down on us in minutes.'

She sat back, smiling. 'You talk like a giant, yet act like a pygmy.'

He cracked. 'Get out!'

Layaley shot to her feet and reached out to him. 'Tensor, please don't speak to my sister like that.'

'Nuliam doesn't give a fig for our servitude. She'd sooner fight me than the enemy.'

Layaley scowled at them both. 'Well, *I* care. If you've got an idea, I want to hear it.'

'I do,' said Tensor, for a plan had surfaced, 'but I've got to be sure Nuliam can be trusted.'

'You question *my* quality?' cried Nuliam, her face going purple.

'You carp and carp, yet offer nothing.'

She stood up, furiously, then sat down again. 'I'm listening. Make it good!'

'What are you thinking about, Tensor?' said Layaley.

Before putting the mirror aside fifty years ago, he had often used it to *see*. First locally, but later, as his control grew, to places hundreds of miles away across Aachan. He was far stronger now, in will and in mancery, and a dazzling possibility had crystallised.

'The greatest prize of all,' he said softly. '*A free Aachan.*'

Layaley gave a little start, and there was such yearning in her eyes that tears pricked his own. How he wanted to give it to her.

Nuliam looked grudgingly interested. 'The enemy's sentinels are alert to the least hint of rebellion.'

'Only on Aachan,' said Tensor.

'What are you saying?' said Layaley.

'Yalkara is about to create a portal to Santhenar.'

'And the Charon won't let you get within a league of it,' said Nuliam.

'I don't need to,' said Tensor.

Layaley jumped up and checked the outside door, then the portholes. As she sat again, shivering, her robe gaped at the front. Tensor averted his eyes. Not even her luscious figure could be allowed to divert him now.

'Spit it out,' said Nuliam, pursing her hard-edged lips.

'One thing my mirror shows very well is *power*,' said Tensor.

'You mean the Secret Art?' said Layaley.

'With the mirror, I should be able to see exactly how Yalkara makes the portal.'

'You're hoping to make it go wrong?' said Nuliam, frowning. 'And destroy her as she goes through?'

'That would destroy the Aachim thralls she takes with her,' said Tensor. 'I want to make a duplicate portal, then lead a force of Aachim to Santhenar – on the greatest adventure of all.'

'How many?'

'Two hundred.'

Nuliam's breath hissed between her square teeth. 'What for?'

'No Aachim knows how to make a portal.'

'Get to the point.'

'Therefore the enemy can't imagine that we could attack them on Santhenar. But with the Mirror of Aachan I can locate Yalkara, Kandor and Rulke there – and we can ambush them.'

Nuliam's eyes gleamed. 'And once they're dead?'

Tensor stood up, quivering with passion. His time had come. 'I'll reopen Yalkara's portal and we'll storm back to Aachan. With the Aachim she's taking, and our troop, we'll number three hundred. Enough to take the leaders of the Hundred by surprise – *and put them down*.'

'Assuming your portal works.'

'Why wouldn't it? I'm planning to copy Yalkara's, in every detail.'

'And you think your mancery is good enough?' Nuliam eyed him shrewdly.

'I don't like it,' said Layaley. 'We don't know anything about portals.'

'We never can, save by making one,' said Tensor.

'You'd be risking everything on a form of the Secret Art we don't understand. At least make a trial portal first. Then, if it goes wrong –'

'There isn't time. Everything depends on taking Rulke, Kandor and Yalkara by surprise, soon after she reaches Santhenar.' He reached out to her. 'Layaley, this chance may never come again.'

'What if the enemy's sentinels detect your portal?'

Tensor looked up and Nuliam's hard eyes were on him.

'Well?' she said.

'Before any Charon can get here to investigate, we'll be gone.'

'But they'll go after our families,' said Layaley.

'It'll take them days to discover who's missing, and who's involved. But we'll come storming back through Yalkara's portal within hours. We'll kill the Charon leaders, then mobilise a hundred thousand Aachim to smash the sentinels and hunt the rest of the Hundred down.'

'It's a bold plan,' said Nuliam. '*If it goes perfectly*. But –'

'What?' snapped Tensor, expecting her to strike another low blow.

'The Charon came from the terrible void between the worlds, where every creature has to fight for existence, every second of their lives.' She paused.

Tensor thought he knew where this was going.

'They've been blooded in a thousand conflicts,' Nuliam continued, 'while we ...'

'Aren't allowed training with any kind of weaponry,' said Layaley. 'How can we hope to beat them, Tensor?'

Having been born hundreds of years after the bloody takeover of Aachan, he had rarely seen violence worse than a punch in the nose. Few Aachim had. But he had already thought of that.

'With overwhelming numbers. From ambush,' he said.

'It'll be bloody.'

'I know,' said Tensor. 'That's why I'll be leading the attack.'

'You'll be killed,' Layaley whispered.

'We have to take this chance – *for our freedom!*'

Layaley was on the front edge of her chair, her gold-flecked brown eyes searching his. He knew she wanted it; they had often talked about overthrowing the enemy, though always with the air of hopelessness that had characterised his people ever since the Hundred had robbed them of their world.

But Nuliam was older and harder. Only cold logic could convince her.

'You know the price of failure for those who lead a rebellion,' said Nuliam.

Tensor had avoided thinking about that, but he must. 'The Charon would put everyone in my family, and yours, to death.'

'And all our relatives, down to our third cousins. Then they would utterly erase our family Histories; it would be as though we had never existed.'

'They wouldn't!' cried Layaley.

'They did it twice, in the early days,' said Nuliam.

Needles speared Tensor's heart. Could the prize for success – freedom and their world back – outweigh the price of failure? Did he have the right to risk the lives of relatives who would never be consulted? Children too young to give consent? The thought almost broke him, and his resolve wavered.

But the lure of freedom was overpowering. 'This chance may never come again,' he said. 'Are you with me?'

'Not without seeing the portal,' said Nuliam.

'Yalkara won't create it until she has to.'

'Why not?'

'It takes colossal mancery to make a portal between worlds – and even more to hold it open.'

'I'm not risking a single life without seeing her portal – and yours.'

'I'm not asking you to. But the moment you agree –'

'If I do.'

'If you do, we have to be ready to go at once. We'll need two hundred volunteers.'

'Yes,' said Nuliam. 'All right.'

'Gather your best people, surreptitiously, and I'll gather mine. You know how to evade the sentinels?'

'Yes.'

'The portal requires a suitable site; a special place that enhances mancery.' Tensor thought for a moment. 'Twin Shards!'

'Good choice,' said Nuliam.

'We've got to move fast. We'll gather there in ... is three hours long enough for you to get everyone together?'

'Yes.'

'The moment Yalkara begins her portal, I'll show you, via the Mirror of Aachan. If you agree the risk is worth it, I'll copy her portal ...'

'If you can,' said Nuliam. 'All right.'

2

Everyone gathered at Twin Shards, a small saddle-shaped hill a league and a half from Tensor's house, at four-thirty in the morning. Aachan's huge orange moon hung low in the sky, casting long shadows across the coarse grey grass and the patches of sulphur-coloured snow. In the shadows, luminous night blossoms glowed like circles of fireflies. Ten yards to either side, the rocky points of the saddle stuck up like two vertical clusters of black glass shards.

Tensor had three lieutenants. Selial, silver-blonde, grey-eyed and extraordinarily beautiful, was the best of them. She was decent, clever and reliable, but small and not physically strong. Nuliam was very strong and, he thought grudgingly, utterly reliable, but too abrasive to be a good leader. Pitlis, a tall, clumsy beanpole of a man, was respected because of his genius as an architect, though he was awkward with people and, having such a high opinion of himself, reluctant to listen to advice or change a plan, no matter how wrong it turned out to be.

Tensor watched the volunteers come together, one hundred and eighty-one young men and women. Not as many as he had wanted, but enough. The Charon did not allow the Aachim to bear arms but, for masters of metal-working as many were, arms were quickly made, and they all bore swords, knives, helmets and chest armour.

They were full of youthful bravado, but his own exhilaration had faded and his armpits were drenched in sweat. There were many ways his plan could fail, and though he had not yet fathered children, Tensor had two brothers and a sister, aunts and uncles and cousins, and three little nieces. Every one of his family – even irascible old Uncle Logor – was precious to him. If this went wrong they would die very unpleasantly. What gave him the right to risk their lives?

An image flashed into his inner eye: their bloody bodies, arranged in a line from oldest to youngest with his three little nieces last. Tensor doubled over, feeling the pain, the loss. Every instinct was screaming: pull out, *now*.

His stomach heaved and he threw up on the grass. He wiped his mouth and looked around furtively. Nuliam was watching, judging him and finding him wanting. He had to regain control of himself; if he started to believe in failure it would become self-fulfilling.

Layaley slipped up beside him and took his hand. In the lurid moonlight, her face was a sickly yellow. 'Are you all right?'

'Just nerves,' he said.

'If this goes wrong –' she whispered.

'It won't. Trust me.'

'What if the portal goes astray? You've never made one before; how can you be sure you can make one *to another world*? What if you can't see all the steps Yalkara uses to make her portal? Or she detects yours?'

He gripped her shoulder, crushingly hard. If he did not stop her, self-doubt would defeat him. He had to present a shell of utter certainty to everyone – including himself.

'If I think it's gone wrong, I'll close it. But we have to plan for success, not failure. *For our freedom, Layaley!*'

Her eyes were huge and wet. 'But ... aunt Sissey's twin boys, Lan and Nurie, are only three ... I can't bear to think ...'

Several people were staring at them now. 'Stop it!' he whispered. 'If the others begin to doubt, we *will* fail.'

'The price is too high, Tensor. Think of the children.'

'I never stop thinking about them, growing up in thrall with no hope of ever escaping it. I'm doing this for the children – and *their* children.'

'Even if it kills them?'

It was like a punch in the mouth. 'How can you say that, *to me*?' he hissed.

'You're going ahead, whatever I say,' she said in a dead voice.

'It's too late to turn back now,' said Tensor.

'No, it's not.'

'Freedom is everything, Layaley.'

'*Life* is everything. We can wait for our freedom.'

'We can't; we're dying!'

'I can't bear this,' she said, her voice aching.

He had to get her out of here. 'I want you to go home. At least you'll be safe –'
Why had he said such a stupid thing?

'If I go with you, I'll die,' said Layaley. 'If I stay, and you fail, I'll be put to death
with the rest of my family.'

'I'm not going to fail.'

'How can I love such a fool?' she cried. 'I'm going with you. But not in hope – in
despair.'

He turned away, his chest heaving. What if she was right?

But if he pulled out he would be a failure in his own eyes, and in the eyes of all
the volunteers here. He would be a man who dreamed big but acted small. He
would be forever in the Charon's thrall, and Nuliam's relentless contempt would
soon infect Layaley. He would lose her too.

'Say something,' said Layaley.

'If I don't go through with it, I lose everything,' he said. 'Including my self-
respect. And you.'

It was as if he had slapped her across the face. 'Do you truly have so little faith
in me?'

Had he made the biggest mistake of his life? No, if he pulled out Nuliam would
make it her business to destroy him. He stumbled away, knowing that whatever he
did would be wrong. How could the glorious moment have been undermined so
swiftly?

'What's Yalkara doing?' he heard Nuliam say, as if through a fog. 'This has to be
timed precisely.'

She had her hand on the right-hand cluster of shards, which thrust up vertically for three times her own height. In the breeze they made an eerie humming
sound that rasped along his frayed nerves. Tensor raised the mirror. His right hand
had a tremor. He had to get a grip.

'Tensor?' she said sharply.

He wrenched the mirror to his will, forcing it not to reflect, but to *see*. That was
easy enough – he had done it many times. But finding Yalkara was not easy, or safe.
What if she sensed him? He put the fear behind him and looked deeper.

'She's at Skyfall Cleft,' he said.

He eyed the image shown on the mirror. Skyfall Cleft, a bare oval hill seven
leagues away, was topped with a lump of sky-fallen iron, like a single knob on the
spine of a long-dead monster. Long ago the black mass of meteoritic iron, which
stood fifteen feet high and twenty across, had split into two pieces with a three-foot
cleft between them. The rocks below it were streaked rust-red.

Yalkara, a big, statuesque woman, stood at the entrance to the cleft, her long black hair drifting behind her in the breeze. There were armed Charon to either side and, gathered between them like sheep between wolves, a throng of Aachim thralls. The image was too small to make out their faces, though their posture was redolent of despair.

Yalkara raised her arms, like a conductor to an orchestra.

'She's about to form the portal,' said Tensor. 'She's using the cleft as the portal-way.'

He showed Nuliam the image. She studied it for a long time, her thin lips moving as she calculated probabilities. She glanced at her sister, whose lovely face was waxen. Nuliam tapped long fingers into the palm of her other hand.

'All right,' she said. 'Make your portal – *if you can.*'

Layaley staggered and almost fell. 'Why are you doing this, Nuliam?'

'Because we're thralls born of thralls born of thralls,' snapped Nuliam. 'We're dwindling to apathetic shadows of our former selves, dying inside, *and I can't bear it.*'

Layaley let out a small, despairing cry, but Tensor dared not go to her – Yalkara had begun and if he missed a single step his portal would fail. He ran down to the level ground at the centre of the saddle and, holding the mirror in his left hand, copied her first hand movement with his right, in reverse.

He drew on the power of the Secret Art, wishing he had worked harder and become a master. He took as much power as his body could stand, and as it built up in him he grew ever hotter until his face was scarlet and he was running with sweat. He read Yalkara's lips, spoke the first words of the portal spell, then allowed the power to flow out through his fingers to begin forming the portal.

Behind him, Selial, Pitlis and Nuliam were organising the attack force. He could not check on them; it would take all his strength to create the portal and endure the massive flow of power through himself, then hold the portal open long enough for a hundred and eighty-one Aachim to pass through.

Every second mattered now. Once they exited the portal on Santhenar he had to locate Yalkara, Rulke and Kandor quickly, and ambush them at once. Every delay increased the risk that the nearest sentinels would detect the flow of power on Twin Shards and alert the Hundred that their thralls were up to something.

One hundred and eighty-one Aachim against three Charon – the odds seemed absurd. Yet fear of the Charon was bone-deep in his people; it had been ever since the conquest of Aachan.

The lantern-lit air in the iron cleft was shimmering like a rusty mirage; Yalkara's portal was forming. She tossed a handful of green leaves onto the coals of a brazier. Smoke belched up and was drawn forwards in lazy coils and eddies.

Tensor's heart began to race. Her portal was starting to open. He forced the fear down; there wasn't time for it.

A small but ominous flash came from the mirror. He checked it absently, and the hair rose on the back of his neck. One of the enemy's sentinel had detected the massive flow of power he was using. What to do? He only had seconds to decide. Call it off and scatter, praying that everyone would get away, though that seemed unlikely, or complete the portal and go. Both options were fraught but only one offered hope – to keep quiet and go on.

'Get ready,' he said, gesturing behind him.

The murmur of voices died away. The air here was perfectly still now, though the shards were humming in a more nerve-rasping pitch.

At Skyfall Cleft, Yalkara thrust out her right arm and pointed into the cleft. Her long hair whipped backwards, forwards, then the smoke from the brazier streamed into the cleft and through it Tensor saw a lush green landscape, so different from the harsh beauty of Aachan.

He was looking across the void *to another world*. To Santhenar! He choked.

Nuliam elbowed him in the ribs, painfully. 'Get it done!'

He mimicked Yalkara's movements, spoke the last words of her spell and thrust his right arm out, his long fingers pointed directly between the twin shards.

Sweat burst from every pore but evaporated instantly. He felt as though he was melting; the surge of power was burning him on the inside. There came a percussive thud, a blast of wind that stung his eyes, then an oval hole appeared in the air ten feet ahead of him.

Power rushed out of him and Tensor staggered a couple of steps. Now he was so cold that he could hardly draw breath. But it had worked! He had actually made a portal, the first Aachim ever to do so. A portal that cleaved the distance between Aachan and another, far-off world. It was the mightiest mancery of all, far greater than anything he had done before. The first step of his bold plan had paid off, and in that moment he knew he could prevail.

He could win their freedom!

There came a great sigh from the Aachim. Even the greatest doubters believed in him now.

'Well?' he said to Nuliam.

She studied the portal for a long time, in silence. His overstrained muscles began to shudder. Despite his great strength, holding the portal open was exhausting him. Should he tell her about the sentinel? If he did, she would surely call it off – but it was too late for that.

Nuliam turned, weighing his fitness for the task. He forced his muscles to relax.

'Yes,' she sighed, and he saw the grudging respect in her eyes. Respect he had not realised he ached for.

Should he go through first? He took a last look at the mirror. At Skyfall Cleft, Yalkara stood to one side, directing her thralls into the portal. As the first Aachim, a stocky fellow with a prominent bony crest, entered, the green landscape vanished, replaced by churning mist with streaks and flashes of mustard-yellow light.

If she was staying back to maintain control of the portal, he should do the same. Tensor turned side-on so he could see his Aachim. They were the best of his people: young, strong, confident and determined.

All but Layaley, who stood to his left, her face bone white. He felt a surge of resentment. Why, when even her sister agreed, could she not support him at this vital moment? He tried to crush the unworthy thought but it would not go away.

'Go!' he said to his lieutenants.

Pitlis, that awkward beanpole of a man, was at their head. He was not troubled by self-doubt. He strode forwards as if he had built the portal himself, nodding condescendingly to Tensor. It took hold of Pitlis, the green landscape vanished and he was hurled into churning whiteness.

Layaley's eyes met Tensor's; she was terrified. He gestured her aside, his stomach muscles clenching painfully. The beautiful Selial came next. She hesitated for a moment as if weighing him up, then went through. A pair of small, pale-skinned, red-headed twins followed – Inneal and Girlor from Clan Elienor. A clan that had always opposed his own.

The Aachim were passing through at a run now. As each man or woman was drawn in, Tensor's temperature oscillated from sweating to shivering, and his strength drained further.

'Hurry!' he gasped.

Holding the portal open was taking a far greater toll than any mancery he had ever done before. Already aftersickness was weakening him, undermining the focus he had to maintain, for their very survival. Should he have waited until he was stronger? What if he could not hold the portal?

That would be catastrophic; he had to, whatever the cost to himself.

Finally, they had passed through but for himself, Layaley and Nuliam. Tensor's knees were thumping together and he was a haggard, sweating wreck; it took an effort just to stand upright.

The glow of achievement had faded; now he could only see the dangers. As long as the Aachim obeyed unquestioningly, the Charon did not treat them harshly. What more would freedom give them? Could rebellion ever be worth the risk?

Layaley stared at him, frozen-faced. There was a question in her eyes but he could not read it. Should he send her home? He tried to speak but his mouth was so dry that only a croak emerged. She ran, stumbled and fell into the portal. Nuliam hurled herself after her sister.

After a momentary hesitation, tormented by the fear that the mission had already gone wrong, Tensor followed.

As he entered the portal he felt a sickening pain low down, as if two fists had clamped onto his intestines and were wrenching them apart. The organs in his belly thrashed back and forth, then something thumped him hard, driving acid up into his gullet. He fell to his knees and pain shot through his heart, his head, his eyes. What was happening to him? Had he lost control of the portal? He wiped his eyes and saw blood in his tears.

He was alone. Tensor prayed that the others were safely on Santhenar because it was getting harder to hold the portal open. But he must, until he left it – an uncontrollable portal might open anywhere, even inside another object. That would blow the object, and everyone in the portal, to bits in the biggest explosion the world had ever seen.

Someone small whirled past, upside-down in the gloom. Red hair and pale skin – it was Inneal from Clan Elienor. Her face was twisted in terror.

'It's gone wrong!' she cried, and vanished.

Tensor's skin crawled. Many of the people of Clan Elienor were sensitives; had she detected what he could not? Should he call everyone back?

He did not know how. He glanced down at the mirror. Its surface, formerly hard, reflective black metal, was now as shiny and mobile as quicksilver. Images appeared and disappeared in the flow, though they were so blurred he could not make them out.

The mouth of the portal was foggy and it felt as though it was moving in a series of spirals. He focused on the destination, the green landscape of Santhenar, and forced with all his remaining strength.

Through the exit he saw a long green slope. Tensor dived forwards, desperate to get out. He could not hold the portal any longer; it spat him out and he fell six feet onto lush, sweet-smelling grass, unlike any he had seen on barren Aachan.

It was close to sunset. The air was warm, the breeze silky on his sweaty skin and scented by sweet blossoms. Santhenar!

He got up. It took a great effort. Either the gravity was stronger here or the portal had sucked him dry. Holding it open had taken a great toll but passing through had been worse. His limbs had little strength and he was so hungry that his stomach ached.

His gaze was caught by a small, dark moon. Santhenar's moon, far smaller than Aachan's bloated satellite, was mottled purple, red and black. It looked ominous now and would be positively baleful at night time. But they need not be here that long; if he found Yalkara quickly they could do the business within the hour then take her portal back to Aachan.

Tensor realised that, all around him, his people were on their knees, gasping, gagging and vomiting. They had suffered in the portal as much as he had. No, for some it had been worse. Ten yards down the slope a tall young woman was moaning; both her legs were broken. As he searched the slope, he saw several more with broken limbs, and two people throwing up blood.

The picture was similar uphill of him. No, worse. Ulix, a handsome, beardless youth, lay dead with his belly burst open and the intestines protruding. He had not died easily, and there appeared to be more bodies beyond him. Fear sheared through Tensor. Why hadn't he called it off when he had the chance?

He lurched back and forth, checking on his people, looking for one person and not seeing her.

Nuliam ran up. 'Why did I listen to you?' she raged. 'I should have trusted my instincts.'

'You wanted our freedom as much as I did.'

'Not at this price. *Where – are – the – others?*'

'What others?' said Tensor, finding it hard to breathe.

'More than forty are missing.'

Terror drove the breath out of him. 'Layaley?' he choked.

'She's down there.' Nuliam pointed down the slope. 'She's all right.'

Tensor picked Layaley out, standing with a dozen others. He drew a gasping breath. 'Maybe the rest came out on the other side of the hill.'

He saw the hope in Nuliam's eyes; though she hated him, she cared deeply about her people.

With a whipcrack, the mouth of the portal reappeared hundreds of feet above them. It curved around in a figure-eight and, to Tensor's gut-crawling horror, the missing Aachim were flung out in all directions. They arced across the sky and fell, arms and legs flailing, some crying out or screaming, others silent. All knowing they were going to die.

He ran back and forth, holding his arms up, though there was nothing he could do. All those young men and women, the very best of the Aachim, thudded into the ground and lay still.

A great wailing began at the lower end of the slope and spread upwards. People ran to their dead and dying friends, but then it got horribly worse – dead, bloody bodies began to rain down. And halves of bodies; and loose limbs and organs. A woman's head landed beside Tensor; it had black, curling hair and a round, pretty face, though her lips were drawn back from her teeth. Lastly came a terrible rain of blood. The smell was like a shambles – it would live with him all his days.

He doubled over, choking. Had this happened because he had lost control of the portal at the end? But how could so many Aachim have still been inside, long after he had exited it? They should have been out long before him.

Whatever had gone wrong, he had to take the blame. His people had trusted him and, despite his best efforts, he had failed them. He fell to his knees, head bowed. *Why, why?*

'Get up!' said Nuliam. Her fists were clenched, her eyes agate-hard. She blamed him.

The agony rang through him; he could find no way past it. 'I – need a few minutes.'

'The longer we delay, the greater the chance that Yalkara will realise we're here. Or Rulke.'

Tensor tried to stifle a gasp but it burst from him.

'You're terrified of him,' sneered Nuliam.

He got up, every muscle and bone aching, struggling to rally his thoughts. 'Got to locate Charon,' he gasped. 'Ambush them. Lead everyone home –'

'Before the Hundred realise what we've done and start putting our families down,' she said harshly. 'I'll get the survivors ready. Find the enemy.'

Tensor staggered around among the shocked and uncomprehending Aachim. He counted forty-seven dead. Some looked unharmed, while others had been broken in the portal, or the fall. His fear deepened into terror. More than a quarter of his force were dead, without setting eyes on the enemy. Another eleven had broken bones and would have to be left behind, temporarily.

As he approached Layaley she turned towards him, then staggered and a red patch appeared on her middle. Tensor's pain spiked and he ran, knees wobbling, but when he was still ten yards away, she crumpled.

He reached her, and froze, for there was blood on the front of her pants, and on her mouth. He fell to his knees beside her.

'Layaley?' He wiped her mouth. 'What is it?'

She did not open her eyes. 'Bad – portal.'

The breath set solid in his throat. What had he done to her?

Tensor yanked up her shirt. There was an odd bulge on the left side of her belly, low down. He put his hand over it, using a diagnosis spell to sense out the damage. He could not tell what was wrong though it felt bad. He began to work the strongest healing spell he knew, fearing that it would not work in time. Healing was a slow process; it usually took days and often failed, especially with internal injuries where the damage could not be sensed clearly.

'No – use,' she said faintly. 'Burst. Inside.'

An awful chill passed through him. No, she was delirious. 'Nuliam!' he roared.

'Don't – use – mirror,' said Layaley. 'Corrupt.'

'Save your strength.' He stroked her brow, kissed her pale eyelids, then put everything he had into the healing.

'It's twisted,' she said urgently. '*Wrong!*'

Nuliam hurtled down the slope, crying, 'What's the matter?'

'She's bleeding inside,' said Tensor, 'but I can't tell where it's coming from'

Nuliam put her hands beside his; as a healer, she was one of the best. He felt the heat as she drew massive power, trying to stem the bleeding.

Layaley opened her eyes and looked up at him. 'Tensor – must – save my family.'

'I will,' he said, putting his hands over her heart. 'I swear it.'

She shuddered, sighed and lay still.

'No!' wailed Nuliam, drawing so much power from herself that her fingertips began to smoke. 'Come back!'

Tensor took Layaley's hands. This could not be. He checked her pulse, her breath, her pulse again, praying that he was wrong. He put his mouth over hers and breathed into her lungs, then pressed rhythmically down on her heart.

But when he checked again there was no breath, no pulse. She was gone. How could her life have ended so swiftly, so *insignificantly*? He clutched her hands, rocking back and forth, his vision blurred by tears. Nothing mattered any more.

A terrific blow to the ribs knocked him sideways. He looked up dazedly. Nuliam had kicked him.

'Get up, you mewling bastard,' she said, kicking him in the neck and knocking him down. 'She loved you! She trusted you! Yet you forced her to come on this ... *adventure.*'

He got up, his neck and head throbbing. 'I did not force her.'

'Your incompetence killed her.' She spat in his face. 'Make sure her life was worth it.'

He stood up, dazedly, wiping his face. 'What?'

'If my sister's death is in vain,' she said coldly, 'I will hound you to the grave – *and beyond.*'

'She said the mirror was corrupt. She said not to use it.'

'Layaley was dying!'

'She seemed lucid ...' said Tensor. He could not go on. He was shattered, incapable of thought or reason. If the mirror was corrupt, all was lost.

'Stop making excuses, you festering mongrel dog! Aoife made the mirror and she was entirely good and honourable. It can't be corrupt.'

'Unless ... the portal did it.'

'You made the portal. If it corrupted the mirror, it's your fault.'

'If it is,' he said numbly, 'how can I fix it?'

'Find the Charon! Lead us to them! Either they die today – or you do.'

Nuliam kissed Layaley's bloody mouth, folded her arms across her chest, closed her eyes and stalked away, shouting at his lieutenants. Pitlis and Selial called the survivors to order.

3

Tensor stood there, looking down at the only woman he had ever loved. Aching for her. Unable to take it in. Had he killed her through reckless hubris, or because he had lacked the strength to hold the portal? He had to take the blame – everything they had done today had been at his urging.

But Nuliam was right – the only way to make amends was to do what they had come for. He checked the mirror and it looked different, greater, almost alive! The shiny surface was quicksilver in slow, rippling motion. Why would it be corrupt? Aiofe had crafted it especially for him, tailoring it to his strengths. He was its master; even if it had become warped in some way, he could force it to show true.

He wrenched it to his will and saw a series of images: landscapes, towns and villages, isolated houses and manors, and many faces, but they were the native inhabitants of Santhenar.

Then he saw a face he knew almost as well as his own, because the Charon had posted a thousand images of it all across Aachan. It was the most wanted man in two worlds – Shuthdar, the genius metal-smith brought to Aachan sixty years ago by Rulke, by the painful and laborious process of *summoning*, to craft a device that would permit him to travel between the worlds without the perils of using portals.

After years of toil, using all the enchanted red Aachan gold that could be found, Shuthdar had finished the golden flute. It was the most perfect object ever created, and he had loved it too much to give it up. Fifty years ago he had stolen it, opened a way between the worlds and fled back to Santhenar. And the Charon had been hunting him ever since.

They had not found him, *but Tensor had*. He could see Shuthdar, an ugly, gnome-like little man, sitting at a black stone table in a bat-infested cave, playing the flute. If Tensor could take the flute, could he bargain with the Charon for Aachan?

No, Shuthdar was far away and there was no way of getting to him. Stick to the plan. Kill Yalkara, Rulke and Kandor, then go home and attack the Hundred before they understood their danger.

He looked deeper into the mirror and saw Yalkara leading the Aachim through a wrought iron gate into a narrow canyon whose sides rose steep and jagged. She must be going to meet Rulke and Kandor. And the range of hills beyond the gate was the same range he could see to his left. The enemy were only a couple of miles away.

Darkness was beginning to shroud the bodies, though in his inner eye Tensor could see every awful detail. He went up to Nuliam, skirting around the shapes in the grass, even Layaley's. Leaving them on alien soil to be eaten by predators was monstrous, but nothing could be done about it now. Once the three Charon were dead, and the Hundred, he would return and take his people home.

Nuliam swung around as he approached, drawing her knife. The hatred in her eyes seared him.

'I've found Yalkara,' he said.

She seemed to be fighting the urge to bury the blade in him. 'Show – me.'

Keeping well back, he handed her the mirror. She looked into it for a long time. 'How do you know this is a true image?'

'I forced it to show true.'

'And the plan?'

'We split in three squads. Mine will creep down this side of the ridge, and yours down the far side.' He pointed to the valley in the mirror. 'Pitlis's squad will attack through the gate and drive the enemy back onto our blades.'

Her doubt was palpable. But he could also see her desperation to make up, in some small way, for the disaster, so that the dead had not died in vain.

'It can work,' she said after a long deliberation. 'And then we storm home and put the Hundred to the sword.'

The Aachim let out a ragged and unconvincing cheer.

They crept through the dark for twenty minutes, then split up. Tensor still felt drained by the portal and his innards throbbed as if they had been damaged. Why had he survived when so many others had died? Layaley, *Layaley!*

He wrenched his thoughts back to the present. Nothing he had done in his life could prepare him for the ghastly reality of the coming battle – heads cleft open, severed limbs pumping blood, disembowelling and unmanning and every other horrible injury that could be imagined. Within minutes he, who had never struck a blow in anger, would be killing another living human being – or dying in agony. What if he could not face it? What if he ran like a coward?

'Are Nuliam and Pitlis in position?' said Selial, twenty-five minutes later.

Tensor checked the mirror. 'Yes.' He showed her.

'How long until we attack?'

'One minute,' he said breathlessly.

It passed far too quickly. He began to pick his way down the rocky slope. It was dark now but his eyes, used to the gloomier light of Aachan, could see well enough. The Aachim moved noiselessly; it was an art thralls were well practiced in.

Tensor worked his brand new sword up and down in its sheath. None of the Aachim had ever used their weapons, yet they were about to attack the three greatest Charon, who had all fought innumerable battles, and won.

He had to take on the greatest of them all, the legendary Rulke. How could he hope to prevail against such a man? In a few minutes he would be dead like his beautiful Layaley, and so many others.

Tensor stiffened his spine. He had sworn an unbreakable oath. The Charon were but three, against a hundred and twenty. It would only take one well-aimed blow to bring Rulke down.

They reached the bottom of the slope, still in thick scrub. Through it he could see the Charon's camp fire on the valley floor, fifty yards away, and three figures sitting there. He raised his hand. Behind him, everyone stopped while he consulted the mirror and checked on Pitlis and Nuliam again. They were still in place. He could not signal them, but they would hear the roar as his squad attacked.

On the mirror, he saw that the three Charon had laid their arms aside. Rulke had his back turned, but Yalkara and Kandor were facing this way, the firelight reflecting on their faces.

'Now!' Tensor said quietly.

He drew his sword and stormed out onto the valley floor. It wasn't until he was within ten yards of the campsite that he realised something was wrong.

'Hold, hold!' he roared, skidding across the dewy grass. 'Where are they?'

The campfire was blazing; a big pan was perched on the fire and pieces of some dark meat were sizzling. The smell made his mouth water. Another pot was boiling, but the Charon he had seen through the trees were straw-filled dummies.

His squad of forty-one formed a ring around the campfire, staring out into the dark. Without warning, Nizitor, who was to Tensor's left, clutched at his forehead. The tail of a crossbow bolt protruded from his skull, then he crumpled and fell, dead. Two more Aachim to the right fell as well, one with an arrow in the eye, another choking on the missile that had torn through his throat.

Tensor kicked the pot over, dousing the fire, and raced in the direction the bolts had come from. A thickset, dark-visaged Charon was weaving through the trees – Kandor. Tensor bounded at him, swinging his sword. Kandor ducked around the trunk of a small tree and the blade embedded itself inches deep in the wood.

As Tensor wrenched it out, Kandor vanished. Tensor looked over his shoulder and saw a swathe of Aachim fall. How could he fight an enemy he could not even see? And where were Nuliam's troop, and Pitlis's?

He stumbled through the darkness into a clearing, and froze. Rulke stood on the other side, only five yards away, apparently unarmed. He was a huge man, as tall as Tensor but inches broader across the shoulders. Tensor was about to charge when Rulke put up a hand.

'You're Tensor,' he said.

'Yes.' How could Rulke, who had left Aachan fifty years ago, know his name?

'How did you make a portal?'

'How did you know –?'

'Great mancery leaves traces – if you know where to look.'

'I copied Yalkara's portal,' Tensor said. 'It wasn't so difficult.'

Rulke's eyes narrowed. 'Given your situation, your pride seems misplaced. How did you copy it?'

'I used a *seeing* device.'

Rulke took a step towards him. Tensor thrust out his sword, watching the Charon's eyes, which were a peculiar colour – indigo and crimson – and his hands. Tensor was surprised to see that his own right hand was steady, for he was quaking inside. Rulke was the most dangerous man in the Three Worlds.

Rulke gestured; the Mirror of Aachan rose from Tensor's pocket and drifted to Rulke's hand. He looked into it for a minute or two.

Tensor shifted his balance and prepared to lunge. One thrust and it would be over.

'If you try,' said Rulke, 'I will gut you with your own blade.'

Tensor had the advantage, yet Rulke showed not a hint of fear. Was he superhuman? Perhaps he was – despite being gravely injured and having a foot-long wound in his side, he had led the Hundred to take Aachan from a thousand times their number.

'This is Master Shaper Aoife's work,' said Rulke.

'My outgift,' said Tensor.

'I commend you; few mancers are capable of making a portal between worlds. But you should have closed it and gone home.'

'Why?'

'Surely you knew that a second portal will always be warped by the first?'

'No,' said Tensor.

'But ... your test portals would have shown that.'

'There was no need for tests. My portal worked the first time ...'

'You ignored the first law of the Secret Art?' Rulke shook his head in disbelief. '*Never use mancery you don't understand.* I assume you lost many of your people.'

Layaley had warned him but he had refused to listen; he had been too caught up in the heroic dream of freeing his people, and his utterly misplaced self-belief. Chills spread down his back. It was his fault that she, and all the others, had been killed by the portal.

'Portals are the most perilous mancery of all,' said Rulke, as if instructing a novice, and a stupid one at that. 'And the art of making them is neither easy nor quickly learned. We first did so in the pitiless void, thousands of years ago, yet portals still go wrong for us, sometimes. Why do you think I never came back to Aachan?'

Tensor mentally rehearsed his attack. Draw, lunge, then thrust his blade through Rulke's heart and out his back, giving it a good twist to make sure of the arrogant bastard. It ought to be easy, yet fear held him back. Fear and self-doubt.

'I – don't – know,' he said.

'Even with all my experience, I could not get a portal to open from here to Aachan.'

Tensor did not want to think about that. 'How did you fool my mirror to make it show you at the campsite?'

'I did nothing to your *toy*,' said Rulke.

'You're lying.'

Rulke laughed. 'Why would I bother?'

'Then – how –?'

'*The second lesson,*' he said as if Tensor was a complete moron, 'is that enchanted objects carried through a portal between one world and another are *always* changed – and rarely for the better.'

'I ... did not know,' said Tensor, stunned.

'It's why we went naked to your world, and came naked here. We could not trust any device we took through our portal. Your mirror will never show true again. You should destroy it.'

The way he talked down to Tensor was infuriating. He leapt forwards, swinging his four-foot blade. Had it been any other man, he would have taken the top of his head off, but Rulke, moving in a blur, ducked, came up inside the blade and his left hand locked around Tensor's wrist, stopping the blow in mid-air.

Tensor strained with all his strength but could not budge Rulke's hand. Rulke squeezed, bone-crushingly hard. The sword fell from Tensor's hand, but his left hand had already found the knife sheathed behind his left hip, and he swung it low and hard.

With a contemptuously casual blow, Rulke struck it out of Tensor's hand, then pressed an iron-hard fingertip to the side of his skull. Vision swam and he crumbled.

When he roused, his hands were tied behind his back and he had been dumped uncomfortably close to the camp fire, which was blazing again. Rulke and Kandor stood nearby. The bodies of a dozen Aachim lay where they had fallen but there was no sign of the rest, and the night was quiet.

Tensor sat up, awkwardly. 'What have you done to my people?'

'Yalkara led them away,' said Rulke.

Fear spiked through Tensor. She was the worst. 'To slaughter them,' he said bitterly.

His plan had been a fool's plan and, because he had convinced his people to follow him, one hundred and eighty-one Aachim would die on alien soil. Then, unimaginably worse, his entire family, and Layaley's, would be exterminated. His unbreakable oath was revealed as the boast of a contemptible loser – a man who had risked the lives of both families based on nothing but hubris.

'Put him down and make an end to it,' said Kandor.

Rulke's right arm twitched. 'After we took their world I was heartsick of killing. I swore I would never again take a life unnecessarily.'

'It'll save us a lot more grief in the end.'

'Tensor's harmless. He doesn't even know how to use his bright, shiny sword.'

The contempt – no, worse, the indifference – was crushing. To Rulke, Tensor wasn't even a flea to be squashed. He was *nothing*.

'He'll learn – if you give him the chance,' said Kandor.

'Let me go,' said Tensor. 'Please.'

'Why?' said Rulke.

'If my family is to be exterminated for my folly, at least let me take my people home so we can die with them.'

'There's no going home – for you *or for us*.'

'Why not?'

'The portal that brought us here made it impossible to create one going the other way.'

'That's nonsense! Yalkara made a portal, and I made another.'

'*To* Santhenar. Not *from* here.'

'Why not?'

'I don't know.'

If Rulke was telling the truth, Tensor's plan could never have succeeded. Or could it? 'What if I could offer you the way home?'

Rulke's strange eyes narrowed. 'Speak.'

'You commissioned the golden flute as a way around the unreliability of portals. It can open a portal from anywhere, *to* anywhere.'

'Not exactly *anywhere*,' said Rulke, 'but go on.'

'If I show you where it is, will you save my family, and Layaley's?'

For an instant, Tensor saw the yearning in Rulke's eyes. He wanted the golden flute desperately, for some powerful reason. Then he blinked and the emotion was hidden.

'How?' said Rulke.

'I saw it in the mirror.'

'When?'

'Less than an hour ago.'

Rulke held out his hand.

'First,' said Tensor, 'I want your word that there will be no retribution on my people.'

'How can I promise that? I may never see Aachan again.'

'You can send messages. Give the order.'

'I don't rule the Hundred.'

'Then beg them; plead with them.'

'Nor do I beg,' said Rulke with a sneer. 'But if your information proves useful, which is unlikely, I will ask the Hundred to leave your people be.'

'I must have your word.'

'My words are my word!'

Rulke took back the mirror and, holding it with both hands, looked into it. The images, far brighter than any Tensor had seen, flickered on Rulke's dark face. Then, for a few seconds, his skin shone gold.

'Ah!' he said.

The images flickered faster and faster, then faded, and he tossed the mirror down at Tensor's feet.

'It lies!' he said flatly.

'But I saw Shuthdar playing the golden flute,' said Tensor.

'You also saw us by this campfire.' Rulke paced back and forth for a minute. 'The mirror does show Shuthdar with my flute, but the *where*, and perhaps the *when*, is a deceit. Only a fool would rely on the Twisted Mirror.'

The implication being that Tensor was such a fool.

'Untie him,' Rulke said to Kandor.

Kandor shrugged, then made a gesture with his fingers and the cords binding

Tensor's wrists behind his back fell away.

'Are you going to kill me now?' said Tensor.

'I'm having mercy on you,' said Rulke. 'You've suffered enough.'

'I don't understand.'

'Fighting you was like fighting a child. Killing you would be like killing a child. I can't do it.'

He snapped his fingers and vanished, as did Kandor.

As Tensor picked up the mirror and rose, he realised that many of his people had gathered in the trees at the edge of the firelight. The blood rushed to his face. Rulke's mercy was an unforgiveable insult – and they all knew it.

They also knew how foolish his plan had been, how reckless and poorly thought through. How doomed, before he began. Layaley had tried to tell him that portals were dangerous but he had refused to listen.

Nuliam stalked forwards in a towering rage. 'Why did you attack before we were in position?'

'But I saw you ...' said Tensor. 'I checked twice. And Selial saw it too.'

'On the Twisted Mirror,' spat Pitlis.

'My beautiful sister died *for nothing*,' said Nuliam with terrifying calm. 'There was never any hope of your plan succeeding.'

'No.' There had been no way of knowing that the portal would corrupt the mirror, but he wasn't going to make excuses.

'Now our families will be expunged.'

A scream of horror built up inside him. 'Yes,' he whispered.

'And we can never go home.' Nuliam punched him in the mouth, knocking him down. 'Curse you for the biggest fool that ever drew breath.'

He lay there for a moment, his whole face aching, then got up.

Nuliam turned to the Aachim arranged behind her. There were about eighty of them, though all had been disarmed and many were battered and bloody. The firelight gave their eyes a haunted look, and the smell of blood brought back the horror of all those Aachim falling from the sky, and the red rain that had followed.

'Does anyone think Tensor should be allowed to stay, after all he has done to us?' said Nuliam.

No one spoke up for him. He saw nothing but contempt in their eyes.

'You are cast out,' said Nuliam. 'Whether you live, or whether you die, is a matter of utter indifference to us ... though personally I hope you live to a very old age, *and every minute is agony*.' She surveyed her people. 'How many of us are left?'

'Ninety-one,' said Selial. 'Counting the injured we left back on the hillside.'

'Half of those who left Aachan two hours ago are dead,' said Nuliam. 'Ninety of our best, Tensor, including my sister. Dead because of you. The rest of us are exiles, and soon our families –' Her voice cracked. She knuckled her cheeks.

Tensor, looking at the stark, staring faces, wished he had died as well. He was foresworn: an oath-breaker and a fool. How, how had it gone so wrong? Because he had been so captivated by the dream that he had refused to listen – to Layaley, to Nuliam, and to his own misgivings.

'Have you nothing to say?' she grated.

Words were useless now, but he said them. 'I'm deeply and bitterly sorry.'

'Go!' she said in a deceptively soft voice.

'But ... I have to bury Layaley.'

'You will not lay my sister out,' she said. 'You will take no part in the rites for any of our beloved dead. You will leave this place now and never come near us again, on pain of death.'

'On pain of death,' echoed the Aachim.

Tensor picked up his *bright, shiny sword*, as Rulke had called it, and jammed it in its sheath. He took the Mirror of Aachan as well, then stumbled away.

Ruined. Lost. Aching with guilt.

Nuliam had been right about him all along. Right to doubt him, and right to do everything she could to separate him from her sister. If only she had.

He was tempted to put his sword to his belly, but death was no answer. He could never make up for the death and ruin he had brought to so many but he must try to atone, and there was only one way to do so: by freeing his people.

After this they would need it more than ever. In punishment for his portal, his people on Aachim would be crushed and crushed again.

Rulke had told him to destroy the mirror but it was the only thing Tensor had left. Could he force it to show true? He must. Maybe it had been corrupted by the passage from Aachan to Santhenar, but it had also been made for him. He would devote his life, no matter how long it took, to becoming a master of every form of mancery there was. Then he would find a way to command the Mirror.

He would use it to find Shuthdar and take the golden flute. Then he would free the Aachim, on Santhenar and on Aachan. He would make them a strong, proud people again, the greatest in the Three Worlds.

After that, no matter if it took a thousand years, he would hunt down Rulke, the architect of all the Aachan's misfortunes. How dare he insult Tensor so?

Fighting you was like fighting a child. Killing you would be like killing a child.

Tensor wished that Rulke had killed him. It would have been a fitting punishment, dealt out by an enemy who had proved more honourable than himself. But Rulke had not, and it was the one thing Tensor could not forgive.

How dare Rulke be merciful!

~

Tensor and Rulke will go on to fight many battles, and appear in a number of the Great Tales of Santhenar — as well as tales that have never been told. Almost four thousand years after this encounter, the end of their monumental struggle is told in **The View from the Mirror** *quartet.*

And two centuries later, the after-effects of their conflict are still shaping the lives and deaths of great people and small, throughout the Three Worlds. The greatest of these stories are told in **The Well of Echoes** *quartet and* **The Song of the Tears** *trilogy.*

STORY II

THE HARROWS

THE HARROWS

A little story from Ancient Times. It is set between the Forbidding (3,000 years before the time of The View from the Mirror) and the beginning of the Clysm (~1,500 years before). Its origin is unknown.

Thanks very much to Lisa Leigh for the seed from which this story grew.

'Why does it have to be me?'

An icy wind whipped Lita's blonde hair around her tear-streaked face, and her green eyes were wide with fear. She pulled the cloak around her small frame but could not stop shivering. Beside her, the waterfall roared. The drop was dizzying, the rocks at the base jagged. She could not do it. She wanted to run back to the safety of her clan but there was no choice.

'Because the other ten girls failed,' said Horler. The old woman was gaunt, almost fleshless, yet she seemed immune to the cold, the drenching spray, and the fatal plunge two feet away.

'They didn't *fail*. They died, broken on the rocks.'

'They let the clan down.'

'You made them dive for the pool. It's your fault they died.'

Horler was relentless. '*You* won't fail our people, will you?'

Sickness churned in Lita's belly. The rocks seemed to be reaching up to her. *Jump, jump!*

'You're the last – *save for your little sister,*' said Horler. 'Would you prefer I used her?'

The threat silenced Lita, as always. Tissy was small, sensitive, special. She had to be looked after. 'What if I don't have the gift?'

'I think you do.'

'Why can't I climb down to the pool?'

'It's protected.'

Lita swallowed. 'What if I can't find my gift in time?'

'You must.'

'Why me?' Lita repeated.

'To atone for our clan's shame.'

Long ago, an unknown woman of the clan had meddled where she had no right, letting loose the *harrows.* Lita looked down. A series of odd streaks, like scorch marks, ran across the algae-covered rocks. How could that have happened when the rocks were drenched by the falls? She counted the streaks. Ten. One for each dead girl.

The old woman drew a glitter-blade. Its edge twinkled in the dawn light. 'Hold out your left hand.'

From here, the pool Lita had to dive for was the size of a coin. She could not do it. No one could.

She hugged her arms around herself, shuddering. 'W-what's the knife for?'

'Price to air, price to water.'

'What?'

'You have to pay both, or neither will support you.'

'The air won't support me. I'll be smashed to bits.'

'You will fly to the pool,' Horler said coldly. 'You will dive to the bottom. You will find the box, and open it, and bring back the cure – and save your clan from the *harrows.*'

Lita rubbed the swellings that ran across her shoulders and down her arms. 'I have no gift,' she lied. 'I can't fly.'

'Everyone in our clan has the gift.'

'I'm not allowed to try. The more the gift is used, the quicker the Change when we grow up. The quicker the Change, the worse the *harrows.*'

Horler curled her wrinkled lip. 'And you think, that if you don't use your gift at all, you'll be spared the *harrows*?'

'Papa said –'

'He's a fool. The *harrows* will get you, gift or not. My way is the only way, and you're the only one left who can save the clan. Hold out your hand.'

Cringing, Lita extended her small hand. Horler grabbed it, thrust it out over the water, slashed the glitter-blade across Lita's palm and shook her wrist violently. Blood sprayed through the air and was caught up in the plunge of the waterfall.

Horler's eyes went a smoky, malevolent black; her lips pulled back to reveal yellow teeth. She dropped the glitter-blade and reached out to grab Lita, who suddenly realised that she wasn't meant to be a saviour, but a sacrifice.

Horler was planning to hurl her over the edge to die, like the ten girls before her.

Her hand was slippery with blood. She wrenched free, threw her cloak in Horler's face and ran. But not back towards clan-hall. She would find no shelter there – only the burden of all those who had grown up, gone through the Change, lost their gift and had been struck down by the unbearable wasting of the *harrows*. Horler was right about that. Lita was the only one who could do it. She had to save her clan.

As she ran, she reached inside her for the gift she had been told never to use and, perhaps because it had been suppressed so long, it rose in a scalding tide. Her face was burning, her vision blurring, the strength draining from her legs as the swellings along her shoulders and arms throbbed and grew. The gift was working. Go, while you still can!

Lita shot past the old woman, whacking her clawed fingers aside, bolted towards the edge of the falls and, sobbing with terror, hurled herself out and over, towards the pool.

Behind her, Horler howled with fury. Lita plunged head-first down the cliff, faster and faster. The rocks were ferocious, the pool tiny. The swellings were opening, the leathery glide-wings she had never used extending behind her outstretched arms. But slowly. Too slowly to save her. She was going to smash into the rocks –

The glide-wings snapped open with a wrench and a burning pain in her shoulders, as if the shock had torn her arms out of their sockets. Had it? What if her wings collapsed? It felt as though they were going to. They thrashed, shuddered, *held*. Then she caught the updraught, lifted and she was soaring, weightless, free for the first time in her life.

And oh! The gift was wonderful. It was worth all the pain, even the cost when the harrows eventually wasted her.

As she turned in a wobbly rising spiral, Lita realised that she could finally escape the burden of guilt that had suffocated her all her life. Escape her dying clan that nothing could save from the harrows. And escape murderous old Horler, too.

But flying was much harder than she had expected. Every flap made her shoulders throb and her muscles burn. As she circled, the streaks seared across the rocks caught her eye. Could they be –?

Crack-crack. Horler's cloak was streaming out behind her, firming and taking on a wing shape. The old woman took three steps to the brink, lowered her head and shoulders into the updraught and the wind lifted her straight up. She side-slipped left, then right, then dived. Lita's mouth went dry. Horler was an expert flier.

She came hurtling down, so fast that the wind hissed over her cloak-wing. Lita tried to get out of the way but she was tiring rapidly. Horler's teeth were bared, her fingers hooked as if she wanted to tear out Lita's heart.

Lita flapped her wings but could not get out of the way in time. Horler shot past, caught her by the ankle and heaved her upside-down. Lita felt a burning pain in her head; her wings were shrinking back into her arms; her gift was fading. No, it was being drawn out of her, stolen from her. She tried to push Horler away but the short flight had exhausted her.

Horler swung Lita around by the ankle until the sharpest rocks were below her. The old woman wore a look of wicked triumph, and only now did Lita understand. Those streaks must have burned across the rock when the dying girls' gifts had been brutally wrenched from them. But where had their gifts gone?

She had to stop this; she had to get the cure from the box. Lita kicked upwards with the last of her strength. Her left heel caught Horler under the jaw, snapping her head back, and she lost her grip. A little of Lita's gift came back and she dived away, praying that she could glide to the pool on her wing stubs. But she was falling like a brick, arcing over and down. She was going to slam head-first into the rocks.

She flapped furiously, churning the air with her useless winglets, and gained a little forwards motion. Was it enough to reach the pool? She dared to hope. But Horler was diving after her, teeth bared. Lita scooped at the air, slipped sideways, shot over the edge of the pool and plunged in.

The shock almost stopped her heart – the water was icy. Lita plunged all the way to the bottom, sending up swirls of grit that scratched her eyes. She blinked them clean and there it was – a small brown box on a bed of white sand.

And the box was calling to her.

She clawed at the lid, wrenched it up and felt inside for the cure.

The box was empty.

Horler's story had been a lie.

There was no way to save her clan from the harrows.

Lita shrieked underwater, creating a storm of bubbles. She pounded the sand until it whirled up in clouds around her. Then a shockwave passed through the water and her ears popped. The old woman was coming; before Lita could move, bony hands closed around her throat from behind, and squeezed.

She panicked and thrashed uselessly. The hands tightened, choking her, Horler's ragged nails tearing her skin. Lita's head spun and her vision blurred. She had to act now or die. She slammed the back of her head into Horler's nose, then scrunched down into a ball and rolled forwards.

Horler went tumbling over her, her nose trailing blood, and her head smacked into the open box. The water seemed to boil around her. Yellow rays – eleven of them – were drawn from Horler into the box, then she slumped sideways and the lid fell shut.

The rays faded. The sand settled. Horler lay on the sand beside the box, motionless.

Not breathing.

Lita, desperate for air, churned up to the surface. She wanted away from here, but first she had to understand. After taking three breaths, she dived. The box was calling her again, and she wanted to open it. She felt sure the cure was there now.

But there was no time. She bore Horler up. The malevolence was gone from her eyes; she was just a bony old woman, close to death.

'What happened?' Lita said, panting.

'*Harrows* – lifted. Clan – saved.'

'How?'

'You – the cure.'

Lita no longer wanted to escape. It was over and she ached for the support of her clan. 'I don't understand.'

'But you – can never – go home,' croaked Horler, sinking beneath the water to her chin.

The pain was worse than being slashed with the glitter-knife. Lita hung on to the rock with one hand, Horler with the other. 'Why not?' she said hoarsely.

'Work ... it ... out.'

Lita stared into the old woman's eyes. 'It was you! You opened the box, ages ago. *You* released the harrows.'

'I was the fool who opened it,' Horler said bitterly. 'But I did not release the harrows – I *became* the harrows.'

'Then why – why did the other girls have to die? Why try to kill me?'

'I'm old. Fading. Harrows failing with me. It needed to feed on their gifts.'

'If it's gone, why can't I go home?'

'You opened the box.'

'But it was empty,' said Lita.

'Not empty now.'

'I don't understand.'

'You should have let me die, but you opened the box and allowed it to feed. Harrows is waiting now. Waiting for you to open the box.'

Lita closed her eyes. The pain was getting worse.

'Go! Fly!' said Horler.

'Where can I go? I'm only fourteen.'

'Too bad!'

'But Tissy won't understand. I've got to see her first.'

'You can't. Never come back – or you *will* open the box. *You* will become the harrows.'

Horler's eyes went blank, she slipped from Lita's grasp, the water closed over her head and she was gone.

Lita lifted off, but as she laboured up past the falls, she heard the box calling and calling. What was worse – to spend the rest of her life in bitter exile, or rejoin the clan she loved, only to harrow them again?

High above the pool she circled. Tormented. Tempted.

She had to say goodbye to her little sister. If she opened the box, just a crack, could she see Tissy one last time?

Lita was strong – surely she could close it again?

A slightly different version of this story was first published in the anthology Trust Me Too *(2012), edited by Paul Collins and published by Ford St Publishing.*

STORY III

A WIZARD'S WAR

1

Perhaps the greatest, unquestionably the most influential, and certainly one of the longest-lived old human mancers has always been an enigma, not least because he made sure that all the records of his early life were erased. But late in his final life he must have regretted it, and took care to set some parts of the record straight. Here, for the first time and in his own words, is the story of the worst deed of his life, and the deed that made him.

This longish story is set late in the Clysm, the 500-year war between the Aachim and the Charon that devastated Santhenar and almost wiped old humans out. The time is around 1100 years before the events of The View from the Mirror.

My original name was Nudifer Spoak, though most people called me Nudie – usually in a mocking, sing-song voice, *Nu-deeee*. How I hated it. Now, unable to take any more, I hunched over the home-made orrery in my smelly cupboard room and plotted my righteous retribution.

Retribution on Blaggart College of the Secret Art; on its sneering Head Master, Trukulus Vish; on my chief tormenter, the popular, wealthy and handsome Head Boy, Haddon Sloon. Retribution on everyone and everything in my miserable life.

Thinking of the new boy, I shivered. Perhaps not quite everyone.

He went by a single name, Yggur, and, though he said little and did even less, even Haddon went in awe of him. Yggur had entered the final year at Blaggart a few weeks ago. He was said to be twenty, several years older than the rest of the final year, though he had an ageless look about him, a sense of self-sufficiency that I could only envy, and an air of supreme confidence in his own abilities.

Yggur was remarkably tall and lean, with unfashionably long hair as black as the wing of a crow and eyes the colour of frost on agate. His mancery, entirely self-taught, was unlike anyone else's and rumoured to be very powerful, though he had declined to demonstrate it to any other student.

I adjusted the rings of my orrery yet again, but divined nothing. My back was aching, my acne-covered face throbbed and I was sweating like a racehorse. 'Stinky Nudie, scholarship boy,' the other students called me.

I washed three times a day but it made no difference. My scholarship only covered tuition and, though I tutored younger students when I could, scrubbed out cauldrons until late in the night, cleaned and mended the equipment used in the alchemy classes, fixed clocks and did whatever other odd jobs I could get, I could only afford the price of a bath once a month.

Retribution!

I shifted on the broken bricks that formed my seat and adjusted the angle of my candle until its feeble light lit the orrery. My room was cold, damp, airless, mouldy and no bigger than a storage cupboard. My drunken parents had been right – I would never amount to anything.

Scholarship boy! I'd been so proud when I'd won it. My teacher had wept, 'Brilliant, Nudifer! Quite brilliant!'

It was the last kind thing anyone ever said about me. I started badly at Blaggart College and never recovered. Though I worked as hard as anyone could, and had an intuitive grasp of mancery, my marks were getting worse each term. I had been called before Trukulus Vish three times this year and I felt sure the chisel-faced Head Master was going to fail me. What would happen to me then?

I could not, would not slink home to my drunken parents. How they would crow! It would prove my failure, and prove them right. Besides, they were more abusive than ever – if I stayed, they would end up killing me. Or the converse, which was unthinkable.

Better that I never saw them again. But if I failed, where could I go? How could I survive? The Clysm, the war between the mighty Charon and the equally powerful Aachim, had been raging back and forth across Lauralin for four hundred years and we old humans, caught between two almost immortal species, were little more than slaves, flung into one hideous battlefield or another, to die.

It wasn't right. Something had to be done.

A month ago each student in the final year had been required to make an orrery, a working model of the planets and their moons, and use it for divination.

I'm good with my hands and my orrery was beautifully made – a series of perfect, pivoting brass rings mounted on a hand-carved wooden base. Amber beads, representing the heavenly bodies, could be slid along the rings to simulate their motions in the celestial sphere. Yet, incomprehensibly, my work had been given a failing mark.

As I sat there, seething, I was struck by a brilliant and original idea: to adapt my orrery to *below* rather than *above*. Instead of showing the mundane and predictable movement of the planets and their moons, what if I rebuilt it to plumb the enigmatic motions of the most important objects in the lower circles? To use the *underworld* for divination.

Good, good.

I sprang up, looking around wildly, but there was no one else in my broom cupboard. I must have imagined that faint, whispering voice. I resumed my deliberations.

I did not know if the underworld actually existed. Though there were stories of demons and imps in every culture, they could have been made up to meet a universal need. Or feed a primal terror. However certain philosophers speculated that a subterranean or chthonian plane, external to the physical world of Santhenar, did exist ... and could be a source of entirely new forms of mancery. Dare I try?

What did I have to lose? All my life I had followed the rules, worked hard and treated other people the way I wanted to be treated, and what had it gained me? Abuse and failure. This time it was going to be different.

Over the next week, working by instinct at the blackest hours, I rebuilt my orrery again and again until, one desperate night, I *touched* something.

I did not know what, though I knew it could not be a source of power. The theory of mancery at that time held that all power came from *within* the person doing it, the only exception being when power had already been stored in an enchanted object such as a ring or talisman. I sensed no power, but I had felt something *unblock* within myself. Something previously sealed off or out of reach – something that had been holding me back all this time – had become available.

And I was going to use it on the first person to cross me.

That afternoon I raked my rapidly thinning hair into a semblance of order and went out, pulling my threadbare red robes around myself, to wander the chilly halls of Blaggart. The college had been built seven hundred years ago, long before the Clysm began and, though it was not a secret, its location in the mountains was not advertised, either.

Originally it had been a fortified castle guarding a strategic pass, and it was a grim place built of dark, weeping stone. Its multitude of steeple roofs were black slate which shone when wet, which it nearly always was. The college was cold, damp and utterly joyless.

Immediately behind it, a range of mountains formed a snowy barrier to the south, briefly interrupted by a broken red cliff with a ruined manse on a ledge halfway up. Two miles north, on the lowlands, stood the dreary town of Gard.

'Nudifer!' said a cold voice behind me. 'My office, four p. m.'

'Yes, Master Vish.' I turned, looking up – being short and bent-backed, I looked up at almost everyone. 'Is something the matter ... *sir*?'

'Four p. m., scholarship boy!' Vish sneered and walked off, his long legs moving like hedge clippers.

I clenched a fist in my pocket. One day!

A very tall boy came striding the other way. Realising that I was hunching my shoulders, trying to make myself more inconspicuous, I stood up straight.

'Spoak,' said Yggur, hesitating in mid-step as if planning to speak to me.

He was strange and scary, and he had such an air of self-sufficiency that not even the toughest bullies or cruellest masters dared take him on.

'Yes, Yggur?' I said politely.

'Be careful where you delve.' He nodded and kept walking.

What was he talking about? Did he know about my underworld orrery? How could he?

But Vish's words haunted me. *Four p. m., scholarship boy!* I almost turned back to my cupboard, to wait out the hour and a half. I felt sure he was going to order me out of Blaggart. But if he was, I had nothing to lose and no reason to go quietly. This once, the mouse was going to roar.

Dare I?

'If it isn't Stinky Nudie, deep in what passes for thought,' said a deep, drawling voice. 'How's your last day going, scholarship boy?'

I spun on one foot, raising a fist in helpless fury. Haddon, who was with half a dozen friends, did not flinch. He wasn't afraid of anyone, and why would he be? He was big and strong, his father was a judge and a close friend of Master Vish, his mother was one of the school governors, and everyone except me liked and admired him.

'Why are you tormenting me?' To my chagrin, my voice went squeaky.

'Because you're not one of us and your family is a disgrace to humanity.'

'Leave my family out of it!' I said furiously.

'But they've made you what you are. What's the matter with your face, anyway?'

I felt my inflamed cheeks. 'I – what?'

'You look like a warthog.'

'You – you –' I spluttered, almost exploding with helpless rage. I was powerless against the likes of him and always would be.

'Go on, get it out of your system,' grinned Haddon.

'I'm going to!' I reached deep inside myself, down to the place I'd found with the orrery in the dark of the night, and whatever it had unblocked. 'You – you –'

Haddon spread his arms. 'Free shot, Nudie, just for you.'

Suddenly the power surged, unlike anything I had ever felt before. It seared its way down my spine into my shoulders, through muscle, bone and sinew, and along my arms until the flesh felt as though it was on fire. I raised my staff and pointed its iron-shod tip at Haddon's mocking features. Then hesitated. The college had an absolute prohibition on casting spells at another student, except under the supervision of a senior master.

'Do your worst, warthog boy,' said Haddon.

I cracked. 'Your *head* is a warthog's,' I cried, directing all the fury of my oppressed existence, and every ounce of power I had found, at him.

The tip of my staff flew off, making a metallic *click-click-click* as it bounced across the flagstones, but there was no flash of light, no sound, no effect at all. The spell had failed.

Haddon's smile faded a little. He looked puzzled. 'What was that about, scholarship boy?'

But on the last two words his voice deepened, the words stretching out until they were almost indecipherable. He doubled over, groaning, then snapped upright and clutched at his cheeks with his big hands.

His face was lengthening, his whole head growing longer. Four wart-like protrusions appeared on his cheeks and swelled to the size of plums. His blue eyes turned mud-brown, dragged to the sides of his face and almost disappeared in masses of leathery brown, wrinkled and bristly skin. His mouth became snout-like. The white, even teeth turned yellow and two on either side grew monstrously, curving outwards and upwards until they were like long, ivory daggers.

I'd burned my bridges this time but I didn't care. The spell would only last for a minute or two, but while it did Haddon would know what it felt like to be a real, suffering human being, oppressed for no reason but his looks. For the first time in my life I had power, and I raised my staff to the sky and roared in exultation.

Haddon's head sagged, then he began to breathe in desperate, strangled gasps as if his neck could not support the massive warthog's head. He reeled around, choking, and fell down, snout gaping, dagger-sharp lower tusks rasping against the massive upper ones. Strings of brown saliva oozed across his hairy lower lip.

'You little bastard, what have you done?' roared Haddon's square-faced friend, Vim.

'Haddon's dying!' screamed Jaelie, a tall girl whose ringlets of yellow hair stuck out for six inches on either side of her face. 'Call Master Vish. Quick!'

'He's putting on an act,' I said, not sure I believed it myself.

A slender, freckled redhead came running, then propped, staring at Haddon in horror. Sissily Bur, his girlfriend, was a quiet, kindly girl, and one of the few who had never been rude to me. She went to her knees beside him, trying to turn his gigantic head into the recovery position so he would not choke.

'Look out for the tusks,' cried Jaelie.

Haddon's warthog head heaved violently and its right tusk speared between the bones of Sissily's arm above her right wrist, impaling her and dragging her towards the champing mouth.

She shrieked. Jaelie heaved Sissily's arm free and dragged her backwards. Blood poured from the inch-wide hole in her arm, running down her hand and dripping from her fingernails. Jaelie wound a scarf around the wound a dozen times and knotted it tightly.

On the ground, Haddon thrashed and choked. Sissily went as white as plaster and slumped against Jaelie, looking as though she was going to faint. She clung there for a few seconds, rubbing her face and leaving streaks of blood across it, then turned to me.

'Undo the spell, Nudie.'

I couldn't speak; it felt as though my tongue was glued to the roof of my mouth.

'Nudie ...' Sissily reached out to me. Blood was dripping through the bandage. 'Undo the spell and we'll pretend it never happened.'

'I ... don't know how.'

'It's a *metamorphism* spell,' said Jaelie. 'A spell forbidden to all save the greatest adepts. No one can pretend it never happened.'

I began to back away. I had no idea how I'd done it; I'd simply spoken the words without having any spell in mind. Now, staring down at the gasping Head Boy, I knew I could no more reverse what I'd done than I could turn an orange into a turnip. Aftersickness rose in me, as it always did after I worked powerful mancery. My head was spinning, my knees were wobbly and I felt an almost irresistible urge to vomit. I turned to run.

'Stop him!' said Vish, striding across the courtyard.

Students surrounded me. I swung my staff out and pointed it towards them with a shaking hand. They froze. 'Don't come any closer,' I said in a high, strained voice.

'Take him!' roared Vish.

Still they hesitated.

'He's weak with aftersickness. He can't do it twice.'

I tried to cast a paralysis spell on the nearest student but I had nothing left – whatever talent the orrery had unblocked before was blocked again. I turned to run. I had no idea where, though if I could not get out of Blaggart I was finished. But before I took three steps someone tackled me and brought me down. My hands were bound behind my back with the sash of my robes, then they sat on me until Vish swept up.

He studied Haddon, who was still panting and drooling, for half a minute, then looked at me sideways. A strange look crept across the Head Master's angular face. He seemed afraid; the flesh sagged beneath his skin. Then the military training of his youth reasserted itself and he snapped out orders.

'Take Haddon to the infirmary. Call the senior masters together. We've got to reverse this curse, right now.' He turned to the Head Girl, forcing a yellow-toothed smile. 'It won't take long, Sissily. Useless Nudie can't have done anything serious.'

He picked up my staff and looked me up and down. 'You're expelled, scholarship boy. But first –' Vish raised his voice, addressing the college guards. 'Take him to the flogging place.'

2

The waiting was the worst, and Trukulus Vish made an art form of it.

I was stripped naked and tied to the flogging rack in the main courtyard. A cutting winter wind was blowing directly from the South Pole and a thin rain began to fall. I had never been so cold. But cold was the lesser of my worries. There was no one else in the courtyard but there soon would be. Vish would make a spectacle of me; he would humiliate and crush me as a lesson to the rest of the school.

Expelled! It struck me hard. All I'd ever wanted was to be a mancer, and now I never would be. I'd thrown it away in an instant of folly, a failure of every mancer's most important attribute – self-control. Had Haddon been sent to test me? If so, I had proven beyond doubt that I lacked what it took. And all for nothing. The masters would reverse my spell within minutes and he would be more popular and famous than ever.

After I was expelled, what would I do? Mancery was all I knew. How could I live without it?

I hung on the rack for hours as the sky grew darker, the rain heavier and colder. The infirmary windows, on the third level of the western tower, were lit by flashes of green and yellow, and an occasional purple, as the masters reversed the curse. Some of the spells rattled the windows and one, a lurid red and black flare, made the paving stones beneath my feet quiver.

Why was it taking so long? How could I, a failing scholarship boy, have worked such a spell, anyway? Metamorphism spells – spells to transform living things –

weren't taught at any college I'd heard of. Besides, I could not even name the spell I'd used. It had just come to me.

The flashes grew duller and further apart, then petered out. They'd done it. Now the whole school assembled in the courtyard to bear witness. Eight hundred and eleven girls and boys, seventy-eight journeymen and women, ten senior masters, twenty-six junior masters, ninety-four cooks, cleaners, bookbinders, glassblowers and workers in a host of other trades, gathered on the sweeping main steps of the college, and the narrower tower steps to left and right. Sissily was out in front, her arm heavily bandaged, her face deathly.

Vish thrust the iron-studded double doors open and stalked out, the grey wings of his Head Master's cloak flapping in the wind. His long face was the colour of the cloak and his eyes had a hollow look. He began to descend the thirty steps, but stumbled and almost fell onto the first-year students to his left.

My unease grew. He looked utterly exhausted, and so did the other masters. How could reversing a student's spell take so much out of them? My bowels knotted. Something was badly wrong.

'It is with the deepest sorrow,' said Vish, staring at a spot above Sissily's head, 'that I must inform you of the passing of our beloved Head Boy, Haddon Sloon.'

Cries and gasps rippled through the assembled students and staff. My left leg started to tremble and I could not stop it.

'Dead?' cried Sissily. She scrambled up the steps. From the step below Vish she clutched at the front of his robes, then released him and swung around, staring at me. 'Murdered!'

'Not dead,' said Vish heavily. 'Haddon's *body* is in fine physical health ...'

Sissily's face cracked. 'I don't understand.' She scanned the faces of the students as if hoping to see his tall blond head above the others.

I was overcome by terror. He was in good health, yet he had *passed*? The way Vish spoke, Haddon's fate was worse than death. But what could be worse?

And where had the spell come from? The Great Spells were guarded jealously by the few masters who could perform them, and learning any such spell could take years. Masters' grimoires were protected by codes and locks and deadly enchantments, and never shown to mere students. It was impossible that I, who had never even seen a Great Spell, could have worked one perfectly.

'But he is no longer Haddon,' said Vish.

'Of course he's Haddon,' said Sissily. Then she drew in a sharp inward breath.

'He has been rendered into a beast from the head up,' said Vish. 'And ... a beast he will forever be. Ah, this is the worst day of my mastership. How am I going to tell –?'

'But I'm just a student,' I whispered. 'Why can't you reverse the spell?'

Vish stalked across and punched me in the face, driving the back of my head into the hard frame. Blood started to drip from my nose. He returned to Sissily, took her hand and tried to speak, but the words would not come.

He tried again, and managed to gasp, 'We tried – all afternoon and evening.' His voice trailed off. 'And failed.'

A stir went through the assembled school. The students and staff stared at one another.

'The masters ... *failed*?' whispered Sissily. A red spot appeared on the thick white bandage around her forearm and spread into a flower with three petals.

Vish's mouth opened and closed. He looked to the masters on either side for comfort, but found none. Spikes of ice started to crystallise in the marrow of my bones. If the spell could not be reversed, if I had destroyed Haddon, I would be put to death as agonisingly as human ingenuity could devise. I jerked uselessly at the manacles until my skin tore.

'We interrogated Nudifer's staff but it did not reveal the particulars of the spell. Though even if we knew exactly what he'd done ... and we could reverse the physical changes to Haddon – the warthog's head, the bristles, the tusks – after all this time it's too late to reverse the mental changes.'

'Why?' Sissily wailed.

'If we could have stopped the spell quickly, when it had only changed Haddon on the outside, we might have saved him. But the spell kept working on the inside until it gave him the brain and mind of a warthog.'

'I don't understand why –'

'A man can be changed into a beast – but a beast cannot be turned back into a thinking, feeling man.'

'Please,' cried Sissily, falling to her knees before him. 'You've got to find a way.'

'I'm sorry,' said Vish, taking her by the hand and lifting her to her feet. I had always believed him to be a hard and heartless master, but now I saw the humanity in him. 'He's lost to us.'

'I won't give Haddon up,' Sissily said in a cracked voice. 'I'll leave school and nurse him.'

'He's a beast,' said Vish roughly. 'A deadly beast. Lord Sloon will have to have him put down.'

Sissily doubled over, pressed her fists into her belly so deeply that the weeping bandage left bloodstains on her pale yellow gown. Then she screamed, her pretty face cracking and cratering as if the flesh had been withdrawn from under the skin. I had never seen anyone in such torment. She genuinely loved Haddon, and I, who had never been loved by anyone, found this desperately moving.

Sissily turned my way. I cringed under her merciless stare, seeing myself as she must: small, stocky, hunched, spattered with muck. Meagre in every way.

'Nudie knows what spell he used!' she hissed.

'He's not smart enough.' Vish spat on the stones at my feet.

'What are you talking about?' said Sissily. 'He gained the highest scholarship ever awarded.

I gaped at her. 'No, it's tuition only. I have to work for food and rent, and every other grint I need.'

'You lying hound! I used to work in the records office. It was a *full* scholarship, with a handsome stipend. You're *rich*.'

'I've never seen a grint of it,' I said passionately. 'Why do you think I live in a stinking cupboard and scrub cauldrons half the night?'

Sissily looked from me to Vish. 'I know what I know.'

'All his coin goes on *slurb* and drink,' said Vish.

'That's a lie!' I opened my mouth wide so they could check for signs of slurb abuse – blackened gums, loose teeth, eroded tongue. 'I've never touched slurb and I don't drink.' I wanted to, though. Right now I longed for the oblivion it brought my parents.

'He doesn't have the look of a slurb user,' said Sissily.

Vish's dark eyes glinted; he clenched a black-haired fist, then gained control. 'Grief has made you forget yourself, Head Girl. Go to the infirmary. Matron will give you a calming draught.'

Sissily thrust out her left hand. A small yellow stone twinkled on her ring finger. 'Haddon and I are ... were ... we *are* engaged, and that gives me rights. Would you sooner Lord Sloon interrogated you about the doings of Blaggart College – in his court?'

Vish fought his fury, then said quietly, 'You have the right to know. But not here. Come inside.' He took her by the left arm.

Sissily wrenched away. 'Here. Now! Or I ride straight to my father-in-law to be.'

He sagged. 'All right. The Council of Santhenar did award Nudifer a full scholarship – the first they've given out in forty years –'

'And Magister Rula personally approved it.'

'But ... just *look* at him.' Vish's tone oozed contempt. 'He's not one of us. And with the Clysm getting ever worse, the college has been struggling. Enrolments are down, fees are down, donations are down. We needed the money more than he did. Besides, adversity is good for the young; it makes them stronger.'

'Or breaks them,' said a deep voice from the left, the enigmatic new student, Yggur.

I hurled himself at Vish, hard enough for the edges of the manacles to peel corrugated layers of skin off my wrists. Agony speared through me but I ignored it. 'You stinking liar! You spent my scholarship on yourself!'

A familiar look of outrage crossed Vish's hard features. He wrenched a knob-ended cane from a belt loop and strode towards me. I tried to stand up to him, but the cold, the hunger, the exhaustion, my humiliating nakedness and the pain in my wrists beat me down again. I cringed, holding up holding my manacled wrists in a vain attempt to defend myself.

Vish swung the cane back, clearly planning to strike me across the face. 'You never belonged here. You will be flogged by the entire school, expelled, and –'

'Stop!' said Sissily.

'You don't believe the lout who destroyed your fiancée should be punished?' said Vish.

'I want to know how he did it. Maybe … just maybe –'

'The whey-faced fool doesn't know.'

'He's the top student,' said Sissily.

I goggled at her. 'What are you talking about? I've never had a good mark in all the time I've been here.'

'You gained top marks every year for seven years. I've seen the marker's reports in the records office.'

'Interim only!' said Vish icily. 'His final marks are uniformly low.'

'I've often wondered why you kept reducing his marks,' said Sissily.

'The markers didn't know the full story.'

'Of your feud with Magister Rula.'

'None of this matters,' said Vish hastily. 'Nudifer used a forbidden spell on Haddon, and destroyed him. Nudifer has become a monster and must be punished.'

'Nudie was turned into a monster – by *you*.'

'Are you saying he should get off?' cried Vish.

'Certainly not,' said Sissily. 'He's been criminally reckless.'

He presented her with the cane, bowing. 'And as the injured party, it's your right to initiate his punishment.'

Sissily took the cane, gripping it so tightly that her knuckles went white. Her green-gold eyes flashed; she swished the cane through the air then took a step towards me.

My teeth were chattering and my feet were numb lumps. In this cold, the cane would hurt more than anything I had ever felt, but I had to endure it. I had destroyed Haddon's life and hurt Sissily gravely. I had to pay. I wanted to pay for my crime.

'Turn around,' said Sissily, shaking almost as badly as I was.

I did so and hung my head, mutely accepting my punishment. I could feel her eyes on me. She must see me as a contemptible specimen. Why had I done it? Haddon hadn't just been picking on me – he mocked everyone. Vish was the real monster; he had done his best to destroy me, purely because of his feud with Magister Rula.

Sissily did not strike. I looked up and saw an offensive kind of pity in her eyes.

'Get it over with,' I muttered. 'I deserve it.'

'Flog the bastard,' someone said from among the staff, then several other people picked it up and soon the whole school was chanting, 'Flog the bastard! Flog the bastard! Flog the bastard!'

Still she did not strike. She was crying silently, tears running down her cheeks. She dropped the cane, gathered her skirts and ran up the steps and inside.

Vish snatched up the cane and brought it down across my bent back with all the force he could muster. The pain was astronomical; it was like having my back hacked open with a blunt sword. I bared my teeth in agony, but locked my jaw so I could not cry out. Even if he flogged me unconscious, I would not give him the pleasure of seeing my agony.

'I'll get you!' I whispered. 'If it's the last –'

'This is just the warm-up,' said Vish, grunting as he laid into me. 'Haddon's father will make you wish your grandparents had never been born, scholarship boy.'

The mocking title no longer had the power to hurt. I was a damned fool, but I had gained the best scholarship of all, and top marks every year for seven years. I was someone. The best at the college!

The flogging took a long time, and never had I experienced such agony. After twenty strokes I could no longer stand up. I hung from my manacles, my back and buttocks and legs a bloody mess, and still he went at me.

Finally the senior masters called a halt. Vish called for a bucket of vinegar and tossed it over me, and as the acid ate into the raw flesh beneath the broken skin, I broke. I screamed so loudly that it rattled the windows, and then I wept.

They left me there, and for a short while I was glad of the freezing rain. It washed the vinegar off and even numbed my injuries a little.

Had they left me to freeze to death? I did not think so. Haddon's father was a judge and – to the extent that humanity's oppressors allowed us to bear arms and carve out small empires – a minor warlord. Lord Sloon was known to be a strong man, and generous to his friends, but hard and pitiless to his enemies.

And I, who had destroyed his only child, the heir he had invested all his hopes in, was now his number one enemy.

3

'Why, Nudie?'

I forced my eyes open. It was dark, still raining and colder than ever. Sissily, now wearing a blue mourning cloak, had a covered basket in one hand and a little storm lantern in the other.

'I did nothing to Haddon,' I said, 'yet he never stopped tormenting me. I was worn out from seven years of humiliation and failure. I couldn't take it anymore.'

She held the lantern up to my face. In its light her eyes were an enchanting greenish gold. She set down the basket, raised a mug to my lips and I sipped. Gloriously hot, sweet tea. Sissily was a saint.

'But you weren't a failure,' said Sissily.

'For seven years I believed I was.'

'You worked that mighty spell. A spell the best masters in the college could not break. Where did you learn it?'

I was reluctant to tell her for fear of incriminating myself more deeply, but she had a right to know. I told her about adapting my orrery to scan the chthonian plane. 'But I didn't know what I was doing.' The moment I spoke, I regretted my words. 'I'm sorry. Nothing can excuse what I did.'

She frowned, rather prettily. 'You know the warnings about delving into dark mancery.'

'Yes.' I understood them as well as anyone. Better, since I'd gained top marks. I had been utterly reckless and criminally negligent.

She put down the empty mug and offered me a small, freshly baked pie, but I could not hold it. She broke off a piece and held it out.

'Why are you being kind to me, Sissily?'

'Haddon is lost to me ... I have to understand why. Would you sooner I brutalised you?'

'I deserve it.'

'Perhaps, after seven years of injustice, you deserve to be treated like a human being.'

'I won't get it in Lord Sloon's hands.'

She bit her lip. 'I can't do anything about that.'

'You could plead for me.'

'I'm not feeling *that* generous.'

'Then set me free. I'll run and never be heard from again.'

'Even if I cared to let you get away, unpunished, the shackles are sealed with an enchantment I could never break.'

'I'll never *get away* with it. While I live, the guilt will live in me.'

'We must all face the consequences of our actions.' She picked up the mug.

'I'm ... a fool. A stupid, reckless fool ... but I'm not a *bad* person.' I had to make Sissily understand that.

'Malice or stupidity, it's all the same to the man I loved.'

She choked. Her eyes went hard and for a moment I thought she was going to strike me. Perhaps she did too, for her clenched fist shook, then she wrenched off her coat, flung it over me, and bolted up the steps.

The coat was of soft green wool that prickled and stung my lacerated back, but it was worth it for the warmth. For a fleeting second I entertained thoughts about her, but cast them away, my face burning. Sissily was just being kind. It was more than I deserved.

I longed for sleep but there was no hope of getting any; I was in too much pain. I had to endure the night, though many times I longed for death. Better I died here than in Sloon's cruel hands. Or sent to be butchered in the endless war between the Charon and the Aachim.

It was after midnight. The puddles on the paving stones were starting to ice over. Judging by the numbness in my toes, I could well lose them to frostbite. The college was dark save for a single small light in the records office. Vish, no doubt, was destroying the papers that could prove he had stolen my stipend and halved my marks.

There was only one way to keep myself going – with hopeless dreams of retribution.

~

At the most miserable hour of the night, when the puddles were frozen half an inch deep, I realised that someone was looming over me. Someone tall. Vish, come to murder me? It was too dark to tell.

I was so cold I could barely move. I put my arms up over my head in a vain attempt to protect myself. The stranger reached out. There was a dull reddish flash, a tingling shock, a moment of pain as my wrists were burned by hot metal, then I fell onto my face.

A few seconds passed before it sank in. My hands were free. The stranger could only be a master – no student could break the spell-binding of the manacles. *Clack-clatter.* My ankles had also been released.

I was hauled to my feet. 'Get dressed.' I did not recognise the voice, though it was not Vish's thin, sour tone.

Dry clothing was pushed into my hands. I took off Sissily's coat and put on shirt, pants and sandals.

'Who are you?' A horrible thought struck me. 'Do you serve Lord Sloon?'

'No,' he said.

Now I recognised the voice. 'Yggur?'

He thrust some small coins in my hand. 'Go!'

I hesitated for a few seconds. 'Thank you. I'll never forget your kindness.'

'Kindness is foreign to me. I serve the cause of justice.'

He created a tiny light between us. I stared at him, trying to fathom him, and for an instant I saw something uncomfortable in his eyes – some terrible pain or loss – that moved me deeply. Then he blinked and the light went out. Yggur swirled his cloak around himself and disappeared.

Yet again I wondered who he was and where he had come from. Justice was not a commodity much in evidence in the world of the Clysm. I hobbled down the road to the college gates, painfully clambered over them and fled up into the mountains. I had no destination in mind; I allowed instinct – or randomness – to guide my lurching steps.

The pain returned, worse than before. I fought it. Two principles drove me on: a determination to visit justice upon Vish, and an even stronger need to atone for my folly.

~

Every tilted paving stone surrounding Manse Muril, every lump of plaster flaking from the mouldy walls, every rotting beam, crumbling roof slate and piece of woodworm-eaten furniture reeked of the fatal mancery that had been done here. I could even read it in the ancient, wind-twisted pine tree outside the back door. The very rocks beneath the manse were saturated with the forces released by its owner's grandiose folly.

Was that why I had ended up here? Had fate led my footsteps to this ruin? Or had I been drawn here to die as horribly as its owner?

I huddled in the driest room, weeping from the pain of my wounds. The manse, two thousand feet higher than the college, stood on a rock shelf halfway up the towering red cliff. A hundred years ago the place had been built by a wealthy but third-rate sorcerer, Vixiline Groeg, who had been mentioned in a cautionary tale back in my first year.

Groeg's ambition had far outreached his talent and an experiment in dark mancery had killed him when he was only in middle age. Since then Manse Muril had been abandoned and the college students were forbidden, on pain of expulsion, from going anywhere near it. It suited me perfectly.

My back was a mass of fire. Many of the flogging cuts were infected and every movement was agonising. The tips of my middle toes had gone black from frostbite; I would have to cut them off or risk a hideous death from gangrene.

My life was ruined. I was an exile and a pariah. Having been expelled from the college for a capital crime, no one would dare take me in or even give me menial work. Anyone who recognised me would report me. If ... when I was caught I would be treated like the worst scum in the world – until I was executed.

Whichever way I went the news would outrun me. Everyone would be watching for me, hoping to get the reward for my capture, and in a world regulated by humanity's warring masters, a world where dissent was not tolerated, I would not be able to escape them. My only hope was to head south to wilderness lands, though with winter on the doorstep wild food would be hard to find, even for people who knew the land. I did not.

I had three options, though they all ended the same way. One – be caught and executed. Two – be sent to the war to be slaughtered. Three – starve to death in the wilderness.

I had to face facts. I deserved to die, and soon I would.

But was I going to die like a whining cur? Damned if I was. If the only thing left to me was retribution, I was going to have it. Retribution on the man who had cynically robbed me of all I had achieved against impossible odds.

I was going to punish Trukulus Vish, whatever it took.

But how?

4

No matter what happened to me, in three respects yesterday had been the greatest day of my life. I had worked a mighty new spell, one that not even the assembled masters knew how to undo. I wasn't a useless, failing fool – I was the best student the college had seen in many years. And Sissily and Yggur, neither of whom had any reason to like me, had befriended me, proving that there was still some good in the world.

But was there any good left in me?

I forced my mind back to Vish, and retribution. My staff had been taken when I was stripped naked, and there was nothing useful here – Vixiline Groeg's grimoire, notebooks and equipment would have been confiscated or destroyed after his death.

Yet the waste products of his profligate mancery remained; the place stank of it the way a dried-up corpse still reeked, years after death. Was there anything I could use to replace my staff?

The manse had been stripped of everything portable. All that remained were pieces of furniture, too heavy to carry down the cliff path, plus some rotting bed coverings, a few kitchen utensils and a number of broken items, including a large wooden clock and a little brass telescope that rattled when I shook it. A wardrobe held a set of moth-eaten sorcerer's robes that would have been unfashionable a century ago, a hat like a crumpled bag and a pair of long boots, the mould on them longer than a wizard's beard. The clock case had been smashed to splinters, the brass mechanism taken apart, and cogs and wheels were scattered across the dusty floor. Some were encrusted with what appeared to be very old blood.

I started a fire in the fireplace, fed it into a blaze with the clock case and a broken chair, and sat in front of it, shivering. The fire began to smoke – the chimney must be blocked. I had nothing to eat but I was used to that. I had often gone to my classes on an empty stomach and, lacking even a copper grint to my name, had eaten nothing for the rest of the day. My stomach had shrunk so much that an apple would have bloated me.

My black toes throbbed. I should cut them off but had no means of doing so save a rusty axe head I had found out the back. Despite the fire, I began to shudder; it was much colder here than at the college. The bed coverings were rotted to shreds, however in a room that, facing south, never saw the sun, I found a pair of heavy red velvet curtains. I wrenched them down, shook out the age-old wasp nests and at least a hundred spiders, wrapped the curtains around myself and returned to the fire.

The room was smoky now, but with the door shut it was a little warmer. I lay on my side in the most comfortable position I could find, enduring the pain I could do nothing about. The room swirled and shivered. I closed my eyes.

The firelight flickered on my eyelids. My feet felt as if they were still frozen, but my head and chest were so hot that I was sweating. The skin of my face was drum-tight.

I reached for my staff to work a pain-relieving charm, then groaned. I had no staff. The loss sheared though me. My first task as a student had been to select a suitable branch from an appropriate tree, carve it to shape and enchant it to give it a simple *persona* that would allow it to enhance my innate gift for mancery. Every year since then I had worked on my staff, subtly honing its shape, imbuing it with all I had learned, and binding its persona ever tighter to me.

My entire history at the college had gone into my staff, and now it was lost. Had Vish broken it? Surely not – I would have felt the psychic pain from a hundred miles away. No, he would have kept it to use against me. He could be working on it now, trying to command its persona to track me down and, in the ultimate agony, kill me with my own staff.

I tried to work a pain-relieving charm with my hands but the room began to weave and wobble and, with my eyes closed, my head spun sickeningly. I fought the nausea and it faded. Now everything seemed to be rocking gently, as if I were on a little raft in a vast ocean. Streaks of light and darkness wobbled up and down; shapes I could not define drifted this way and that.

A darker layer crystallised out, and upon it a globular shape went whirling around a sinkhole of blackness. As I dreamily followed its orbits, the pain began to recede. I imagined I *was* that spherical shape, endlessly following its elliptical path, concerned about nothing, affected by nothing, until finally the path embedded itself into my mind like a marble wearing a groove in a tile.

Other layers appeared, other shapes. Some were like world globes, one colour or another, while others were spinning discs or tumbling rocks. I kept following them until the pain of my back and feet slipped away to another world – or I slipped away from it ...

A flash and a clap of thunder hurled me back into my tormented body. A storm was shaking the manse. I must have been away for a long time because the pain was excruciating now. My gangrenous toes were filling my blood with poison. How long did I have left? Days, or only hours?

Panic flashed through me. I had to act at once or die a failure. Needing something to do with my hands, I took the little telescope apart. It wasn't broken; the lenses had simply come out of their mountings. After warming some gum scraped from the pine tree, I fixed the lenses in place and put the telescope back together. It worked, but it could not save me.

My frantic eye fell on the scattered cogs and the rest of the clock mechanism. Like everything else in the manse it was imbued with waste mancery resulting from the sorcerer's death.

Suddenly I knew what to do.

～

The clockwork-driven orrery was a far superior device to the one I had made in my cupboard in the college. It was beautifully built, mounted on a circular ebony-wood platter I had found in the kitchen, and when I wound it with the clock key it began to run. Best of all, every atom of my orrery was enchanted, and I hoped to use it as a substitute for my staff.

But it did not resemble any orrery ever made before, for its worlds and moons had never been seen in the skies of Santhenar. They were as dark, mysterious and impenetrable as the fevered vision I'd used as a blueprint and, now that I considered them rationally, it wasn't clear that they were planetary bodies at all ... or what they were.

Or where.

A shiver passed through me. Hadn't I learned my lesson? But how could my life get any worse? The pain in my infected back was now worse than the pain in the live parts of my toes. My head and back were boiling, the rest of me freezing. I was slipping back into a fever from which I might never wake.

My life had to mean something; before I died I had to do something worthy. Trukulus Vish was an evil man, and I was going to cut him down in the name of justice.

At least, I convinced myself that it was justice.

I know better now.

The room was wavering again, the fever beating on me like a desert sun. I had to do it now.

I tried to get up, and screamed. The pain in my black, bloated feet was excruciating. I groped in the firewood pile, caught hold of a three-foot-long piece that had once been part of a wooden chair and used it to lever myself upright.

After several attempts I managed to pick up the orrery. I staggered through the manse to the rear door, then out onto the narrow terrace. A broken stone railing ran along part of the cliff edge. I was afraid to go close but had no choice – for the best spell-work, I had to be able to see the college and the office window of Trukulus Vish. I also had to be outside – given the manner of Groeg's death, the manse would be tainted with all manner of resonances that could interfere with my spell.

It was seven in the morning. The sun had not yet risen and, though it was growing light, Blaggart was still a black outline, a mile away and two thousand feet below. I was pleased to see, however, that a light burned in the upper window of the northern tower. That bastard Vish was in his quarters.

I fixed the little telescope to the orrery with dabs of warmed gum and sighted on Vish's window. If all went well the orrery would serve to *locate* the power I needed and direct it at my enemy.

And then, righteous justice would be mine!

Overhead, the dark clouds thickened. The light in Vish's window shone out more brightly. I felt a sharp pain in my empty belly. My hands, holding the heavy mechanism, were shaking. I dragged out a chair, the only unbroken one, and sat down to wind the mechanism. The cogs of the orrery made a gentle whirring sound. The tension increased as the spring tightened.

Holding the orrery on my lap, I focused on the slowly creeping globes – enigmatic bodies from an unexplored underworld that had unblocked some power or gift in me before, enabling me to create an unbreakable spell. Could I do it again? I must.

First I had to reach the part of me that had briefly unblocked last time. It was even harder now but I used the pain the way a jockey uses his whip. As I strained to reach that closed-off place I had touched before, pain speared up my littlest left toe. Then up the right middle toe. And then the others, over and again, like a tune picked out, one-fingered, on a keyboard.

I forced myself to swallow the pain, to sit upright and focus harder than I had ever focused before. To reach into the core of the place that had unblocked my gift last time, *and prise the door open.*

And then it came, so powerfully that it was almost unbearable: hot prickles surging along the nerves running across my shoulders, up my arms and into my hands until they felt as though they were ablaze.

They were! Cold blue fire began to drip from my fingers and the heels of my hands, while a darker blue luminescence streamed up from the orrery. Indigo lightning arced between a small, dark planet and a large ringed world with three moons. I sighted on the lighted window again and focused the telescope until the window filled the field of view.

Then, as if my luck had turned at last, my nemesis appeared there, looking out. Looking up at the red cliff. At Manse Muril. At me?

Could he see me? Not with any normal sight. But Vish slowly reached backwards and I knew he was going for his staff. He had sensed danger. Was he going to attack?

With a soft, organic *click*, my gift, whatever it was, unblocked. 'Die!' I said, focusing on Vish's chest and drawing every speck of power the orrery had revealed within me. I felt a boiling hot flush; my hands turned crimson; my face was burning and huge drops of sweat formed all over me.

But as I released the power, the clockwork mechanism jammed. The orrery shuddered wildly; the small dark planet jerked, unseated itself and crashed into the large ringed planet, knocking it off course and sending its moons flying in all directions. I tried to hold my aim true but the front of the orrery was flung downwards and a torrent of power roared from it, striking the base of Vish's tower with almighty force. Jets of dust shot out from between the stones, then the lower half of the tower blurred.

A second later a tremor passed through the ground, shaking loose tiles off the roof of the manse to shatter on the terrace. Shards stung the back of my left knee. The orrery slid from my grasp, between my spread legs and hit the ground. I half rose to my feet, staring, fearing.

I realised I was holding my breath. The tower did not seem to be harmed, and Vish had vanished from the window. As I exhaled, the door at the base of the tower was flung open and students began to stream out.

In an instant, the wall where my blast had struck crumbled. Cracks zigzagged up the sides of the tower, all the way to the top. With nothing holding it up, the stonework above the arch collapsed on two students coming through the door.

Dust obscured the scene.

5

How could the orrery have jammed when I'd made it so carefully? I picked it up but my hands were shaking so badly I could not hold it. I put it on the chair and checked the mechanism once, twice, thrice. There wasn't a speck of grit or debris that could have affected it, yet it had jammed at the crucial moment ... as if something had *forced it* to go astray –

Stop looking for excuses! It had gone wrong and it was my doing. I removed the telescope and examined the scene at the college. It looked bad.

Hundreds of students had gathered on the lawn outside the tower; several black-gowned masters kept them well back. The stonework had collapsed for ten feet above the arch but the remainder of the tower, though badly cracked, was still in place. Two masters stood on the rubble-littered steps, staring at the mess.

A rope was thrown from a broken window halfway up. A man with a long bundle strapped to his back stood there for a second, then clambered out and went hand over hand down the rope. He reached the ground, staggered, and turned. Trukulus Vish!

His face was bloody, though he did not appear to be seriously injured. He gave a series of orders and the senior masters gathered around. Vish unstrapped the long object – two staffs, his and mine. The agony of separation sheared through me once more.

He pointed his staff at the rubble and a broken stone, two feet long and a foot high, lifted. He swung the staff to the side; the stone moved out over the lawn, and fell. Moving such heavy blocks with mancery must have been hard work, for the sinews stood out in Vish's neck each time he raised one. Under his direction, the other masters also began to work.

After half an hour, by which time most of the rubble had been moved and it was clear that all the masters were exhausted, he held up a hand. Two of the senior boys went up the steps, carrying a stretcher, and eased someone onto it. A tall boy who appeared to have a badly broken leg. As they brought him down, I focused on him. It was Yggur.

I felt sick. But there had been another student in the doorway. The masters moved three more pieces of rubble. Again Vish stopped the work and they gathered, looking down. Someone was lifted onto a second stretcher and, sombrely, carried out onto the lawn.

Matron Ulice, who had been tending to Yggur's leg, came running. She fell to her knees beside the stretcher, looked up, then angrily shooed the throng of masters and students away. She bent down and tried to raise the head of the injured student. I caught a glimpse of carroty hair.

No! No!

Ulice's broad figure blocked my line of sight. I lurched to the other end of the terrace, past a diamond-shaped, half-frozen pool, frantically focusing the telescope. My heart was beating erratically –heavy thumps were followed by whispering ticks, like the movement of a butterfly's wings. Move, damn you! They moved, and I looked down at the red hair and pale, freckled face of Sissily Bur.

Let her be all right. I could not bear it if she, of all people, had been badly hurt. The healer lifted her until she was sitting upright. Sissily's mouth opened, as if she were trying to speak, then a torrent of blood poured forth and her head sagged. The healer turned her on her side and waved her staff, calling for help. The masters gathered, looking down, then slowly walked away. The healer drew a sheet over the body.

Sissily, who had always been kind to me; Sissily, the one person I would never have wished harm on, was dead. My reckless stupidity had killed her.

And injured Yggur, who had allowed me to escape. Was the world out to get me? Even in the moment of my triumph, things twisted around to bring me down.

No! In a shattering instant of realisation I saw myself for who I really was – a meagre, whining fool, all too ready to blame everyone but myself. I hadn't been seeking retributive justice at all, but a cowardly, sneaking revenge. And good people had paid for it.

It wasn't going to end there. Vish was stalking around the broken tower, pointing his staff this way and that, trying to divine how the collapse had happened. I had no doubt that he would. Finding out who had done it would take a little longer, but the assembled masters could bring colossal forces to bear and they would soon know the truth.

Once they did, my life would be measured in hours. And if I could see them, with a telescope they could see me out here. I crawled back to the chair and the orrery, and hauled them inside.

I huddled by the fire, so sickened by what I had done that I scarcely cared whether I lived or died. Let them put me to death. I deserved it. I had ruined three lives, and two of them had been innocent. Anything would be better than this awful guilt.

There was no way out for me; no allowances were made in the harsh world of the Clysm. I would be tried, convicted and sentenced to the cruellest, most agonising and drawn-out death it was possible for any human being to suffer.

Unless ...

I shot upright. It was the soft voice I'd heard in my tiny room a week and a half ago, when I'd first had the idea for an underworld orrery. 'Unless what?' I said dully.

What have you got to lose?

Nothing, but I was justifiably wary of voices in my head. 'Who are you? And why would you help a monster like me ... if you *are* offering help.'

Santhenar is a jewel among worlds. I can't bear to see it ruined in this endless Clysm.

I thought it was a woman's voice, but could not be sure. It was very faint, as if she was an impossible distance away. 'What's that got to do with me?'

Purely by instinct, and with no resources save your own gift and intellect, you've worked mancery that no one else has ever done.

'So?'

You love Santhenar with all your heart.

'Yes,' I said, realising it for the first time. 'I do.'

Imagine if you could weld your people into a third force, equal to the Charon and the Aachim.

'That's preposterous!' Then, slowly, 'How?'

By ending the petty squabbling among your own people that is keeping them weak. By putting an end to the Clysm that is destroying your world.

'What makes you think I – a condemned, dying wretch – could do any of that?'

You will because you must. It's the only way you can relieve your crushing guilt.

'I'll be captured within a day, then executed.'

Unless you take renewal.

Hysterical laughter bubbled up in me. I held it at bay. 'Whoever you are, you're mad!'

Renewal can give you a new body, new face, new voice, new identity.

'It's the most agonising spell any mancer has ever used – and a death sentence to all who have tried.'

And therefore, the perfect escape.

'The greatest mancers in the world have failed to work a renewal spell.'

The voice was silent.

'Failed and died gruesomely,' I added. 'Their bodies exploding ... or being turned inside-out.'

A quick and pleasant death compared to what you're facing.

She was right. What *did* I have to lose? But I was not such a fool as to think the offer came at no price. 'What do you want?'

Santhenar ... free of war.

I laughed hollowly. In this empty room, I must have looked like a madman. 'The renewal spell is a deadly secret; I've never even *seen* such a spell.'

Look under the floorboards where you found the telescope.

I levered them up and found a crinkled sheet of beaten silver, blackly tarnished. I rubbed it with a rag. It was a page from a grimoire and impressed in the metal was the mostly deadly and unworkable spell ever invented – the renewal spell.

I put it down, very carefully. This was far too convenient. Had I been *led* to Manse Muril? Had the idea of the underworld orrery been *put* into my mind? What for, and why me? Because I was a brilliant student? Or because I was at the end of my rope?

Or had I been *driven* to the end of my rope, so I would have no choice?

I was in a very dangerous situation and I had no idea what to do, though one thing was obvious. The soft voice represented someone incredibly powerful and utterly ruthless, and they weren't doing anything for my benefit. If I had any sense I would take the easy way out – crawl to the edge of the cliff and topple over it.

I considered it. But now that I wasn't a useless failure the faint prospect of escape, of life, was too tantalising. I picked up the renewal spell, which was going to kill me.

But if, I vowed, by some miracle I did survive, I would devote the rest of my life to paying for my crimes. I *would* work tirelessly to end the War of the Clysm, protect my people and my world, and imprison or banish its enemies. But not because a voice in my head told me to. Because it was the right and only thing to do.

'How do I use the spell?' I said.

There was no answer. The voice was gone. It was up to me now.

I read the spell three times. The first necessity was food and water, as much as I could cram in, otherwise my body would consume its own flesh to feed the process of renewal. Since I had no food, my chances of a successful renewal were even slimmer.

I went out to the pool on the terrace, smashed the ice and gulped tooth-achingly cold water until my belly throbbed. Then, lying there gasping, I saw something move below. Fish!

I wove a crude net from the curtain cords and scooped out two fat fish, which I ate raw: eyes, organs, fins and all. I went back for more but the others had hidden and my further attempts at netting them proved fruitless. It wasn't near enough food but it would have to do.

I dare say you've read about the process of renewal, so I won't go into the revolting details. I don't care to relive my shattering screams, the explosive shedding of hair and nails and teeth, the eruptions of shit and piss, blood and vomit and bile. The turning of a living man into a gigantic body-blister encapsulating raw, roiling flesh ...

I groaned. Every bone ached, every muscle, every finger and toe joint. What had happened to me? It felt as though I had fallen from a cliff.

I tried to open my eyes but my eyelids were stuck together. I raised my hand; it moved in a series of jerks, missed my face, and my fingers raked through a mane of thick, coarse hair, as different to my own stringy, thinning hair as it was possible to be. I felt down my forehead and carefully rubbed my eyelids until the seal broke. Light flooded my eyes, so bright that I flinched. Sunlight was shining in through the grimy eastern window.

How could it be morning again? It had been midday. Had I slept all afternoon and night?

I caught a whiff of blood and other, disgusting smells, and the day-long agony flooded back. Renewal! Was I still in it? Or was I immersed in a hallucinogenic nightmare?

No, it was horribly real. I had survived. The very first mancer to do so.

My eyes were gritty. I could barely see, and I stank of piss and crap and blood. I was naked and very cold. I tried to stand up but fell. Pain stabbed through my toe joints, ankles, knees and hips. My arms and legs felt strange; my body did not belong to me. And I was utterly, *utterly* exhausted.

I crawled a couple of feet and had to lie down, panting. Then another foot, and another. I don't know how long it took me to reach the terrace and the ice-covered pool; I'd lost all sense of time. I cracked the ice with my forehead, washed my face and cleaned out my eyes, then slid in. Fire and ice, burning me all over! I sank to the bottom, took handfuls of the gritty mud and scrubbed myself until all the muck was gone.

I hauled myself out and lay there, gasping and shuddering, my skin burning with cold, unable to move. The renewal of a human body – tearing it down and rebuilding it bone by bone and organ by organ, save only the brain itself – burned an incredible amount of energy. Never before or since have I felt the desperate hunger I felt at that moment. I was literally starving to death. Since there had been no fat on me, my body had consumed some of its own tissue to survive the spell.

A small golden fish darted to the surface, escaping the mud I'd stirred up. I grabbed it, killed it and took a bite. Pain spiked through my belly as if I'd swallowed a nail and I threw up fish and blood, into the water. My renewed stomach was not ready for food.

Lying on my side, I examined myself. Previously I had been short and stocky, with muscular arms and heavy thighs. I suppose all that muscle had saved me. I was a good six inches taller now, but lean, almost emaciated. My feet were long and skinny, with no trace of gangrene, and my back was straight. But what about my face? Would it give me away?

I crawled inside and, using a piece torn from one of the red curtains, polished the back of the silver spell-sheet until it shone. I gingerly examined my features, and started.

My face was long, hollow-cheeked and clear-skinned – not a trace of the pimples that had troubled me these past five years. My nose was thin, with a slight arch, my lips thinner, my eyes no longer blue but dark brown, and a dense beard, as black as my hair, shadowed my jaw. I was not a handsome man but I could not give a damn.

I was unrecognisable as Nudifer Spoak.

I felt a little better, though I was not up to walking any distance. Nonetheless, I could not stay here, because sooner or later Vish would identify the manse as the origin of the attack spell. I burned Nudie's clothes and sandals, cleaned up the mess from my renewal, shook the dust and spiders out of Vixiline Groeg's robes, scrubbed the furry mould from his boots and put them on. The leather was hard and cracked and would undoubtedly let in water, and the boots were a poor fit, being too wide but not long enough. They pinched my toes, though after what I had been through the pain was insignificant.

I was preparing to leave when I heard the clack of a stone striking another, not far away. I eased my head over the cliff. Trukulus Vish and three of the most senior masters, all armed and angry, were climbing the path. They were only minutes away.

'There he is!' cried Master Abberie, an absurd little fellow with a round, leprechaun-like face and a urine-yellow rat's tail on his plump chin. 'After him!'

I cursed. It was too late to run. I would have to brazen it out. The orrery – it must not be found! I thrust it beneath the floorboard, threw the silver sheet in after it and replaced the board. What else?

Nudie's clothes weren't quite burned. I poked them into the coals and put the rest of the wood on. The fire blazed up. I went out onto the terrace to await the masters, not without a sickening feeling of panic.

What if the renewal was only temporary? Or illusionary? What if I began to revert to Nudifer Spoak? What if it was only skin deep? What if – I thought in horror – I still had Nudie's voice?

There was no time to test it. The masters turned the corner twenty yards away and headed up towards the terrace, their staffs raised. I stood up straight, fighting exhaustion, then turning to meet them as if I had every right to be here.

'Good day, gentlemen,' I said. My voice was deeper than Nudie's, and I managed to keep a quaver out of it. 'May I assist you?'

'Who the hell are you?' said Vish.

A name! I hadn't thought of that. Names mattered in mancery and they had to be absolutely right – I couldn't make one up on the spot. 'I'm an itinerant wizard.' Given my success with two forbidden spells, I could justify the name. 'You may call me Thaumat.'

Vish sniffed. 'We're looking for a renegade student, a stumpy, bent-backed villain, freshly flogged. Have you seen him?'

They might know that Nudie (I no longer thought of myself as him) had been here, so I dared not deny it. 'Spotty chap? Stringy hair? He tried to hide here yesterday when ... I was out. I chased him away.'

'Where did he go?'

'Up into the mountains.'

'Why the hell didn't you stop him?' snarled Vish.

I didn't bother to answer. Exhaustion was a boulder on each shoulder, and it was all I could do to remain upright.

'What are you doing here?' said Vish.

'Resting. Meditating.'

'It's a dangerous haunt. Its only owner –'

'I read his fate in the splatters on the walls.' How confident I felt. How utterly changed from poor, pathetic Nudie. 'He was a fool, interfering in matters he knew nothing about.'

'I'd advise you to take it as a caution and move on,' said Vish coldly.

I almost bowed, almost cringed, as Nudie would have done. But I wasn't a failing, persecuted student. I was a master who had wielded real power, and I was going to act it.

'Should I ever be in need of your advice,' I said, meeting his stare, 'I'll be certain to look you up. Good day!'

Rage fleeted across his face. 'Hold it!'

'Yes?' I said. It was a struggle to stop my knees from shaking. I had to get rid of the masters as quickly as possible. If I collapsed, and they examined me with mancery, they might find traces of the renewal spell.

'Stand aside.'

'You wish to search?' I moved out of Vish's way, surreptitiously supporting myself on the broken railing. 'Go ahead.'

He pushed past and went in. The other masters followed, and so did I.

'What's this all about?' I said to Abberie.

'Forbidden mancery. Nudifer left one student dead, another injured, and another ... mindless.'

'If only I'd known, I would have held him for you.' I leaned against the wall, controlling my breathing with an effort.

They searched the place hastily but thoroughly. I followed them from one ruined room to another, worrying all the while. What if they could detect Nudie's renewal spell? They might have ways of detecting him in me. I was sweating like a pig; what if I smelled like Nudie? I could be exposed in so many ways.

Shortly, after giving me several more assessing glances, Vish led the masters out and up the cliff path. When they were out of sight I prepared to leave. Last night's rain would have washed all footprints away but they might be able to track Nudie by mancery. If so they would soon realise that he had gone no further than the manse, and suspicion would fall on me.

I had to get away. In my starving state I dared not risk a full, wizardly interrogation. But first I had to have a staff – a magician without one would seem suspicious.

The ancient pine tree out the back was small and twisted, as if every one of its hundreds of years had been a fight for survival, and it also bore an enchantment from the profligate manner of Groeg's death. Its wiry wood would make a fine staff.

I twisted off a suitable branch, roughly shaped it using the axe head as an adze until the staff was my own height, and rubbed soot into the pale wood, ageing it to a dark brown that outlined every layer and knot-hole. Doing mancery would be difficult until I had time to imbue the staff with a persona, but it made me look the part.

I lifted the floorboard and took the orrery apart, reducing it to the clock parts from which I had made it and dumping them down the hole. I thought of leaving the renewal spell there as well, but it seemed too valuable to abandon, and too dangerous. I put it in the secret pocket of my robes, along with the little telescope.

Then, fearing that Vish might be able to divine what I had done here, I raked the coals out of the fireplace into the middle of the room, piled more dry wood on, and when the floor was well alight I headed down the cliff path. I only had the small coins Yggur had given me, enough to live on for a week or two.

After that I would have to survive on my wits.

~

It was only a three-mile walk to Gard, the closest town to the college, but it took me five hours because I had to rest every hundred yards. My robes, old though they were, attracted no attention – the town was used to visiting mancers and most were eccentric in one way or another. I paid for a cheap room and went to a bar for a bowl of stew and a mug of small beer. The stew vanished into the cavern that was my belly, making it throb but leaving me hungrier than before I'd started on it.

I had another bowl and sat there, trying to digest the astonishing events of the past days, that had changed me beyond recognition inside and out, and wondering how to begin on my impossible vow. It would take time. The renewal spell had left me so weak that a flight of steps exhausted me, and there was no way of knowing how long the weakness would last.

A group of students entered, talking sombrely about the fate of the Head Boy and Head Girl. They passed me without a second glance, heading for a long table at the rear. I was idly watching them when I realised that someone had stopped by my table. I looked up and my heart began to race. It was Yggur, his right leg in plaster, supporting himself on crutches.

He was staring at me. Why? Had he recognised me despite the renewal? His gift was a strange one. No one knew where it had come from, and not even the masters understood how it worked.

'Can – can I help you?' I said breathlessly.

'Do I know you?'

'I don't believe so,' I lied. 'I've not been to Gard before.'

His eyes roved over me. I struggled to breathe normally. If he recognised me and denounced me, I had no hope of escape. Nor if he attacked with his fists or the Secret Art; either way he was far stronger. He stared at me for a full minute, then turned aside without a word and made his painful way down to the table with the other students.

I reached out for the beer but could not lift it. My arm was shaking and I was overcome by gut-clamping, head-spinning terror. I felt a desperate urge to bolt, but forced myself to overcome it. Self-control! Now! I must do nothing to attract suspicion.

I dragged the mug across the table, lifted the mug and spilled beer down my front. I wiped myself down, wanting to check on Yggur, but fought the urge and sat there for another ten minutes, sipping my drink, my mind racing. I had planned to stay for a few days, but that was too dangerous now. I would leave in the middle of the night, heading north, and avoid every town and village until I was fifty miles from here.

I pushed the empty mug away, stood up shakily and headed for the door. Only when I reached it did I dare to look sideways. Yggur was staring at me as fixedly as before. I went out, trying not to run.

Back in my room I collapsed on the bed, so worn out from climbing the stair that I could not stand up. As soon as I was able, I wedged the chair under the door handle, opened the window as a way of escape and lay on the bed fully dressed. I had to sleep, for a few hours at least. I closed my eyes and sank into a well of darkness.

You'll do very well.

I roused slowly, still in the paralysis of sleep, and so slug-witted that at first I thought it was Yggur, for he had haunted my nightmares. Yggur and Sissily, with blood pouring from her mouth.

'What?' I said in a dry creak.

I've watched half a dozen brilliant mancers attempt that spell. You're the only one who didn't decorate the room with his internal organs. You'll do very well.

It was definitely a woman's voice. 'For what? Who are you, anyway?'

My name is Murgilha.

'Are you a ... demon? In the underworld?'

She laughed. *There is no underworld. And I already told you my price – Santhenar, free of war.*

'How?'

By welding old humans into a third force, equal to the Charon and the Aachim. By taking over the so-called Great Council and turning it into a cabal of the most powerful old human mancers in the world. A cabal strong enough to take on humanity's greatest enemies, kill or imprison them – and put an end to this Clysm that is destroying Santhenar.

'I'm only seventeen!' I said scornfully. 'And penniless, and powerless.'

If you listen to me, in three days' time you will have earned all the wealth you can ever spend – and a fortnight after that you will have more power than you can ever use. In return ... you will do one little thing for me.

I should have known something was terribly wrong. Anything that seems too good to be true almost certainly is. And even if the offer was genuine, why would it be made to me? But I was young, all too human, and everything I'd gained by my own blood and sweat had been stolen from me. The offer was too tempting; I could not resist it. I ignored my misgivings.

'What must I do?'

Go to the stables at the end of the street and buy a horse and cart –

'I don't have the money.'

You have a staff – use a simple Mesmer Spell on the owner. You can send him the coin later … if your conscience troubles you. Ride east along the range for fifty-four miles to Nuggetty Hill, and I will tell you where to dig.

The voice was gone. I gathered my gear, the work of a moment, and went out into the dark. I bought food, a knife and spoon, a pick and shovel and a small cooking pot. I needed a sleeping pouch but my coin was exhausted, so I headed to the stables.

I'd never used a Mesmer Spell before though I knew how it was done, and the mancery-imbued wood of my staff did the rest. The bespelled proprietor gladly sold me a horse and wagon, to be paid for next week, and gave me directions to Nuggetty Hill. I left Gard immediately and planned not to come back; it represented a past I never wanted to think about again.

Three days later, in the mid-afternoon, I reached Nuggetty Hill, a long, low rise topped by two lines of small rocky knobs, like the teats of a sow. The hill was pocked with hundreds of little diggings and shafts, long abandoned and overgrown.

Turn your back on the diggings and head east towards the small hill a quarter of a mile away.

I did so, until I reached rough ground which the cart could not cross.

Leave the cart. Turn left and walk twelve paces.

I did so, wearily. I was far from comfortable in my new body and still tired easily. And I wondered, not for the first time, if this was all a cruel joke.

Stop. Dig.

The ground was hard and stony. I attacked it with the pick, shovelled the loose earth and stones away, then used the pick again. It was exhausting work but I kept going. If I stopped, I wouldn't be able to start again today.

Two hours later and four feet down, the pick sank into something softer, and stuck. A shiver made its way up my backbone. I wrenched the pick free, shovelled the dirt out and scraped a rough surface clean.

And saw the gleam of gold. I cleared around it and discovered a monster nugget, two feet long and a foot wide. Shaking as if with ague, I began to excavate it.

It was too heavy to lift, so I hacked the soft gold in half with the pick, along a natural weakness, and dragged the pieces to the cart. Using one of the side boards as a ramp, I forced the gold up to the bed of the wagon and shoved them into a canvas sack. There may have been more gold in the hole but I didn't bother to check.

Two days later I sold the nugget to an assayer in Garching for eleven thousand gold tells – a staggering fortune; enough money to keep a family for an equivalent number of years. I told him where I'd found the nugget and he grew rich on what I had left behind. We were friends for a while, after that, though it did not last. My friendships never have ...

I sent money back to the stable owner, for the cart. I pay my debts to the last grint.

Ride west to the estuary of the River Ching. There is a greenstone lighthouse on its northern headland, once occupied by the mystic, Calliat, and his lover, the notorious Collector Arcana, Daliet. They died in a suicide pact and Daliet's collection has never been found ...

Properly outfitted this time, I did as I was instructed. The land west of Garching had been scalded by repeated war and was largely empty, its manors and steadings abandoned, its towns in ruins. It hurt to see my beloved country in such a state, and I knew it was repeated right across Lauralin. The Clysm had been going for four hundred years now and, without something to break the deadlock, might continue for another four hundred. We old humans paid the price. If the war continued, what would be left of us?

The greenstone lighthouse, though only a hundred years old, was crumbling, the soft, unsuitable rock fretting and flaking away.

Look behind the fourth stone of the third course, directly opposite the entrance.

I cut the mortar away on all sides and eased the green block onto the floor. Behind it, in a small wall cavity, was a book-shaped package wrapped in a sheet of lead whose edges had been beaten together to make a perfect seal. I opened it carefully, knowing that magicians always protected their treasures. Though Daliet had been a collector, not an adept.

The book was unprotected, and immensely heavy. Its covers were of serpentinite, the same dark, oily green stone as the lighthouse. It had no title and no name on the cover, and contained only eleven leaves, each a sheet of brass hinged into the spine. Etched into each sheet was the formula, or recipe, for a spell of dark mancery. Spells that uncomfortably reminded me of the unknown place I had twice plumbed with my orrery.

'Mancery of command, control and domination,' I said.

How else will you tear down the useless Council and rebuild it? How else will you unite your small-minded and fractious people? You must be as strong as Pitlis the Aachim, as unyielding as Rulke the Charon. Nothing less can save your world – as you already vowed to do.

Murgilha was right. To pay for my crimes, this was what I must do, though I did not have the faintest idea how to begin. 'How can *I* hope to influence Magister Rula, or any of the great lords and barons?'

The art of seduction takes too long to learn. You must train yourself to domination, using the eleven spells.

She was right. The members of the Council were old, arrogant and set in their ways. They would never listen to an upstart young wizard with no past or pedigree, who had simply appeared out of nowhere. My task was even greater than I had thought. I would have to tear the Council down, even the once-great Rula who had awarded my scholarship, and start afresh with brilliant young mancers that I could control. But first I had to master the eleven spells.

This crumbling tower in an empty land would do as well as anywhere to begin my study. I fed and watered my horse, gathered my gear, bolted the door and climbed two hundred steps to the top of the lighthouse. Its brazen mirror, ten feet high, was dusty. There was a table and chair, an iron bed and an empty water jug. It was more than I'd had in my life.

My whole body ached for sleep but I set the brass grimoire on the table and opened it at the first page.

And now, my price.

I jumped. *One little thing,* she had said the first time. I had convinced myself that we had a common purpose in saving Santhenar. Fool!

'Yes?' I said wearily.

You will find something for me.

'What is it?'

It's called the summonstone. And once you find it, you will wake it. You will find that the method you used to unblock your own gift will do nicely.

'What is this summonstone?'

A lost artefact.

'What does it do? And why, if you're so powerful and so far seeing, can't you find it yourself?'

Questions a prudent mancer would have asked before *making a binding vow.*

'I didn't make it to you.'

Ah, but you did, and you are bound to me until the vow is fulfilled – or you lie dead and full of worms.

'Be damned!'

When you turned your orrery away from the planets, thinking you were turning it downwards, you entered my realm, and from that moment I began to shape you to this end. But I can break you just as easily, and start again.

'You put the spell into my head that destroyed Haddon?' I cried.

I did, though you freely chose to use it.

'You diverted my blast at Vish's window and it killed Sissily.'

I diverted it. But you chose to use a needlessly destructive blast.

'This is why you brought me all this way.'

Everything you have – your life, a new and better body, more wealth than you could ever spend, the most important grimoire in the world – you have because of me.

'I never promised to find this summonstone. I'm going to fulfil my vow my own way, in my own time.'

Trukulus Vish will be most interested to know your new identity. As will Lord Sloon and Magister Rula –

'I'll go to the far side of the world.'

There is no place on Santhenar distant enough to escape Yggur's vengeance, if I should tell him who you are. He almost sensed Nudie in you, that day in Gard. He is a most determined young man. Implacable, in fact.

I walked to the nearest window and, after a struggle with badly corroded hinges, heaved it open. Cold air struck me in the face, making my eyes water. I dashed the tears away and stared out blindly. Murgilha was right – Yggur would find me, wherever I went. My life was in her hands and I had to pay her price. I had to find the summonstone, whatever that was, and activate it for her.

But what then?

I had been used, and I had a feeling that this *one little thing* would not turn out to be little at all. Murgilha had said she wanted Santhenar free of war. Why? She wanted old humans united into a third force as strong as the Charon and the Aachim. Why? Did she really want to save Santhenar – or did she want to break the power of the Charon and Aachim, forever? To what end?

Who was she, anyway, and why, if she had such vast power and insight, could she not act directly?

I had to find out. The future of Santhenar might depend on it.

Before I did anything, I had to have a new, appropriate name. I dusted the great mirror and stood in front of it, staring at my distorted reflection.

'I am Mendark!' I roared, 'and these things I do vow –

'I will do everything in my power to give humanity back its pride and self-respect. I will do whatever it takes to weld the Council into a force capable of taking on the Charon and the Aachim, and break their power forever. I will devote my life to protecting Santhenar, no matter what it should cost me.'

Only then did it occur to me that, to rebuild the Council with young and determined talent, I would have to bring the most gifted and enigmatic young mancer I knew to it. And find a way to work with him.

My implacable enemy, Yggur.

It is not recorded if Yggur ever discovered what happened to Nudie, or where Mendark came from, however there can be no doubt that Yggur took a heated dislike to Mendark at the instant of their first meeting. And in every dealing the two great mancers had afterwards, even before Mendark, for a noble cause, betrayed Yggur at the time of the Proscribed Experiments, Yggur suspected a hidden agenda behind everything Mendark did ... and was right to do so.

For Mendark's entire life, which lasted for more than 1100 years, and in which he took renewal an unprecedented thirteen times, was shaped by the vow he swore before his first renewal.

He spent many of those lives trying to unravel the mystery of the summonstone, and to decipher 'Murgilha's' true purpose, a deadly conspiracy he was still wrestling with at the time of his death.

One that finally comes to fruition ten years later in Book 1 of **The Gates of Good and Evil**, The Summon Stone. *You can read Chapter 1 at the end of this book.*

STORY IV

DARKNESS VISIBLE

DARKNESS VISIBLE

This short story was first published in Rich and Rare, *a collection of Australian Stories, Poetry and Artwork, edited by Paul Collins and published by Ford St Publishing (2015).*

The story is set about ten years before my epic fantasy quartet, The View from the Mirror, *and features Karan, the hero of that series, her friend Rael, and a particularly nasty ancestor.*

~

'We'll see it as we round the bend,' said Karan. Her chest was so tight with expectation that she could hardly draw breath. She turned around the bluff of zigzag-patterned rock and there it was, only a couple of hundred yards away. 'Oh!' she said, clutching at her heart. 'It's even worse than I remember.'

Rael, her young guardian and mentor, stopped dead, staring at the ruined tower. Baleful waves seemed to issue from it. 'I don't think we should go any closer.'

She looked up at him. He was tall and slender, with carrot-coloured hair that hung in ringlets to his shoulders, and sad green eyes. 'But it's taken us nine hard days to walk here.'

'We can take our time on the way back. Enjoy the mountain scenery. Spend a couple of days fishing.'

'Fishing?' she cried. 'My father died here when I was eight, and I've spent the past seven years wondering why. I've got to know.'

'Has it occurred to you that you might be better off *not* knowing?'

'He's the only good family memory I've got. I have to know why he came to this terrible place ... and what he got up to.'

Rael's extraordinarily long Aachim fingers clenched around his walking staff. 'At a guess, Galliad came here because he was only half-Aachim – and my people would never accept him.'

'He was desperate to belong,' said Karan.

'He would have been better off looking after his poor, troubled wife and his little daughter.'

'His little daughter was fine!'

She tossed back her long, tangled hair, which was the rich red of sunset in a smoky sky, and glared at him, defying him to mention her mother again. Vuula had suffered from the family curse, madness, and a few years after Galliad's death it had claimed her.

Now Karan was fifteen and almost grown up, in her own mind at least. She studied Carcharon, a madman's tower built on a knife-edged ridge. The afternoon sun lit the ruins like dripping blood.

She headed down the narrow ridge-top path. To either side, the ground fell away steeply for hundreds of feet. Twenty yards from the front of the tower she stopped abruptly. The tortured stone, which was an unsettling purple colour, had been laid in mad curves and distorted angles that raised her hackles.

'My father came here to prove himself,' said Karan. 'To your father.'

'It would never have worked,' said Rael. 'Tensor clings to the old beliefs. We pure-bloods are up high, and everyone else is down below.'

'I'm only a quarter Aachim, yet he took me in.'

'But all you claimed on our kinship was shelter until you come of age.'

She wiped sweat off her brow. 'It shouldn't be this hot. Not here!'

'We've been walking hard.'

'It's *never* hot at Carcharon. That's why Basunez built the tower here – because it was the coldest, windiest and most miserable place he could find.'

'He was insane.'

There was no wind, and that too was strange, because it was always windy in these knife-edged peaks. The air felt sticky, brooding.

Crash!

Karan jumped. 'What was that?'

'Ice.' Rael's eyes were darting; he wasn't as calm as he pretended. 'Falling off one of the roofs.' He weighed her up. 'You're absolutely determined?'

'Was Father a good man – or did he come here to do black-hearted magic? And if he did, knowing the terrible history of this place, *why*? I've got to know, Rael.'

He nodded. 'All right. Keep well back.'

'Why?'

'Because you don't have the gift for magic.'

'But I *am* a sensitive.'

'It might be better if you were an *insensitive*,' he muttered. 'Now listen – if my spell goes wrong, there's nothing you can do. You must head straight back to Shazmak –'

It was the stupidest thing he'd ever said. She glared at him. 'How would I explain *that* to Tensor?'

'I agreed to escort you here on one condition – that you did exactly as I said.'

She looked up at him, quivering, afraid. 'But –'

'You do realise that if this goes badly you'll never be allowed to see me again?'

It hit her like a blow to the stomach. In her girlish daydreams she had seen Rael as more than a friend, once she had grown up. 'What are you talking about?'

'Tensor isn't happy that I'm friends with a girl who's only one-quarter Aachim. Give him the excuse and he'll send me to the far side of the world.'

'All right. I'll do exactly what you say.' She went back down the path for ten steps.

'Further,' said Rael.

She took another few reluctant steps. The air seemed to be hotter now, and stickier.

He glanced at the sun, which was already low. 'I'd better be quick. We've got to be gone before dark.'

Carcharon was a desperately haunted place and, if he did raise something, they would need sunlight on their side. After dark, things could get awkward.

He conjured something from his pocket to his hand. An object made of dark metal, twisted into a complicated shape that Karan could not make out.

'What's that?' she said.

'A twistoid. I'm not supposed to have it ...'

He touched his forehead with it, then moved it in a swirling pattern. The base of Karan's skull tingled: *magic*. Her father had been able to do it, and her evil ancestor, Basunez, had been a master, but she lacked the gift. She yearned for it, though.

As she peered through the broken front door of the tower, something flitted across the inside. It was the yellow-brown colour of old bones, but it was not the ghost of her tall, handsome father, nor that twisted old lunatic, Basunez.

It was the spirit of a girl Karan's own age, and she was trying to drive Karan away. Another five children appeared, four boys and a girl, all silently screaming, *Go! Go!*

Rael hugged himself. 'Are they –?'

'My ancestors,' Karan said, shivering. 'Centuries ago, six of Basunez's seven grandchildren were picnicking in the forest a few miles below here. It's said they were torn to pieces by a mountain cat ... though he was always blamed.'

'You're descended from the seventh grandchild?'

'She had been naughty; she wasn't allowed to go on the picnic.'

'Lucky for her.'

'It haunted her until the day she died. That she'd survived because she'd been bad, and they did not.'

Karan, unnerved by the children's ghosts, clamped one hand over the other and squeezed hard.

Rael swirled the twistoid in a different pattern and another ghost appeared. Karan choked. Her father's spirit was as thin as mist, with a reddish tinge that echoed the western sky. Over there, the sun was hurtling towards the horizon. Should she tell Rael to stop?

There was still time. She had to know.

Her father's spirit was bent over a white, circular pedestal with a series of red glyphs running around its circumference and a ragged black symbol in the middle.

'What's he doing?' she said quietly.

The tendons stood out in Rael's neck. The spell was taking far more out of him than she had expected. 'He's trying to raise someone – or *something*.'

'Not – *Basunez*?'

An image flashed into her mind – deep below, in solid rock, a jagged, spinning clot of darkness shot with crimson flames. Then it vanished. Rael doubled over, gasping.

'Rael?' she cried.

'Stay where you are!'

'Father, what are you doing?' she whispered.

Galliad looked up and saw her standing there, seven years after his death, and his face twisted in agony. His lips formed the words, *Karan, run. Never come back!*

'Rael!' she yelled. 'Stop, now!'

'*I – can't.*'

The sun plunged below the horizon like a diver off a cliff. The light faded, the sweaty heat became a clammy chill and tendrils of fog rose in a hundred places.

Rael was trembling wildly and brown smoke was rising from his fingers. Then, as she watched in horror, something began to separate from him. Something as misty as her father's ghost, though it had the shimmer of life – Rael's life. His spirit was being dragged out of him.

'Run for your life!' he gasped. He was shuddering from head to toe and the smoke rising from his hand was turning black.

'But –'

'You – gave – your – word. Go!'

But his spirit was being drawn down through the rock towards that spinning clot of darkness. He was dying. Whatever the consequences, she had to break her word. Karan stumbled forwards.

'Go back!' he screamed.

She had to stop his spell. She went for the twistoid, but Rael was a lot taller and she could not reach his upstretched hand. She darted behind him and kicked him in the back of his right knee. It collapsed, he slumped sideways and she drove her knuckles into the funny bone of his right arm. His fingers opened but the twistoid did not fall; it was burned onto his palm.

Karan struck at it with the side of her hand. A shock shot up her arm, then she felt a sickening pulling sensation within herself, and a shadowy outline started to separate from her. A dreadful weakness came over her, but she had to fight it.

It was getting dark; time seemed to be speeding up. Inside Carcharon the little spectres did a bone dance, awaiting their hour.

Rael fell to his knees, choking. His spirit had almost completely separated from him and without it he would die ... *or worse*. She whacked the twistoid again and again, and each time felt the shock, the burning sensation and the nausea as her spirit separated further.

She clamped both hands together and struck at the twistoid with all the strength she had left. The charred skin of Rael's palm tore away and the twistoid fell to the ground, still smoking. She picked up a heavy rock, raised it above her head, and froze there. She could not move; her own spirit was holding her wrists; that clot of darkness was trying to stop her.

Karan could not move her arms, but she could relax her fingers. She leaned forwards and let the rock fall onto the twistoid. The rock split with a bang, like a river stone in a camp fire, then the brittle metal of the twistoid snapped and her spirit slipped back inside her. She picked up another rock and slammed it down onto the broken twistoid over and again, smashing it into pieces. She kicked them over the edge and doubled over, heaving.

Rael's ghostly outline – at least, most of it – had returned to him, but he had fallen. Was he dying? She staggered to him, her legs barely holding her up. His right hand was still smoking, badly burned. She squirted half the contents of her water skin onto it.

'Told you to run,' he said faintly. He rolled onto his side and drew his knees up, making small choking sounds.

'How could I abandon my closest friend?'

She dug a little jar of ointment out of her pack, smeared it on his hand and tied a strip of cloth around it. They headed back the way they had come, as fast as he could manage.

'What was that *thing*?' she said.

'Not here!'

Only when the madman's tower was out of sight, and the clean, pure stars were coming out, would Rael sit down long enough to take some food and water. He was still trembling.

'What happened?' said Karan. 'What was my father up to?'

'There's a great, unknown power deep below Carcharon. I suppose that's why Basunez built the tower there – to draw on it.'

'What kind of power?'

'Not a good kind.'

'And that's what my father wanted?'

'Perhaps he thought it would help him prove himself to Tensor.'

'So Galliad used the forbidden art of necromancy,' she said bitterly, 'and raised the spirit of that evil man, *just to gain the power for himself.*'

'We don't know what he wanted the power for. It could have been for a noble purpose.'

Karan could no longer hope for that; her faith in her father had been crushed. 'But that spinning clot of darkness stopped him.'

'You saw it? What did it look like?'

The eagerness in Rael's voice disturbed her. 'I couldn't tell,' she lied. 'Was that what ...?'

'Tried to draw the life-force out of us? Yes.'

'What for?' said Karan.

'I don't know,' said Rael. 'Though I'm afraid –'

'What?'

'That it was trying to *feed*, and grow.' He looked up at her. 'Your father's ghost was right. You must never come here again.'

'I don't plan to.'

'And when I get back to Shazmak,' he choked, 'before my father sends me east, *never to return –*'

She let out a cry of anguish. 'No!'

'I did warn you, Karan. But before I go, I'll beg Tensor to come here and raze Carcharon to the ground. No, to a hundred feet below the ground. He's the only one with the power to do so. It's the only way this evil thing can be destroyed.'

'Good!' said Karan.

'But he won't,' Rael said softly.

'Why not?'

'History has ground my people down. After all the defeats, and all the failures, they no longer care about the fate of the wider world – only about their own tiny part of it.'

'But that means –'

'The darkness will fester and grow, until one day it breaks out. I pray that I'm not alive to see it.'

'I don't understand,' said Karan.

'The first lesson in magic is *Never meddle in things you don't understand.* Basunez woke something at Carcharon, centuries ago. Something very dark. And when your father tried to draw on it, he made it stronger.'

'Now you and I have fed it,' said Karan, feeling sick. 'But what does it want?'

'A question better asked before we came here. It's too late now.'

STORY V

THE PROFESSIONAL LIAR

THE PROFESSIONAL LIAR

Spoiler alert!

*If you haven't read my fantasy quartet **The View from the Mirror**, and intend to, you should do so before reading* The Professional Liar.

    This short story is set five years after The Way Between the Worlds, *the final book of the quartet, and background details in* The Professional Liar *necessarily reveal part of the ending.*

Llian was halfway up the volcano when, out of nowhere, he caught a whiff of wood smoke and heard a faint, phantom cry. His heart skipped several beats and he reeled off the track, gasping for air. But it was a bright, cloudless day; he was safe here, wasn't he? He forced the memories down, slammed the lid on them and increased his pace until he was breathless and burning hot – just like the trapped prisoners.

He smelled smoke again and the scream rang out in his mind. *Help, it's burning!*

Llian groaned, thrust his clenched fists skywards and roared, 'Go – *away!*'

He pounded up the rock-littered slope, the gritty soil rasping underfoot. It was a sweltering afternoon and, even at this altitude, the breeze was hot. The sky was a brassy bowl and the black boulders radiated heat; it was blistering his feet through the soles of his worn-out boots. Everything was baked here: the bare ground, the occasional tussocks of yellowing grass, the little horned lizards lurking in the shade. From the look of them, it had been a long time between meals.

He reached the crest of the volcano, panting, with his knees trembling. He ached for a cool drink and a rest in the shade, but the water in his bottle was hot and there was no shade here for any creature bigger than a rat.

Help! We can't get out!

Flashes of yellow and red flame through the brown smoke; smoke so thick that he could not breathe. His eyes were watering, the tears flooding down his cheeks; the fumes was burning the inside of his nose and the back of his throat. The crackling of fire ... the crash of falling timbers ... the pungent smell of burning hair ... the awful reek of charred flesh ... the screams as all those prisoners burned to death.

And it was his fault.

Llian dropped his pack and fell to hands and knees, clawing at the dirt and howling in horror. Though five years had passed, the nightmares – and the guilt – would not go away. He wailed, he shrieked, he pounded his fists and banged his forehead on the stones, hard enough to tear the skin. The pain broke through the flashback, scattering it like mist; the ground rocked and the real world reappeared.

He rolled over and lay on his back, staring up at the blistered sky. His head was throbbing and blood was running down the left side of his face. The nightmare was worse every time. No wonder Karan – no, *don't go there.*

He got up, caught his pack by one strap and lurched across the rock-littered rim of the crater for twenty yards, at which point it sloped down steeply. It was a mile across, and mostly arid and lifeless, yet a few hundred feet down he saw a dark blue lake, half a mile in diameter, with a tree-clad island in the centre. Somewhere on the island was his one hope and last chance – the hermitage of Wisemon Elgarde.

If she could not help him, no one could.

Once a great teacher and the principal of a college for brilliant girls, as well as a renowned herbalist, poet and philosopher, Elgarde had turned her back on that life in her early thirties, to live alone on this barren volcano in the middle of the Sea of Thurkad. She was said to have mysterious powers and great influence, which was why Llian had made his desperate, weeks-long journey to see her. Though it was also said that she rarely used her influence.

It was too hot to stand still; he heaved the pack onto his shoulders, adjusted the straps from one chafed strip of skin to another, and slipped and skidded his way down to the water. The air was deathly still inside the crater and smelled of baked rock, and the humidity rose with every step. By the time he reached the bottom it was choking him.

Bushes and small trees dotted the shore, and patches of brown grass. No doubt there would be snakes as well and they were bound to be venomous. He squinted through the heat shimmer, looking for signs of life on the island. Grey-leaved trees rose high above the rock but there was no evidence of a building, and this did not look like cave country.

The ground quivered. It had been doing so ever since he had landed here, and it made him uneasy. The volcano had blown its top off a hundred and twenty-three years ago, raining blistering ash on towns and villages thirty miles away, and creating a twenty-foot-high tidal wave that had washed whole villages into the sea, then collapsed part of the ancient wharf city in Thurkad, a hundred and thirty miles south of here, with the loss of hundreds of lives.

Patches of steam rose from the ground in half a dozen places, and fifty yards away Llian could see the distinctive yellow of sulphur, crusting the rocks. The air reeked of it. Was that a bad sign? If the volcano had blown up once, it could do so again.

There were clusters of blue freshwater mussels under the water, and bright green streamers of algae. He scooped a handful of water but it was warm, and bitter. He spat it out, gathered another double handful and washed his face with it.

After looking vainly for a boat or even a floating log, he concluded that he would have to swim to the island. He was a competent swimmer, and it was only a few hundred yards, but the prospect of going into these unknown waters did not enchant him.

He took off his boots and socks, tied them around his neck, secreted the carefully wrapped gift in a secure pocket, put his pack up on a boulder where it might be safe from predatory lizards, then waded into the water.

It was the first time his feet had felt cool since he set out from the landing cove six hours ago; it was bliss. But away from the shore the water was almost blood-warm. Too warm, and when he stopped fifty yards out to tread water and catch his breath, he could feel a warm current rising around him, coming up from the searing heart of the volcano.

A shudder passed through the water and enormous, dish-shaped bubbles broke in an arc across the surface, emitting a sulphurous reek. Llian put his head down and swam the rest of the way in one long, gasping burst. He had to get out of the water.

There was far more green algae here – the whole shoreline was coated with it, and the rocks down as far as he could see, and it was so slippery that it was hard to get out. He fell twice, the second time gashing his left knee on a sharp edge of rock. Blood poured down his leg.

He went down on hands and knees and crawled out into the cool shade of the trees, his sodden boots thumping him in the chest with every movement. He stood up, emptied the water out, tied a rag around his bloody knee, looked around, and started.

A little old woman, dressed in baggy yellow pants and smock, and wearing a wide-brimmed hat woven from fern fronds, sat cross-legged on a black boulder eight feet above him, a small brass telescope in her left hand. She had small hands with short fingers, and bare feet. Her round face was as wrinkled as a crumpled piece of paper, yet her grey eyes were piercingly bright.

'W-Wisemon Elgarde?' he said, bowing.

'Llian, formerly of Chanthed,' she said in a throaty voice, inclining her head. She came nimbly down the steep face of the rock.

In her bare feet she would not have been five feet tall, yet she had a presence he found intimidating. He took a step backwards, which sent a painful throb through his knee, then withdrew the wrapped gift and, holding it in both hands, palms upwards as he had been instructed, held it out to her.

'The price of entry,' she said with a secret amusement, but did not take it. 'What did they tell you to bring me?'

'Twenty-years-aged bamundi,' said Llian.

The preserved fish, a rare treat, had cost him even more than the passage from Thurkad to Ganport, then east to Lubley, the volcanic island next to the fishing port of Horn Island.

'Have you tried it?' said Elgarde.

'Certainly not!'

'Were you tempted?'

'Judging by the aroma,' he said, 'it's a delicacy for which I have not yet acquired the taste.'

'If you mean it stinks, say so.'

'It smells ... disgusting.'

'It's made by putrefaction. I hope you didn't pay dearly for it.'

He bit his lip.

'Oh dear,' she said. 'Thank you.' She took the package and, without unwrapping it, tossed it out into the lake.

Llian stared at her. Was she mad? The trip had cost more than Karan could afford; how could he go home and tell her the money had been wasted?

'Someone played a practical joke on you,' said Elgarde. 'In any case, I don't ask for payment in advance.'

'What about afterwards?' Llian fingered his meagre purse.

'Only when I judge I've been of service.'

'I ... may not be able to pay your price.'

'It's never more than my supplicant is *able* to pay ...'

'But?' said Llian.

'Sometimes it's more than he's willing to pay.'

'Ah.' He sensed a trap.

'But we won't talk about that now.'

The ground shook more strongly than before, creating ripples that lap-lapped against the shore. Llian felt the hairs rise on the back of his head.

'Could the volcano erupt again? And blow us to pieces?'

'At any time,' Elgarde said placidly.

Llian hunched his shoulders, as if making himself smaller could make a difference.

She looked at his forehead, and at his knee. 'Sit down.'

He perched on a triangular rock. She put down the telescope and disappeared into the trees, shortly to return with a small, cylindrical wooden container. A daisy flower and several leaves were carved into the pale yellow wood. Squatting in front of him, she removed the bloody bandage and applied a thick green paste, which smelled almost as offensive as twenty-year-bamundi, to the wound. The gash burned for a few seconds, then his knee went numb. She smeared the paste on the cut on his forehead. His head began to ache.

Llian thanked her. She studied him in silence. He cleared his throat and she smiled. She had a charming smile and must have been remarkably attractive when she was young.

'You're thinking that we should get on with it,' said Elgarde.

'I wouldn't want to waste your time,' he said lamely.

'Not a second of my life is wasted – even when I'm doing nothing. But I can see you're an impatient man. You'd better make your confession.'

'My – *what*?'

'Before I consider a supplicant's case, I require her – or him – to unburden himself of his failings and secrets.'

He squirmed at the thought. 'You want me to confess my *sins*?'

Elgarde laughed. 'I'm sure they're many and varied, and highly entertaining, but I couldn't care less about them. However, I require absolute honesty about the problem that brings you here. Honesty, with *brevity*. So ...'

Being a master teller, Llian could tell a tale in any length and a variety of forms, including poetic ones, though he was used to taking his time. He thought for a minute.

'Five years have passed since the Way Between the Worlds was opened, and Santhenar –'

'No need to tell me what everyone knows,' said Elgarde. 'This is about you and your problems.'

'I was a master chronicler,' he said bitterly. 'And a great teller. I wrote the *Tale of the Mirror*, the first new Great Tale in hundreds of years ...'

He trailed off; that was common knowledge too, but she waved an age-spotted hand, and he continued.

'Five years ago, when I was only thirty-one, I had everything. Respect, universal acclaim –'

'The love of a remarkable woman.'

'That too,' he said, almost inaudibly. 'Then Wistan, the ugliest and most malicious little creep in all the world, cut the world from under my feet.'

'Wistan, the Master of the College of the Histories at Chanthed?' she said in a distinctly cool voice. 'Wistan, who has devoted his entire life to the good of his college and the safety of the west? Wistan, my old friend, on whom you hope I will use my influence?'

Llian was making a hash of things, as usual. 'I'm sorry. I –'

'*Absolute honesty*, I said. You were not being honest about Wistan – *or* yourself.' She looked at him, enquiringly.

'He banned me from practicing my profession, for seven years. I'm not allowed to study or even write the Histories. I'm forbidden to write a new version of any existing tale, or a new tale, or even tell a tale in public.' The pain burst out of him. 'I can't bear it any longer. Telling is my life!'

'Have you learned your lesson?' said Elgarde.

'Excuse me?'

'You haven't told me the reason you were banned.'

His heartbeat accelerated. 'It's ... common knowledge.'

'If you don't want to tell me, perhaps you can't admit it to yourself. Doing so is the first step on the long path to redemption.'

Could he say it aloud? He must. 'Wistan banned me,' Llian said slowly and clearly, 'for *corruption*. I broke the chroniclers' first and most important rule.'

'Not *rule*,' she said. 'The first *law*. There's a big difference.'

'If you know everything about me, why do I have to say it?'

'If you can't, I can't help you.' She looked into his eyes.

Llian could not face her; he looked down first. 'I broke the first law – I failed to remain an impartial chronicler. In order to find the answer to a historical curiosity, I interfered in the Histories. I manipulated people; important people. And ...' He could not say it.

'You have to confess it,' she said. 'Out aloud. You have to *own* your failings, Llian.'

For the past five years he had been trying to *disown* them, but they only got worse.

'The first time I interfered,' said Llian, almost choking on the memories, 'a hundred prisoners in the Citadel burned to death.'

'Don't take more on yourself than is your due,' said Elgarde. 'You did not kill them.'

'But I manipulated Mendark. Had I not –'

'Had you not broken the first law, *the law you swore as a chronicler to uphold*, those prisoners might still be alive.'

'I have nightmares about them almost every night, and sometimes in broad daylight.'

'I know,' said Elgarde.

'How could you know?'

She touched the telescope with her toes. 'I saw you, up top.'

'I've tried to block them out but they only get stronger ...' Llian's voice dropped to a whisper. 'They're eating me alive.'

'Go on.'

He had to purge himself. 'But had I learned my lesson?' he cried. 'No, I was far too arrogant and full of myself.'

'Just the facts, Llian.'

'It wasn't enough for me to have the blood of all those prisoners on my hands,' he said in a voice thick with self-loathing. 'Oh no! Nothing less than *genocide* was good enough for a chronicler as arrogant and self-important as I was.'

'Now you're overdoing it. Leave the moral judgements to me.'

'Because I provoked Tensor, a great and noble human species, the Charon, were driven into extinction. I don't deserve ...'

There, he had said it. He had admitted to the one thing that made him irredeemable.

'So we come to the root of the problem,' said Elgarde. 'Sick with guilt, and overwhelmed by flashbacks where you relive the awful consequences of your folly, you believe that no one could love a monster like you.'

'Yes,' he whispered.

'Yet you ache to be loved. Tell me about your everyday life.'

'What?'

'You have a wife, Karan. And a four-year-old daughter ...?'

'Sulien,' said Llian. Before she came along he had not thought much about children. Llian had been astonished to discover that he loved her more than his own life, and he was terrified that he was going to lose her.

'You live at Karan's drought-stricken estate, Gothryme. What does a banned chronicler do all day?'

'He tries to be a farm hand,' said Llian, studying his scarred and work-worn hands. 'He does his very best, but he's all thumbs. Always has been; always will be.'

'And this makes you feel ...?'

'Frustrated. Angry. Desperate. I'm not made to be a farmer; I'm only good for one thing but I'm banned from doing it. I'm cranky, depressed ... a drain on the family ... and Karan ...'

'She sent you to me?'

'She said, "Don't come back until you've sorted yourself out ..."'

'The implication being?'

'If I can't sort myself out, *don't come back*.'

Elgarde did not speak for some minutes, then said, 'Is that everything?'

'Yes. Can you help me?'

'What did you have in mind?'

His heart was racing now. 'I was hoping you could ask Wistan to lift the ban.'

'Even though it still has years to run?'

'Yes, though now I've learned my lesson –'

'I'm not sure you have,' said Elgarde. 'Curiosity is your fatal flaw, Llian. If you were released from the ban, you might break the chroniclers' laws again – with even worse consequences.'

He slumped on his rock, staring at the water. She was probably right. He could not bear to look into her grey eyes for fear of what else she would read in him.

He stood up. It took an effort, for his gashed knee was still numb, and bowed. 'Thank you for hearing me, Wisemon Elgarde. If you would tell me your price, I will send –'

'I haven't finished with you,' she said sharply.

He sat. What sanction was she going to impose on him? Wistan was an old friend and Llian had insulted him. What if Elgarde had the ban lengthened, or made permanent?

'As I understand your ban, you're not permitted to work on the Histories in any form,' said Elgarde. 'Nor to tell or retell any of the tales great or small, old or new.'

'That's right.'

'But the ban doesn't stop you from making up stories.'

Llian fell off the rock. 'Are you suggesting I become a contemptible yarn-spinner?' he cried. 'A *professional liar?*'

'Surely any form of storytelling is better than nothing?'

'No, it's not!' He scrambled to his feet and limped back and forth in agitation.

'Making up stories, out of one's unfettered imagination, is utterly wrong. I could not even consider –'

'*Don't come back until you've sorted yourself out*, Karan said.'

He sat down hard, his nails digging into his palms. 'You rightly criticised me for breaking the chroniclers' laws, yet now you're undermining them.'

'How so?'

'The first thing I learned, when I arrived at the College of the Histories as a boy of twelve, was that all stories must be based on historical truth.'

'Is that one of the laws you swore to obey?' said Elgarde.

'No – but it might as well be.'

'Why must all tales be based on truth?'

'Because they're the very foundation of human life on Santhenar.'

'Strictly speaking, it's the *Histories* that are the foundation of our civilisation.'

'And the Great Tales exemplify and illustrate the Histories, and make them accessible to all. They must be based –'

'I'm not sure the Great Tales *are* all based on truth,' said Elgarde.

Llian jumped up. 'No! This goes against everything I've ever believed in.'

'The rule of historical truth was imposed by the master chroniclers long ago –'

'Why?'

'To devalue all kinds of storytelling save the ones they controlled through the Colleges of the Histories.'

'Are you saying ...?'

'The rule is all about power, control, and *money*. The uncouth yarn-spinners, who had never been to college and simply made up stories for the public's entertainment, had to be devalued and driven underground –'

'Why?' he repeated.

'So the chroniclers and tellers could maintain their power ... and their obscene wealth.'

Llian rocked back on his heels. It was hard to take in; even harder to digest. Yet Wisemon Elgarde had an unblemished reputation for probity and clear thinking.

'Even your friend, Wistan?' he said quietly.

'He's a good man, in many ways. But he clings to power long after he should have relinquished it, and will share it with none.'

She looked out across the lake, shading her eyes with her hand. In the middle, bubbles the size of wagon wheels were bursting, and the ground was shaking again. The volcano could erupt at any time, she had said.

'Are you advising me to become an *uncouth* yarn-spinner?' said Llian quietly. How could he sink that low?

'You say that you're no good at anything else. And it would help you to maintain the skills you spent so long learning; skills that must be dwindling from misuse.'

'It would be a hideous comedown.'

'You've already come down, Llian,' she snapped. 'Every College of the Histories in the world uses your example as a cautionary tale to their students.'

It struck him hard. 'A *cautionary tale*! Is that how the world sees me?'

'It's how the masters and students see you. I assumed you knew.'

'I – don't go out much.'

'My point is, do you really have far left to fall?'

'I suppose not, but ...'

'Perhaps your reputation, as the only living teller to have created a Great Tale, means more to you than your own family?' she said slyly.

Hot blood rushed to his cheeks. 'Certainly not!' Yet he had an uncomfortable feeling that she was right, and what kind of a man did that make him?

'You take Karan and Sulien for granted. Even though you can't go home without sorting out your problems, you hesitate to consider my suggestion.'

'It seems I have no choice,' said Llian. 'Though I can only do so at the cost of my self-respect.'

'Why?'

'Yarn-spinners are no better than liars.'

'What utter poppycock,' said Elgarde. 'Tales based on the Histories *may* be a superior form of storytelling –'

'Of course they are!' Llian said furiously. 'The Histories are based on pure, unvarnished truth ...'

She gave him a strange, almost pitying look – a look, he realised, akin to the one Rulke had given him five years ago. From Llian's perfect chronicler's memory, he could hear Rulke speaking.

Dear boy! You have failed the final test. You believe what you were taught. Everyone else may believe, but the masters must know the truth. History is as it is written, that is the only truth.

'In any historical event there can be dozens of truths,' said Elgarde, 'but the winners pick the truths that support the version of events they want people to believe. Then they choose malleable chroniclers to write the Histories – and sometimes they distort the truth to fit the facts. So ...'

Llian swallowed bitter gall. 'Yes?'

'One could argue that a made-up story, one written solely to entertain its audience, is a purer and more truthful form of the art than any tale based on the winners' version of the Histories can be.'

'A made-up story can also be used for dark purposes.'

'Which brings me to the price of my advice,' said Elgarde.

'Whatever it is,' said Llian, 'if it's in my power, I will pay it.'

'Without even hearing what it is?' She shook her head in disbelief. 'Very well. My price is absolute truth.'

'What do you mean?'

'I should have thought it was clear enough.'

'Make it clearer.'

'You can say whatever you like when your story is created solely for entertainment ...'

'But?' said Llian.

'If you make up a story *for any other purpose*, it must be based on truth, as you know it.'

'Are you saying that I may never lie again, in my entire life?'

Elgarde rolled her eyes. 'When I say a *story*, I'm not talking about an excuse for coming home late from the tavern. I mean a *proper story*, and you, who are already under a ban for corruption, must obey truth – or pay the price.'

'What price?'

'How would I know? I can't see the future – save this: if you fail to obey truth in your yarn-spinning, you will pay the very price you have come all this way to avoid.'

'Thank you,' said Llian, though he felt less than grateful. He began to tie his boots around his neck. The lake seemed to be bubbling more than before and he was anxious to be gone.

He looked up. 'Are you sure you're safe here?'

A curious expression crossed her wrinkled face; surprise at his concern. 'From the volcano?'

'Yes.'

'Is anyone ever safe, anywhere?' said Elgarde.

'Maybe not.'

'We've had many years of peace now,' she mused, 'and the signs are it won't last much longer. All the more reason for you to sort out your affairs. As for myself – if the volcano should erupt, I won't know anything about it.' She bent over, scratching her small brown toes. 'To your biggest problem.'

'Yes?' said Llian.

'Trying to block your nightmares and flashbacks will only make the trauma worse.'

'What else can I do?'

'The opposite. Write them down, then use your gift to explore every terrible detail. Immerse yourself in your nightmares until they lose their power over you.'

At the thought of deliberately exposing himself to those horrors, of exploring every ghastly facet of the torment of his victims, flames exploded in Llian's mind. Then the screams began; awful, despairing screams. His fingers and toes curled, a howl rose up his throat and he began to shudder so wildly that his teeth rattled.

Elgarde sprang forwards and put her open palms on his cheeks. 'Breathe – *slowly*. Focus on every breath, just the in and the out; eliminate everything else.'

He forced himself to do so; he bit down on a howl, turned away from the flames, held back the horrors, but only just. Had she not been holding him, he would have cracked; he would have hurled himself into the water like a madman.

After an eternal interval the nightmare retreated, for now.

'You've got it bad,' Elgarde said softly.

Llian's skin was crawling. 'What if the nightmares don't lose their power over me?'

'The human mind is a curious thing; what works for some people fails for others – and, for an unfortunate few, makes things worse. But you have to try or it will consume you.'

'I'll try,' he whispered.

'Begin with tiny steps. Focus on small and unimportant details – the shape and colour of the prison door, say, or the dank smell of the Citadel underground. Once you feel safe with the minutiae, move on to more confronting images. But know that healing can take a long time. Years.'

He nodded. He felt burned inside, not up to speaking.

'Remember the breathing,' said Elgarde. 'It's your refuge.'

'I will.'

'I wish you well, Llian,' she said. 'You *can* recover from this.'

Could he? He could see that she cared, and it helped. He could also see that she was disturbed.

She handed him the small cylinder of ointment. 'Reapply this when you get to the other side, then twice a day until your knee heals.' She turned away.

Llian got up, staggering a little on rubbery legs, and headed down to the water.

'If you do become a yarn-spinner,' said Elgarde, 'and choose to sell your stories, I suggest you do so under an assumed name.'

He turned. 'Why?'

'Being a professional liar, as you put it, could one day be used to destroy your career.'

She nodded and disappeared into the trees.

'Thank you,' Llian called.

He swam back to the slope of the crater. The water felt warmer than before, yet thicker. It clung to him as if trying to hold him back, and he was glad to reach the shore and climb out. The sun was halfway down the western sky, the air cooling at last. He reapplied the ointment to his knee – a sharp burn, followed by numbness – wrung out his smelly socks, put his boots on and scrambled up to the rim. There he looked back and thought he saw the wisemon on her rock, watching him. He raised an arm, then turned away.

As he made his way down the arid outer slope of the volcano towards the cove where he was to meet Tessariel, the fishing boat captain who had brought him here, Llian reviewed his choices. He would give almost anything to work again. If the ban was not lifted, could he bear to become a contemptible yarn-spinner, a man who made up stories with no basis in historical truth?

Was Elgarde right? He considered the question, trying to shake off the prejudices the college had taught him. He supposed that made-up stories, if done well, could convey a different kind of truth – the truth of human nature in all its myriad complexity.

For his own sanity, Llian had to write; he had to tell, and if yarn-spinning was the only form of writing and telling permitted to him, he would do it. But not cynically, like others he had heard of, manipulating their audience with cheap emotion and melodrama.

Some of the greatest moments of his life had been at the end of a telling, when his audience sat in breathless silence for a minute or more, digesting the tale, then erupted in applause. He had not had such a moment in five years. He would craft the very best stories that it was possible to write; he would transport his readers to entirely new worlds.

Though if he did become a yarn-spinner, there would be no going back. He would have betrayed his calling and nothing he wrote as a chronicler or a teller would ever be taken seriously again. He would be seen as a professional liar.

That was for the future. Before anything, Llian had to prove to Karan that he was sorting himself out. He had to show her that he was coming to terms with the nightmares, the flashbacks, the trauma and the guilt. Elgarde had shown him the way, though he did not plan to take the cautious path she had suggested. There wasn't time. He was going to try and heal himself with made-up stories that explored his life, his situation and his flaws, and the disasters and traumas his reckless arrogance had created – his *truth*.

By the time he saw the red masts of Tessariel's fishing boat sticking up from the little cove, a story idea was coming together – a condemned man, a decent but very flawed man, seeking redemption for a great wrong he had done. A story that, if Llian was ruthlessly honest, could be the first tiny step in his own recovery.

Flames exploded all around him; desperate cries for help; the stench of burning hair and skin. Llian threw himself down and focused desperately on his breathing – in and out, in and out, trying to eliminate everything else. Had he tried to do too much, too soon?

It was going to be a long haul.

~

This story hints at some of the problems Llian faces in **The Gates of Good and Evil,** *the sequel to* **The View from the Mirror** *quartet.*

STORY VI

THE SEVENTH SISTER

1

Minor spoiler alert.

T his story, a novella, is set seven years after the end of my epic fantasy quartet **The**
View from the Mirror, and features several characters from that series, plus some
new characters who will appear in future books. There is no need to have read **The View**
from the Mirror first, however this story does reveal one detail from the ending.

The man without a right thumb opened his master's note.

I've got to have it.
Make sure you get everything.
Leave no witnesses.

He tore the note to shreds, chewed them to pulp, and swallowed. After picking
shreds of paper out of a hollow tooth and eating them, he curled one end of his
black moustache around a fingertip, then smiled.
He loved his work.

Aviel's big sisters weren't going to ruin this birthday. Not her thirteenth. It was special – a lucky day for the unluckiest girl in the world.

It was time to begin the day's drudgery but she lay back in the straw of her bed-box, one of her herb pillows over her face. The scent of lavender and lemon balm almost disguised the reek from the goat pens at the other end of the crumbling barn. She cleaned out the pens every night, and every morning they stank like a troll's armpit.

Scrub out the pens; weed the garden; dig the potatoes; try to clean the collapsing ruin where her six older sisters – lazy cows! – lived with Father. Cook their meals, make balms for their sores and boils, sole their man-sized boots ... then hobble down to sleep with the animals because Aviel was so unlucky they would not have her in the house.

Drudgery was her life, and always would be, but just once she was going to have a special day.

She hummed the tune that had been passing through her head as she went to sleep last night, then slipped a hand under the straw, where her birthday present lay hidden. Aviel had spent weeks making it, carefully concealing what she was doing from her sisters. She wasn't going to open it yet – she was saving it until after lunch, when all her chores would be done, her sisters would be belching and snoring on the mouldy sofas, and she could sneak away to the forest for an hour, just for herself.

She indulged in the daydream – the flask of herb cordial she had made specially, a little sweetcake she had baked at midnight, then lovingly unwrapping her present –

Thump, right behind her head, so hard that it rattled her bed-box. Aviel yelped and shot upright. What were her sisters doing up so early? How had they crept so close without her hearing them?

The slatterns rose around her, grinning like the idiots at the Casyme fair. She clenched her fists helplessly, because fighting them always made it worse.

'Get up and cook our breakfast, Twist-foot,' said gap-toothed Sniza.

'The pigs' swill is already in the trough,' said Aviel. Though she could not beat them, she always fought back.

'Get up, get up!' they chanted, whacking the sides of her bed-box.

'We hate you, Twist-foot!' said the oldest, cross-eyed Razel. 'You're a horrible little runt!'

There was nothing runt-like about Razel – she could have lugged sides of beef in a slaughterhouse.

'That's not true,' cried Aviel. 'People say I'm just like Mama, and she was really nice.'

'How would you know?' said Vishel, who would have looked homely enough but for the perpetual scowl. 'She ran away when you were a squalling little poo-bag.'

'Mother took one look at you and threw up,' said Sniza.

It hurt every time, though Aviel did not blame their mother. Aviel wanted to run away too. But her best form of defence was attack.

'You look like a sack of hairy turnips,' said Aviel. 'That's why you're twenty-four and every man you've proposed to has turned you down.'

'Get her!' shrieked Sniza.

They lifted Aviel's bed-box off its posts and turned it over, dumping her onto the dirt floor. She gasped as her bad foot twisted back on itself, and tears formed under her eyelids, but she screwed them shut; she wasn't going to cry in front of her sisters. Someone put a big, unwashed foot on her head and ground her face into the dirt. She spat out muck and rolled over, trying to conceal her presents.

'She's hiding something,' said Razel, her crossed eyes darting.

'Birthday present,' grinned Gidgel, who was six-foot-one and could wrestle a mule. 'Get it!'

Aviel felt in the straw and brought out her little flask of herb cordial. 'You can have this.'

Gidgel froze.

'Don't touch it,' said Razel. 'It's one of her black potions; it'll give you carbuncles in nasty places.'

Aviel had never made a potion, but went with it. 'It's perfectly safe,' she said, forcing a smirk.

Razel smacked the flask out of her hand, smashing it on the wall of the barn. 'Everything went bad the day you were born, Twist-foot.'

'A seventh sister is rotten bad luck,' said Vishel. 'Father should have drowned you like a kitten in a bag.'

Sniza yanked Aviel's gown up, exposing her slender calf, lumpy right ankle and angled foot. 'Twist-foot, twist-foot! It's because of you that Father spends all our money dicing in the tavern with –' She broke off, looking scared.

Aviel had seen desperation in Gybb's eyes when he'd come in last night. And terror. What had he got himself into?

Razel rubbed Aviel's silvery hair into the dirt until it took on the same dun colour as the sisters' hair. A silver-haired child was the unluckiest omen of all, but that wasn't the real reason they hated her.

'Why are you doing this to me? I do everything for you.'

'This is going to be the worst day of your life,' Vishel said gloatingly. 'I can't wait to see your face when Father –'

'Shut it!' Razel thumped Vishel and she broke off, scowling. 'It's a ... surprise,' said Razel.

'What do you mean?' said Aviel, looking from one hostile face to another.

'You'll see soon enough.' The sisters' eyes shone with malice.

They wanted her to ask. If she did it would ruin her birthday, but she had to know what was going on. 'Please tell me,' she said feebly.

Razel dragged Aviel back and forth across the floor until her gown was as filthy as her hair. Each of her sisters thumped her for the fun of it, then they pawed through the straw. Gidgel stamped on her sweetcake.

Vishel found the small, velvet-wrapped present and gleefully held it aloft. 'Look what I found.'

Aviel tried desperately to get it but she wasn't tall enough. Vishel tore the scrap of embroidered velvet off to expose a little phial of jasmine essence. It was the first perfume Aviel had ever made and it had taken her weeks to prepare. Vishel wrenched the stopper out, sniffed, made a face, then ran up to the goat pen and, while Aviel vainly tried to stop her, poured it onto a pile of manure.

'Smell that,' said Vishel, and dropped the phial into the muck.

The sisters lumbered out. Aviel looked down at the phial, now embedded in filth, and felt stabbed to the heart. Her birthday present was gone and her dreams with it. Her hopes of a better life, of becoming a perfumer and bringing a little beauty into a foul and ugly world, had been erased.

'I hate you!' she screamed after them.

'Ha, ha!'

The back of Aviel's head hurt and pain throbbed through her bad ankle. She wanted to crawl back under her covers and hide from the world but she could not bear to be so filthy. She broke a chunk off the slab of yellow soap she had made last week and hobbled out to the well, the frost crunching under her bare feet, to draw a bucket of water. She stared at it for a full minute, trying to find the courage.

When she plunged her head to the bottom of the wooden bucket, the shock took her breath away. Aviel pulled out, gasping, the icy water running down her back and front. After soaping up her hair, she scrubbed until her eyes stung and her scalp burned. She wasn't going to be like her sisters in *any* respect.

A headache started at the base of her skull and spread upwards. She drew a clean bucket of water, rinsed her hair, then put her right foot in, hoping the cold would numb the pain. It made it worse.

She dried her foot and gave it a heave, as if to force it into alignment. If only there was a spell to straighten it so she could walk normally, without it hurting all the time. But even if there had been such a spell, her father had no money to pay for it. And if he'd had the money, he would never waste it on an unlucky seventh sister.

Aviel put on her boots, brushed her hair and dressed, fretting. Clearly, Father was up to something bad, and she had to find out. Her sisters weren't in sight; they would be inside, huddled around the smoky fire, trading insults and hogging the gritty porridge. Father was bound to be a'bed, nursing a headache from last night in the tavern, and a guilty temper at dicing away the pittance he earned by raking muck out of the town's gutters. When she was born he had been a professional man, a bookkeeper, and the family had been well off. How had it come to this?

Soon after her mother ran away, when Aviel was just seven months old, the western wing of the big house had burned down. The roof of the eastern wing had also been damaged and there had been no money to repair it. Now, twelve and a half years later, only the kitchen, the salon and Gybb's squalid bedroom were habitable.

Aviel's right knee and hip ached with every step; her fall must have wrenched the bones out of alignment. She was looking for a stick to use as a cane when she noticed a furtive movement up near the front gate.

Gybb, a big, saggy sack of potatoes on legs, was creeping down the path. What was he doing up so early, and why would he creep into his own home? She slipped behind a dead pine tree and peered around it. Gybb's fat head darted this way and that, looking out for her, then he turned and beckoned.

A scrawny old woman followed, stepping carefully on the rutted path. Magsie Murg! If she had ever had a prime, she was well past it. She had a hooked nose, a sour mouth, eyes like raisins soaked in vinegar and breath that would eat through cast iron. And Magsie, who was so mean that she only ate five meals a week, was thoroughly nasty. What was she doing here? Surely she and Father weren't *seeing* one another? No – even the thought was disgusting.

Gybb offered Magsie his arm. She knocked it away with her bag, then followed him down to the ruined house, her nose in the air. They disappeared inside.

Aviel's stomach clenched. Magsie Murg was rich and could only be here on business ... though what business could she possibly have with Father? Her tannery was so revolting that when the wind blew from the west the reek could be smelled in the village of Thimbel, four miles away. Her gaunt, desperate workers carried the stench with them and nothing could wash it off. The mere thought of the place made Aviel gag –

A premonition struck her and she doubled over, struggling for breath. *Run, now!*

No, she had to know what was going on. She eased the back door open and crept along the roofless hall to the salon. It had once been panelled in burr walnut but most of the panelling had been used for firewood and the rest was water-stained and rotting. Her sisters were gathered at the door into the kitchen, spying. Father and Magsie Murg were sitting at the yellow pine table, talking in low voices. At least, Father was talking. Magsie was gobbling the oatmeal biscuits Aviel had made for the family last night.

Aviel crouched; she must not be seen.

Her father said something she did not catch, then, 'And worth every grint.'

'Isn't she small for her age?' said Magsie. Her screechy voice sounded like a ferret caught in a mangle.

Aviel gulped. Were they talking about her? Why?

'She's a hard worker,' said Gybb grudgingly. 'The girl never stops.'

'I'll give you thirty tars for any one of those heifers of yours,' said Magsie.

The six sisters cried out in outrage. Gybb lurched up from his chair and banged the door in their faces. Aviel slipped out of the house, around the side, and peered through the gap in the rotting kitchen windowsill. What was Father up to?

'Lazy slatterns,' he said. 'Never done a day's work –'

'I know how to make people work,' said Murg, in tones so cold they might have issued from a corpse.

'*My* girls aren't on offer. Only the youngest ... she's not one of mine.'

Aviel swayed backwards. If Gybb wasn't her father, *who was*? She picked the rotted wood away, the better to see his face, to read the truth there.

Magsie rose, shaking her head. Aviel ducked down.

'All right,' Gybb said desperately. 'Twenty-five tars, as long as –'

'She's a twist-foot! I'd never get the value out of her.'

Aviel's heart stopped, then gave three frantic thumps as if beating on a locked door. Father was trying to *sell* her?

'Twenty, then,' he said hoarsely. 'I've got to have twenty by tonight, or –'

'No cripple is worth twenty tars,' said Magsie.

'Hide scrapers don't need to walk.'

Aviel hugged herself desperately, rocking from side to side. Scraping down – scouring the rotten scraps of flesh off hides before they were tanned – was one of the most disgusting jobs ever invented. How could Father do this to her? How could her sisters laugh about it? Why did they hate her so? She clutched her stick, fighting an urge to run in and whack the evil old woman over the head.

But what could she do? She had no money and nowhere to go.

'They have to stand up fourteen hours a day, seven days a week,' Magsie said coldly.

'Please, Magsie,' said Gybb, clutching at her stringy arm. 'If I haven't got the money by tonight I'm a dead man.'

She shook him off, a disgusted look on her face. 'Fifteen silver tars, and not a grint more. But I'll need a longer indenture or there's no profit in it – I'll need her for seven years!'

After a long pause, Gybb said, 'All right!'

Aviel's sisters, who were back at the salon door, let out a ragged cheer.

'Bring her tomorrow, an hour after noon,' said Magsie.

'You can take her now if you want,' said Gybb. 'The moment you pay me the money.'

'And feed her for an extra day?' Magsie cried, as if Gybb was trying to rob her. 'Tomorrow, after noon, when the indenture is ready. Is there any more tea in that pot?'

Gybb poured it for her.

Aviel slumped back on her heels in the shrubbery. How could her own family so betray her, after all she had done for them? She could not endure seven years in the stinking tannery, being flogged on the hour to make her work harder. Few of Magsie workers lived that long.

Happy birthday!

2

Aviel had to bolt, *now*; every second mattered. If she ended up in Magsie's talons there would only be one way out – an unmarked grave among all the other graves down the back of the tannery.

In the barn, she made a bundle of her spare clothes, a mug, flint striker, candle, knife and spoon, a bag of oatmeal, a jar of herbal ointment and her precious box of tiny scent bottles. She knotted everything into a blanket, put on her coat and her weathered old hat, and slipped out the rear door. As she scurried down through the garden she plucked up a bunch of onions and headed for the forest.

Aviel felt dazed, undermined, robbed. Her father was not her father, her sisters were only half-sisters, they all hated her – and she had no home any more.

Where could she go? Casyme was a small town and everyone knew Gybb and Magsie. No one would give a thirteen-year-old runaway a job; they would send her home or hold her until he came for her. She would have to go much further, though Aviel had never been outside Casyme and had little knowledge of the lands beyond. As far as she knew, only two cities in Iagador were big enough for someone as distinctive as herself to disappear: Thurkad, forty leagues north-east, and Sith, fifty leagues to the south.

Thurkad, the biggest city in Iagador, if not the whole world, was a vast, wicked cesspit of a palace. She could certainly disappear there, but would she ever come out again? Sith, the free city built on an island in the middle of the River Garr, was Thurkad's opposite, a place where the rule of law meant everything, and honest people who worked hard might do well. But with no trade and no money, would the gate guards let her in?

The question was moot. Aviel could not walk fifty leagues, or forty. If she managed one league – three miles – in a day she would be in agony. Besides, her food would barely last five days and her savings were only eleven copper grints, enough for a few days more. Or one night in a cheap inn.

Despair settled over her. If she had to live rough, her clothes would soon be so filthy that everyone would take her for a vagrant. No one would give her work and she would fall prey to the predators who lived on such unfortunates.

Aviel let out a sob. It was hopeless.

'Sniza! She went this way!'

It was Razel's voice, and there was such malicious glee in it that Aviel choked. They were cunning hunters: how could she get away? She slipped behind a trunk, gauging where best to go. The trees were large here and widely spaced, and there was little undergrowth.

Only a few hundred yards up the slope, a track led up and over the mountains to Chanthed and western Iagador, but if she went that way, they would catch her within minutes.

Downhill, the land became a series of gullies, with many little streams that flowed into the river Yome. If she could cross the river she might reach the caves up near the top of the next ridge ... though they were an obvious place to look for a fugitive.

All that mattered now was staying out of her sisters' hands, but she had left a clear trail. Aviel headed down to another large tree, walking carefully so as to leave no tracks. It slowed her even more.

She crept down to another tree, then another, and peered around its corrugated trunk. She could hear them coming, making no effort to conceal themselves. Terrorising her was their main pleasure in life.

Only another hundred yards and she would be into the gullies, rocky country where it would be harder to track her. Fifty yards to go. Forty. If she could get behind the big tree up ahead, and use its cover to slip down –

'Got you!' Gidgel, the third oldest, and biggest sister, caught Aviel by the shoulders.

She hurled herself forwards, but Gidgel's grip was too tight, and Aviel ended up flat on her back with her half-sister leering down at her. She rolled over and sank her teeth into Gidgel's bristly shin. She shrieked, kicked out and sent Aviel flying. She scrambled to her feet and ran, ignoring the agony in her ankle.

'The runt's getting away!' screeched Gidgel. 'Quick, quick!'

The other sisters came pounding down the slope, their heavy breasts bouncing and huge thighs wobbling. Aviel reached the first gully, dived over the edge and scrambled down on hands and knees, heading for a clump of bushes.

With a great bound, Sniza caught her by the hair and dragged her back.

'Aaahh!' cried Aviel. It felt as though her scalp was going to tear off.

She kicked and scratched. Sniza held her out by the hair, drew back a fist and punched her in the belly. Aviel doubled over, gasping. The other five sisters surrounded her and slapped her about the face until her head was ringing.

'Get her purse,' said Razel.

Gidgel emptied it into a meaty hand. She frowned as she counted. 'Eleven lousy grints.'

'Where did she get eleven grints?' said Glika, the youngest of the six, incredulously.

'I earned it,' said Aviel. 'Selling herb pillows.'

'That's stealing,' said grubby Gidgel. 'Everything you earn belongs to the family.'

'Then why does Fath– Gybb spend all his money in the tavern?' She was never calling him Father again.

Whack, across the face. 'How dare you criticise Father, you little bastard!'

'I'm not a bastard!' Aviel's whole cheek stung but Gidgel's words were worse. It was as if she had robbed Aviel of her very identity.

'You're not Father's daughter! Bastard, bastard, bastard!'

'Please let me go. If I have to work in the tannery, I'll die there.'

'If Father doesn't get the money his enemies are going to *kill* him,' said Razel, white-eyed. 'You've got to save him.'

'So he can do it all again,' Aviel said bitterly. 'Who's he going to sacrifice when I'm gone? You?'

'Don't be stupid. I'm his firstborn.'

Razel studied her five younger sisters, in a calculating kind of way. They stared at one another, their mouths gaping.

'Father would never sell *us*!' cried Glika. 'Twist-foot is trying to turn us against him. Let's give her to Magsie now.'

'Magsie won't take her until tomorrow,' said Sniza, grinning. The gap between her front teeth was wide enough for an earthworm to crawl through. 'I've got a better idea.'

'What?'

'She's scared of the dark. And evil ghosts. And, especially, *hungry rats*.'

'So – am I,' said Glika, her eyes darting.

'*We're* safe. They don't come out in daylight.'

Sniza drew her sisters close, whispering, then they roared with laughter. Aviel looked at their malicious faces and shivered. She wasn't scared of the dark, but she loathed rats with a passion that only someone forced to sleep in a filthy barn could.

'What are you going to do?' she whispered.

'Pick her up,' said Sniza.

Glika heaved Aviel over a brawny shoulder. Aviel kicked and thrashed. Sniza's big hand came down on the back of her neck and squeezed until she cried out.

'I can hurt you as much as I want,' hissed Sniza.

Aviel had to save her strength, though she did not hold much hope. Her sisters weren't smart, but they were exceedingly cunning.

'Where are you taking me?'

The barn wasn't haunted. The ruined temple on the other side of town definitely was, but children played in its graveyard and sometimes dared each other to creep inside. Her sisters wouldn't hide her anywhere she might be discovered.

Glika, who was carrying her effortlessly up the slope, veered left and headed diagonally towards the track to the west, but a hundred yards below it she turned left again and continued through the forest.

Shivers ran down Aviel's back as she realised where they were taking her. The shivers became shudders; she felt a scream building up and fought to contain it. She would not show her sisters how terrified she was – they would love that.

'Stop,' said Sniza.

Glika stopped.

'Look at her!' chortled Sniza. 'She's practically wetting herself.'

They gathered around, prodding her with their pudgy fingers. She fought the terror with all her will, but it built up and up until it burst out in a despairing howl. They were taking her to the place she feared more than any other – the sacrifice tree.

'What a sooky little cry-baby you are,' said Gidgel.

'Hurry up,' said Razel. 'I'm hungry.'

The sacrifice tree was said to be more than a thousand years old, and it was gigantic. Its branches covered an area fifty yards across and its trunk was eighteen feet through the middle, though it was just a shell; the inside had rotted out long ago. There was a tall, narrow crack in its downhill side, and rumour said that human sacrifices had once been made there. Some people still used the tree for animal sacrifices, and it had a horrible stink. At night it was said to be so thick with ghosts that they fogged the air around it, though Aviel had never been game to go near it.

She struggled furiously. 'Please don't give me to the tree.'

The malice on their faces was palpable now. They climbed the mound around the base of the tree. Its bark was mottled grey and brown, with hundreds of grub holes, and a variety of animal skins – weasels, rats and a big-eared hare – had been nailed to it.

The crack that led into the trunk was lens-shaped and eight feet high, though only a foot wide at its widest point. Any of the sisters would have had to squeeze to get in, but Aviel would fit easily. The bottom and lower sides of the crack were dark brown with dirt where rats and other vermin had scurried in and out for centuries.

It smelled as if something had died and was rotting away, deep inside.

'Do it!' said Sniza.

Glika pushed Aviel through the hole. She screamed, fell a lot further than she expected and bounced off soft, spongy ground. Pain speared through her ankle.

'Nighty-night, Twist-foot,' said Glika. 'Sweet dreams!'

Someone hurled her bundle in, striking her on the back of the head. She rolled around a corner onto a mound of rotting wood, then heard them laughing as they left. It was dark here, a good ten feet below ground level, and the crack was out of sight. The heart of the tree had rotted away, right down into its roots.

Aviel lay there until the pain in her ankle became bearable, then pushed herself to a sitting position. Rat skeletons snapped under her palms, and little, raspy creatures squirmed beneath her fingers. Beetles, she thought, or cockroaches. Ugh!

Oddly, the stench wasn't so strong here; she could mostly smell damp earth and rotted wood. Then, all around her she made out the movement of little feet and the scratching of tiny claws. If she could not get out the rats would eat her too.

She stood up and felt around. The inside of the tree was the size of a small, oval room with a number of bulges in it. The trunk was surprisingly smooth – almost as if it had been planed off to serve as a prison. In places, rainwater seeping through cracks had pooled in little depressions in the wood.

She walked around the inside, stretching as high as she could reach, but found no foot- or hand-holds that would allow her to climb out. She was trapped in the sacrifice tree until her sisters came to get her.

Aviel leaned against the trunk and closed her eyes. What would it be like after dark, when the rats would be bolder ... and the ghosts came out? It was a lot easier to believe in them now.

As she was thinking these dire thoughts, she heard a faint, whispering breath. Goose pimples crept along her scalp. A ghost? No, ghosts did not breathe. Could they make sounds at all? She did not know. She held her own breath. Had she imagined the sound? Could it have been wind, stirring the leaves? But there was no wind.

Something cold and clammy closed around her bad ankle and gave a jerk that pulled her off-balance. Aviel clawed at the side of the trunk, desperate to get away, but could not break the hold.

She fell towards it.

3

'Put it over there,' said Shand, late the same afternoon. 'That's where I'm having the compost heap.'

Wilm, a tall, hungry-looking youth of 14, wheeled a barrow piled five feet high with scythed grass to a bare patch of the overgrown garden, dumped the load and went back for more. Shand, a stocky man closer to old than to middle-age, took off his battered hat and rubbed his sparsely haired scalp with thick fingers. He was about to take up the scythe again when someone on horseback turned in at his front gate, a good eighty yards away.

He leaned the scythe against a tree where Wilm, who was notoriously clumsy, would not trip over it, and headed up the driveway past the big house, a monstrosity with undulating walls in intricately-laid polychrome brickwork. The figure on horseback had a familiar, tall carriage, though Shand could not be sure who it was from here. Then she took off her hat, her black hair cascaded down to her shoulders and he knew her instantly.

'Tallia,' he said as they met. 'It's good to see you. I wasn't expecting visitors.'

She dismounted wearily. 'Given that you neglected to tell anyone you were leaving Tullin, how could you be?' She was half a head taller, and slim, with dark eyes and skin a rich shade of brown.

'I suppose it was expecting too much that the Magister wouldn't find out.'

'You could hardly have forgotten that I inherited the best spy network of all.'

She studied the house, smiling at the eccentric design. 'The place doesn't quite suit you. It ...'

'Looks as though its architect had been eating magical mushrooms.'

'Something like that.'

'I sort-of inherited it,' said Shand. 'It's growing on me.'

She led her horse down to the stables and saw it fed, watered and rubbed down. Shand introduced her to Wilm, who shook her hand awkwardly, flushing and staring at his big feet, then hurried back to his wheelbarrow.

'A quiet lad,' said Tallia.

'He's got no father,' said Shand, 'and a chip on his shoulder about it. But he's a hard worker and eager to please.'

They went inside. 'This is a big change for you,' said Tallia, looking around.

The interior design was equally strange – rooms whose proportions changed from one end to the other as if they belonged in a house of mirrors; walls stepped from bottom to top, and top to bottom; rooms with five, seven and even eleven sides. It was empty apart from various outlandish pieces of furniture that had come with it, and a clutter of crates and chests, still full. Every surface was thick with dust.

'Old Quintial left it to me,' said Shand. 'Did you know him?'

'Only by reputation. A recluse, wasn't he?'

'In his final years. He dabbled in his alchemical workshop, read the philosophers and smoked the disgusting pipes that killed him.'

From a cobwebbed pantry Shand collected a wedge of blue-veined cheese, a thick black sausage and a jar of pickled leeks, which he handed to Tallia. He carried a knife, bread and a battered wooden platter into the most normal of the rooms, a rectangular chamber with a long table up one end and a fireplace in the middle of each wall, though only one was burning.

Tallia eyed the water-stained ceiling and grubby walls. 'It's going to keep you busy, fixing all this up.'

'I'm planning to get people in to do the work while I watch them, glass in hand.'

Tallia snorted. 'How long have you been here?'

'A week.'

They sat at the table and ate. 'What brings you here, anyway?' said Shand.

Tallia's face lit up. 'I'm meeting a courier.'

'He must be carrying something special, to bring the Magister on a two-day ride in the middle of winter.'

'You could say that.'

She was glowing and Shand, who had read a face or two in his time, smiled. 'Or it's the courier who's special,' he said slyly.

'I should have known I'd never keep it from you. It's Ryarin!'

Shand frowned. 'I've heard the name before ... years ago.' He looked into her eyes. 'Is he from your own country?'

'Yes, I ... knew him twenty years ago, before I left Crandor. He's bringing something that's going to change my life.'

'All that way?'

She waved a dismissing hand. 'No, the package comes from Yggur, in Fiz Gorgo. It's going to free me.' She took a deep breath. 'Shand, *I'm going home!*'

'But ... you lead the High Council,' said Shand, stunned and a little disturbed. 'You can't just up and leave.'

'My assistants are trained and experienced; they're ready to take over.'

'I doubt that.'

'With what Ryarin is bringing they will be.'

'How mysterious.' But she was an old, reliable friend, so he simply smiled, cut the bread and sliced the leeks diagonally, and said, 'Tell me more.'

'I'm homesick, Shand. I've always hated Thurkad – filthy, pestilential place that it is. I ache to be back with my own family, among my own people. And I want children, but I don't have long to have them.'

'Well,' said Shand, 'this is a surprise.'

'A shock, you mean. But the west has prospered under Yggur's rule these past seven years; there'll never be a better time for me to hand over.'

'He hasn't been entirely himself lately ...'

'Nonsense. It's time, Shand.'

'Then I wish you the very best,' said Shand. It wasn't his business to talk her out of a decision she must have spent years coming to. 'I hope Ryarin gets here soon. There's bad weather on the way.'

'When?' said Tallia.

'Tomorrow, or the next day. Though if the two of you are back here by tomorrow night you'll miss the worst of it.'

'You'd better clear out the guest bedroom.'

4

Aviel kicked out, and whatever was holding her ankle let go. She was scrabbling in her blanket bundle for her little knife when she heard a thud, a groan and a shallow, gasping breath.

'Hello?' she said, clutching the hilt. 'Who are you?'

After a long pause, a deep male voice said softly, 'Help – me.'

It was too dark to see anything but the vaguest outline on the floor, though he looked big. She backed away. 'What – are you doing here?'

'Stabbed. Dumped.'

He raised a hand and her sensitive nose caught a number of smells at once: fresh blood, horse, leather, then something rank that was vaguely familiar. Lastly, coming from his clothes, a faint, foul odour she did not recognise.

'Stay where you are,' she said.

'Not – going – anywhere.'

He sounded very weak, though he might have been putting it on. Aviel got out her flint striker and candle, and struck sparks expertly until one caught. She held the candle up.

Her first impression was size: he was a tall, muscular man. The second was his colour – the deep brown of a chestnut, though his eyes were amber in the candle-light. And the third – he looked in a bad way.

'Don't – afraid,' he said. 'Couldn't – hurt.'

There were few foreigners in Casyme, and none who looked anything like him. He was a handsome man with a broad, open face, a mouth that looked as though it had spent a lot of time smiling, dark, curly hair and thoughtful eyes. Not young, though; he could have been forty. There was a well-worn scabbard on his left hip, but no sword.

'What – name?' he said.

'Aviel. Where are you hurt?'

'Back. Nothing – can do.'

'I know some healing,' said Aviel. He smiled and it irked her, as if he wasn't taking her seriously, though she was small for her age and might have passed for a kid of ten or eleven. 'I'm *thirteen*! And I've been looking after my family's ills since I was little.'

The smile broadened. No doubt he thought she was still little. 'Thank – you.'

She rolled him over and pulled up his coat and shirt.

'You're strong,' he said.

'I'm the only one in my family who does any work,' she muttered.

There was a gash in his muscular lower back, on the left side. It was a couple of inches long and an inch deep, though it did not appear to have reached any vital organ. The rank smell was stronger around the gash.

'It's not a bad wound,' said Aviel. 'I'll clean it up.'

'No! Blade – poisoned. Don't risk –'

He was struggling to breathe, and though life had taught her that not even her own family could be trusted, she could tell she had nothing to fear from him. She tore a strip off her shirt, dipped it in one of the little pools of rainwater and carefully washed around the wound, wiping away from it so she would not get any more poison in.

She dabbed her herbal ointment on the gash but could not bandage it – another strip from her shirt would not go close to knotting around his broad back.

'Thank you.' His words were a breathless sigh.

'Who did this?' said Aviel.

'Don't know.'

'Why did he dump you here?' It would have been hard work carrying such a big man down from the track.

'Questioned me – long time,' he wheezed. 'Looking – something. Forced – poison – throat.'

'Why would anyone do such a wicked thing?' she cried.

'Make me – die – slowly.'

'When?'

'Hour – ago.'

His breathing was getting slower and his arms had a tremor. Aviel felt his forehead, which was worryingly cold. She smelled his breath. Again that rank smell, some poisonous plant, but which one?

'What's your name?' he said for the second time.

'Aviel.' She pinched the candle out in case she needed it later.

'Pretty name. Will – stay? Don't – want – die ... alone.'

She wasn't going anywhere, but that wasn't what he was asking. 'I'll stay,' she said, deeply moved.

'Talk.'

'What about?'

'Your life.'

There was little to tell, though that wasn't what he was asking for either. 'I don't fit in.'

'Why not?'

She told him about being a seventh sister, a twist-foot and a silver-hair, how desperately unlucky that made her, and how different she was from everyone else in the family. While she was speaking, he hummed a mournful little tune, soft and low.

'Unlucky – but gifted,' he said.

'What do you mean?'

'Each ... problem comes – gift. Balance – bad luck. You – trebly gifted.' He hummed the tune again.

Aviel snorted. 'My mother ran away when I was a baby. My father has just sold me to the tannery to pay his gambling debts. My sisters chucked me down here because I'm scared of rats.'

'What – you want?'

'Just a place of my own, and good work.'

'What work – you like?'

She was reluctant to speak about her dream for fear of jinxing it. 'Gardening, and making things that smell nice: herb pillows; healing balms ...'

'Good at it?'

'If it wasn't for my garden, my family would starve.'

He began to hum the tune again. Now it was running through Aviel's head as well. His breath caught in his throat and he struggled to breathe. She got out her little box of scent bottles, counted along until she found the right one, and wafted it under his nose. He gasped, then sneezed.

'What – that?'

'I also make scented oils. This is mustard oil –'

'A gift.' His breathing came a little easier. 'What you *really* want, Aviel?'

Dare she tell him? Why not? He would not mock her dream, or use it against her. 'Since I was little, I've wanted to make perfumes; proper ones. Though I don't think –'

'You – *will*.'

'Once Magsie gets me,' she said miserably, 'I'll never smell anything nice again.'

She sat by him, trying to work out what the poison was. Without knowing, there was no way of helping him ... or was there?

With her little knife, she prised half a mug of wood chips from the trunk, then the blade snapped. She set them alight with her candle and when they were burning well she covered them with clay dug from beneath the rotted wood on the floor.

'What – doing?'

'Making active charcoal. It's an antidote to many poisons.'

'Thank – you.'

'It takes a long time to make,' she fretted.

'Not going – anywhere.'

Suddenly she recognised the rank smell. Hemlock, a deadly poison. But antidotes should be taken quickly and he had been poisoned well over an ago. What if she was too late? The moment the wood was reduced to charcoal she crushed it with the back of her spoon and mixed it with half a cup of water.

'Drink this.'

He struggled to get it down. 'Horrible!'

She gave him some water. His throat moved. He closed his eyes. She watched him anxiously, praying the antidote would work but fearing it was much too late. He seemed to be getting worse, not better; every breath was a struggle now. It hurt her, too. She felt closer to this dying stranger, who knew her secret dream, than she ever had to her family.

After a long period of silence, he said, more clearly than he had spoken before, 'If – in my power, I would help you reach your dream ...' His voice trailed off. He was fading away.

'Hush,' she said. 'I don't ask for anything.'

'I do. Would you – take my hand?'

She held his big dark hand with her small pale one. With his free hand he made a complicated movement in the air. Some kind of magic? He felt in a secret pocket, she heard a faint rustle and he pressed something into her hand. A ring.

'Will you – give – her?'

By this time tomorrow Aviel would be an indentured slave, but how could she refuse a dying man? 'Yes,' she said.

'Tell her ... I loved ... to my dying ... dying ...'

'What's her name? Where does she live?'

He did not reply. His cold fingers, which had been gripping hers tightly, slowly relaxed.

'Please don't go,' she whispered.

She wafted the mustard oil under his nose again but it had no effect this time. She clutched his hand, praying that he would come around, though after several minutes she knew he was gone.

Aviel stayed by him. He'd had such a fear of dying alone that it did not feel right to move away. She felt bewildered and lost. How could such a powerful, vital man, who had travelled the world and must have dealt with many dangers, have been killed so easily? And since he had, how could there be any hope for a little twist-foot who was already condemned?

After a respectful time had passed, she lit her candle and checked the inside of the great tree, a space about three yards by four. The thought of spending the night down here with his body, and the rats, and the ghosts that were bound to come out as soon as it was dark, was too much to bear.

If she had not snapped the blade of her knife she might, with great labour, have cut foot- and hand-holds into the hard wood.

Without them, she had no way out.

5

Tallia had left with the dawn, without waking Shand. When he rose an hour later it was bracingly cold, with a keen southerly blowing and big snowflakes drifting on the wind. He was out on a morning walk, familiarising himself with the lands and paths around Casyme, when he heard a faint, desperate cry.

After scouting around in the forest below the road he traced the cries to a gigantic and clearly ancient tree. Around its base were dozens of stone markers, some with worn writing carved on them, others blank. Many more markers were almost buried in the humped-up soil.

It was a sacrifice tree. A deeply unpleasant place where the credulous, the superstitious and the downright nasty gathered to do unpleasant things to innocent creatures in the hope of staving off an injury or gaining an advantage. Or for the pleasure of inflicting pain, which he guessed to be the situation here.

He scrambled up the mounded earth to the crack, but it was dark inside and he could make nothing out. 'Hello?' he called.

'*Get – me – out!*' A girl's voice, beyond hysteria.

He stretched an arm down as far as he could reach. 'Grab hold.'

'I can't reach that high.'

'Wait here.' A stupid thing to say, he realised.

'Don't leave me!' she said desperately. 'Don't leave me!'

'I'm not going anywhere.'

He cast around in the forest for a suitable fallen branch, then carried it to the tree. 'Watch out.' Shand inserted it into the crack and lowered it. 'Jam the end into the ground.'

He heard her choke back a sob. The top end of the branch moved around. He held it steady. 'Take it slowly.'

She climbed up into the light, a small, elfin girl with huge blue-grey eyes and fine, flyaway hair that was a remarkable shade of silver. Her clothes were of home-spun cloth but fitted her well, though they were covered in dirt and her threadbare coat would be little use in this piercing cold. He went to lift her down but she held a hand up, palm outwards. He stepped back and she scrambled down, awkwardly.

'I'm Shand,' he said. 'I'm new in Casyme; inherited old Quintial's place.'

'Aviel.' She checked all around as if used to watching for danger.

'Aviel who?'

She hesitated before answering. 'Just Aviel.'

'How long were you –?'

'All yesterday.' Her voice rose. '*All last night.*'

'I'd better get you home before your parents start to worry.'

She let out an hysterical laugh. 'I've run away. My sisters threw me in there. And ... and there's *a dead man.*'

'In there?' said Shand.

'He died yesterday. He was stabbed in the back, then poisoned. A big, dark man.'

Prickles started at the backs of Shand's legs and crept all the way up to his shoulders. 'A dark man?'

'With a foreign accent. He was dumped down there to die, poor man.'

'I'd better take a look.'

'Don't go down,' she cried, terror vibrating in her voice. 'If my sisters come back –'

'Be damned!' roared Shand. She rocked backwards and he could see the fear in her eyes, and the wonder. 'Be at ease, child,' he said gruffly. 'I won't let anyone harm you.'

'My sisters are big, strong women – and there's six of them.'

'You're a *seventh sister?*' He did not hold to the superstition about it being bad luck, though why else would they take her to a sacrifice tree?

'Yes,' she whispered.

'Well, I'm also more than I appear. Stand guard, and call out if you see anyone, all right?'

'Yes.' A little of the darkness leaked from her. She shivered.

It was bitterly cold now and getting colder by the minute. He took off his coat. 'Put this on.'

'I can't take your coat.'

'I lived in the mountains for twenty years. I'm used to cold.'

She put it on. It would have wrapped around her twice, and came down to her ankles. 'It's so warm!'

'Ten geese gave their down for it.'

Shand clambered through the crack, down into the humid, reeking darkness, and conjured a wisp of light from a fingertip to check the body. Everything was as Aviel had said. Could the dead man be the courier that Tallia had come so far to meet? The man who had been far more than a courier to her?

He climbed out. 'Do you know where Quintial's house is?'

'The weird-looking place,' said Aviel. 'Everyone knows it.'

'Could you run there for me? It's only a mile. There's a lad works in my garden, Wilm –'

'I know Wilm. But I can't run. I've ... got a bad ankle.'

She instinctively tried to hide it behind her left foot, though in one swift glance Shand saw all he needed to know. 'I'll go; it'll do me good. Can you wait here?'

She hugged herself, then looked left and right and over her shoulder. 'If my sisters come back, they'll beat me and take me to Magsie.'

'Who's Magsie?'

'A rich, evil old woman. Father's sold me to be an indentured slave in her tannery.'

Shand's smoky eyes hardened. 'You'd better come with me. I won't let anyone touch you.'

He could tell that she desperately wanted to go with him, but she looked back at the split in the tree and her small jaw lifted. 'The poor man was afraid of dying alone. It wouldn't be right to leave him now.'

She was so young, handicapped and downtrodden, yet something fine and noble shone out of her. 'What if your sisters come back?' said Shand.

'I –' She swallowed. 'I'll go back down.'

Given the awful shrieks that had brought him here, it revealed a rare kind of courage. 'I'll be as quick as I can.'

Shand went up to the track and began to jog. He could not remember when he had last run any distance and the sensation was a trifle uncomfortable. He was getting old.

'Wilm?' he yelled as he reached his backyard.

Wilm, who was digging the patch of ground Shand had scythed down yesterday, came at once.

'Dead man, in the forest,' said Shand, panting. 'Bring the biggest horse out of the stables. He's called Thistle.'

Wilm asked no questions. Shand threw a coil of rope over his shoulder and they headed back.

'Do you know a girl called Aviel?' said Shand.

'We were friends when we were little,' said Wilm.

'Fall out?'

'Never!' Wilm cried. 'Her father took her out of school when she was nine and wouldn't let her have any friends. He's a rotten–' Wilm bit off whatever he was going to say.

'What do you think of her sisters?' Shand said mildly.

Wilm stiffened, but refused to be drawn. Ah well, there was injustice everywhere, and it was none of Shand's business. Shortly he turned off the track and they headed down to the sacrifice tree.

'I wouldn't go there,' said Wilm.

'That's where the body is. And Aviel.'

When Shand turned around the tree, she was sitting with her back to the trunk with a long, pointed stick in her hands, humming an unfamiliar tune. Her eyes lit up when she saw them. Perhaps she had thought Shand would not come back. Or, more likely, it was seeing Wilm.

They stared at each other. Wilm was nearly six feet tall, a gawky beanpole, while Aviel was well under five feet. Something passed between them but neither spoke. Wilm turned to the split in the tree, swallowing hard.

'It's down there?' he said hoarsely, as if thinking Shand wanted him to go in.

Shand nodded. 'It's all right. I'll go down.'

'You'll never lift him out,' said Aviel.

'I don't plan to.'

Shand tied the rope around the victim's chest to form a harness, then heaved the body upright. Rigor mortis had set in and it was quite rigid. With considerable effort he propped it against the inner wall of the trunk, climbed up with the rope, kicked the branch out of the way and tied the rope to Thistle's saddle horn.

'When I say so,' he said to Wilm, 'walk Thistle away, very slowly.'

Wilm did so. Shand had to keep freeing the rope, which was constantly snagging on the bottom of the crack, and it took all his strength. However after ten minutes the body reached the level of the crack.

'Wilm, I'll need your help. Aviel, Thistle has to hold the weight. Keep him steady.'

'How do I do that?' said Aviel in a quavery voice.

'Sing to him – if you can sing.'

'My mother was a singer.'

'And stroke his nose.'

She stared at the huge, cross-eyed beast. Thistle looked down his nose at her. Very softly, she began to sing a folk song about tragic love, and her high, pure voice reminded Shand of times, and loves, he would sooner have forgotten.

He and Wilm levered the body out and heaved it onto Thistle, who rolled his eyes and whinnied. Aviel's singing calmed him and Shand led him up to the road. An icy wind blasted along it and the snow was falling thickly, the visibility down to fifty feet.

'I'd better look for clues now,' said Shand, 'or we'll never find any.'

Aviel gave the reins to Wilm and joined Shand. 'Clues to the murderer?'

'Yes.'

'I tried to save him and I couldn't. I want to help.'

Shand studied her small, determined face. Perhaps it would alleviate her feelings of helplessness. 'All right, but tread carefully. Don't walk on any tracks.'

'What are you looking for?'

'Where he was attacked, the killer's footprints ... anything that can tell us who he is.'

'He wouldn't have carried the ... body far.'

'No,' said Shand.

'Here's where the killer carried him down,' said Aviel shortly, standing by the trampled bank. 'And here's where he came back.'

'A big, broad boot, worn down on the left side of the heel, with a bent-over boot nail in the shape of a question mark.'

'Yes.'

'Deep tracks,' said Shand. 'Big feet but a short stride. What does that tell us?'

'A fat man?'

'Or a big-bodied man with short legs.' He walked around, frowning at the ground, then saw several small spots of blood. 'The victim bled here, though only a little.'

'The knife wound didn't kill him,' said Aviel. 'It didn't go through the muscle.'

Shand spun around. He hadn't had the chance to check. 'Then what did?'

'He said his attacker poisoned him. From the smell, it was hemlock. I made some active charcoal and gave him a big dose but it was too late ...'

What a remarkable child she was. Shand followed the prints, trying to reconstruct the crime. 'The killer knew his victim was coming and hid in the trees, here where the ferns are tramped down. He threw a poisoned knife and struck the victim in the back, but not a bad wound. Why throw a knife? It's hard to do accurately.'

'He was afraid to get close,' spat Aviel, 'because he's a stinking coward.'

'If the poison brought the victim down, why didn't the killer stab him? Why carry him all that way?'

'Maybe he didn't want the body found.'

'Why not?' Shand glanced at Aviel. 'Did he say anything about that before he died?'

She thought for a moment. 'He said, "The man who stabbed me, robbed me." And, "Questioned me – long time. Looking – something."'

'Looking for what?'

'He didn't say. It was hard for him to talk; he didn't have much breath.'

She was holding something back, but now was not the time to interrogate her about it. 'Let's get the body home. Then I'll tell the town constables ... though I don't think they'll find the killer after all this time.'

6

ere it is. It's all he had, and he told me nothing. I searched him, interrogated him, poisoned him and left him to die.

I await your instructions.

~

Aviel emerged from Shand's wash room with her skin glowing after scrubbing herself in icy water, wearing the clean clothes she'd had in her blanket bundle. Wilm was by the door of the back room where they had laid the body. She stopped, biting her lip. She had no idea what was going to happen now but feared the worst. Should she slip away, while she still could?

She was considering it, for the snow had let up, when she noticed the peculiar colour of the sky. The clouds were the blue-black colour of the roof slates on Shand's house and the wind had turned due south. It felt as though it was blowing all the way from Noom, where the sea was frozen solid. It was not a day for running anywhere, or being lost out of doors.

Shand appeared. 'Wilm, show Aviel around, then get her some breakfast.'

'I'm not hungry,' she lied. She was starving, but did not want to be beholden to him. Whatever she got from this day forth, she would have to earn.

'Nonetheless,' said Shand.

Wilm led her outside. 'It's nice to see you again,' he said tentatively.

'Yes.'

Aviel did not know what to say. When they were little, Wilm had defended her from the taunts of the other children, and she would always think kindly of him for it, but she had not seen him in five years. During that time he had doubled in size and she had no idea what to make of him.

'Did your sisters throw you –?' he began.

'Yes.'

'That must have been horrible.'

She did not want to talk about it. She tapped her left foot. 'Gybb wants to sell me to Magsie. He – he said he's not my father –' Too late she remembered that Wilm had no father. 'Do you know who –?'

'My father abandoned us,' he said coldly. 'I don't want to know. *I hope he's dead.*'

There was a very awkward silence. She looked around the huge yard, which ran down past the stables for a hundred yards and became increasingly overgrown. Behind the stables was a cluster of sheds and cages and, further down on the right-hand side, an odd-looking stone building with seven sides, small leaded windows and a pointed slate roof like a witch's hat.

'What's that for?' said Aviel.

'It's old Quintial's workshop. Where he did his alchemy stuff, until he got too sick.'

Something stirred in her. 'Can I see inside?'

Wilm shrugged. 'Shand said to show you around.'

They went down and he unlocked the door with a black iron key as long as his hand. The door groaned open and she put her head in.

Benches around the walls were covered in dust and cobwebs and thousands of rat droppings, plus the decaying corpse of a crow that had found a way in and died there. On the left side a vine had grown in through a broken pane and writhed around for yards, bleached of almost all its green. Shelves held bottles and jars with the labels peeling off. Under each bench was a long drawer, and a cupboard below that.

Quintial's alchemical equipment – a mortar and pestle, a number of flasks, pots, dishes and retorts, and other items she did not recognise – was a filthy mess. But then she saw it, sitting by itself, and her breath caught in her throat, for it was a treasure more valuable than a chest full of gold.

It was a beautiful copper distillation apparatus: a cylindrical heating vessel connected by a dozen cooling coils to a round condensing chamber. Greed stirred in her amateur perfumer's heart – if she had one of those she could make almost anything.

At the rear of the workshop, through an archway, was a long, narrow room. On the left a square washing tub had running water from a tap, a small miracle in itself. There were draining pegs above it and to the side was a laundry copper with an iron firebox underneath, then another bench. To the right, the rest of the narrow space was full of boxes and crates covered in dust and cobwebs. A ladder ran up to a trapdoor in the ceiling.

Aviel stared around her in wonder, daydreaming.

A wild gust blew snow flurries in through the door. Wilm shivered. 'I've got to go home soon, and cut the firewood.'

His mother was even poorer than Aviel's own family, though unlike them she was proud and hard-working. Back in Shand's house, Wilm cut bread and cheese and carried it into the long living room. Aviel stood by the fire, awkwardly, holding her little bundle. He returned with a pot of tea, a piece of honeycomb and a mug, and handed it to her.

'What are you going to do now?' he said.

Reality crashed down on her. She had no money, no work and nowhere to go. 'I don't know.'

'I could ask my mother –'

'No!' she said sharply. Wilm's mother worked her fingers to the nubs, just to survive. How could Aviel impose on them?

He reacted as if she had struck him. 'Got to go.' He ran out.

'Sorry,' she said belatedly, but he was already out of hearing.

Not wanting to sit on an armchair in her dirty clothes, she perched on the raised hearth, sipping sweet tea and nibbling on bread and cheese. Her stomach hurt. What was she to do? Running away had been a failure. But if she went home she would be sold to Magsie.

Then there was the dead man's ring. *Tell her ... I loved her ... to my dying ... dying ...* Aviel had promised to do so, though she did not even know the woman's name.

Shand came in, carrying a mug and looking worn out. He poured tea and sat in the chair on the other side of the fire. Aviel studied him surreptitiously. He looked really old, sixty at least. But, she thought, a good man. Dare she ask? She had to. She leaned forwards but the words would not come.

'Whatever it is,' said Shand tersely, 'say it.'

'Do you need a servant?' she said in a rush. 'There's mess and dust everywhere. It'll take you years to clean this place all by yourself. Or a gardener? I can grow anything and you wouldn't have to pay me. I'd work for food and a board to sleep on. Please –'

'How old are you?' said Shand.

'Thirteen,' she whispered.

'Really? You look about ten.'

'I'm a year and a half younger than Wilm,' she said, on her dignity. 'You can ask him.'

'When was your birthday?'

'Yesterday.' The pain burst out of her. '*It was yesterday!* I so wanted to have a special day. I had it all organised, but my sisters smashed my presents and rubbed me in the muck. Then Father *sold* me.' Aviel scrunched herself into a ball and wept.

Shand did not speak for some time. 'I can't interfere in your family. You have to go home.'

She got up, trembling. 'If I'm sold to Magsie, I'll die there. She flogs her workers to death, then buries them down the back of the tannery. Please, I'll do anything.'

'I'll talk to your father,' said Shand.

'He's not my father. He said so yesterday.'

'What about your mother?'

'She ran away when I was a baby, so I don't belong to them. Please, Mister Shand.'

'Since they fed and sheltered you all this time, the law would say otherwise.'

'I fed them!'

'I'm sorry.' He rose. 'Come on.'

Aviel stood there, quivering but very upright, then took off his coat and laid it neatly over the arm of the chair.

'You'll need that, outside.'

'I don't want *charity*. Besides, I won't have a coat in the tannery.'

'As you wish. Come on then.'

He put the coat on and shepherded her down the hall to the front door. As she opened it, the wind tore it out of her hand and slammed it back against the wall. Outside, the snow was blowing horizontally and she knew she had run out of options. If Shand took her back to Gybb, she would die in the tannery. If she ran away, she would freeze to death in the coming blizzard. She might survive the cold by hiding in the sacrifice tree, but sooner or later the hungry rats would eat her.

Shand strode off. Aviel laboured after him. She had already walked a mile today and her ankle bones were grinding together with every step. He had gone a hundred yards before realising that she could not keep up. He came back.

'Sorry,' he said. 'Wasn't thinking.'

They went slowly down the steep road towards the centre of Casyme. It was a very old town, and long ago must have been a wealthy one, for the four wide streets that ran off the circular market area had many fine buildings of three and even four storeys, all built from buff-coloured limestone. In recent centuries, however, the population had declined and some of these buildings, long empty, had fallen into ruin. Outside the centre, the streets were narrow, higgledy-piggledy, and the homes and shops were small and jumbled together.

'You'll have to tell me where to go,' said Shand.

Aviel was so afraid that she could not speak. She pointed the way and finally, on the other side of town, they came to the ruined shell of a house that had once been grand.

Shand studied the unkempt yard, the burnt-out ruin that had been the west wing, and the largely roofless mess where the family still lived. A muscle knotted in his jaw. 'Will your father be in?'

'Still in bed,' she muttered, shivering in her threadbare coat.

'At this time of day?' he exclaimed. 'When there's work to do?'

He went down the path and thumped the front door. Shortly a big, grubby slattern opened it, Grizel. Her eyes widened when she saw Aviel behind Shand.

'Get your father,' said Shand.

'He's in bed.'

'Now!'

Grizel jumped and went to bang the door in his face. Shand held up a hand and, though he did not touch the door, it stopped and she could not budge it. She disappeared down the roofless, mouldering hall. Shortly Gybb appeared, his eyes bloodshot, hitching his pants up over his bulging belly. Aviel flushed for shame.

'Who the hell are you?' snarled Gybb.

'I'm Shand. How dare you sell this girl into slavery, you disgusting oaf?'

'She's thirteen. It's a legal indenture.'

'Not when all the money goes to you.'

'You said I'm not your daughter,' said Aviel to Gybb. 'You've got no rights over me.'

'Get in here, you little bitch, and cook my breakfast,' said Gybb.

Aviel's teeth started to chatter. Inured to obedience, she made a convulsive movement towards the door, but stopped. 'I'm – not – coming – back.'

'Girls,' said Gybb to Aviel's half-sisters, who were crowded in the door behind him, 'bring the brat home and give her the thrashing of her life. If the interfering old fool gets in the way, thrash him too.'

They were all bigger than Shand and if they rushed him he would not have a chance. Aviel could not allow them to hurt the old man. She stepped forwards, her small shoulders slumped.

'Stay where you are,' said Shand from the corner of his mouth.

'Get him!' said Gybb.

The sisters burst out. Shand held up his weathered hand and Gidgel stopped as if she had run into a cliff. The other sisters piled up against her massive back, trying to get to him but unable to pass some unseen barrier. Their helpless thrashing-about looked so ridiculous that Aviel laughed. Gybb directed a hate-drenched glare at her and she broke off.

'Aviel isn't coming back,' said Shand.

'I'll have the law on you for stealing my daughter,' said Gybb.

'But she's not your daughter; anyone can see that.'

'Maybe she's *your* daughter, you fornicating bastard.'

Shand did not bother to answer. 'Since she's thirteen, she can legally leave for work.'

'Not without a contract.' A look of slimy cunning crossed Gybb's unshaven face. 'Thirty silver tars and she's yours.'

'You liar!' cried Aviel. 'Magsie Murg only offered fifteen for me. For seven years!'

'Magsie's a friend,' said Gybb. He met Shand's eye for a couple of seconds. 'It's thirty tars or I beat her black and blue.'

'Touch her and I'll punch every tooth out of your ugly head,' said Shand.

Gybb started forwards, swaying from side to side, but suddenly lost the courage.

After a very long hesitation, Shand said, 'Be at my house at five p.m. and I'll sign a contract. For twenty tars and not a grint more.'

7

Aviel followed Shand back, trailing so far behind that she could not see him through the whirling snow. Her ankle always hurt worse in cold weather and in the past day she had used it far more than usual, but she was in such turmoil she barely felt it.

How dare Gybb sell her like an unwanted kitten? She had never been happy there, she had never felt wanted, yet until he disowned her she had belonged. Now he had erased her life.

Why, why had Shand agreed? Though clearly he was not a poor man, twenty tars was a lot of money. Why had he offered to pay it for a child he barely knew? Her debt would be enormous, an obligation far beyond anything she could ever repay.

A shocking thought struck her – could he be her father? What other reason could he have? But he had not said a word afterwards, nor had he looked around to check on her. Of course he wasn't her father – he'd just come to Casyme from far away. He must be having second thoughts, and he would soon try to find a way out. Perhaps he was hoping she would disappear.

Suddenly the suppressed pain exploded through her ankle. She lurched to his gate, wincing with every step, saw him standing just inside it and stopped dead.

'You don't have to do this,' said Aviel.

He made a dismissing gesture, as if to say that it could not be undone. 'In, out of the cold!'

She followed him to the front door. 'You don't owe me –'

'I've got business to attend,' he said curtly, waving her past.

He must be regretting his rash offer. Was he going to repudiate it? 'What do you want me to do?'

He peered at her. 'Did you get any sleep last night?'

She shook her head. 'I had to protect the poor man's body from the rats.'

He opened the door and pointed down the hall. 'Go in. Curl up by the fire and have a nap.'

As she went in, Aviel had the unnerving feeling that someone was watching her. Shand nodded as though she was a casual acquaintance and pulled the door closed without coming in.

Only lazy slatterns slept in daytime. Aviel could not even bring herself to sit down. It was early afternoon. Four hours until five o'clock, when her fate would be sealed, one way or another.

She stood in front of the fire until the throbbing in her ankle became bearable. She had to do something to distract herself, and the place was a mess. There were half-opened boxes and chests all over the place, the table up the far end was piled with books, blankets, wrapping paper, a pair of old boots and sundry other items. The floor had not been swept in years and every surface had a thick layer of dust, spotted with dead blowflies and an occasional black or grey moth.

She found a broom and swept the far end of the room, then dragged the boxes and chests up there, arranged them neatly and swept the rest. After dusting an empty bookcase, she wiped it down with a damp cloth and shelved the books – the Histories at the top where they belonged, then the Great Tales in second place. Shand had copies of seven Great Tales including the latest, the twenty-third, the famous *Tale of the Mirror*. They looked well read. Further down she put his books on plants, animals and the natural world, then tomes on healing and horticulture, an atlas, three books of poetry and the other titles at the bottom.

Aviel lost track of time and her own torment; she was singing when the front door opened and Shand came in, followed by a big, red-nosed man. She might have thought he was a bartender, except that his robes had the blue sash and red tassels of a notary.

'What in botheration are you doing?' said Shand, gazing around the remarkably clean and tidy room.

'Anything I get, I work for,' she said stiffly.

He scowled. The notary allowed himself an arid smile, then sat at the freshly cleaned table. Shand fetched a bottle of wine and filled two goblets. The notary drank his in a single gulp, unrolled a length of heavy fawn paper and uncapped a bottle of purple ink. He eyed the wine bottle. Shand refilled his goblet.

'Are you absolutely sure about this?' said the notary. 'It's a trifle irregular.'

'Yes,' Shand said curtly.

The notary began to write. Aviel rinsed her cleaning rags in a bucket and wiped down the mantelpiece, then the door and the windows, as high as she could reach.

'Will you stop that infernal cleaning?' said Shand.

'No,' said Aviel in her most polite voice.

It was dark outside; it must be past five o'clock. What was the notary writing? What if it was a trick? How could she tell? She could read, though haltingly, and she had good reason not to trust people.

A thump shook the front door. Shand went up and shortly returned with her father – no, with Gybb, who was not her father. His face was flushed and he looked meaner than ever. Clearly he had already been in the tavern, celebrating the sale of an unwanted non-daughter.

Aviel slipped her rags into the bucket, put it in a corner and limped up to the table. She did not want him to see her as a scrub girl.

'Where's my money?' said Gybb. The notary handed him the paper. 'What's this?'

'It's a contract,' said the notary. 'In essence, for the consideration of twenty silver tars –'

'Thirty!'

'*Twenty* silver tars, the girl Aviel, who is not your daughter but lives in your house, will be bound in service to Shand for a period of five years, until she comes of age – or weds, whichever is earlier.'

'*Weds!*' cried Aviel, as if he had suggested she paint the other side of the moon.

'Sign here.'

Gybb squinted at the paper, his lips moving. 'Where's the money?'

Shand counted twenty tars onto the table, in a single stack. Gybb eyed it, licking his lips, then, as if realising how desperately he needed it and afraid it would be taken away, scrawled his name on the contract and made a grab for the coins, scattering them everywhere.

The notary examined the signature, then nodded. He indicated to Aviel that she should sign, below Gybb's signature, and Shand below that. The moment Gybb had collected the money, Shand dragged him out by the ear and, as Aviel peered up the hall in wonderment, booted him off the front steps into the garden.

The notary wrote another paragraph below the signatures. 'I, Shand, of Brickery House, Casyme, hereby state that, for the consideration of one copper grint, I have sold this indenture to Aviel Foyl. Sign, please.'

'I don't understand,' said Aviel.

'It means exactly what it says,' said the notary.

Aviel signed, then Shand. 'Pay him a grint,' said the notary, 'and the contract is in force.'

Aviel felt quite breathless. 'My sisters stole my eleven grints.'

The notary frowned, then ostentatiously went through his pockets, piling several gold tells on the table and a small bucketful of tars, before finally finding a long neglected copper grint. He pushed it across the table to Aviel, dated the contract and added large blue wax seals in half a dozen places.

'I can't take your money,' she said.

'He'll cheerfully add it to the bill,' Shand said drily.

Aviel reluctantly took the grint and gave it to Shand. He handed her the contract.

'You're free and Gybb can never take you back,' said the notary. 'Congratulations.' He nodded to Shand, shook Aviel's hand, drained his goblet and saw himself out.

Aviel slumped onto a hard chair. Too much had happened and she could not come to terms with it. Why had Shand done this? If he wanted to help the unfortunate, he could find hundreds, even in a small town like Casyme. Why her?

Could Shand be her father? What other explanation could there be? But if he was, where had he been all her life?

8

'What do you want from me?' said Aviel.

'Nothing,' said Shand. 'You're free to do whatever you wish.'

'No, I'm not. I owe you twenty silver tars and one grint. And the notary's fee.'

'The debt is wiped.'

'Not to me.' No one had ever done anything for her, for nothing. It was a monstrous obligation and she had to repay it as soon as possible. 'This place is a horrible mess. I'll work for nothing until the debt is paid back.'

'I prefer my solitude,' said Shand in an off-putting tone.

'Wilm said you lived in the inn at Tullin for years.'

'Which is now why I want to live alone.'

Was it a subtle way of telling her to go? But it was dark and a blizzard was coming; she had to have somewhere warm and safe to sleep. 'I could make a nice bed in your stables,' said Aviel, 'with a blanket and some straw.'

It would not be nice. It would be dusty and scratchy, and the straw was bound to be full of blood-sucking vermin, but it was all she was used to.

'You're not sleeping in the bloody stables! All right, there's a little storeroom out past the kitchen. I'll put a mattress in there and you can stay – but just until things get better for you.'

'I'm not staying in your house,' said Aviel, shaking at her boldness. She had to sort things out, right at the beginning. Dare she ask him? She must. 'What about the old workshop down the back?'

'What about it?'

'Can I have it? Rent it, I mean,' she said hastily.

'It's a rat-infested abomination,' said Shand. 'I was going to pull it down.'

'No!' she cried. 'It's beautiful! Perfect!'

'Perfect for what?'

'I like the shape,' she said lamely. 'It's ... interesting. I could clean it out and fix it. Easily.'

'That's a downright lie,' said Shand, with a faint smile. 'It'd take an enormous amount of work.'

'Can I rent it?'

'How do you mean to pay?'

'I've been feeding my family since I was seven. I'll tend your garden; I can grow anything.'

'Why the workshop?'

'A place of my own.'

'No, there's a good reason why you want old Quintial's workshop,' said Shand. 'Is it your ambition to become an alchemist?'

She laughed scornfully. 'You have to be apprenticed to a master. I could never pay the fees.'

'But you do want to use the workshop?'

'How can you tell?' she said miserably.

'Your face lights up every time I mention it.'

'I've got to have a trade. One I can do sitting down.'

'What kind of a trade?'

She was afraid to say it aloud. 'Making ... perfumes,' she whispered.

'And you're thinking that you might use Quintial's alchemical equipment.'

'Can I?' she said eagerly.

'How good are you?'

'I can tell the ingredients of a perfume by its smell.'

'Any perfume?' he said curiously.

'As long as the ingredients are ones I've smelled before.'

'I don't have any perfumes, but ... '

He went across to a tall, narrow cupboard and opened its doors. Aviel saw a number of bottles and flasks inside. He came back with a glass flask whose contents glowed golden-red as it passed in front of the firelight. He took the bung out and offered her a sniff.

'What's it made of?'

'Grape spirit,' said Aviel. '*No*, brandy spirit. And cably-fruit, and –'

He frowned. 'What's cably-fruit?'

'It grows on the cably tree, a big tree with black bark and little round leaves.

The fruit is oval and as big as my hand, with a thin skin, yellow or orange, and a long flat seed.'

'Where I come from we call it gellon,' said Shand. 'What else do you smell?'

'There's dried kumquat, vanilla, and cinnamon – just a hint. And spearmint. Honey, of course, black-bee honey.'

'Anything else?' said Shand, grinning.

'Pepper.'

'Pepper!' he cried. 'In a fruit liqueur?'

For a moment she doubted herself. She took a long sniff. 'Yes. Pepper, a trace.'

'What kind of pepper?' he said in a curious voice.

'Green.'

He poured himself a small glass, then offered the flask to her, absent-mindedly.

'I'm only thirteen!' she said in a school-mistressish voice.

'Quite!' He corked the flask and put it back, then sat down and stared into the fire, sipping his liqueur thoughtfully.

'Was I right?' said Aviel, unable to keep the anxiety out of her voice.

'Extremely.' He took another sip. 'All right,' he said. 'You can rent the workshop.'

She fell to her knees, her hands clasped. 'Thank you, thank you!' Then caution prevailed. 'At what rent?'

'Two days gardening a week in the growing season and one in the fallow season. A fortnight of pickling and preserving when we harvest the fruit and vegetables, and a week when we do the sausages and cheeses. You can also make me a gallon of this liqueur each year, when the cably-fruit is ripe.'

'That's not enough work.'

'You can look after things when I go away, and that's all I'm asking. It takes a long time to learn a trade if you have to teach yourself.'

'I'll make you herbal balms and lotions and pillows,' said Aviel. 'And when I blend my first perfume, I'll give you the best bottle.'

'I don't use perfume,' said Shand.

'Then you can give it to your girlfriends.'

'I don't have any girlfriends.'

'You will when you've got a bottle of my perfume,' she said cheekily.

He stared at her, open-mouthed. Aviel bit her lip; where had that come from? But she was so happy she could have leapt into the air and flown around the room. She was free! She had a place of her own, and honest work to pay her way, and a place where she could learn the trade she knew she was going to love. And, a miracle to top all miracles, the use of that beautiful copper still.

'I beg your pardon,' she said quickly. 'I'm sure you're long past the age of girl-friends.'

He scowled; somehow, she had made things worse. 'For someone who's asking for favours,' said Shand, 'you're awfully presumptuous.'

She had to get away before she said something really stupid. 'I'm sorry. I – I'll get started.'

'On what?'

'Cleaning up the workshop.'

'It's dark outside.'

'I can't wait.'

He sighed and went looking for the key. She was standing behind him when the back door opened and a very tall, dark woman stood there, plastered in snow.

'You look like you've had a long, hard ride,' said Shand.

'For nothing,' she said wearily. She took off her hat, shook it outside the door, looked down at Aviel and smiled. 'Hello, I'm Tallia. Who are you?'

'Aviel,' she said, studying Tallia surreptitiously. She was a big, attractive, confident woman, everything Aviel would have liked to be.

Tallia took off her coat and hung it on one of the hooks inside the back door. They went in to the fire, closing doors behind them.

'Aviel is renting old Quintial's workshop,' said Shand. 'She's going to be a perfumer.'

To Tallia's credit, she did not look the least bit surprised. 'What kind of perfumes do you make?'

Then it hit Aviel, out of nowhere. She felt a stab of pain in her heart and a powerful feeling of compression around her chest. Tallia was *the one!*

Aviel could not speak. She just looked up at Tallia, dumb with agony.

'I'm sorry,' she cried. Impulsively, she took Tallia's brown hands and clutched them to her. 'I did everything I could for him, but it was too late.'

9

Tallia's smile petrified. 'What's going on, Shand?'

He did not speak for a moment. Perhaps he had not thought it before. Perhaps he had thought it but had not been certain, but Aviel could tell that he was certain now.

'Yesterday, Aviel found a dying man. A big, dark man from the north.'

Tallia's face crumpled, ageing her twenty years in a heartbeat. 'A *dying* man. Who?'

'I don't know,' said Shand. 'I brought his body back here.'

Tallia tried to speak but the words would not come. She caught hold of the back of an armchair with both hands and sagged there. She tried again. 'How – did he die?'

'He was stabbed, robbed, interrogated, then poisoned.'

Aviel felt that she was, in some odd way, responsible; that she had done Tallia terrible damage. 'Maybe it's not your friend,' she said in a tiny voice.

Tallia began to shiver and shudder. Shand got out the flask of golden liqueur.

'No,' she said bleakly. 'Nothing pleasant. Nothing good.' She looked around dazedly. Her fingers were hooked and her face had gone a bloodless grey. 'Show me.'

'He's – out the back,' said Shand. 'Aviel, stay here.'

He went out, his back bent. Tallia followed. After a moment's hesitation, Aviel went too. Shand took a lantern from a shelf in the kitchen and lit it. He had laid the body out on a table in the frigid back room. The dead man's eyes were closed, his big hands by his sides.

Shand held the lantern up so it fell on his broad, handsome face.

Tallia let out a single, despairing cry, 'Ryarin!' and slumped over him.

Aviel stood frozen, sick with guilt at her failure to save him. Shand put the lantern on the table and caught her by the shoulder, urging her towards the door.

'Give me a hand in the kitchen.'

They washed their hands and cut up bread, cheese and salted beef. Shand sliced some wrinkled tomatoes and three green onions. Aviel carried the tray in to the fire. He followed with two large mugs of ale, and another mug which, from the smell, was a brewed ginger drink. He handed it to Aviel. She sipped it, grimaced and put it down.

He brought an extra chair over. She sat, staring at her thin fingers.

'You've had virtually nothing for two days,' said Shand. 'Eat! And that's an order.'

She tried a small piece of bread but could not get it down.

'It's not your fault,' Shand said quietly. 'It's the fault of the killer.'

'If I'd been quicker to think of the active charcoal –'

'You did everything you could.'

Yet it had not been enough. There must be a way to make up for her failure. Was there a way to identify the killer? It seemed the only thing she could do for Ryarin and Tallia. Aviel went over the clues again. A heavy, short-legged man. A coward who attacked with a poisoned knife, from behind. A man who had left Ryarin to a lingering death rather than killing him quickly. The boot print. It wasn't enough.

Shand had finished his ale. He opened a bottle of wine, filled a goblet, sipped, then abruptly hurled the wine into the fire. Aviel jumped. He went upstairs, his feet heavy on the treads, and she heard a series of thumps, a cry of rage or pain, then silence.

Tallia came in silently. Her eyes were swollen and the skin of her face sagged as if the muscles underneath had lost all their tone. She looked at the platter and the mug of small ale but did not touch either. She sat on the floor next to Aviel's chair.

'Tell me from the beginning,' she said. 'Take your time.'

Shand came in and sat in his chair. He looked grim, unapproachable. Aviel began with her triply-bad luck, her birthday and the little presents smashed by her half-sisters, and went all the way to being dumped in the sacrifice tree. Tallia held up her hand.

'May I see your ankle?'

Aviel was used to hiding it. She hated being judged as a cripple because of it, but how could she refuse? She extended her right leg. Tallia put her hands around Aviel's lumpy ankle and the nagging pain, which was there most of the time, eased.

Tallia released her, then gave Shand a curious, almost *knowing* look that Aviel could not fathom. 'Go on.'

Aviel told her about the shock of discovering an injured man in the sacrifice tree with her, and how she had tended the wound in his back and made the charcoal antidote.

Tallia's eyes blazed. 'That was good thinking.'

'It didn't work; I wasn't quick enough.'

'It may have been too late when you got there.'

Aviel was relating what Ryarin had said to her when the memory came surging back. 'There was a ring!'

'A ring?' said Tallia.

'I put it in the secret pocket of my pants. Then I washed them.'

Aviel took a lantern and went out to the drying line. Her clothes had not dried during the day and were frozen stiff. She felt in the secret pocket, retrieved the icy ring and warmed it in her palm as she went back.

'He asked me to give it to you,' she said, holding out the ring.

She had not seen it clearly before. It was a beautiful object made from three, no, four bands, each a different metal, beaten together until they fused.

Tallia stared at it, clenched her hands around it, and wept.

'It's exactly like,' she said, choking. 'Like the one I gave him when I left Crandor, twenty years ago. What did he say?'

'*Tell her ... I loved her ... to my dying ... dying ...*' said Aviel.

'He – waited – all – this – time. While I've been wasting my life, serving a Magister who was no better than he should have been. Playing at being Magister myself,' she said bitterly, 'thinking that what I did was important.'

'It is important,' Shand said quietly. 'And so was your work with Mendark, all the years you served him. It saw off Santhenar's greatest enemies and made the world a better place.'

She rose abruptly, took the lantern and went out.

Shand took another flask from the cupboard and poured a tot into a glass with a globular bowl. Aviel smelled brandy spirit, though not the harsh stuff Gybb had brought home after one of his rare wins. She sipped her ginger cordial, which bit the back of her throat, and took some bread.

Suddenly realising how hungry she was, she ate a huge piece. 'May I – have some more?'

'Eat it all,' said Shand, staring into the fire.

She ate as much bread and meat as she needed, and a bit more. Shand drank his brandy and poured another. He seemed disinclined to talk. It was not late, but after the sleepless terrors of last night Aviel felt unutterably weary. She curled up in the big armchair and closed her eyes, listening to the crackling fire and the wind howling outside in the eaves. How her life had changed; she could not believe it.

An icy draught woke her. A door banged in the wind and, for a moment, she thought she was back in her bed-box in the stables with her half-sisters creeping up on her. She jerked upright, crying out and expecting a blow.

Tallia came in, bleak-faced, with snow in her hair. She went up the other end of the room to the table. Shand was sitting there, writing in a journal.

'You've been to the sacrifice tree,' said Shand.

'And the road. I had to see both places; I had to know them.'

She slumped at the table, then let out a brief, incongruous peal of laughter. 'Since Ryarin wrote a year ago to tell me he was coming, I've pinned all my hopes on him. Expectations are the death of happiness, Shand.'

He said nothing.

'We've corresponded, over the years. Not an easy thing when you're separated by a hazardous sea voyage of two or three months. A couple of years ago I belatedly realised that he was my true soul mate. Ryarin realised it many years earlier and waited all this time for me, poor man. Now he's dead, and I'm utterly, utterly alone.'

Aviel could tell that Shand had no idea what to say. Perhaps there were no words that could make a difference. He put an arm across Tallia's shoulder, then came away. She laid her head on her arms.

No one spoke for a long time.

'What about the package?' Shand said quietly.

'I don't know.' She came across to the fire, warmed her hands, then squatted in front of Aviel. 'Aviel, this is very important. Ryarin was carrying a small package for me. Did he say anything about it?'

'No,' said Aviel. 'He said, *The man who stabbed me, robbed me.*' And also, *Questioned me – long time. Looking – something.*'

Tallia looked up at Shand. 'If he'd robbed Ryarin, why would he need to question him?'

'I have no idea.'

'Ryarin gave you no message?' she asked Aviel. 'Nothing at all?'

'Only what I told you when he handed me the ring.'

'What was he carrying?' said Shand.

'A lost secret.' Tallia glanced at Aviel, frowned, then added, 'Lost no longer. Seven years ago, after Mendark was killed in Shazmak, Yggur took something from his body because he didn't trust anyone else with it – *not even me.*'

'Took what?'

'The Magister's Key.'

'Never heard of it,' said Shand.

'Neither had I until Yggur wrote to me about it a month ago.'

'He's a secretive man. What's it do?'

'It allows the Magister to use certain secret powers and devices in defence of the land. I've always been hobbled as Magister because I couldn't command our most powerful weapons, and it appears our enemies now know this.'

'What is the Magister's Key?'

'Something that unlocks those secret powers.'

'How?'

'I don't know. Yggur dared not commit it to paper. That's why he sent the key with Ryarin. Yggur was planning to tell Ryarin how the key is used, then destroy his own copy of the secret.'

'So unless the killer made Ryarin speak, the secret died with him.'

'There should also have been a letter,' said Tallia. 'Yggur was going to send one.'

'Ryarin said he was searched,' said Aviel.

'How come the ring wasn't taken?'

'He made a funny movement with his fingers before he gave it to me. I thought he was using *magic*.'

'Maybe that's how he hid it.'

Aviel started. 'As Ryarin took the ring from his pocket I heard a rustling sound, like paper. But it was so dark –'

'I'll go,' said Shand.

He and Tallia went out, and shortly Aviel heard them ride down the drive. She was dozing when they returned. Tallia cleaned a filthy, rat-chewed piece of paper and held it out so the firelight fell on it.

The top and bottom of Yggur's letter was gone. What remained was only two short paragraphs. One said, *Ryarin knows the key.*

And the next –

Over the past year my old ailment has begun to torment me again, and it's getting worse each day. Soon I may have to relinquish all my positions and go away. I've fought this mental disability before, as you know, but it takes solitude – and a very long time. It is a comfort to me, however, that you are leading the Council so ably, and with the Key you'll be able to take on my role as well.

'This is bad,' said Shand. 'Very bad.'

'The past seven years have been good years,' said Tallia. 'The best in more than a century.'

'Largely because Yggur has grown into a strong, just overlord. If he pulls out –'

'He'll make arrangements for the transition to a new leader, surely. He won't just disappear ... will he? You've known him longer than I have.'

'His arrangement for the Key has just been disastrously undermined,' said Shand. 'Who's to say his other arrangements won't be?'

'Or his choices prove bad ones.'

'We've got to find Ryarin's killer.'

'I fear he's already fled with the Key – and probably the secret of using it as well.'

'To Thurkad?' said Shand.

'I imagine so. With the key, the killer's master could gain access to Council secrets I've never been able to use,' said Tallia. 'Spells from the spell vault that I've never been able to open. And devices locked away since the Clysm because they were perilous to use. This is a disaster, Shand.'

10

'What am I going to do?' said Tallia.

'In the morning, we'll have to bury Ryarin,' said Shand.

Again her face crumpled; the blow kept striking her, over and over. Aviel had to look away.

'To bury him, so far from home, is bitter,' said Tallia in a dead voice. 'I'll stand vigil over him tonight –'

'Would you like me to take a turn with you?' said Shand.

'No!' she said sharply. 'It's my duty, and my honour.' She turned Yggur's note over and over. 'Once I've seen Ryarin buried, with all the proper rituals, I'll ride for Thurkad.'

'Without any sleep?'

'Nothing could bring me sleep, tonight or tomorrow. Besides, the Magister's Key won't wait. If I can't intercept the killer, I've got to make sure our secrets are protected.'

'It'll be bitterly cold in the back room,' said Shand.

'Not as cold as it is for Ryarin.' Tallia put on her coat and went out.

Shand handed a blanket to Aviel. 'Are you comfortable there?'

'Yes,' she said, curling up in the big armchair and tucking the blanket around her. It smelled of camphor wood.

'Good night.' He blew out the lamps and headed upstairs.

She lay there, listening to the howling wind, which rattled the windows and drove gusts under the ill-fitting doors, and watching the slow movement of the red coals. For the first time in many years she felt warm and safe. Out of the depths of despair, the whole world had opened up to her.

But it had closed for Tallia. It was a reminder, not that Aviel needed one, that anyone's life could be turned upside-down in an instant.

And Tallia was standing vigil in that freezing room, alone in the world. Aviel could not bear it. She got up, the blanket around her shoulders, and padded out to the back room. The door was open but the room lay in darkness. All she could see was the rectangle of the table with the body on it and, at the nearer end, a tall, still shadow.

Aviel went in and stood beside her. Tallia did not move. Aviel reached up and took Tallia's cold hand in her own warm hand. Tallia squeezed it and they stood together for a long while. Aviel could feel the tension in her, the grief, the agony of loss.

Tallia sighed, stroked Aviel's hair and said, 'Go to bed.'

Aviel gave her the blanket. Tallia wrapped it around herself. Aviel went back to her chair and was asleep within seconds.

~

When she woke, the blanket was tucked around her and it was broad daylight, a cold, grey day. The wind had dropped and it was snowing hard. Neither Tallia nor Shand were to be found and there was a fresh mound of earth, partly covered in snow, on the right side of the backyard. They had buried Ryarin and Tallia had gone, despite the weather.

Aviel ate some stale bread and cheese, making a mental note that her debt to Shand was increasing, then found the key to the workshop and went down. The yard was empty. Wilm would not be working in the garden in this weather.

She went into the frigid workshop, closed the door and her heart sank at the enormity of the task. She wiped down a stool and perched there, gazing at the beautiful copper distillation apparatus, and daydreaming. What wonderful perfumes she could make with it once it was cleaned up. It was in sad condition, covered in caked dust and mottled with blue-green verdigris.

She gave herself a little lecture – the best way to get a job done is to start *now*. Next to the tap and tub in the narrow room at the rear was a laundry copper for heating water. She cleaned out enough rat droppings to fill a soup bowl, filled the copper with water and lit a fire in the firebox. One tiny job done.

Aviel returned to Shand's house for a broom, scrubbing brush, soap and cleaning rags. She gave the copper still a loving pat as she went past. She was saving it until last – her reward for getting everything else done.

She swept out the workshop, cut off the vines that had sneaked through the windows, tossed the dead crow and the rat droppings onto the compost heap, then carried all the equipment to the bench by the copper.

Old Quintial had left his equipment in a disgusting state and the only thing to do was boil everything in the copper until the worst of the muck softened. She put the glassware in first, while the water was cool.

Aviel scraped various unidentifiable crusts off the benches, singing to herself, scrubbed them down and rinsed them with clean water. She was admiring her work when she realised that she had not done the high shelves. After she had taken all the bottles and jars down – more rat droppings – she had to wash the benches and sweep the floor again. Plan the job, you ninkypoo!

She made temporary plugs for the gaps around the windows with garden clay, so absorbed in her work that even her ankle had stopped hurting. There were long drawers under each bench and cupboards below them. The first drawer she opened contained rat-chewed journals and notebooks, nests of shredded paper and more rat droppings. She closed it hastily and opened a cupboard. More mess. Later!

The door opened, letting in a blast of freezing air. It was dark outside; many hours had passed in her frenzy of cleaning.

Shand stood in the doorway, gazing around in amazement. 'I'd have thought it would take weeks.'

'It'll take a month to do everything properly, but it's going to be a wonderful workshop when it's done. I can't believe it's mine – to rent,' she added hastily. 'Down the back, where all the crates are, I'm going to make a little bed.'

'What with?'

'Bits of spare timber. And straw. It'll be nice and cosy.' That was an exaggeration. Even with the copper fire going the workshop was cold.

'It'll be freezing,' said Shand. 'You'll need a brazier, at the very least. Anyway, it's dinner time.'

'I can't keep eating your food.'

'You can do what you're damn well told!'

'I'm a free woman,' said Aviel. 'I've got a contract to prove it.'

'You're not a woman, you're a thirteen-year-old girl, and if you want to rent my workshop you'll follow my rules.'

She glared at him, then suddenly realised what she was doing. 'Yes,' she said in a humble voice. 'Thank you.'

'Harrumph!'

She followed him in and they sat at the table. He pushed a breadboard towards her. It contained a freshly baked loaf shaped like a triangle and a piece of butter the size of a horse's hoof. She cut neat, thin slices of the grain-flecked bread. He ladled red stew into two bowls. It smelled glorious.

'What is it?' said Aviel.

'Buffalo, onions, turnip and beans.'

The meat was chewy, but the stew tasted better than anything she had ever eaten at home. She warmed her cold hands on the bowl then ate slowly, savouring every mouthful.

'Go on, then,' said Shand after she had scraped her plate clean.

'Sorry?' said Aviel.

'You haven't said a word, and you're aching to get back out to the workshop,' he said gruffly, 'so you might as well go. I never wanted any conversation anyway.'

'I'll clean up –'

'Go, go! I can wash a couple of bowls by myself.'

The cold struck her like a fist the moment she went out the door, and it was snowing so heavily that she had to feel her way down the path. And yet, she had an uncomfortable feeling that someone was out there. She dismissed it; only a bigger fool than herself would be out in this kind of weather. Nonetheless, Aviel was glad when she closed the door and put the lantern down on the clean bench.

With a pair of tongs she fished a big flask out of the bubbling copper, scrubbed it with soap and sand, rinsed it and put it on the draining rack above the tub. When all the glassware was done she studied it in the light of her lantern and saw specks and stains everywhere. Perfume-making required the highest standards of cleanliness and everything would need another scrub, but it was a start.

Many hours had gone by and her fingers were raw. All the stoneware and metalware still had to be done but she was sagging with weariness. Aviel made sure the fire under the copper was out, gave the beautiful still a quick wipe-down, locked the door and went back to Shand's house, and the armchair she had slept in last night. Today had been the best day of her life.

But as she snuggled down in the dark, she could not shake the feeling that someone had been watching her. It must be her half-sisters, out for revenge!

11

The killer opened the message awkwardly with his thumbless hand.

You stupid corn-hopper, the Magister's Key is locked. The courier must have had a separate key to the Key.

Find it – then kill the cripple!

He held the message to the wick of the lantern and, when it was well alight, put it in the empty fireplace. He watched it burn, coiling his moustaches and thinking. Once it had burned away he ground the ashes to powder under his boot, sharpened his wavy blade and went out.

Crash, crash, CRASH.

Aviel woke with a start and sat up, her heart fluttering. What was going on? Outside, the wind was shrieking around the chimneys and rattling the windows. The crashing stopped. There must be a loose shutter, somewhere upstairs. She put some wood on the fire, it blazed up cheerfully and she went back to sleep.

Again she slept later than usual, and more soundly; again there was no sign of Shand when she rose. She ate the pottage he had left on the stove and cleaned everything in the kitchen, longing to get back to her workshop.

It was still snowing heavily and the backyard was covered so deeply that the mound of earth above Ryarin's grave had disappeared. Tracks showed where Shand had gone back and forth to the stables, and a single set of hoof marks indicated that he had ridden out. It would be bitterly cold in the workshop and she was tempted to go back to the fire. Surely, after the last couple of days, she deserved a break.

But the sooner the place was cleaned up, the sooner she could begin learning her trade. Aviel waded through deep snow to the workshop, then stopped. The door was ajar, though she could remember locking it. Could Shand have looked in and forgotten to close it? No, the wood was splintered around the lock. The door had been prised open.

It must have been done a long time ago, because the snow near the door was unmarked, but Aviel, remembering that crashing in the night, was afraid to go in. She eased the door open, looked in and froze, pierced to the heart.

The shelves, and the drawers and cupboards below the benches, had been emptied onto the floor. Many of the bottles and jars had smashed and everything was covered in a variety of liquids and powders, all mixed with shredded paper and rat droppings. She stared at the mess, her chest heaving. It would take a full day to clean up.

The glassware! She scrambled across the debris, praying that she had seen the worst, then stopped dead.

Terribly, disastrously worse – the glassware she had so carefully cleaned was smashed on the flagstones, along with all the unwashed stoneware and porcelain, and the big mortar was split in half.

She looked down and let out a cry of anguish! Partly buried by the wreckage, the beautiful copper distilling apparatus, that had made her heart race every time she looked at it, was a ruin of flattened pipes and burst seams. The intruder must have attacked it with a hammer, deliberately battering it beyond repair.

'Aviel?' Wilm called, from outside.

She plodded to the door. Defeated. Numb.

Wilm had a bucket full of cleaning rags in one hand, and wore a big smile. 'Shand said you might need some help –' The smile faded.

'It's *ruined*.' She slumped on the snow-covered step, put her head in her hands and wept.

Wilm put down the bucket and looked in, then his big fists clenched. 'Who would do such a wicked thing?' He grabbed a long stick from the wood heap, swung it around and smashed it to bits against a corner of the workshop. Bits of wood went everywhere.

'I'll bet it was my sisters,' Aviel said dully, staring at her feet. All the energy had drained out of her.

'In the middle of a blizzard?' said Wilm. 'They're far too lazy.'

She felt so discouraged that she was tempted to take to her bed – but that was how Gybb dealt with problems. Aviel forced herself to get up; she had to think this through. If it had not been her sisters, who could it be? And what did they want?

She went in, and this time caught the faint, foul odour she had smelled on Ryarin's clothes. She still could not identify it but an ugly suspicion stirred. On three separate occasions she had thought she was being watched.

'Where's Shand?' she said.

'I don't know. He said he might be out all day.'

She worked her way back through the mess, sniffing the air and checking every surface for evidence. Then she saw it – a clear boot print on the floor where the intruder had stepped in a puddle of glycerine, then in white alum.

She crouched beside the print. 'Wilm,' she whispered, 'it's the killer!'

'How do you know?'

'Shand and I saw the same footprint where Ryarin was stabbed.'

'Why would the killer want to smash this place up?'

The motivations of adults had always been a mystery to Aviel. What drove Gybb to gamble every grint he earned? Why did her half-sisters hate her when she did so much for them? Why – the biggest mystery of all – had Shand paid her indenture?

'I don't know,' said Aviel.

'What if he's looking for something?'

'Like what?'

Wilm shrugged his bony shoulders. 'Maybe the killer thinks Ryarin gave you something.'

'Only the ring for Tallia.'

Aviel began to pick up the stuff on the floor, sorting it into one pile that could be put back where it had come from, another pile that would have to be cleaned first, and stuff to be thrown out. But after a few minutes the heart drained out of her; it was too cold and too depressing. The killer had set back her dream immeasurably, because she did not have the money to replace even the smallest piece of broken equipment.

They went into the house. She made mugs of lime tea and they sat in the kitchen by the little round stove. Aviel stared into the firebox, her heart thudding leadenly. It was all too hard –

'No!' she cried. 'I'm *not* letting him get away with it.'

'Aviel?' Wilm said anxiously.

'Ryarin was carrying something important for Tallia,' said Aviel, thinking it through. 'And the killer stabbed him in the back with a poisoned blade – but not to kill.'

'Why not?'

'He needed to question him without getting caught. He carried Ryarin down to the sacrifice tree –'

'So no one would find the body after he'd finished with him,' said Wilm.

'Why, though?'

'I suppose he didn't want anyone to know he'd stolen Ryarin's parcel until he'd given it to whoever wanted it –'

'That must be why the killer is still here,' Aviel said excitedly. 'He thinks Ryarin told me something important.'

'But the killer could be anyone,' Wilm said.

'He's a heavy, short-legged man and we know his boot print.'

'It's not enough.'

'Wait, there's another clue. I smelled an odd, foul on Ryarin's clothes, and again in the workshop a few minutes ago.'

'What kind of a smell?'

'Really stinky. And ... a bit like bird manure.'

'What sort?' said Wilm.

'Like goose poo, after they've been eating meat – but fouler.'

'Skeets eat meat,' Wilm said thoughtfully, 'and their poo smells disgusting.'

'I've never seen a skeet,' said Aviel.

'Come down to Shand's skeet house and I'll show you.'

'I didn't know he kept them.'

'They're the fastest carrier birds of all. He's always sending messages back and forth. He knows a lot of important people –' Wilm broke off, as if he had said more than he should have.

They went out. 'Skeets are dangerous, aren't they?' said Aviel.

'Very. If you give them a chance, they'll go for your eyes – or your throat.'

Aviel stopped in the middle of the yard. She did not want to go anywhere near such creatures. There were three roofed cages, each eight feet wide and nearly as high, with solid walls between each cage and wooden gates with horizontal viewing slots. A heavy chain ran through the latches of each gate and was closed with a padlock the size of a turnip.

'They must be huge,' said Aviel.

'Wingspan of seven feet. If they weren't kept in separate cages, they'd tear each other to pieces. You can look through the slots. Don't go too close.'

She approached warily. The smell was revolting. Two of the cages were occupied; the dark brown birds were at the back, on perches. They were the size of eagles, with viciously hooked beaks and massive claws. Each perch had a blood-stained wooden feeding platform, a foot square. She wondered how Shand fed them without being attacked.

She backed away. Wilm looked at her questioningly.

'That's the smell,' said Aviel. 'The killer uses skeets.'

12

Where was Shand? Aviel was desperate to tell him what she had discovered so he could send the town constables after the killer, but he had not come back.

Before going home, Wilm had told her that only three people in Casyme kept skeets: Shand, the mayor, and Jel Tandy, a wealthy gem trader who had been away at his mines in the north for months. The killer could not have used the mayor's skeets, which were in a locked compound, nor Shand's. But Tandy's big house was empty save for old Tod, the caretaker.

Aviel sat by the fire, gulping cup after cup of mint tea. What was the killer looking for, and why had he wrecked her workshop? It could have attracted attention to him. She could only think of one reason – he was an angry, violent man who could not control himself. *And he was watching her.*

She felt a sudden pounding in her ears and her heart was racing. If the killer was watching the house, he knew she was alone; he could come for her at any time. The doors were locked but he could easily break in and no one would hear her screams. Aviel armed herself with the biggest knife in Shand's kitchen and sat so she could see both doors.

Crash! She jumped, scrambled to her feet and looked around desperately. Which way to run? *Crash!* It was coming from upstairs. It was just that blasted shutter banging in the wind.

She could not bear to sit here, waiting for him to come. She had to identify him first, so Shand could have him arrested. Dare she go down to Tandy's place and look for clues? It was a big old house set in several acres of grounds, on the western side of town, though it would be a miserably cold and painful walk in this weather. Aviel did not want to go, but how it be more dangerous than waiting here?

She put the knife in her pocket and went out. On the street, the wind was so strong that her eyes kept watering, and the air was full of drifting snow; she could only see ten yards ahead. Trees, bushes and people blurred into formless shadows, any of which could have been the killer. If he came after her, he could catch her as easily here as inside, and no one would ever know – until they found her body.

She limped on, her heart pounding and her ankle more painful with every step. *Thump!* Behind her! Aviel whirled, staring around wildly, but there was no one in sight. It must have been snow sliding off a roof.

Aviel trudged across the trodden snow of the market circle, keeping watch for a big-bodied man with short legs – and for predatory sisters. There were few people around and most of the shops and market stalls were shuttered, though the taverns were busy. Gybb would be in one of them. She pulled the hood of her coat around her face, not that it would make much difference – he would recognise her lurching walk at a glance.

Tandy's house was huge and eccentric in design. Built of red stone with black inserts around the round, leaded windows, it had half a dozen turrets, many pointed little roofs and hundreds of leering gargoyles, alternately carved from red and black stone. Along the outside wall, below the line of the main roof, white marble busts of famous poets and philosophers were set in blue-black niches.

The snow up to the house showed only a single set of tracks, going out. The killer's footmarks? She could not tell – the prints were already partly infilled. Then, in the sheltered area in front of the huge right-hand gatepost, she found a clear footprint – so complete that she could see the mark of the bent nail in the heel.

The killer had been here, not long ago.

Where had he gone? There was no way of knowing; his tracks were lost in all the other tracks on the footpath. Aviel stood there, her weight on her left foot, wondering what to do. The sensible course was to find Shand and tell him. But what if she could not find him, and the killer disappeared? Shand would not know enough to track him down.

She kept going past Tandy's estate, which was surrounded by an eight-foot-high wall, then headed up the lane to the right and around the back. At the rear, snowdrifts reached almost to the top of the wall. Aviel scrambled up the biggest drift, which had a hard crust, and onto the wall. She was kneeling there, staring at the house, when pain speared through her ankle and she overbalanced, slipped on the icy surface and fell into the foot-deep snow inside the wall.

Snow went down the back of her neck. Aviel rolled over and lay there, cursing herself for the biggest fool in the world. She had pushed her luck too far and it had betrayed her, as it always did. She was dangerously exposed here. She looked up at the wall, then along it, left and right, and ice formed around her heart. The wall towered seven feet above her and there was no way she could climb over it.

As she stood up on shaky legs, her head spun and the strength drained out of her. She slumped back in the snow, her heart going so fast that it was painful. Why, why had she done such a foolish thing? She should have gone straight to the mayor's office, or the constables. Now she had no choice but to go down past the house and try to sneak out the driveway – and if the killer came back, she would die.

Her mouth was as dry as paper; she was afraid to move, to even raise her head. What if he was watching, smiling in anticipation? She sucked on a lump of snow but it only made her colder. Fear closed like a fist around her heart. She had to get out, *now*.

Ahead, a patch of large trees would give her some cover until halfway down the gentle slope to the house. She crept down from tree to tree. From the last one, she saw sets of tracks running from the back door to the skeet houses, and to a cluster of sheds and outhouses, though they were old tracks, partly filled by the drifting snow. She was desperately cold now and her feet, in her thin boots, were freezing. She would sneak down to that long stack of firewood, thirty yards from the rear door, see if she could pick up any clues, then go.

She ducked behind the stack, watching the driveway, the caretaker's cottage and the rear of the manor. Tracks ran from the stack to the back door, but were they the caretaker's tracks, or the killer's?

She could not tell; the tracks were dusted with fresh snow. Dare she go closer to the house? If she did not find a clue to the killer's identity, coming here had been a dangerous waste of time.

Aviel crouched there, her cold hands pressed into her armpits. She *really* did not want to go any further ... but the back door was not far out of her way. She checked all around; no one in sight. Placing her feet in the killer's footmarks, she crept down to the back door and tested it. It was unlocked; why would a murdering thug care about another man's property?

To go in, or leave? Leave, you fool! But from here she could not see the driveway. What if she turned the corner of the house and the killer was right in front of her?

As though a death wish had possessed her, she eased the door open.

13

Aviel saw an empty coat room, with coats and cloaks on hooks, and a neat line of boots against the wall. Cobwebs showed that they had not been used in a long time. She shook the snow off her coat and hat, slipped in and pulled the door shut.

Then she stopped; she had to have a plan, in case he came back. She would creep out the front door, wade through the fifty yards of snow down to the gates, and out onto the street. And pray that she could reach safety before the killer caught her.

The door in front of her was closed. She edged through into a rear hall. On the right an enormous kitchen with an vaulted black brick ceiling was dominated by an iron stove that had six ovens and eight cooking plates. Next to it was a fireplace with a spit long enough to roast a whole cow. On the left were pantries, larders and storerooms, and a set of stone steps that ran down into darkness, perhaps to a cellar. Ahead, a massive door, cut from a single slab of green slate fixed in a brass frame, kept the workers in their place.

Aviel crept through the door. Beyond, a sweeping staircase ran up to a second level; above that, a smaller stair went to the third floor. She bypassed the stairs and checked the next room, which was the size of a ballroom. Its carved wooden ceiling depicted a battle scene in gruesome detail, in dozens of different kinds of timbers: brown, yellow, white, black and, in places, far too much red. The timber floor was partly covered by a series of magnificent rugs, though the scenes woven into them were equally disturbing.

The rooms around the ballroom were smaller, though similarly grand and unsettling. All the curtains were drawn and the rooms were dimly lit. There were cobwebs in the corners and the furniture was covered in yellow dust sheets. Aviel, who was keeping careful watch for escape routes, noted that some of the rooms had multiple doorways, while others had only one.

She reached the front door – and it was locked. Aviel's heart missed a beat. She was heading back, checking the rest of the rooms for clues, when the door she was opening stopped a third of the way, as if blocked by something. She pushed harder and the door moved enough for her to slip through.

She barely managed to choke back a scream. A dead man lay on the floor; an old man with the back of his head bashed in. Tod, who had been the caretaker here for decades, still clutched a knobbly stick in his left hand. His toothless mouth was stretched wide as if he had been shouting.

Aviel sank to her knees beside him. Poor old Tod. He had been a crotchety old fellow, quick to shout at kids who threw stones over the wall, but he was not a bad man; he did not deserve this.

And if the killer found her here, she would die just as horribly. Instinctively, she reached for her knife. Her pocket was empty! The knife must have fallen out when she toppled off the fence. She was defenceless. Why, why had she come in here? Then suddenly Aviel knew, with the certainty of a lifetime of bad luck, that the killer was on his way. She had to get out!

But as she reached the green slate door she heard the distinctive double click as the heavy latch on the back door was lifted. She was trapped. Unarmed and trapped with a brutal, malicious killer.

No, the house was huge; there must be a way out. She had been careful coming in and, unless he had been up past the wood heap where she had left clear tracks, he might not know she was here.

Aviel returned to the room where Tod's body lay. The long room had two doors and at least a dozen large pieces of furniture, covered in dust sheets. She rejected the long table as a hiding place; it was too obvious. A pair of dressers were no good either; there wasn't enough space under them.

Then she saw something that struck her like a blow to the heart – a small, curving piece of ice beside Tod's body. It must have broken off her heel, and if the killer saw it he would know someone had stood there only minutes ago. Someone with small feet. Her!

Aviel was tiptoeing across to pick it up when heavy footsteps came up the rear hall. She squeezed in behind a dresser with a huge oval mirror on top. If he approached, she could slip out the other side. She realised that she was sucking at the air, almost gasping. Aviel forced herself to breathe slowly, though it left her feeling light-headed and panicky.

The killer came in and bent over the body before she could see his face. He was even bigger around the middle than Gybb, but with stubby legs. His black hair was cut short and he had a circular bald patch with edges so neat that they might have been shaved.

He picked the piece of ice up, rather awkwardly; he had no thumb on his right hand. His square, pudgy face might have been handsome before he put on so much weight. He had extravagant black moustaches, waxed and up-curled at the ends. He traced the curve of the ice with a fingertip, then let out a small, chilling laugh. He knew she was here.

He wore a long woollen coat, deep blue with scarlet stitching. An embroidered yellow and black waistcoat, bulging out over his chest and belly as if over a barrel, made him look like a fat bumblebee. He dropped the ice, drew a wavy-bladed knife and she saw such a savage look on his face that all thoughts of a bumblebee vanished. This bee had a stinger.

Aviel did not think he could see her in the dimly-lit room but he could probably track her down by the thumping coming from her chest. In all her life she had never been so terrified, or so sure that her desperately bad luck was about to claim her for the final time.

14

If Aviel had any luck at all, the killer would check the furniture on the other side of the room then continue to the far door, allowing her to escape. Naturally, she had no luck. He came directly towards the dresser she was hiding behind.

She slid around the end furthest away from him, crouched and peered out through a gap. Her feet felt deathly cold and her right hand had developed a tremor. What would he do if he caught her? There had been no need to hurt poor old Tod; the killer could easily have overpowered him and tied him up. Instead, he had hit him so hard that it had caved his head in.

It would be worse for her. He was looking for something and she did not have it. Shivers crept down her back. Whatever she said, he would not believe her.

'You can't get away, you hideous little cripple,' said the killer. Aviel flinched. His voice was flat, almost dead, and chilling. 'Give it up and I won't hurt you.'

She wasn't tempted to answer. He was a deadly version of her sisters and wanted to hurt her in every way. Yet she wondered what 'it' was.

He came three-quarters of the way towards the dresser then spun around, scanning the gloomy room. He flipped up the dust cloth on the big table and peered under it; he turned abruptly and lumbered towards a glass-fronted display cabinet.

Aviel was about to dash for the door, which was ten yards away, when she noticed an expectant tenseness in the killer's broad back. He was waiting for her to move. It took all her courage to stay where she was, knowing he could catch her in a few bounds.

'I'll be doing the world a favour,' he sneered.

His head turned left and right, then whipped around. His belly stuck out in a dome but it was not saggy like Gybb's; it did not wobble at all. She could hear his fast breathing. Then he turned and came straight for her.

Could she outrun him? Not for long. She tensed, counting his steps. He was five yards away; four; three. Again he turned abruptly and this time she had to take the chance. She bolted for the door.

But the killer had been shamming again. He spun on one foot, lunged and caught her by the back of the coat. Aviel heaved desperately, tore it from his thumbless grip, staggered and nearly fell. He scrambled upright but did not come after her.

'I'll get you, you little bitch.' He drew the wavy-bladed knife and hurled it, rather awkwardly, at her back.

She flung herself to the left and the knife embedded itself, quivering and thrumming, into the architrave on the right side of the door. She snatched at the hilt but could not pull it out; it was in too deep. She half-ran, half-hopped into the next room, the bones of her ankle grinding together, sobbing with pain and terror.

The blade squealed as he wrenched it out. He came after her, moving quietly now, though she could tell where he was from his heavy breathing. Fabric whispered as he pulled the dust cloth off a table set with ten dainty carved chairs. The back of each chair was carved to depict a different kind of bird, all birds of prey or carrion-eaters.

Aviel moved from one piece of furniture to another, desperately trying to control her own breathing. Her options were running out with every dust cloth he stripped away.

'I'm not going to kill you immediately,' he said softly. 'First you'll tell me everything you know.'

She sensed that he wanted her to reply; that it was a game and if he provoked her into answering, he won. He loved the hunt and he was feeding on her terror. There was plenty to feed on; she was practically wetting herself.

He had controlled his heavy breathing and she could not tell where he was. Which way should she go? This room had less covered furniture than the last and too late she saw that there was only one way out – the door she had come in.

Aviel heard a soft *rasp-rasp*, rising and falling. Then again, and again. She knew the sound; he was running a sharpening stone up one side of the knife blade and down the other.

Rasp-rasp. Rasp-rasp. It was a threat. A terrifying one.

'You'd be a pretty girl,' he said, 'if you didn't have that repulsive ankle.'

It struck at the heart of her. Her ankle was the measure of her life, the cause of her pain and disability, and one of the sources of her bad luck. It was the thing everyone remarked on, and the other children had picked on, all her life. *Twist-foot, twist-foot!*

All except Wilm, her defender. She used the thought of his quiet loyalty as a shield.

Rasp-rasp. Rasp-rasp.

'I can't bear to look at it while I question you,' he said, conversationally. 'I'll have to cut it off.'

His words were an assault; they hurt more than a punch in the teeth.

'If you still haven't given it up,' he added, 'I'll cut higher.'

Rasp-rasp. Rasp-rasp.

Terror was turning her bowels liquid and her knees to jelly. His sneering words were a form of attack she could not fight, while the *rasp-rasp, rasp-rasp* was a subliminal terror that leached her courage away. She felt like a poor dumb animal, hearing the slaughterer coming and unable to do anything about it.

'The courier gave you a key,' said the killer.

What was he talking about?

'If you hand it over,' he added, 'I might let you go.'

Liar! He'd killed twice and enjoyed it. He had smashed up her workshop just to hurt her. He wanted to see the terror in her eyes. And if she let him control her, she would die.

Aviel used the image of the beautiful, ruined copper still to stiffen her resolve. She had to distract him long enough to get to the door.

Rasp-rasp. Rasp-rasp.

It was coming from behind a precious lobster-wood cabinet, a weirdly beautiful scalloped piece with etched glass doors, behind which she could see a collection of tiny books, each no bigger than her thumb. He was waiting for her to move, though if she did he would cut her off before she reached the door.

Aviel went down on her belly and, taking advantage of all the cover she could, wriggled towards the table. She was taking a big risk – if he burst out, he could dive on her before she could get to her feet.

She almost made it. She was only a yard from the table when he lunged out from behind the cabinet, swinging the knife underhand. She came to her hands and knees, hurled herself under the table and scurried away.

He thumped up, breathing hard. Aviel's heart was bursting with terror; she could see his legs at the other end and she must not let him get near. He ducked, his face appearing upside-down, then let out a bellow. She shrieked and went the other way, but it was another feint and he came pounding around after her.

She scrambled to her feet, too late. His arms were spread; he was grinning under his black moustaches as he came for her. Without thinking, she grabbed one of the delicate chairs, the one whose carved back depicted a carrion crow. Just like him! It was lighter than she had expected and she thrust it at him, legs first, with all the strength gained from years of labouring in the garden.

Aviel had been aiming for his face but he closed in too quickly and the two slender back legs struck him in the belly with such force that they pushed it in a foot. The knife skimmed past her nose and the fingers of his left hand were about to close on her throat when he went, 'Oof!' and his face turned purple.

Aviel threw her weight behind the chair, forcing its legs further into his belly, and felt something tear. A folded piece of paper fell out of his waistcoat pocket. He took several staggering steps backwards, gasping, and landed on his back. She threw the chair at his head, snatched up the piece of paper and ran for the door. By the time she reached it her ankle was spearing pain up her right leg with every step. She hopped through the great house, heading for the back door, then stopped.

She did not think the killer was badly hurt; if he was just winded, he would soon recover. And if he had seen her tracks outside, he might have locked the back door on the way in. There were no windows in the boot room so she would be trapped there. She turned left and headed across the central hall with the staircase to a pair of round, leaded windows. But they did not open.

He was grunting and gasping as he staggered after her. She only had a minute; how could she break the window? There – a brass lampstand, taller than she was, with a heavy circular base. She lifted it with an effort and, as the killer turned the corner, slammed the base through the centre of the window, tearing out a dozen small panes. She rolled the lampstand at him and scrambled up onto the windowsill.

She was halfway through the tight gap when his hand closed around her left boot.

15

The killer's face was a deeper shade of purple than before and there was blood on his belly where a chair leg had torn into him. Aviel kicked furiously, catching him in the mouth, and dived out. She landed in deep snow, though not so deep as to protect her from a jagged piece of glass below her left palm. It went in until it hit bone, and it hurt desperately.

She pulled it out, gasping with the pain, and blood poured from a nasty gash an inch and a half long. She clenched her fingers over it, feeling faint, and floundered around in the snow. As she came to her feet, the killer's face appeared at the window. Her kick had split his lip and blood was running down his chin. He raised the knife as if to throw it and she flinched, but he must have thought he would miss. He turned and she heard him lurching away. He was heading for the back door.

The grounds here, on the opposite side of the house to the driveway, were two feet deep in snow and it would be very slow going. But if she ran up and around the back of the house, where the snow was thinner, she would be heading towards him.

Aviel stumbled along the side of the house in deep snow, blood spotting the ground behind her, only to see that a deep drift rose ahead of her, blocking her way; she would be trapped in it. She had to risk the long way; if she could get past the rear of the house and head down the far side, onto the driveway, she might have a chance.

As she turned along the back, she heard a clatter as the killer jammed the great iron key in the lock and tried to turn it. Judging by the rattling sound, his hand was shaking, but it would not take him long. She ran harder, but as she passed the back door he shouldered it open and lurched out, gasping. He made a wild grab for her, his fingertips grazed her cheek, then she was past and careering towards the far corner of the house.

As she reached it, she risked a glance over her shoulder. Blood streaked the killer's cravat and there was a red, seeping bulge under the lower part of his waist-coat as if the chair leg had torn into his belly. She prayed that it was serious. He ran a few steps, doubled over, spitting blood, then came after her.

It was a hundred and fifty yards from here to the gates and her ankle was already excruciatingly painful. Worse, it was giving every time she put weight on it, and her right knee was wobbling. It had slipped out of alignment again and, if she kept abusing it, it was liable to collapse without warning. But she had no choice.

He stopped to throw up, then came after her. He was gaining; she would not reach the gates. At the driveway corner of the house she looked around desperately. The cluster of sheds and outhouses was fifty yards ahead. Next to them but a bit closer was the skeet house – the reason the killer had come here in the first place.

She wasn't going near the skeets. But – if she was incredibly lucky – she might be able to escape him by ducking through narrow gaps between the sheds, where he would not fit. She staggered towards them, sobbing with the pain.

He put on a burst of speed; he was only ten yards behind. His purple face looked maniacal, the black moustache tips quivered and the wavy knife stabbed up and down. She wasn't going to reach the sheds.

Aviel turned sharply on her good foot to duck past the skeet cages. The hungry skeets began to shriek and flap their wings wildly – they had caught the scent of blood. Their hooked beaks tore at the timber poles and their evil claws shredded the hardwood of their feeding platforms.

Without thinking, without hope, Aviel yanked on the bolt of the first skeet cage and pulled the door open, trying to swing it into the killer's face. He side-stepped to the right, cursing her. The skeet, the biggest of them all, let out another shriek and its eight-foot-wide wings propelled it through the door. It was going for her! She dropped flat, covered her head with her hands and prayed.

It soared over her and kept going, straight for the blood-covered killer. He screamed, 'Get away!' and struck at it with his knife.

The skeet swerved in the air and, with an expert slash of the claws on its right foot, tore his throat open. Blood erupted six feet into the air and he dropped the knife. He stared at Aviel in astonishment, as if he could not believe that a crippled girl had beaten him. His expression turned to wide-eyed, moaning terror when he understood what was going to happen next.

He tried to beg for help but he had no wind. His lips formed the word, 'No!'

The killer toppled, landed on his back and lay there, his eyes wide with horror, his pudgy fists beating feebly at the skeet. It landed on his chest and began to feed with horrible tearing and gobbling sounds. Aviel could not bear to look.

The other skeets, maddened by the smell and the sight of so much blood, battered at the doors of their cages so furiously that she feared they would break free. She grabbed a stick leaning against the side of the empty cage and, using it as a cane, staggered down towards the gates.

As she passed through, Shand came pounding up on Thistle. Some distance behind she saw Wilm, running as fast as he could go through the snow, then two of the town constables.

'Aviel!' Shand swung down, landing with a thud. 'Are you –?'

She was drenched in the killer's blood. Shand must have thought she was dying.

'I'm all right,' she said weakly. 'Found – killer. Skeet got him. Careful.'

Shand held her up until Wilm and the constables arrived.

'Take her home,' said Shand to Wilm.

'There will be questions,' said the leading constable.

'Later!' snapped Shand.

He headed up the drive, following Aviel's blood-speckled tracks. The constables went with him. Wilm lifted Aviel onto Thistle. He looked over his shoulder and stamped a hoof; he did not like the smell of blood. Wilm stroked his muzzle and led him home without saying a word.

16

'I recognised him at once,' said Shand that evening, 'even after the skeet had ... remodelled him. His name was Berenet and he was one of Mendark's people, years ago. They fell out and Berenet joined a bad crowd.'

Aviel sat on the hearth by the fire, her badly swollen ankle strapped and extended to the warmth. She had scrubbed Berenet's blood off, bathed in hot water for the first time in her life and dressed in her only clean clothes. Shand had put five stitches in the gash in her palm, and the constables had come, questioned her, and gone.

She felt a deep melancholy. Two good people had been murdered, and Tallia's dream had been shattered. For what?

Wilm sat beside her. It was good having her oldest and only friend there. She did not count Shand as a friend; he was something else entirely but she still did not know what. Could he be her father? She remembered that odd, knowing look Tallia had given him. She had to know, but how was she to ask?

'I sent a message to Tallia,' said Shand. 'It'll help her to know that justice has been done – rough though it was.'

Aviel wrapped her arms around herself. 'I keep seeing the moment when the skeet –' Her voice cracked. '*And how it fed.*' She looked up at Shand. 'I didn't mean it to kill him; just stop him ...'

'If Berenet had got away, he would have killed again. You did the world a service.'

'What was he after?' said Wilm, speaking for the first time in an hour. 'What did he think Aviel had?'

'I don't know,' said Shand.

Wilm rose. 'I'd better go. Dinner will be ready.' He went out.

'There was a note,' Aviel remembered. 'It fell out of the killer's waistcoat when I hit him with the chair.'

She felt in her pockets, but they were empty.

'Those aren't the clothes you were wearing,' said Shand.

She began the painful process of standing up. Every muscle in her body ached, all the way down to the bones.

'I'll go,' said Shand.

Shortly he returned, carrying a collection of small items, including the folded piece of paper. 'You left it in the wash house.'

'Can you read it?' Aviel felt utterly emptied out.

Shand unfolded the paper. 'It says, *The Magister's Key has to be unlocked every time, before it can be used. There's a key to the Key. Find it, fool!*'

'Who's it from?'

'It doesn't say.' He put the paper down on the arm of her chair. 'But Tallia said the Magister's Key is a micrast –'

'A what?'

'A kind of fossil. It's solid stone – there's nowhere to insert a key.' Shand poured himself an unhealthily large drink. Aviel frowned; he drank too much. 'Unless it's a *magical* key – a spell or charm that must be cast on the Magister's Key each time ... though charms can leave a residuum that a skilled mancer might be able to decipher ...'

Aviel started. 'What if it's a *musical* key?'

'Why do you say that?'

'Ryarin kept humming a little tune, over and over.'

Shand leaned forwards, eyes alight. 'Do you remember it?'

'I can never forget it. It sounded so sad.' She sang eleven notes, high and pure.

Shand got a piece of paper and a pen. 'Sing it again.'

She did so and he made a series of marks on the paper.

'And again.'

He checked the marks, scribbled a note on the bottom and sealed it with candle wax. 'I'll send this to Tallia right away. It might be just in time.'

'How do you mean?'

'Berenet was well known in Thurkad, and her spies will soon discover who sent him – who he stole the Magister's Key for. With the key to the Key, she'll be able to turn it against him. You've done us a great service today, Aviel.'

She felt a small glow of pleasure. 'It's really that important?'

'Yes it is. The signs say that our long peace is coming to an end –'

'Do you mean war is coming?'

'Yggur is a mighty warlord and a fine leader. If he suddenly withdraws, it'll leave a vacuum that every villain in the west will try to fill.'

Aviel shivered and scrunched herself up into a ball.

'But what you've done today has really made a difference,' he added. He headed for the door.

She had to clear something up, right now. 'Shand?' she said, her heart fluttering.

'Yes?'

'Are – are you my father?'

He froze, then came back. 'No. Why do you ask?'

'Then why have you been so good to me?'

'Does there have to be a reason?'

'The world is full of poor, unlucky people. Why me?'

He sighed, then sat down. 'I had a lover once, Yalkara. She was a Charon, one of the very greatest of that superhuman species. Too great for me, as it turned out ...'

He looked old and sad, and so very lonely. 'You must miss her.'

'I do, but after I discovered that she had committed a terrible crime I could never take her back. *Not even if she were to beg!* Not that she would.'

'It must have been really bad,' she said softly.

'It was a very long time ago – the Charon can live for thousands of years. She murdered an innocent girl called Fiachra, only a couple of years older than you ... Yalkara stabbed her in the back.'

Aviel jumped. 'No!'

'She killed Fiachra for a higher purpose but I could not forgive her. The girl was helpless and Yalkara was brilliant; she should have found another way.'

'I don't understand what it's got to do with me.'

'Fiachra's legs were withered; she was crippled and could never have defended herself. It was a monstrous crime.'

Suddenly Aviel understood. 'And that's why you helped me.'

'Perhaps I'm trying to atone for Yalkara's crime the only way I can. Are you offended? Do you feel like a token?' Shand looked anxious.

'Not at all,' said Aviel. 'I'm honoured. Though I'd like to know –'

'Fiachra's story begins the Great Tale called the *Tale of the Mirror* ... and is finished near the end of it. You can read it if you want.' He waved a hand towards the bookcase.

'I will,' said Aviel, longing to know more about that crippled girl from so long ago whose life, tragically cut short, had so changed her own.

A thought struck Shand. He went to the table and picked up a small, wrapped package. 'This is for you.'

'What is it?'

'If you open it, you'll find out.'

She did so, careful not to tear the paper. Inside was a small, battered old book bound in faded green leather. *Arte and Crafte of Perfumerie.* She sat there quivering, tears of joy blurring her vision. It was a treasure beyond her imagination.

'You can't give me this,' she said in a croaky voice.

'Can't talk,' Shand said hastily. 'Got to send the message to Tallia.' He headed for the door.

'Shand?'

'Yes?'

'Be careful at the skeet house.'

He smiled. 'I will.'

She opened the book but her eyes were too wet to read. Later, she thought. When things have settled down. She would ration the book, one page a day.

Aviel lay back and closed her eyes, trying to put the events of the past days out of mind. It wasn't easy, for the images were burned into her: the glee on the faces of her half-sisters as they broke her birthday presents; Gybb betraying her to Magsie; Ryarin clutching her hand in the sacrifice tree as he died; Shand giving her the indenture and offering her the workshop; Tallia's agony when she was told of Ryarin's murder; Aviel's discovery that the killer had smashed all her equipment.

Berenet hunting her through the empty house.

The skeet throwing its head back to swallow bloody gobbets of him –

With an effort, she forced the images into her subconscious. Tomorrow she would start again. Some simple perfumes could be made with everyday equipment – plates, bowls and pans, the right oils. She was going to master the trade, no matter what it took.

Two weeks later, on a cool, sunny morning, Aviel was pruning the rosemary hedge at the back of Shand's garden when a laden cart came down the driveway and stopped in front of the stables. Shand, Wilm and the driver lifted down a large crate. The driver turned his cart and went out. Shand and Wilm hauled the crate down to the door of the workshop.

'What's that?' said Aviel, carrying a bag of clippings up. She sniffed her fingers, which were pungent with rosemary oil.

'Open it.'

She did so and found, carefully wrapped, a large number of flasks, a copper distilling apparatus and another one made from glass, three mortars and pestles in varying sizes, tubes and phials and bowls large and small, and other items that she did not know the use of.

She turned to Shand. 'You can't give me this. I owe you far too much already.'

'It's not from me,' Shand said blandly.

'Then who?' she said suspiciously.

'I dare say there's a note somewhere.'

She gave him a disbelieving look, but took everything out and found an envelope at the bottom.

My dear Aviel,

You have done more for me than you can ever know – both personally and as Magister. Shand's message came just in time and the matter has been sorted out to my satisfaction.

This is the least I can do in return, and I wish you joy of your trade. Work hard and master your gift – and whatever it may lead to in future – for I fear we may need your talents again before too long.

Your friend, Tallia.

Aviel sat down on the workshop steps, dazed by her good fortune. 'What does Tallia mean by, *and whatever it may lead to in future?*'

A shifty look crossed Shand's weathered face. 'Let's leave that to the future.'

That question is answered in **The Gates of Good and Evil**, *set a few years after this story. Aviel and Wilm play important roles in this series, and Shand and Tallia will be back as well, plus a number of other characters from* **The View from the Mirror**.

Most notably, of course, Karan and Llian.

STORY VII

ONE THROW OF THE DIE

1

*If you haven't read my epic fantasy quartet **The Well of Echoes**, and intend to, you should do so before reading this novelette,* One Throw of the Die, *since it begins immediately after* Chimaera, *the final book of **The Well of Echoes**, and necessarily gives away the entire ending.*

When Jal-Nish, shockingly burned though he was, reached Gatherer and Reaper first, Flydd knew it was over. The two enchanted tears were too powerful. The war, and perhaps the world itself was lost, and all the allies could do was run for their miserable lives.

'Come on!' Flydd ran, his cloak trailing smoke, for their one hope of escape – Jal-Nish's air-dreadnought.

Yggur, a very tall, lean man, took off like a hare through the smoke. Klarm raced after him, the dwarf's stubby legs making three strides to Yggur's one. The others followed, not looking back.

As Flydd reached the air-dreadnought, a huge craft with a sausage-shaped cabin sixty feet long, suspended by cables below three long airbags, Sergeant Flangers came running around the edge of the crowd, carrying the pilot, Chissmoul. She was a small, painfully shy young woman who became a laughing extravert at the controls of a flying machine, but she was not laughing now.

Yggur blasted down one of the guards with jagged white fire. Fyn-Mah, a slender, black-haired woman in her thirties, killed the other with a backhanded blow to the throat. She and General Troist scrambled inside. Klarm was not far behind.

Flydd took the weapons from the dead guards – two swords and a stubby, red-handled knife – and panted up the wobbling plank. 'Chissmoul! Can you fly this thing?'

'Nodes dead,' she said dully. 'Fields gone. No power!'

'I've got a charged crystal,' said Klarm, producing it. It was two inches long and half an inch through, yellow-green at one end grading to red at the other. 'Will it do?'

She snatched it as if it was a lifeline, and it was, for flying was life and soul to her. She tied the crystal onto her forehead with a brown bootlace. Her hands were shaking. She took hold of the control levers and closed her eyes, drawing power from the crystal and, in a process no one but pilots understood, funnelling it to the triple rotors at the stern. They began to revolve.

Flydd handed one sword to Flangers, buckled on the other and gave the knife to Troist. The general, a stocky, handsome man, was slumped in a canvas seat, head in hands.

'You all right?' said Flydd.

Troist stared at him, frozen-faced, then nodded stiffly.

Flydd did the count and came up short. 'Where's Nish and Irisis?'

'Taken!' said Klarm in the tone a judge would use to pronounce sentence of death.

Pain sheared through Flydd's scrawny chest. 'We've got to go back –'

'No, we agreed,' said Yggur. 'Anyone who falls behind must be abandoned to give the others hope of escape. The struggle is going to be a long one.'

Flydd knew it, but bridled at the lecture. 'But Irisis – Nish! Without them, none of us would be here.'

'If we go back, Jal-Nish will take us and all hope will be lost. Besides, he won't harm his own son ...'

'But Jal-Nish hates Irisis more than anyone in the world.' The thought of her in his hands was unbearable.

'They're coming!' yelled Klarm. 'Pilot, get this thing up! Flangers, Troist, cast off the rear ropes. Yggur, you take this side, I'll do the other.'

Everyone ran to their posts. Flydd stood beside the pilot, looking back at the town square of Ashmode and its litter of bodies, people he'd fought beside for years. In the middle of the square, Jal-Nish was doubled over in agony inside the protective barrier he had conjured around himself. But the moment he recovered, all the power of the tears would be at his disposal.

And only Flydd, a small, skinny, ageing man, to stand in his way.

He could see his distorted reflection in the curving binnacle around the controls. Deeply sunken black eyes, shaded by a continuous eyebrow. A face that appeared to have had all the meat pared from it, leaving mere bone, skin and sinew. Fingers twisted as if they had been broken in a torture chamber, then set by someone who knew nothing about bones. And they had.

How was he to stop Jal-Nish? With the fields gone, Flydd could not use the Secret Art. Yet there had to be a way to save Nish and Irisis. Think, think!

The air-dreadnought lifted at the stern, drifted towards a patch of trees, then the bow ropes were cast off and the airbags full of floater-gas propelled it upwards.

Yggur yelled at Chissmoul. 'Get us out of sight!'

She worked her levers, directing the big craft away from the square.

'Hold it!' said Flydd. 'There's one chance, but we've got to act right now.'

'How?' said Yggur.

'Dive at Jal-Nish, full bore, and smash him against the wall of his barrier. I doubt that anyone could survive such an impact, but if he does cling to life we cut him down and grab the tears.'

'It's risky –'

'If we give him the chance to recover he'll take the whole of Lauralin within a year. What do you say, Klarm? Troist?'

Flydd looked at each of the six in turn. Troist nodded absently. He did not appear to be listening.

'Yes,' they said, and finally Yggur agreed.

'Go!' Flydd said to Chissmoul.

She let out a wild whoop. The rotors roared and she wrenched on her levers, skidding the huge craft into a manoeuvre it had never been designed for. The cabin wobbled from side to side, tossing Troist off his chair; they shot over the trees, heading back towards the town square.

'There he is!' Flydd pointed. '*And the barrier is down.* Fly, Chissmoul!'

Jal-Nish was doubled over, clutching his face and clearly in great pain. Irisis was on her knees, neck bared, her yellow hair flying in the wind, watching him in an attitude of proud defiance. A guard held her down. Nish was several yards away. A second guard handed him a sword, and it was clear what he was supposed to do with it.

Suddenly Nish leapt at his father, swinging the sword in a violent arc.

'Faster!' Flydd roared. 'Brace yourselves.'

The rotors howled. The air-dreadnought dived. Wind whistled past the cabin, which began to shake wildly. A cupboard door flew open; bags of dried peas fell out and one burst, scattering yellow peas everywhere.

But then Jal-Nish stood up, renewed the protection with a single gesture and a luminous blue sphere surrounded him. Nish's sword glanced off it in a spray of red-hot sparks and he was thrown backwards off his feet.

Jal-Nish turned to face the hurtling air-dreadnought. He raised the tears, two silvery, grapefruit-sized globes, the residuum of an exploded node. Even over the sound of the rotor Flydd could hear a high-pitched hum, the song of the tears.

They were made of *nihilium*, the purest substance in the world, and it was coveted by mancers because it took the print of the Secret Art more readily than any other form of matter, and bound it far more tightly. The tears were worth the value of a continent – and Jal-Nish planned to use them to take one.

He plunged his hand into Reaper and the left-hand airbag burst with an ear-stinging bang. Chissmoul let out a howl. The air-dreadnought rolled onto its side and hurtled off course; she fought desperately to prevent it from plunging at high speed into the trees.

The second guard, the one with Irisis, drew his sword. Nish ran at him but he was not going to get there in time. The air-dreadnought wobbled again and, momentarily, Flydd lost sight of the scene. He turned to see.

'Don't look back,' grated Klarm, catching Flydd by the arm and trying to haul him away.

He looked back.

2

Flydd was a hard and ruthless scrutator who had done whatever it took to win the war against the alien lyrinx. For thirty years he had schemed, manipulated, threatened and blackmailed. He had sent many a prisoner to be flogged or tortured, had ordered his country's enemies strangled in the dark, and commanded whole armies to what turned out to be their doom. Most of his friends and allies were dead and he had long expected his own bloody demise.

He had thought himself inured to death, but he was wrong. He could neither bear Irisis's death, nor accept it. 'She was the bravest of us, and the best,' he said brokenly. 'Why did *she* have to die?'

The question had no answer.

Chissmoul regained control and levelled out, only twenty feet above the trees. To Flydd's right, a few hundred yards away, the dry plains of Ashmode ended in a cliff. Below it was the monumental slope, broken into sections by seven more sets of cliffs and incised from top to bottom by gigantic canyons, that descended twelve thousand vertical feet to the greatest gulf in the Three Worlds – the Dry Sea. Until two thousand years ago it had been the beautiful Sea of Perion and, at the rate it was refilling through the recently unblocked Hornrace, it would soon be a sea again.

Klarm, the dwarf scrutator, a good-looking man with a mane of swept-back brown hair and dazzlingly blue eyes, sat Flydd down and put an arm across his shoulders.

'If I'd got us going ten seconds sooner –' said Flydd.

'There's no point, old friend! Irisis faced her death as magnificently as anyone could. I hope I can do the same.'

Yggur limped up to them: tall, lean, hard, and *beaten*. His face was grey. 'We tried.'

Flydd tried to rouse himself from the overwhelming despair. 'We've got to try again.'

'No, we've got to survive so we can fight Jal-Nish when we're strong again – if that ever happens.'

'If we let him recover he'll never give us the opportunity. It has to be now. Chissmoul, go around.'

The little pilot did not move. Her face was bloodless, her knuckles white.

'Chissmoul?' Flydd said sharply.

'Can't!'

'Why not?'

'Crystal – draining. Soon finished.'

'How soon?'

'Ten minutes. Five?'

'There's got to be a way to get more power. Surely someone has a crystal?'

'Jal-Nish's guards took everything we had,' said Fyn-Mah.

'They couldn't take Yggur's *gift*,' said Flydd. 'And it doesn't rely on fields. Yggur, can't you channel power to Chissmoul?'

'I don't know how,' said Yggur. 'Besides, given that Jal-Nish will soon rouse the whole world against us, I'm keeping my power in reserve.'

'But we've got to attack!' cried Flydd. Why couldn't they see? 'This is our last chance.'

'If we go near him again he'll burst the other two airbags, and we'll all die. Chissmoul, how far can you go before the rotors stop?'

'Few leagues.'

The air-dreadnought was now tracking east along the cliffs, towards the chasm of the distant Hornrace. With every lurch the spilled peas rattled back and forth across the floor.

'Once we set down, Jal-Nish's riders will catch us within the hour,' said Flangers, a lean, even-featured man with a shock of fair hair and a strong, jutting jaw.

'We don't have to set down,' said Flydd. 'This craft can stay in the air for days on two airbags.'

'But without rotors it's at the mercy of the winds,' said Fyn-Mah. 'And whether they sweep us north, south, east or west, we're liable to end up in the sea. Then, sooner or later, we'll drown. We've got to split up. Some of us might survive.'

'Never fly again,' wailed Chissmoul. 'Might as well be dead.'

She yanked on the left-hand control lever. The suspended cabin jerked wildly from side to side, for the cables, previously taut, had gone slack when the airbag burst. The air-dreadnought plunged down steeply, throwing everyone but her off their feet.

Flydd's foot came down on several of the hard yellow peas, which rolled under him. He fell backwards, cracking the back of his head on a bulkhead. The others slid down towards the rear of the cabin. White dots whirled before his eyes. He lay there, head downwards, dazed.

Flangers, favouring a twisted wrist, scrambled up the steeply sloping floor towards Chissmoul. She was clinging to the control levers, eyes closed and teeth bared.

'Chissmoul?' he said gently.

Flydd was amazed at his self-possession. But then, Flangers, good soldier and all-too-human man that he was, a man to whom duty was everything, often surprised.

Flangers reached her feet. 'Chissmoul? It's me.'

Through a porthole, Flydd saw yellow cliffs streaking past, perilously close. Chissmoul had lost it. The wild plunge had taken them over the edge, but even if they survived a crash, on the mostly barren slope down to the Dry Sea the air-dreadnought would be visible for miles.

Flangers caught her ankle. Her eyes sprang open and she tried to kick him out of the way. He leapt up, grabbed the right-hand lever and yanked hard. The air-dreadnought lurched the other way. Chissmoul let out a shriek and began beating at his face with her small fists.

'How dare you touch my controls!' she shrieked. 'Get away!'

One fist caught him on the nose. The air-dreadnought lurched again and now no one was at the controls. Flangers fell, slid across the sloping floor on his back and crashed head-first into the cabin door.

The catch clicked, then the door began to slide open. He slipped inexorably towards the gap, clawing at the smooth floor but unable to get a grip. The door slid a little further open. As he slipped closer, he managed to dig two fingers into a join in the floor, but his injured wrist could not hold his weight on such a steep slope.

He was going to fall out.

3

As the air-dreadnought spun, the cables creaking and groaning, Flydd dragged his way up to the controls. Chissmoul's eyes were tightly closed and she was keening to herself.

He shook her. 'You're killing your best friend! Do your bloody job – or jump out before I throw you out.'

Chissmoul's head flashed around and she focused on Flangers, half out the door. Letting out a milk-curdling moan, she flung the air-dreadnought into a corkscrewing left turn that hurled him across the cabin into the opposite wall.

'I'm sorry!' she wailed.

Her eyes widened and she pulled the craft up so sharply that Flydd's knees buckled – it felt as though he was three times his normal weight.

A red shadow flashed past, too quickly for him to make it out. As the craft climbed, he slid to the rear of the cabin. Fyn-Mah swore as his bony elbow struck her eye, and shoved him aside.

The rotors were shrieking, drawing far more power than they had been designed to use. Chissmoul stood the air-dreadnought on its tail and it rocketed up, passing so close to the yellow cliff that the landing skids scraped moss off the rocks. Higher, higher they climbed, the big craft shuddering as if it was about to tear apart. The remnants of the burst airbag were lashing the bag next to it, *whack-whack*, and that wasn't good either.

It must have been hell to control at this speed. Flydd had no idea how Chissmoul was doing it, since she had never flown an air-dreadnought before. Though she was an instinctive flier, the finest pilot he had ever seen.

'What the hell is she doing?' cried Troist. 'Has she gone – *uggh*?'

She hurled the air-dreadnought into another wild manoeuvre, one Flydd would have thought impossible for such an unwieldy machine. It looped the loop, plastering everyone to a floor that had become the ceiling, then curved left and right, and dived again.

'You stupid little –' Yggur broke off, looking down.

Flydd followed his gaze and spotted the craft Chissmoul had been trying to avoid, below and ahead – a sleek little air-cutter, designed for attack. It had one bright red airbag and two over-sized, swivelling rotors that made it both fast and manoeuvrable. An open platform at the front held a small but deadly javelard, a spear thrower shaped like a gigantic crossbow.

It was incredible that Chissmoul could have evaded the cutter with a lumbering dreadnought, but the end could not be in doubt. The cutter curved away to the left, whirled and climbed towards them. Its pilot knew the air-dreadnought was unarmed and could do them no harm. Flydd took a set of spyglasses from a rack, steadied himself with his free hand and studied their attacker.

The pilot was partly concealed behind the javelard operator, a dark and wiry fellow whose shaven head was painted yellow, identifying him as a Lurile from the desert of eastern Faranda. He hefted a six-foot-long spear studded with jagged, fin-like blades, kissed the shaft and seated it in the slot, then wound the crank of the javelard. A good operator could skewer half a dozen men in a row with its heavy spear, though Flydd imagined he would aim for the airbags.

And then they would go down.

The screaming rotors missed a beat. 'What was *that*?' yelled Flangers.

'Either Chissmoul is drawing more power than the rotors can take,' Yggur said quietly, 'or the crystal is failing.'

'Either way, we've not got long,' said Flydd. 'Get ready.'

Flangers turned and ran. Chissmoul looked around wildly, her eyes the size of blood plums. Her fingers clenched on the controls. She bared her teeth, let out a shrill yell, half shriek and half war cry, and turned towards the little air-cutter.

'What are you doing?' shouted Fyn-Mah. 'Turn away!'

'There's no point,' Flydd said softly. 'He'll just shoot us down. Brace!'

No point to that either. If they lost the airbags, they would go down so fast that the impact would break all their bones. Flydd took a firm grip on the nearest strut and looked for somewhere safe to land.

To their left were dry plains. Beyond them stood two ranges of round brown hills, one after another, and semi-desert after that. Behind the air-dreadnought, four leagues away, was Ashmode. Directly below, the upper slope of the Dry Sea held a scattering of orchards, vineyards, farms and, where seeping groundwater provided enough moisture, patches of forest. Elsewhere it was arid and stony, and further down the slope everything was encrusted in wind-blown salt. The bed of the Dry Sea, which had been fathoms deep in salt for two thousand years, was now covered by wild water.

Ahead, invisible from this distance, an unimaginable torrent hurtled through the chasm of the Hornrace that separated the island of Faranda from the continent of Lauralin, ending in a waterfall ten thousand times bigger than the next biggest falls in the world. Magnificent though it was, it was not a sight Flydd was anxious to see from a craft falling out of the sky.

Flangers came racing back, carrying two crossbows.

'Where'd you get those?' said Flydd.

'Armoury.'

He considered Flydd and Troist, who was still pale and listless, then tossed one crossbow to Flydd and began to wind the crank of the other.

'Bolts?' said Flydd, catching the crossbow awkwardly.

Flangers threw him a small bundle of crossbow bolts tied with green twine. Flydd yanked one out, pocketed the bundle and loaded his weapon.

'I'll aim for the pilot,' said Flangers, taking the more difficult shot. 'You go for the javelard operator. If we're quick ...'

The cutter was racing up at them. Chissmoul wove the air-dreadnought through the sky. The javelard operator tracked them with his weapon.

'Not an easy shot,' said Flangers, 'to hit a flying target from another racing craft.'

'We're a big target,' said Flydd. And Jal-Nish demanded the highest standards of his troops.

'Not yet. Not yet – *fire!*'

Flangers fired. A second later, so did Flydd. But the operator had already released his spear – Flydd saw the arms of the javelard snap back as the tension was released. If the spear was aimed at him he would die without ever seeing it.

Chissmoul hurled the air-dreadnought into the wildest manoeuvre yet. The contents of Flydd's belly turned to lead as the air-dreadnought zoomed up from its dive, then was hurled up into his throat as the craft went into a looping roll. He felt a floating sensation and a momentary dizziness.

Bang!

The spear had gone through the middle airbag. Its rubber-coated canvas made a *flub-flubbing* sound as it deflated, then the fragments lashed around in the wind, cracking like dozens of whips. The control levers jerked in all directions, flinging Chissmoul off her feet.

'Can't hold it!' she moaned. 'Going down!'

Flydd's shot had missed but Flangers fired again and the operator jerked backwards, clutching at his face.

'Great shot!' said Flydd.

'Think I hit the javelard and it threw up splinters.'

'Either way, he won't be firing again.'

But the operator did not need to. The air-dreadnought was going down rapidly.

'Did you hit the pilot?' said Flydd. From where he was standing he could not see.

'Yes,' said Flangers, 'but he's still flying.'

'Cut the burst bags free,' snapped Chissmoul. 'Only the *slack* cables.'

Yggur yanked the long-bladed emergency axe from its brackets and went to the left-hand side, where the heavy airbag cables ran into sockets in the base of the cabin. Flangers headed for the other side, drawing his sword. Yggur's axe rose and fell.

The cabin lurched wildly; the floor jerked up and down, then from side to side. The air-dreadnought leapt forwards as the cables and torn airbags fell away. Chissmoul revved the rotors up and down, trying to keep the craft in the air on one airbag, but the controls weren't answering. One of the severed cables had tangled around the rudder.

'Find somewhere to set down!' rapped Flydd.

At last he had a clear shot. He fired. The pilot of the cutter slumped forwards and it zoomed upwards into their path. Chissmoul, unable to use her controls, threw one rotor to full ahead and the other to full astern.

There was a colossal grinding and crashing as one of the mechanisms tore itself to pieces and hurled fragments into the second rotor, smashing the blades. The air-dreadnought was now uncontrollable. She wailed and slumped back into her despairing trance.

The air-dreadnought arced gently down in near-silence. For a second Flydd thought it was going to miss the cutter, until their left skid tore into the top of the cutter's airbag, bursting it. The cabin rocked under the gush of floater-gas. One spark and they would die in a cataclysmic explosion.

The air-dreadnought jerked around to the left, the remains of the cutter swinging below it from the airbag cables. The two craft, locked together, sank in a slow, deadly spiral. The cutter's airbag must have had two compartments, for only one had deflated. Its huge rotors, now hanging vertically below them but still spinning, were helping to slow their descent, though the slope was rushing up at them.

The javelard operator was hanging half out of his seat, his face covered in blood. The pilot, whose left shoulder was blotched red, had taken his hands off the useless controls and was raising a small black crossbow, sighting on Flydd. Flydd stared at him, momentarily unable to move or think.

Snap!

A bolt, fired from behind Flydd, whistled over his shoulder. The pilot's head was slammed backwards and he slid out of his seat and out of the cutter, still clutching his crossbow.

'Thanks,' said Flydd.

'You owe me one,' said Troist.

Flydd looked around sharply. The general, formerly so energetic, had barely moved since boarding the air-dreadnought. Flangers' crossbow hung from Troist's hand and his jaw was set, his eyes staring.

There was no time to ask what the matter was. They were spiralling down, spinning faster and faster. A red cliff flashed past only yards away.

'Arm yourselves,' said Flydd, indicating the armoury. 'And grab what you can from the galley – it could be a long time between meals.' He filled a pot with dried peas, then tied the lid on and the handle to his belt.

'Hold tight!' said Chissmoul, coming to life again.

Below the cliffs Flydd could see treetops – a narrow strip of forest growing on steeply sloping land at the base of the red cliff. The forest ran east and west for a mile or two before petering out. He braced himself.

They struck the treetops with a grinding crash and a snapping of timber. A jagged length of trunk speared up through the floor of the cabin beside Flydd's left foot. He yelped and threw himself aside. The cabin, which had almost been torn in half, slid down for ten feet and jammed in the fork of the tree.

Flydd looked down, swallowing. It was a good fifty feet to the ground and the long, straight trunk was unclimbable by anything that did not have claws.

4

There was another crash and the remains of the cutter's airbag dropped several feet. The cabin of the cutter swung back and forth, grinding the air-dreadnought against the trunk.

Chissmoul screwed up her face in agony, then stumbled back to the ruined rotors. Flydd could not imagine what she hoped to do; they were beyond repair. She screamed, each cry lower than the one before, until the last died away in a howl of despair that shivered the skin on his spine.

'How the hell are we supposed to get out of here?' said Klarm.

'The last airbag!' said Flydd.

'What about it?'

'We hang onto one of the cables, cut the airbag free and float away.'

'We'd never hold on. And if we could, we'd probably end up a hundred miles out to sea.'

'Beats waiting here for Jal-Nish.'

'I've got an idea,' said Flangers.

He inserted a long bolt in the crossbow, half wound it, then fired into the nearest cable, which was two inches thick. The bolt went straight through. He tried again, with one-third tension this time, and the eight-inch bolt stuck midway.

He fired another six of the long bolts into the cable at intervals. 'Each of you, hang onto one!'

They did so, though without enthusiasm save for Klarm, who had the upper body strength of a normal man but only half the weight, and had once worked as an acrobat in a troupe of dwarves.

'Hold this.' Flangers thrust the crossbow at Klarm.

He hooked it over his shoulder. Flangers severed the other cables with single blows of the axe. The airbag drifted up, now only held by a single taut cable.

The air-cutter jerked and slipped down another couple of feet. Now its cabin was pointing straight up at them. The javelard operator, who was still in his seat, thumped himself on the side of the head as if to clear it, wiped blood out of his eyes and reached back for a spear.

'How are you going to cut the last cable?' said Troist to Flangers.

'Tie on first,' said Flydd. He looked down. 'Better be quick.'

It appeared that the javelard operator had been blinded in one eye, but he was determined to carry out his orders. Flydd had to admire his tenacity – or rather, Jal-Nish's ruthless training methods that did not permit failure. The operator loaded the spear and wound the crank part-way, then covered his left eye and tried to aim. It would not be easy with only one eye, though the range was very short. There was nothing Flydd could do – he could not wind his crossbow one-handed.

Chissmoul let out a howl of anguish. The operator had aimed at Flangers and was giving the crank of the javelard a last wind.

Klarm swung upside-down, holding on with his legs and winding his crossbow furiously. Flangers tied a rope around his own waist and knotted the other end around the cable. He checked the knots and raised the axe.

Klarm fired as Flangers swung at the rope, severing it. The air-dreadnought's airbag shot upwards and the rope jerked him with it, upside-down. Klarm's bolt struck the operator in the shoulder as he fired the javelard. The six-foot-long spear went astray, tore through the inflated compartment of the cutter's airbag and its floater-gas exploded with twenty-foot-long tongues of blue fire. The cabin plummeted to the ground, crushing the operator beneath it.

The freed airbag was buffeted wildly. Chissmoul lost her grip and fell, screaming. Yggur's long arm caught her and dragged her to him.

'Lock your arms around my neck!' he snapped. 'And shut your stupid face.'

She did so. He put his arms around her and clamped onto the bolt with both hands.

As they hurtled upwards, Flydd saw a new danger. 'Klarm, shoot the airbag!'

'Why?' said Klarm, who seemed remarkably comfortable hanging upside-down.

'With so little weight, it'll rise so high that we'll freeze, then we'll be carried out over the ocean. We've got to go down while we're over dry land.'

Flydd fumbled out a bolt and passed it down to Klarm, who aimed carefully and fired into the centre of the airbag. Floater-gas seethed out. Ice formed around the little hole and Flydd thought it was going to seal itself, then the ice was blown off and the airbag tore in a star pattern. Their upwards motion ceased; they began to sink slowly, then faster as the airbag continued to tear.

They were past the forest now, swinging from the cable a few hundred feet above the ground and slowly descending. They drifted towards a steep scree slope below a black cliff, a strong breeze carrying them along. Flydd was alarmed to see that the slope was littered with boulders as big as cottages.

'When we're five feet above the ground, everyone *jump*, otherwise we'll be dragged into the boulders.'

Lower they sank, and lower. The scree slope was a dangerous place to land – there were few suitable spaces among the boulder fields. Wait! A small clear patch had opened up not far ahead.

'Jump!' said Flydd as they skimmed a trio of black boulders.

Klarm dropped his crossbow and jumped, then Yggur, with Chissmoul still clinging onto him. They landed with a rattle of loose gravel and skidded for several yards. Troist dropped off the cable, then Fyn-Mah. Flydd was about to let go when he realised that Flangers was struggling to untie the knot around his chest.

Flydd went down the spikes, hung on with one hand and his knees, and attempted to undo the end tied around the spike, which had pulled tight under Flangers' weight. With one hand he could not budge it.

'Look out!' bellowed Troist.

They were being dragged towards another boulder. 'Use your sword,' said Flydd.

Flangers hesitated. Flydd saw the disaster coming and could do nothing to avoid it. He jumped, landed in gravel, skidded and struck the boulder with his left shoulder and knee, hard enough to hurt.

Above him, a thud was followed by an involuntary groan. Flangers had been slammed into the side of the boulder, then dragged over its rough top. And there were more boulders beyond it.

'Cut him down, quick!' Flydd roared.

He limped around the boulder, the pot thumping his hip with every step. Troist and Klarm caught Flangers by the legs and tried to hold him but they had no hope against the pull of the huge airbag, which was gathering speed under the strong breeze. Flydd could not run fast enough in the deep gravel to catch them. They were being dragged towards another boulder, and the impact would probably break Flangers' back.

'Let him go!' said Yggur.

They did so. He thrust out his right hand and a white flash zipped forth. The uppermost crossbow bolt glowed white-hot, the rope burned through and Flangers fell free, hit the side of the boulder, crashed to ground and lay there, unconscious.

Or dead.

5

Flydd scanned the sky for more flying craft. It was empty. 'At least Jal-Nish won't know where we landed.'

'He knows where to start looking,' said Klarm, who was facing west.

A couple of miles back, smoke rose from the forest where the wreckage of the cutter was burning.

Chissmoul was crouched over Flangers, cradling his head and crooning to him. Flydd squatted beside her. She gave him a resentful glare. Flangers' eyes fluttered, then came open.

'How's your head?' said Flydd.

'Bloody awful.'

'Can you walk?'

'No, he can't!' Chissmoul said furiously.

She and Flangers had been friends for a long time, and perhaps his injury was fortuitous – it would occupy her mind and ease the torment of her own loss.

Pilots were usually women, and small ones at that, since every ounce of extra weight mattered. The psycho-mechanical bond between a pilot and her craft had to be close, otherwise she could not control the flow of power, though this meant that the loss of her craft was devastating. Some pilots had gone insane from it.

'They'll be well on the way by now,' said Flangers. 'We've got to get out of sight.'

'Which way?' said Yggur.

'Due east along the mid-slope,' said Flydd.

'Why?'

'There are more hiding places down here than up on the plains.'

It was late afternoon and the sun, which set north-west at this time of year, had long since disappeared behind the black cliffs. The sky was cloudless and it would be a cool autumn night. They headed towards another patch of forest, leaving no tracks on the gravel-covered slope. It was the one positive aspect of an utterly disastrous day.

Every time Flydd thought of Irisis, tears formed in his eyes and his throat went so tight he struggled to draw breath. He could still see the bodies of all the other dead, friends and allies, known and unknown, in the town square. And now Jal-Nish, the foulest man Flydd had ever met, was planning to reshape the world in his corrupt image. It could not be borne.

At the densest part of the forest, where the tall, widely-spaced trees were wreathed in vines, they built a small fire from dry wood, so it would not smoke, and attended their injuries.

While Klarm cooked their pilfered food in the coals, Flydd limped up to the cliff in the semi-dark, carrying his pot. The ground at the base of the cliff was damp from seepage; he dug a small hole and it soon filled with water. The air smelled of fragrant herbs, crushed underfoot.

He gathered herbs and, back at the campfire, made tea with the leaves of a salty, grey-leafed bush that smelled like lemon thyme. Klarm covered the coals with turf, in case of aerial patrols, and they perched on logs and lumps of stone in the gloom.

'Well?' said Yggur, after they had eaten.

'Jal-Nish must be cast down,' said Flydd. 'If we give him time to consolidate –' He broke off, for everyone was staring at him in astonishment. 'What?' he muttered, knowing what they were going to say.

Yggur, who was sitting across the smouldering coals from him, said it. 'We're powerless, penniless, poorly armed and hundreds of miles from anywhere we can get help – assuming that anyone would help renegades with a gigantic price on their heads. Jal-Nish has taken command of our army and there's only one thing we can do. Run and hide.'

'*You're* not powerless. Your mancery doesn't rely on nodes or fields.'

'It's severely weakened. He's going to hunt us with everything he's got, Flydd, and it'll take all my power to escape him.'

'There are older forms of the Art,' said Fyn-Mah. 'Kinds of magic scarcely used since Nunar discovered how to draw upon the power locked in fields, a century ago.'

'But few mancers know how to use them anymore.' Yggur quirked his right eyebrow at Flydd, questioningly.

'I studied the theory of the older Arts as an apprentice,' Flydd conceded.

'Though not the practice. Fields offered many times as much power, with better control, for a fraction of the effort.' Now he wished he'd made the effort.

'Then how do you suppose to take on Jal-Nish?'

'I don't know!' Flydd cried. 'But we have one chance to bring him down, and it's right now. When that globe burst – well done, Klarm! – Jal-Nish was struck in the face with hundreds of droplets of boiling quicksilver. He must be in agony and he won't be able to focus on anything else. And there's another thing ...'

'What?' said Yggur, irritably.

'Quicksilver is a poison. If we strike now, before the healers clean all the droplets out of his face –'

'If you've got a plan, spit it out.'

'I don't,' said Flydd. He felt an utter failure.

'Then I vote we split up,' said Yggur. 'That way, some of us may survive.'

'We'd better arrange a rendezvous,' said Klarm. 'Otherwise we could spend the rest of our lives looking for one another.'

'Where do you suggest?'

'Lugg.'

'Where the blazes is that?'

'It's a town on the Sea of Thurkad, a little way south of the Hornrace.'

'Why there?'

'It's a port town and it gives us options. We can meet at the fish markets – I know a woman there who can be trusted with messages.'

'You know a woman in every town,' muttered Flydd.

'What can I say?' grinned the dwarf. 'Her name is Rableen. Rableen, *Rableen!*' he sang. 'Blue-black hair, big –'

'We get the picture.'

'No you don't. Big *smile*, I was going to say.'

'All right,' said Yggur. 'Those who want to meet up, be in Lugg in fifteen days. I'm leaving at first light.' Then, grudgingly, 'if anyone wants to come with me ...' It was clear that he wanted to go alone.

'Go with him, Flangers,' Flydd said quietly.

'Surr,' said the good soldier, 'I swore to you.' His eyes drifted to Chissmoul, who had eaten nothing and was scrunched up in the foetal position, eyes closed, rocking back and forth.

'*Until the war should end, or death take you,*' said Flydd. 'The war with the lyrinx has ended and I release you from your oath. Chissmoul is going to need a good friend.'

'Thank you, surr. And may we meet again in happier times.'

'Indeed. What about you, Fyn-Mah?'

'I'll go alone.'

Flydd was not surprised. She had always been a loner and every aspect of her manner said, *Keep your distance*. He glanced at Klarm.

'I'll make up my mind in the morning,' said Klarm.

'Troist?' said Flydd.

He was slumped on a log, head in hands, and did not appear to be listening. 'General?' said Flydd, 'What is it?'

Troist looked up. His handsome face was pale, his eyes tormented. 'My wife, Yara. And my daughters ...'

'Surely they're safe in Borgistry?'

Troist's head jerked back and forth. 'Yara heard the war was ending, and my twins were desperate to see me. They arrived in Ashmode on an air-floater, *yesterday*.'

No one spoke, but they all knew what would happen. Jal-Nish ruled by fear and knew no other way. Years ago, when he'd held far lesser power, he had been famous for hunting down the friends and families of his enemies and putting them to death.

In times like these, lucky was the man who had no family.

'I'm sorry,' said Klarm. 'If there was anything I could do, anything at all ...'

Nothing could be done. Jal-Nish was a methodical man and he would have arrived at Ashmode with his lists drawn up. Yara and the fourteen-year-old twins, Liliwen and Meriwen, would surely have been taken by now. The public executions would begin very soon.

'I'm going back for them,' said Troist.

'There's nothing you can do.' Flydd despised himself for speaking the truth aloud and destroying Troist's faint hope.

'My wife and daughters are everything to me. If I can't save them ... I'll join them in death.'

6

The darkest hour of the night was always Flydd's worst. It was the time when his failures were sharpest, the flaws in his strategies most obvious, and the consequences of his bad decisions fell into diamond-sharp focus. The most catastrophic decision of all had been his assumption, almost two years ago, that Jal-Nish had been killed and eaten by one of the enemy, the winged lyrinx.

Irisis, Irisis!

Flydd had not allowed himself to love a women since his youth. As a ruthless scrutator, and then a member of the Council of Scrutators who controlled the known world for the good of the war against the lyrinx, a war that had raged for one hundred and fifty years, it had been incumbent on him not to form attachments, either romantic or of friendship.

But Irisis had been different. Reckless, cranky, tormented, quixotic, brave, brilliant and loyal in equal measure, she was the most remarkable woman he had ever met. Though their brief physical relationship was long over, he had loved her as a true friend. Now Jal-Nish had wantonly and maliciously destroyed her.

Tears welled and, for the first time since his torture at the hands of the scrutators three decades years ago, Flydd did not hold them back. Why should he? He was a scrutator no longer; he was just an ordinary, feeling man, and the emotions he had been forced to suppress for so long welled up uncontrollably.

Not here! He choked back a sob, pulled his boots on and rose silently. The camp was dark but he knew where everyone lay and picked his way between them.

A pair of eyes gleamed, though there was no light to reflect from them. There was no getting past Yggur unnoticed but he did not speak. Neither did Flydd; let Yggur think what he wanted.

Flydd pressed his fists into his stomach, holding back the agony that threatened to burst out any second, and headed diagonally upslope until he reached the edge of the forest. It was cold here, and the clear sky shone with thousands of stars.

His chest was heaving, his guts aching. Flydd raised his fists to the sky as if to smash it down. The pain surged again; he wanted to scream.

But dared not – in the still air, the sound might carry for a mile. Following a lifetime's habit, he scanned the slope and the cliffs above for danger. Finding none, he let out a small, stifled cry of anguish, all that the scrutator in him would allow after all.

Then he saw it, away to the right – a shadow shifting in a way it should not have. The cry died in his throat. It could have been a large animal, though he knew it was not. It was a man. A local farmer or poacher about his business?

No, for his night-sensitive eyes had picked out another figure a few yards further off, and another. An attack force. How had Jal-Nish found them? Flydd's eyes roved all around, then up.

Had it been a still night he would have missed it, for it was cunningly disguised by paintwork, enhanced with illusions, to mimic the night sky. It was a brilliant job, but the little air-floater's rotors were still and there was just enough breeze to drift it out of position, shifting the painted stars against the night sky.

It had carried an attack force right to their hiding place. There wasn't time to wonder how it had located them; Flydd edged back into the forest and went, at the fastest pace he dared in the dark, back to the camp.

'Get up!' he hissed. 'Air-floater, half a mile away. Troops are coming our way.'

Seasoned by years of war as they were, they roused instantly. He heard people dragging their boots on and drawing weapons. All except Chissmoul, who let out a whimper and clutched something faintly glowing to her breast. Flydd snatched at it but Klarm got it first.

'What's *that*?' said Flydd.

Klarm made a disgusted sound in his throat. 'It's the heart of the air-dread-nought's power controller. That's how the bastards found us.'

He put it on a stone, hefted another stone and smashed the crystal to glowing fragments that scattered across the campsite, shedding a faint bluish light. Chissmoul wailed and thrashed. Flangers clapped a hand across her mouth and held her close.

'Shh!' said Flydd. 'They're only minutes away.'

'How many?' said Klarm.

'The air-floater could carry a dozen, I expect.' Chissmoul was still struggling, trying to bite Flangers. Flydd stalked across and thrust his face against hers. 'Shut it!' he snarled, 'or I'll cut your stupid little throat.'

She went still. Flangers sucked in a whistling breath. 'You'll have me to deal with first.'

Flydd had never known a more honourable or loyal soldier than Flangers. How had they been driven to this? That bastard, Jal-Nish! 'Then keep her quiet, or we're all dead.'

'What's your plan?' said Yggur.

'Without mancery, six of us can't beat a dozen soldiers.' Flydd did not count Chissmoul; even had she been of sound mind, she was not a fighter.

'Meaning that you're relying on me,' said Yggur.

'You're the only one who can use the Art, right now.'

'All right. But it's too risky to try and deal with them individually. Clean up those shards, then everyone lie down as if asleep.'

'What if they shoot us in our bedrolls?'

'It'll be the easiest death we can hope for.'

Flydd pressed the glowing shards into the earth with his boot and kicked leaves over them. They lay down in their former positions. Yggur pulled his black cloak around himself and sat some yards away, leaning against a tree trunk, almost invisible.

Flydd stared into the dark, gripping the hilt of his blade so hard that it hurt. He was an accomplished swordsman but well past his prime and he had little hope of beating a soldier less than half his age. At least, in a fair fight.

Another worry intruded. 'Breaking the crystal may have given them warning,' he said quietly.

'Nothing we can do about it,' said Yggur. 'Shut up; I need to focus.'

The night was unnaturally still. No breeze stirred the treetops, no night birds called. If the enemy were closing in, they were remarkably skilled at moving in the dark.

'They're coming,' whispered Klarm, who was next to Flydd.

It was a comfort, for the dwarf could fight in ways no normal man could.

Something arced through the air towards them. 'Cover your eyes!' hissed Klarm.

Flydd clapped a hand over his eyes, but not quickly enough. A small object landed on the turfed coals and burst with a brilliant flash that lit up the campsite and the ring of trees around it, dazzlingly white against black. And in that instant his night vision was gone.

'Take them!' said the enemy leader.

Flydd scrambled to his feet but all he could see was shadows coming from every side. Yggur had vanished and Flydd could not see Klarm either. Could they have killed him already?

Flangers was on the right, and in normal circumstances he was a brilliant fighter, but after the head blow he had taken, and with Chissmoul to protect, Flydd could expect nothing from him.

A glancing blow to the back of the skull drove Flydd to his knees. His sword was kicked out of his hand and a sharp point pressed to the back of his neck.

'Move,' said the leader, 'and I'll sever your spine.'

Flydd blinked three times and a little of his vision returned. Their attackers had also taken Flangers, Chissmoul, Fyn-Mah and Troist.

'Only five,' said Flydd's captor, a squat, over-muscled captain with a missing left ring finger. 'Where's Yggur, and the dwarf?'

'Yggur went his own way last night,' Flydd lied.

The captain spun him around and drove a bronze-hard fist so deep into his belly that Flydd thought his teeth were going to be blasted out of his mouth. '*Where's Yggur?*'

'Don't know,' gasped Flydd. 'Here – five minutes ago.'

'What about the dwarf?'

'I don't know.'

His hands were tied behind his back; he was searched with clinical thoroughness and his knife taken. The other four were also searched and bound.

'Take them to the air-floater,' said the captain to his four nearest troops. 'If they try to speak to each other, given them an inch of blade. If anyone tries to escape, give them six inches. Go!

'You lot,' he said to the others, 'spread out. Yggur is the big threat and Jal-Nish wants him alive and well. Don't give him a chance to use his power, just shepherd him towards ... *you know what*. He can't be far away; we can search this whole patch of forest in half an hour.'

'What about the dwarf?' said a rail-thin soldier with a mass of rat-like hair and the smell of a male ferret.

'Shorten the little bastard by a head.'

7

The captain hurled a flare to each of the four compass points, lighting up the surrounding forest with harsh white light. He and his seven men formed a spread-out line and began the search.

The other four soldiers prodded the five prisoners into a line, Fyn-Mah first and Flydd last, then two soldiers led the way, one holding a lantern up. The other two formed a rear-guard. Flydd stumbled along, still winded from the blow. How easily Jal-Nish had beaten him. And how, after all these years, could the great struggle of his life end in so pathetic a way?

He had to escape. He tested the bonds, but they had been professionally tied and he had no hope of freeing himself in the few minutes before they reached the air-floater.

It was shocking how Tiaan's perverse act, of setting off a chain reaction through the nodes to destroy them all, had robbed Flydd of his gift for mancery. There had been times when it had been insufficient, and many times when it had gone wrong through his own failings or the sheer perversity of the Secret Art, but his gift had always been there.

Now it was gone. He was no longer an adept who could work miracles with hand or voice. He was just a skinny old man with only his wits to rely on.

And soon he would be put to death.

But not Yggur. Why not? Jal-Nish wanted him *alive and whole*, presumably to investigate his unique gift for the Art. And whether it represented a threat, or an opportunity.

Where the hell was Yggur, and why hadn't he done anything to help them? He was a strange fellow at the best of times, a powerful but troubled man whose reliability was uncertain. What if he had simply disguised himself and slipped away?

After they had marched for another minute or two Flydd heard a faint swishing sound, a little thud, a hiss like a fountain, and felt warm rain on the top of his head. How could it rain from a clear sky? Rain that had a thick, metallic tang.

The *swish*, *thud* and *hiss* were repeated and he looked back to see the second guard standing only a yard behind him with blood gushing from his headless neck. His head lay on the ground and the other guard, also headless, was sprawled a few yards back. How had Yggur done it so cleanly and noiselessly, without alerting the guards at the head of the line?

Swish. Not Yggur – Klarm came hurtling out of the trees, clinging one-handed to the severed end of a vine and holding his beheading sword in the other hand. As he passed behind Flydd he gave a dextrous little flick, slicing through the ropes and taking an inch of skin off Flydd's wrist.

He was glad to donate it to the cause. Taking the sword of the first guard and the knife of the second, he went forwards, cutting the bonds of the prisoners one by one. As he freed Fyn-Mah's wrists, the second guard turned. Acting on instinct, Flydd hurled the knife into his throat.

The guard clawed at it, making an awful gasping sound, and wrenched the knife out. His slit windpipe whistled, then bubbled and gurgled as it filled with blood. Flydd ducked around him and went for the leading guard, who slashed wildly. Flydd managed to block the blow but his sword jarred from his hand.

He dived for it. The guard came after him and as Flydd's hand closed around the hilt he slipped and fell, exposing his back. He was bracing for the thrust that would kill him when Flangers, who had scooped up the dead guard's blade, drove it through the soldier's back into his heart.

Klarm swung back and dropped to the ground beside the bodies.

'Nice work,' said Flydd, shaking the dwarf's callused hand. 'Where's Yggur?'

'Wouldn't have a clue.' Klarm's face and right arm were spattered with the blood of the beheaded. 'Maybe he took an early mark.'

'I've *generally* found him to be a man of his word – within his limitations.'

Klarm gave a sceptical grunt. 'Reckon we can take the air-floater?'

'Depends on how well it's guarded.'

A flare exploded through the trees to their right and Flydd heard pounding feet, shouts and yells.

'There's Yggur!' roared the enemy leader. 'Go out, left and right. Steady, *steady*.'

'Troist, Flangers, Chissmoul and Fyn-Mah,' Flydd said quietly, 'check on the air-floater and secure it if you can. We'll help Yggur.'

They separated. 'I'll go through the treetops,' said Klarm. 'The enemy haven't thought to look up there.'

He scrambled up a fissured grey trunk, making the climb look easy, and was lost to sight. Flydd slipped from tree to tree. The captain and his seven men were spread out in a funnel shape, moving slowly forwards, but where was Yggur? Ah, there, forty yards away, though even in the light of two flares he was barely visible and his bent figure appeared to shift from side to side. Illusion!

What was the *you know what* they were driving him to? Some kind of trap or snare? But surely there had not been time to install any such device? Flydd crept closer. The soldiers were closing in on Yggur, step by careful step. He had not moved. Did he suspect the trap?

He stood up straight, extending his right arm towards the captain.

The captain bellowed, 'Take him!'

A blast of white fire slammed him backwards against a tree. The other seven soldiers fanned in on Yggur. He turned, ran twenty yards and skidded to a stop.

The trap had closed.

A mancer stood there, a portly, hook-nosed dandy who had been with Jal-Nish in the town square. Flydd had also met him many years ago. What was the name? He wore a scarlet cape, yellow waistcoat and pink knee britches bulging over massive thighs, and carried a staff shaped like a trident. Its three prongs were pointed at Yggur's face and the mancer was smiling. Clearly, facing the oldest old human mancer to have ever lived – and one of the most powerful – did not faze him.

The name popped into memory – Lurimon Gant, an adept from Jal-Nish's home province of Einunar; a proud and arrogant man who did not suffer fools. The five black jags on his shoulders indicated that he was one of Jal-Nish's deputies. The presence of so important a mancer, here, showed how desperately Jal-Nish wanted them.

Again Yggur raised his right arm, though this time it had a slight quiver.

'Like to see you try,' smirked Gant.

Cone-shaped bundles of pink rays, the lurid colour of his knee britches, lanced from the prongs of the trident staff and touched Yggur on the face, chest and shoulders.

He began to shake so uncontrollably that Flydd could hear his teeth chattering and his joints clicking. Every muscle in Yggur's body was jerking; he was bouncing on his feet, his arms and legs flying out in one direction, then another, his fingers clenching and unclenching. He had lost control of his body.

Grunts were forced out of Yggur, 'Ungh, ungh, ungh!' Flydd could not tell if he was trying to speak or the sounds were involuntary.

Gant grounded his staff. The seven soldiers moved in and the man in the lead swung a long stick, with a bag on the end, over Yggur's head. They held him, bound his arms to his sides and the first soldier tied the bag on.

'Ungh, ungh, ungh,' said Yggur.

'So falls the last of Jal-Nish's enemies,' said Gant, 'grunting like a pig for slaughter. How such incompetents beat the lyrinx I'll never know.'

Yggur teetered and almost went down. 'Hold him upright like a toddler,' grinned Gant. 'Walk him to the air-floater.'

The troops tried to do so, without success; he was jerking so wildly that it was all they could do to keep him on his feet.

'Carry him,' said Gant. 'Where's Captain Yarb?'

Flydd could not see him and dared not move closer in the bright flare light. He hunched down. Had the captain been injured by impact with the tree, or was he creeping after Flydd? He looked around. There was no sign of Yarb, but the forest had many hiding places.

'Ungh, ungh, *unnnngh!*' Yggur's grunts had an edge of panic now.

'Squeal, long tall piggy,' chortled Gant.

Long ago, in a terrible betrayal, Yggur had been *possessed* by Rulke and had never fully recovered. Over the succeeding centuries Yggur had suffered a number of breakdowns, and after the worst of them he had lived as a witless beast for a very long time. Had Gant's blast brought on another episode? How long would it take Yggur to recover this time? Weeks? Years?

It was a bitter blow. Flydd longed to bring the sneering mancer down but, unarmed and without mancery, how could he? If they were to escape, he and Klarm had to engineer it before Gant got Yggur into the air-floater.

One of the soldiers appeared from the shadows between the trees, supporting Captain Yarb, who had blood on the back of his head. The way he was supporting his dangling right arm with his left hand suggested a broken collarbone.

Shouting erupted from the direction of the air-floater, then a thin little scream – Chissmoul, surely – and a skyrocket blasted up on a column of yellow flame. Flydd watched it appear and disappear behind the trees, then burst high up in a red flower. It was a signal – but was it announcing a triumph or calling for reinforcements?

He had to act now. Where the hell was Klarm?

Yggur began to thrash his legs so violently that the two soldiers could not hold him up. A fist came free and struck the leading soldier in the face; he let go and Yggur hit the ground, his flailing limbs scattering leaves and gravel everywhere. Gant trotted back, pointed the trident staff at Yggur, then frowned and shook his head. Was he afraid to damage the mancer Jal-Nish wanted so desperately?

'You four, carry him,' he said to the soldiers. 'And this time, *hold onto him.*' He swung the staff towards the man who had dropped Yggur – the bony fellow with the rat-like hair and rank smell. His left eye was swelling rapidly, almost closed. 'Not you, Zlide! You're already on a warning.'

A narrow pink ray, emitted from the central point of the trident, meandered across Zlide's right hand. The skin in the path of the ray turned crimson, as if it had been burned. He wrung his hand and began to curse Gant, but thought better of it.

'On guard!' said Gant to the other three soldiers. 'You,' he pointed to a giant of a man, well over seven feet tall, whose little nose and eyes were lost in a pumpkin-sized face, 'check on the air-floater and come straight back.'

The giant slipped away. Gant held up his staff, created tongues of fire like pink candle flames at the tips, and ordered the little troop on.

As Flydd watched them go, helplessly, Klarm swung down from a tree behind him. The light was dim here, and fading as the distant flares died down.

'Where the hell have you been?' Flydd muttered. 'They've got Yggur.'

'I saw. What did Gant do to him?'

'I don't know, but I don't like it. Where could he have come by a spell that affected Yggur so easily, and so badly?'

'Who knows what Jal-Nish worked on in the two years he was gone?' said Klarm. 'With the power of the tears, mancery that used to be impossible could now be easy. Or he might have tailored a spell to Yggur's known weaknesses.'

The thought was disturbing; Jal-Nish might also have made a spell to attack Flydd's weaknesses. 'What's happening at the air-floater?'

'No idea ... but I've got a bad feeling.'

'So have I. We've got to attack. Do you still have your crossbow?'

Klarm shook his head. 'Taken when they attacked our camp.'

'Then how the blazes are the two of us going to deal with eight soldiers, an all-powerful mancer and the guards at the air-floater?'

Klarm unbuckled his belt.

'I don't see how dropping your strides is going to help,' said Flydd, 'prodigious though your –'

'Find some nice rocks! Size of an orange.'

Flydd cast around on the forest floor, which was scattered with stones large and small. After much groping in the leaf litter he found a couple of suitable ones. Klarm considered the first, put it down and took the other, which was roughly round.

'More like this one. Bring them.'

He bent low and scurried out to the left, up the slope, presumably planning to intersect Gant's party as they left the forest. Flydd gathered another three round stones and followed. It was dark here and Klarm made no sound; all Flydd could do was head in the direction he assumed the dwarf had gone.

The assumption proved sound and he emerged from the forest only a couple of yards away. Klarm held out a meaty hand. Flydd put another stone in it. Klarm held the two ends of his belt, which was slightly elastic, to form a sling and inserted the rock.

'It's a dual-purpose belt,' said Klarm. 'Sometimes the most useful weapons are ones that don't look like weapons.'

In the circumstances, Flydd could not argue. He crouched beside the dwarf.

'I'll aim for Gant,' said Klarm. 'If I hit him, do ... whatever you do best. I'll try to knock down a couple of the soldiers, then we go for them with our blades.'

'Doesn't sound like the world's best plan,' said Flydd, 'but I'll take what I can get.' The forest was dark in all directions. 'Don't suppose we could have missed them?'

'No.'

Another couple of minutes went by. There was no sound from the direction of the air-floater. Flydd took that as a bad sign. Tension grew along his shoulders and the back of his neck. He was way too old for this; too old and too slow.

At the victory lunch, his friends had laughed when he had talked about retiring to a cottage with a garden. He wished he was there now, feet up, a good book in his hand and a long, cool drink at his elbow. He massaged the knots in his jaw, trying to think himself back into the mindset of a ruthless scrutator. It failed; that part of him felt like another life and a different man. Almost a stranger.

'They're coming,' murmured Klarm.

As he rose, Flydd saw faint, moving pink flames, then Gant emerged from the forest fifty yards off, still holding his staff up to light the way.

'Hell of a throw with a sling,' said Flydd. 'You used one before?'

'Not lately.'

Next came the four soldiers, carrying Yggur, who was still jerking, then another man supporting the injured captain, and finally Zlide, the soldier Gant had punished. The giant guard had not returned but no doubt he would at the worst moment. Gloom settled over Flydd. Klarm was a small but powerful spring beside him, under great tension, but what could he do with a sling, against so many? It was utterly hopeless.

The enemy would pass within ten yards. Too close. Better to attack now and take the risk of missing than hit one man only to be surrounded by another seven.

Sling it, damn you!

Flydd kept his mouth shut. Klarm was reliable, and touchy.

When Gant was fifteen yards away and the leading soldiers, carrying Yggur, were a few yards behind him, the dwarf slung his stone with tremendous force.

It struck Gant in the face like a half brick, knocking him onto his back. The trident staff discharged tongues of pink light backwards, hitting one of the leading soldiers in the midriff. He convulsed and doubled up, letting go of Yggur, and the other soldiers could not hold him. He hit the ground head-first, his arms and legs thrashing more violently than ever.

Flydd raced for the staff, which was shooting pink flares across the grassy ground. A soldier reached it first, but then stood there, gaping, afraid to touch it.

Flydd dived and caught it by the three-horned end. The back of his hand was grazed by a ray which fried his nerve endings and made his whole right arm shake. He wrenched the shaft out of the groaning mancer's hand and swung it at the soldier, who backed away. From the corner of an eye Flydd saw Klarm hurl another stone as he ran, but lost sight of him.

Flydd had not used another mancer's staff since the time of his apprenticeship, and dared not try to bond to the inner *persona* that gave it its power – that would be far too dangerous. He simply used it as he would have used any enchanted object, as a source of stored power. He swung the staff horizontally at the soldiers, trying to think himself into a state of controlled violence and, to his surprise, pink beams roared from the three tips, passed over Yggur and slammed into the soldiers, hurling them in all directions.

Gant let out a pitiful moan. The rock had smashed his proud nose and his face was a swelling, bloody mess. He jerked upright, desperate to regain his staff, his lifeline. Flydd jammed the prongs against his chest, and thrust. Gant went over again.

All the soldiers were jerking and twitching except for Yarb, who had taken his sword in his left hand and was lurching towards Flydd. Flydd tried to blast him down but nothing happened. The staff had gone dead to him – its persona had cut the power off.

Then, in a rush, Yarb was on him. Flydd did not have time to draw his sword; he had to defend as best he could. He swung the staff at Yarb's head. He ducked. Flydd swung again. Yarb parried once, twice, thrice; he was as good with his left hand as most swordsmen were with the right. Flydd tried to thrust the trident points into his eyes, but Gant reached up and whispered a word of command.

The staff reversed in Flydd's hands and came spearing at his face.

8

F lydd hurled himself sideways but not quickly enough. A trident point tore
through his left ear with a stinging pain and a shock that rattled his brain.
When he could see again the captain was charging, his sword raised like a cleaver
to split Flydd's skull in two. And the staff was coming at him again, now from the
left.

He wove aside to avoid the sword blow, ducked under the staff, caught its shaft
with both hands and swung it horizontally at the captain, calling on the power he
had used before. At the same instant Gant's right arm shot to the vertical and he
tried to snatch control.

Yggur let out a mad roar. A white ray burst from his fingertips, burning an arc
across the sky and hitting the staff at the same instant that the captain's sword
struck it. All these intersecting forces proved too much for it – as the sword
sheared the trident off the shaft, a baleful pink and black fire erupted from the
severed ends. It combined to form a roiling ball of light that hung in the air, then
swelled and extended black tongues for several feet before falling back into the
ball.

Flydd felt a psychic blow, as if something spiky had crystallised in his brain and
was piercing through it in all directions. He froze in place – he could not think,
could not move, could do nothing but stand there, his throbbing fingers locked
around the severed staff, and endure the agony.

The sword blade glowed white and turned molten in the captain's hand,
spraying red-hot drops across the ground and setting fire to leaves and grass. He

dropped the hilt and shook his burned hand. A breeze drifted the little fires towards the forest.

Gant, suffering the unmitigated agony that came when the emotional link between a mancer and the *persona* of his staff was severed, screamed. The pain in Flydd's hands faded. The trident end lay on the ground and the churning pink and black ball, whatever it was, was drifting at head height. It was three feet across and so bright it would have been visible a mile away.

The captain attempted to draw a knife with his right hand but, having a broken collarbone, could not hold it. He fingered it out of its sheath with his burned left hand, grimacing, and crept between the patches of blazing grass towards Flydd.

The giant soldier appeared out of the darkness. Blood was spattered across his front, though it did not appear to be his. He propped, staring at the floating ball, his mouth hanging open to reveal that he had only two teeth, one top left and one bottom right. His eyes moved from the ball of light to his fallen comrades, to Gant, the captain, and to Flydd. The giant had a sword in each hand and he began to swing them back and forth towards one another like twin scythes.

'Cut him down,' said the captain.

The giant took a step towards Flydd, but stopped when the severed staff was pointed at him.

'Klarm?' Flydd said hoarsely. 'Where the bloody hell are you?'

Klarm did not answer.

Something tried to insinuate itself into Flydd's mind. A thin, cold probe that, in his inner eye, had a silvery shimmer. Naked terror crept over him. Was it the touch of Gatherer? Had using the staff been the biggest mistake of his life? Was it linked to the tears? Had they located him? If Gatherer had found Flydd, could Reaper strike at him across the twenty miles that separated him from Jal-Nish?

On the ground, Gant lay still, but it seemed an alert stillness, as if he was biding his time. The captain's burned left hand was dripping fluid and he could barely hold the knife. He moved towards Flydd, who retreated. To his right was the roiling ball; on his left, the giant soldier with the two swords blocked his way. Behind him, two of the soldiers were starting to recover.

There was no way out.

Then Flydd had a desperate idea. The cut-off trident had been formed from three layers of metal – grey, silver, and copper-coloured – beaten together until they fused, and it had been fixed to the shaft via a circular socket which still contained a stub of splintered wood. He picked up the trident, receiving another painful shock, prised the splinters out and jammed the end of the shaft in.

'It's dead,' said the captain, thickly. 'Like you.' Then he hesitated, looking alternately at the staff and at Flydd's face.

'Back off,' said Flydd. He felt a sickening lurch in his belly – the beginnings of aftersickness. After misusing another mancer's staff it was bound to be bad. 'You too,' he said to the huge soldier.

'No pink fire,' said the giant, and rushed him.

'Come on, you mongrels!' roared the captain. 'Zlide, get over here!'

Zlide and another man rose, still shaking, and the four of them advanced on Flydd from all sides. His only hope lay in the one source of power he might be able to use, the unfathomable force they all feared: the pink and black, churning ball.

He plunged the trident deep into the ball – and roared, for every nerve in his body burned like a white-hot wire. Then he sensed, in a way he had never sensed anything before, someone's agony. *It was in his head!* Someone was screaming and thrashing, clawing at his ruined face and begging for death. Could it possibly be *Jal-Nish*?

It cut off. The nerve pain also faded and the insinuating probe vanished. Flydd raised the ball of light, which had begun to shrink; it was only a foot in diameter now. Holding it out at chest height on the prongs of the trident, he swung it back and forth to cover the big soldier and the captain.

'If he gets away,' choked the captain, 'we're dead and so are our families. Kill him!'

He staggered at Flydd. The giant came too, timing his approach to reach Flydd at the same time. He was the greater danger. Zlide and the other soldier hung back. Both were unsteady on their feet and Zlide's left eye was closed by a massive black bruise.

Flydd's strength was fading; aftersickness from using the staff was building in him. He had to end this quickly or he never would. He went for the giant, thrusting the churning ball of light at the scissoring swords. They passed into the ball, there came a scream as of tortured metal and the blades of both swords boiled away, hurling arcs of red-hot metal for twenty feet to either side and creating more little fires. The two soldiers froze, gaping.

Flydd had expected the giant to go into convulsions as the others had, but he was unaffected save that his lips now had a bluish tinge. He hurled the hilts at Flydd, who ducked, thrust the staff out and the pink ball touched the huge soldier on the breastbone. He brushed it aside, shuddering but unaffected.

A scrutator's most necessary skill was the ability to dominate all kinds of people, and Flydd had been a master at it. Now he called upon that skill. He intoned a nonsense phrase – *Girrili insunnan hrork!* – as if it were a spell.

'You've got ten minutes to live,' said Flydd. 'Make amends for all your wrongs before it's too late.'

The giant opened and closed his enormous hands. 'You're lyin'!'

'Your heart is racing but you can barely move. You feel like you're going to vomit but the poison is in your veins. It's already killing you.'

The huge soldier tried to sneer but it was beyond him. Flydd thought he had him. The captain stopped, then edged closer.

'That terrible thing you did is going to send you to damnation unless you atone for it right now,' said Flydd to the giant.

He was on safe ground here – most soldiers were superstitious, and all had done terrible things; it came with the trade. He turned to the two men behind him, thrusting out the ball of light to send them the same message. They backed away.

'Don't listen to him,' said the captain. 'Knock the little bastard down, Risper, then pull his head off his scrawny shoulders and shove it up –'

'You've done awful things in Jal-Nish's name, *haven't you*, Risper?' said Flydd. 'See the faces of all the innocent people you've killed, brutalised, ruined. *They're accusing you!* Beg forgiveness now – or pay for eternity.'

Risper clutched at his belly, looked down into Flydd's blazing eyes, then away.

'He's a lying scrutator!' cried the captain. 'Take him down!'

9

Risper threw himself at Flydd, swinging fists the size of cabbages. Flydd jerked the trident up and the points speared into the big man's chest for an inch before hitting ribs. The churning ball of light almost disappeared inside him.

'It's claiming you,' said Flydd. 'Feel the pain in your heart.'

Risper went rigid, his two teeth bared. He knocked the staff aside, knuckled his chest, let out an incongruous, high-pitched cry, then the air rushed out of him and he fell. Flydd swayed out of the way as Risper crashed at his feet, dead.

Flydd rotated, holding up the staff and the ball. Zlide bolted, leaving only a rank stench behind him. The other soldier backed away. Flydd did not think the ball of light had killed Risper; men his size often had weak hearts and he suspected the giant's heart had stopped from terror. But it was what the captain thought that mattered.

'If you put down your knife and go,' Flydd said quietly, 'I won't touch you.'

The captain, though he was in great pain, stood firm. 'Jal-Nish will get me wherever I go.'

'He's a dying man.'

'He's been hurt before. He always comes back.'

'Not from quicksilver poisoning. Jal-Nish is doomed, captain, and so are you if you stay with him.'

Flydd could see the despair in the captain's blue eyes. 'I'm doomed either way, but I swore a binding oath and I can't go back on it.'

In his way, Yarb was an admirable man, but it had to end here. As he rushed forwards with the knife, Flydd thrust the staff at him. The ball disappeared into Yarb's chest and he gasped and toppled forwards, as dead as Risper. The left-hand prong of the staff, perfectly aimed, had penetrated his heart.

But the other soldier did not know that. 'You can't beat mancery,' said Flydd. 'Put down your sword and go.'

The soldier slipped away. The ball, which had shrunk to the size of an orange, was entirely pink now save for a tiny, churning core of black. Flydd raised it high and, in its lurid light, checked all around, but not quickly enough.

Gant rose from behind a bush and hurled himself at Flydd, punching and kicking, trying to snatch the staff. It flew out of Flydd's hand, landing ten feet away. Gant drove his head into Flydd's belly and would have winded him had he not clenched his stomach muscles in time. The blow drove him backwards, though, and Gant dived for the staff.

He got a hand to it and tried to draw a killing power, only to cry out in dismay, 'Where are you?'

Gant groped his way up the staff, towards the pink ball of light, and Flydd knew that if he reached it he would have all the power he needed. Flydd kicked out desperately, knocking the staff out of Gant's hand. It struck him across his broken nose, he screamed, and Flydd snatched back the staff and ran.

Gant fell to his knees, groping all around himself and whimpering. Every so often he reared up and felt around in the air, his eyes staring. Flydd had seen it before with mancers who had lost a staff – being severed from its persona had been too much for him.

The remaining three soldiers were twitching but Yggur, whose head was still bagged, lay motionless. Flydd heaved him onto his back and removed the bag. In the pink light, Yggur's eyes had a worryingly vacant look.

'Wherever you've gone, come back,' he said, touching Yggur on the forehead with the head of the staff. Flydd had little hope of reversing the effects of the spell, since he did not know what it was.

Yggur murmured gibberish for a couple of minutes, then slowly the blankness seeped from his eyes and Flydd saw a hint of the normal Yggur there. But only a hint, and how long would it last?

He sat up. 'Aah! I ache all over.'

'You were in convulsions for a quarter of an hour,' said Flydd. 'Come on. We need to find Klarm and rescue the others, at the air-floater ... if they're still alive.'

They collected all the undamaged weapons. Flydd covered the pink ball with the bag that had been over Yggur's head. After some minutes of searching in the dark they found Klarm under a bush, his handsome face so swollen that he was almost unrecognisable.

'What happened?' said Flydd.

The little man groaned. 'Saw the big bastard coming. Tried to take him down, man to man. Mistake! Lucky to get away.'

'You're a moron,' Flydd said fondly. 'He's three times your size. At least, he *was* ...'

'You got him?'

'Someone had to.'

'Should have been me,' Klarm grumbled.

Flydd helped him up and gave him a sword and a knife. When he looked around, Yggur was trembling again. Flydd revised his hopes downwards.

'Can't help noticing that you're still alive,' said Klarm, trying to make light of things.

Flydd briefly described what had happened.

'You astonish me,' said Klarm. 'You beat the whole troop by yourself?'

'You took Gant down. I just made use of the power in his staff.'

They approached the air-floater, warily. 'Guards,' whispered Yggur. 'Three of them.'

'What about Troist and the others?'

Yggur rose up onto his toes. 'No sign. Wait! They're tied up by the stern of the cabin.'

Klarm fitted a stone into his sling. 'Creep as close as you can. I'll hurl two stones, then you rush them and I'll come after.'

They separated. Flydd wasn't sure they could rely on Yggur; he was still trembling and every so often his eyes went blank. Flydd, exhausted and beaten down by aftersickness, did not think he was up to the job either.

A pair of lanterns burned at the air-floater, revealing two guards at the bow and one at the stern. All were on high alert. Flydd crawled to within twenty yards, and waited. He could not see Yggur, but Klarm was twenty yards further back. The distance was long and Flydd wasn't counting on him to take any of the guards down – only to make a diversion.

He waited. And waited.

Thud. The guard at the stern toppled over backwards, cracking his head, and fell. Three seconds later one of the guards at the bow clutched at his shoulder, gasping. Klarm had excelled himself.

Flydd yanked the bag off the pink ball and charged. The uninjured guard ran forwards several steps, saw Flydd, turned and raced for the prisoners, drawing his sword. Was he planning on killing them? Flydd could not get there in time to stop him.

The guard thrust at Chissmoul. Flangers shouldered her out of the way and ducked a blow at his own head. The guard stabbed at Fyn-Mah, piercing her in the shoulder, then whirled and thrust his sword deep into Troist's belly.

10

Troist doubled over, blood pouring from the terrible wound. The guard came for Flydd, who smashed him across the face with Gant's staff, sending the trident end and pink ball flying off. The guard hacked viciously but missed. Flydd jammed the end of the staff into his belly, doubling him over. He swung at Flydd's knees.

Flydd stumbled backwards. A rock hurtled over his shoulder and struck the guard on the forehead. He reeled around, dazed; Flydd drew his sword and put the guard down. Klarm came panting up, swinging the sling.

'What's happened to Yggur?' said Flydd.

Klarm flipped a hand towards the right. Yggur was frozen in mid-stride and his eyes had gone vacant again.

'The guard got Troist,' said Flydd. 'Doesn't look good.'

'See what you can do for him,' said Klarm. 'I'll do the housework.'

Sword in hand, he headed to the bow to deal with the injured guards. Flydd cut the bonds of the prisoners, then squatted in front of Troist. One glance told him that nothing could be done. The belly wound was a hand-span across and had gone through vital organs.

'I'm sorry,' said Flydd, taking the general's hand. 'It's the end.'

'I thought so.' Troist's face twisted with the pain. No, a deeper pain. His grip tightened. 'Flydd ... you won't refuse a dying man, will you?'

Flydd knew what Troist was going to ask and he had to refuse. It was utterly impossible. He said nothing.

'Flydd, I'm begging you.'

'You want me to save Yara and your daughters.'

'Will you do it? *Will you?*'

It was too much for anyone to ask; a death sentence. Not to mention that if he, Flydd, was humanity's last hope, going anywhere near Jal-Nish would utterly extinguish that hope.

But Troist was desperate, and his terror for his family was palpable. 'You've met Yara and my twins. If you can't say yes for the sake of my wife, then please, *please* do it for my innocent daughters.'

Troist was weeping, and blood was draining from his belly wound as he threw everything into his despairing plea. 'Remember my twins, Liliwen and Meriwen? Remember their faces, and the way they laugh and cry? You know better than anyone what Jal-Nish will do to them ... for being my children.'

Flydd remembered the twins very well. They were pleasant, well-brought-up, comely girls on the verge of womanhood. Could he really allow Jal-Nish to take them? It was utter folly – but he could not say no.

'I will.' Flydd squeezed Troist's hand. 'I swear that I will do everything in my power to rescue Yara, Liliwen and Meriwen, and get them to safety.'

'You're a true friend.' Troist slumped over, breathing weakly, then looked up, his face wet with tears. 'Liliwen loves those little brown mushrooms with the red gills. Ninkies, they're called.' He was rambling. 'And Meriwen always wanted to see the caves.'

'She'll have plenty to choose from at Ashmode,' said Flydd.

He squeezed Troist's shoulder and went to confer with the others. Flangers, who had some skill as a battlefield healer, was bandaging Fyn-Mah's shoulder. Yggur lurched across, his frosty eyes blank.

'Last night we had a plan,' said Flydd. 'Has anyone changed their mind?'

'Jal-Nish found us too easily and too quickly,' said Fyn-Mah.

'Because Chissmoul kept the crystal,' said Klarm.

'Whatever the reason, I'm going with the one person I can rely on – myself.'

Considering that Flydd and Klarm had just saved her life, her words were offensive, but Flydd was too weary to say so. Everyone had their limit and Fyn-Mah had reached hers. Let her go.

'What about you, Yggur?' he said.

Yggur looked around blankly. 'Where are the others?'

'What others?'

'Nish ... Malien ... Irisis ... Tiaan ...'

Had it been anyone else, Flydd would have thought they were playing a macabre joke, but Yggur was not a joking man. 'You don't remember?' How could he not? The events of the past day and night were etched into Flydd's bones.

'I remember having lunch in Ashmode,' said Yggur in a voice as empty as his eyes. He gazed at the dark sky, the grass fires slowly burning towards the forest, then the air-floater. 'And then, *nothing*.'

'Jal-Nish happened, and he's got the tears! You were attacked by his chief mancer, Gant. We're splitting up and running.'

'Clearly ... I'm ... not myself,' said Yggur.

'Gant's attack must have woken an old trouble of yours, an ailment of the mind ...'

Yggur stiffened. '*I remember that.* It comes from the time Mendark betrayed me and used me ...'

'To trap Rulke and imprison him in the Nightland.' The ancient story was part of the Histories; it was one of the worst deeds the great Mendark had ever done.

'It still hurts,' Yggur whispered. 'It ... it's almost unbearable at times. But if anyone wants to come with me –'

'I will,' said Flangers. He looked down at their pilot, who had assumed the foetal position again. 'And Chissmoul. Can we take this craft?' Her eyes sprang open.

'Given that it belongs to Jal-Nish, and may be linked to the tears,' said Flydd, 'that would be risky.'

'I prefer to go on foot,' said Yggur.

'Better put some distance between yourselves and here before dawn, then. When Jal-Nish's chief mancer doesn't come back ...'

'We'll go at once.'

Yggur, Fyn-Mah, Flangers and Chissmoul shook hands with Flydd, Klarm and Troist, and walked away without another word. Only Flangers looked back. He saluted Flydd, and within seconds they had vanished in the darkness.

Flydd slumped to the ground, feeling as if all his bones had dissolved. 'And just like that, the fellowship of years is broken.' How swiftly the little company had come apart. Would he see any of them again?

'Well, old friend?' he said after several minutes of silence. 'Are you going too?'

'Haven't decided,' said Klarm.

They went back to Troist. The life of that compact, handsome, clever man was slipping away, and it wasn't right. He should have died valiantly in battle, doing what he did best, or surrounded by the family that meant everything to him. He should not be dying from a coward's blow, struck while he was helpless.

Flydd knelt down and took Troist's hands. The general tried to speak but could not; there was no breath left in him. His eyes opened wide and Flydd saw his most desperate fear – that Flydd would not keep to his word. That Troist's unprotected family would be brutalised for Jal-Nish's revenge.

'If they can be saved,' said Flydd, putting his hand over the wound, 'I swear on your life's blood that I will save them.'

A faint light appeared in the general's eyes. He gave a tiny nod and his life was gone.

There should have been a fanfare; surely something should have marked the passing of so great a man. Was life ultimately meaningless? Was there no point to anything?

Flydd closed Troist's eyes and stood up. It took an effort; he felt old and depressed. 'So dies another of the best of us. And for what?'

'Where is justice,' said Klarm theatrically, 'when good people die yet wicked old scrutators survive and prosper?'

'Prosper!' Flydd exclaimed. Between aftersickness and lack of sleep it was a struggle to say upright.

'How are you going to keep your promise?' said Klarm.

'I haven't got the faintest idea.' It was an unbearable burden, yet one he could not put down. 'Though I fear that Jal-Nish will have taken Yara and the children by now.'

'Yara is a clever woman, and she plans ahead. The instant he turned up she would have taken the children away.'

'If she got the chance. They would be high on his list.'

'But Jal-Nish only had the eighty-eight troops he brought on the air-dreadnought, and they had their hands full controlling the town square.'

'Only until he took command of our armies,' said Flydd. The more he thought about it, the worse it became.

'Our soldiers may obey him out of fear,' said Klarm, 'but Jal-Nish can never command the loyalty of good men. They loved Troist. They won't betray his family.'

'Jal-Nish can always find people to do his dirty work. '

'And there are a thousand hiding places near Ashmode.'

'Then how can I hope to find Yara and the twins?'

'She would have left a trail Troist could follow.'

'Unfortunately we can't ask him.'

'Well,' said Klarm casually, 'I dare say you'll work it out.'

'What are you going to do now? You've never said.'

'I reckon I might be able to fly that air-floater.'

'We just told the others –'

'They wanted to fly away in it. We want to go *towards* him.'

Flydd choked. 'You're planning on coming with me?'

'A turnip-head like you would never do it on your own.'

Such a feeling of relief swept over Flydd that he felt momentarily light-headed. He sat down abruptly. 'Thank you.'

'Not doing it for *you*, you ugly old bastard,' Klarm said gruffly. 'Good man, Troist. Nice kids.'

Flydd studied the air-floater. 'Do you reckon Jal-Nish will be able to tell it's us?'

'Right now I reckon he's so sick, and in such pain, that he won't be able to concentrate on anything.'

'I think you're right,' said Flydd. 'I sensed his agony when I jammed the trident into that pink ball. But we've got to be quick.'

'I'd better deal with the witnesses,' said Klarm. 'Why don't you go through the dead men's pockets?'

'What for?'

'Coin for travel expenses, bribes and so forth. We're going to need plenty.'

Robbing the dead, Flydd thought as he went from man to man. Was there a depth he had not plumbed in the past thirty years? Last of all he went through Troist's pockets, hoping to find some keepsake to give his girls, but all his possessions had been confiscated in Ashmode.

Flydd found bread and sausage in the air-floater. He made a fire, toasted a stack of sausage sandwiches and made tea. Then he sat with the shaft of Gant's staff across his knees and the tri-metal trident in his lap, trying to work it out.

Klarm came back, ran water from the air-floater's barrel and washed the blood off his face and hands.

'All dead?' said Flydd.

'Yes, including the rank fellow who ran away.'

'What about Gant?'

'I took the precaution of removing his head. He relinquished it most reluctantly, I have to say. Then I dragged the bodies to the forest, into the path of the fire.'

Flydd shivered. Sometimes Klarm could be too efficient. 'He was one of Jal-Nish's deputies.'

'And since Jal-Nish is reluctant to trust anyone, Gant's death will set back his plans tremendously. What are you up to?'

Flydd indicated the pink ball, which had shrunk to the size of a lemon and now clung to the broken end of the staff like a nail to a lodestone, as if trying to get back in. 'Trying to work out what this is.'

'I'd say it's the persona that controlled Gant's staff ... though I've never heard of a persona being ejected before – or taking on a visible form. How did you do it?'

'Yggur and I blasted simultaneously, at the very moment Gant was trying to call the staff back to him, and the captain's sword hacked through it.'

'And all that proved too much for the persona,' said Klarm. 'It was forced out of the staff and the power took on the most efficient form it could, to survive. I wonder if we can we use it?'

'For what?' said Flydd.

Klarm did not answer at once. He was staring into space, his mouth slightly open. He gave a little shiver and said, 'Yes! Lie down.'

'What?' said Flydd.

'As if you're dead.'

'What are you up to?'

'Shit!' cried Klarm. 'The fire!'

He raced down the slope, and shortly returned with Gant's luridly-coloured clothing and long boots, plus a heavy purse that he put to one side.

'Have you lost your mind?' said Flydd.

'Probably. Lie down!'

11

K larm arranged Flydd's 'corpse' artistically, smirking, then collected a mug of congealed blood from one of the dead soldiers and smeared it all over his shirt. He then dragged Troist's body down next to Flydd.

Flydd winced. 'Must you be so disrespectful?'

'His belly wound makes the scene look authentic.'

'Is 'Gant' going to send Jal-Nish an image of our corpses?'

'Great idea, don't you think? It'll make Jal-Nish's day. And give us a small advantage – if you can recover the link from the time you saw his pain.'

'I'll try.'

Flydd flicked the ball off the end of the shaft, fixed the trident there and plunged its central spike through the ball. Again his nerve fibres burned like a white-hot wire; again he experienced Jal-Nish's agony. He was raking hooked fingers down his burned, mutilated face, and screaming.

'Got it!' said Klarm.

He propped the broken staff up above Flydd and Troist, decorated his own throat with clots of blood and threw himself down beside Troist, his eyes open but unfocused. Klarm did something with a device concealed in his hand and there was a dim white flash from the staff.

Flydd waited until Klarm said it was safe to move. 'What exactly did you do just then?'

'Gant had to report to Jal-Nish once a day, via his staff. I showed him our bodies.'

They buried Troist, dragged the other bodies down to burn and boarded the air-floater. Flydd broke open the air-floater's strongbox and Gant's purse and divided the gold equally. By then it was three in the morning and the night was overcast and very dark. Klarm searched the craft, removed a needle-shaped green crystal and a yellow one with hexagonal sides and flat ends, and tossed them into the burning forest.

'Are they location devices?' said Flydd.

'Possibly. Wouldn't want to take the risk.'

'Why not smash them?'

'Gatherer might find that suspicious. If fire destroys them, it may conclude that this air-floater crashed and burned too.'

Klarm did not say how he planned to fly it and Flydd was too exhausted to ask, but it did not surprise him. He had seen Klarm use all manner of strange devices, some of his own invention. He was also skilled at concealing his little contraptions from a search.

'Any ideas about the persona?' said Flydd.

'Don't chuck it away.'

'Why not?'

'Gant was one of Jal-Nish's few deputies. His staff's persona might know all kinds of useful things.'

'It could also be dangerous.'

Klarm shrugged. 'It's up to you.'

'I don't suppose there's any platinum in this craft?'

'None I can spare. But there would be plenty in the air-dreadnought.'

Ten minutes later, Klarm hovered over the wrecked craft. It had been partly burned in the fire, along with the treetops around, but half of the broken cabin had been spared and, following Klarm's directions, Flydd obtained enough platinum sheet to tightly wrap the plum-sized pink persona. Platinum was impervious to all known forms of mancery and should isolate it, even from Gatherer.

Flydd left Klarm at the controls and lay down on the floor. Even an hour's sleep would revive him, and he was going to need it ...

The dwarf was shaking him. 'Approaching Ashmode. You've been out for an hour and a half.'

Flydd lay there, eyes closed, longing for another ten hours of sleep. 'How are we going to do this?'

'I'll drop you on the slope half a mile below Ashmode. It's still two hours until dawn. I'll hide the air-floater in one of the deep canyons a few miles west, and walk up to meet you tonight, an hour after dark.'

~

Flydd heard the grim news within minutes of sneaking into Ashmode, heavily disguised.

The streets were crowded and there were soldiers on every corner, though few wore Jal-Nish's distinctive uniform, red with black jags. Most of the troops were from Flydd's former armies.

It was the one piece of good fortune he was to have, though it only lasted until he entered the first tavern, where the terrible business of last night was the sole topic of conversation. He was to hear about it another hundred times before it was time to head back to the rendezvous.

'Dead?' said Klarm. 'All of them?'

'Yara, definitely. She was taken only hours after we escaped in the air-dreadnought. Jal-Nish hanged her in the town square at sunset, along with another sixty-seven men and women – including our most loyal army officers.'

Flydd would have given anything to erase that mental image – Yara, a tall, stern advocate, a noose around her neck, sweating blood for the children she could not protect. He groaned.

'So it begins,' said Klarm.

'And my unforgiveable blunder two years ago –'

'Don't start! What about the twins?'

'There's no word of them. I think Yara got them away.'

'Leaving Ashmode would be too risky; they'll still be in hiding.'

Flydd started. 'And I think I know where.'

'Go on.'

'Troist said it before he died, but I thought he was rambling. *Liliwen loves those little brown mushrooms with the red gills. Ninkies, they're called. And Meriwen always wanted to see the caves of Ashmode.*'

'It's limestone country. There are dozens of caves here.'

'But ninkies are rare and hard to find. If I can locate a cave where they grow, that's where the girls will be. Wait here.'

At the vegetable markets, Flydd asked where he could obtain a basket of ninkies. He was given directions to a small, obscure cave that could be entered below a vineyard a mile and a half west of Ashmode.

By the time he returned and they found the cave in the dark it was after midnight, and he was footsore and heart-worn. 'If they haven't been taken ... if they are here ... how are we going to tell them?'

'That both their parents have been killed,' said Klarm, 'and they're being hunted by the most vicious monster on Santhenar, so he can hang them too?'

'Yes.'

'There's only one way to break news like that. Directly.'

Flydd, hard-hearted scrutator though he had been, was dreading it. What if the twins went into hysterics? Or were inconsolable? He had little experience of girls their age and did not have the faintest idea how to deal with them.

The cave was oval, twice as wide as it was high, and stank. Water trickled along thread-like channels in the floor and bats roosted under the roof, their eyes red in the lantern light. Every so often Flydd and Klarm squelched across a stinking mound of bat dung packed with the white skulls and skeletons of frogs, mice and other small creatures, and crawling with feeding cockroaches.

As they went on, the cave narrowed steadily. It was warm, there were seeps everywhere, and the humidity was stifling.

'Not seeing any ninkies,' muttered Klarm.

Flydd grunted. He was struggling to come to terms with the new reality. Only forty-two hours had passed since the Lyrinx War had ended, a war that had lasted for 150 years and changed Santhenar immeasurably.

Less than thirty-six hours since Jal-Nish had turned up in his air-dreadnought to shatter the peace. Thirty-four hours since Tiaan had destroyed all the nodes and fields, unwittingly handing him Santhenar on a plate …

'It doesn't help to dwell on it,' said Klarm, who must have divined what Flydd was thinking. 'We can only deal with what *is*.'

'The floor of this cave is a miniature of Jal-Nish's new world,' Flydd said sourly.

'Not even Jal-Nish can see the future.'

'He doesn't need to – he *makes* it.'

'Don't be such a miserable old sod.'

They rounded a corner. The cave here was only six feet high and ten wide, the limestone a mustard yellow with hundreds of weeping cracks and fissures. Clusters of little crystals flowered green and yellow and red along some of the fissures.

'Hello, Mister Flydd,' said a young voice.

Flydd blinked, choked and wiped his eyes. Two girls were perched side by side on a rectangular block of limestone, watching him. Identical twins, and on the small side for their age, they had shoulder-length wavy hair the colour of polished copper, dark brown eyes and well-fleshed figures that owed more to their compact father than their lean, horsey mother.

'It's not *Mister* Flydd, Liliwen,' said the girl on the right, Meriwen. 'It's *Scrutator* Flydd.'

'Not anymore.' Flydd was so relieved to see them that he was breathless. 'The age of the scrutators is over. Do you know my friend, the former scrutator, Klarm?'

They did not. Liliwen shook hands with him, then Meriwen.

'Don't stare like that!' Meriwen said out of the corner of her mouth. 'It's rude.'

'Stare all you like,' Klarm said with a chuckle. 'I'm not easily offended.'

'Have you come from our mother?' said Liliwen.

And there it was – the question Flydd dreaded. There was a strangled pause. He took a deep breath.

Liliwen's face crumpled. She shot a desperate glance at her sister, who let out a tormented cry, '*No!*'

'I'm so sorry.' Flydd wished he was on the other side of Lauralin.

'What happened to her?' Liliwen's young face hardened. 'It was Jal-Nish, wasn't it? He –'

'Don't say it!' sobbed Meriwen. 'It's not true! *Don't say it.*'

'It has to be said,' Klarm said firmly. 'Your mother is dead and Jal-Nish, that evil monster who is the enemy of us all, killed her.'

Meriwen let out an eardrum-shivering wail. Liliwen gave a single dry sob, but drew herself up and choked the next one back. She went very still, her eyes as hard as garnets.

'Mother will be avenged,' she said with deadly menace. 'As soon as Father gets here –'

Not even Klarm could meet her eyes this time. She stared at him, then at Flydd, her mouth slightly open. Her throat moved. Her eyes slipped to her sister. Liliwen flung her arms around Meriwen, squeezing her as if she were the only real thing left in the world.

'Father *is* coming?' said Liliwen. 'He'll be here soon, *won't he?*'

12

Liliwen had absolute faith in her father. All her life, Troist had been the one to make things better. But there was no way of putting it kindly or gently.

'I'm afraid Troist ... won't be coming,' said Flydd.

'Why not?' said Meriwen, as if she had no comprehension of what he meant. 'What's holding him up?'

'Your father ... is dead.'

It was as though she had been cut off at the knees. 'He's not dead,' she shrieked. 'He's not, *he's not!*'

His useless words of comfort congealed in his throat. Fighting an irrational urge to bolt, he looked at Klarm, pleadingly.

'We were attacked by a dozen of Jal-Nish's soldiers only hours after we escaped,' said Klarm. 'Most of us were injured ... and Troist was killed.'

Liliwen pressed her forehead against the side of her sister's head and both faces disappeared behind masses of coppery hair. She held that position for a minute or two then sat up straight. She looked so very young and out of her depth, but desperately determined.

'I was born first; I'm the head of the family now. Tell us everything, and then we'll decide what to do.'

Flydd did not question her astonishing statement. As economically as possible, he related the story of the past two days, including Troist's death, and what he had heard about Yara's fate. Liliwen's eyes remained fixed on him the whole time. She asked no questions.

'They died bravely,' she said at the end.

'They did,' said Klarm, 'and never stopped thinking of you two. Yara refused to say anything about you. In Troist's last words, he made us promise to save you.'

'Save us from what?' said Meriwen, raising her swollen, tear-stained face at last.

'Jal-Nish wants to kill us too,' said Liliwen.

Meriwen began to shiver violently. 'Don't – be – silly. Why would he want to kill children?'

'As a lesson to the rest of the world. But we're going to kill him first.'

'We're not going to kill anyone.' Meriwen spoke the way a parent would speak to a silly child.

'Yes, we are. Aren't we, Mister Flydd?'

Flydd could see utter determination in her eyes. Though she was not yet fifteen, he knew there was no way of convincing her otherwise.

'It's too dangerous to discuss plans here. Sound carries in caves and anyone could overhear us. After we get you to safety we'll talk about what to do.'

They headed out and down to where the air-floater was hidden. A long, wearying trudge down the slope of the Dry Sea, then a two-hour climb down the canyon, it took most of the night. They stayed there all day, hidden by the towering walls of layered red, brown, purple and yellow rock. The girls kept to themselves. Flydd and Klarm took it in turns to keep watch. The following night was clear, with a bright moon, so they remained where they were. Flydd dared not risk being seen; if they were to have any hope, Jal-Nish must believe them dead.

He used the time in preparation, first fixing the trident solidly back onto the shaft of Gant's staff. Despite its persona having been ejected, the staff retained a small amount of power and, once he had recalled the lessons of his apprenticeship decades ago, he was able to work some minor spells, though he would not be able to perform anything powerful. Flydd spent the rest of the time practicing, learning the idiosyncrasies of the staff and painfully applying long-forgotten lessons.

Klarm, who had been his cheerful, acerbic self until they reached the air-floater, had withdrawn. He became a silent shadow, staring into the distance and replying in monosyllables. Something was wrong but Flydd had no way of finding out.

The following night was overcast and they flew south-west to the rugged coast of the Sea of Thurkad, south of the Hornrace, where Klarm set down on an isolated headland. They disembarked, he removed the device that had allowed him to fly the air-floater, cut the anchor ropes, and it rose and drifted north with the wind.

'Wherever it ends up, near or far, there's no way of tracing it back to us,' he said.

Five days later they reached the coastal town of Lugg. The girls, well disguised, went to the public bathhouse. Flydd and Klarm headed to a tea house which was almost empty at that time of day.

'We'd better talk,' Flydd said quietly.

Wearing lifts in his boots, a padded coat and a bushy beard, all subtly welded together by illusion to turn him into a bigger and much fleshier man, he would have fooled all but the most experienced spy. Klarm had cut his hair short and given himself the appearance of a far older man, though it was of limited benefit. Dwarves being rare, he attracted attention wherever he went.

'Don't tell me your plans,' said Klarm.

'Why not?'

'I don't want to know.'

'But we've got to stand up –'

'I've been fighting since I was born, Flydd, and I can't do it anymore. I want an ordinary life – at least, as ordinary as a dwarf can hope to have in this world.'

'You're running away too!'

'If you like,' Klarm said coldly. 'I was planning to leave a week ago, but I could no more abandon Liliwen and Meriwen than you could. Now they're safe – safer, at any rate – I'm boarding the first ship out of Lugg and I'm not coming back.'

'Where are you going?'

'Wherever the ship is going; it's all the same to me. And when I get there I'll take the next ship, and the one after that. I've a hankering to sail unknown seas, even to see the fabled Great North Land on the far side of the world.' He forced a smile. 'Let's not part in rancour. You've chosen your path and I'm taking mine.'

He was right. Life had not been easy for Klarm, and he had served faithfully for many years. He was entitled to do whatever he wanted with the rest of his life.

'I'll miss you,' said Flydd.

'Don't go all maudlin on me, you ugly old bastard.'

Flydd smiled. 'Clear out then, short-arse.'

'That's the spirit. Fare well, my friend.'

'You're not going to say goodbye to Liliwen and Meriwen?'

'I've had too many goodbyes lately. Say mine for me.'

Klarm extended his hand, they shook, then he walked out of Flydd's life.

And all the burdens of the world descended on his shoulders, as they had when he had been a leader in the Lyrinx War. But he'd had armies at his disposal then, subordinates ready to carry out his every command, and friends and allies. Now there was only himself. Under the padding his shoulders felt smaller than ever, his bones more fragile, and his driving determination had been eroded to nothing. How could he go on, alone? How could one man fight a dictator who planned to own the world?

But he had sworn to Troist. Until the twins were safe, he must fight on.

He could only make them safe by hiding them in some far-off land where Jal-Nish would not think to look, *or by killing him*. Both were fraught. How could he hide the twins where Jal-Nish, with the power of the tears and the wealth of the world, could not track them down? Were they doomed to a life of fear, afraid to make friends who might betray them, or be condemned with them? Was the price of life to be constantly running, forever hiding and always alone?

The better solution, for the twins and the world, was for Jal-Nish to die and the tears to be destroyed. But how?

Flydd wandered down to the harbour, keeping watch for spies, but saw no one to arouse his suspicions. He was not surprised; these were early days and Jal-Nish had few people he could rely on. Why would he waste a spy on this little backwater when he had armies, cities and rebellious nations to take control of? Nonetheless, Flydd assessed everyone he saw, just in case.

A dozen small fishing boats were tied to the jetty, and many more had been drawn up on the shore, a black mudflat stinking of rotting fish guts. At the warehouse end of the harbour a decrepit two-masted brig was unloading bags of grain, while beside it a trim, blue-sailed schooner loaded dried fish and salt. Neither vessel looked suspicious. A third ship, a round little yellow tub sailing a flag he did not recognise, was anchored out in the bay.

Flydd took a turn through the fish markets but saw no one he knew. A blue-black-haired, buxom woman working there had to be Klarm's friend, Rableen, but Flydd did not approach her. It was a week too early for Yggur or any of the others to come to the rendezvous, not that he expected they would. If they had any sense they would have gone south to hide in the rugged lands around the Burning Mountain, or across the sea to Meldorin Island, which had been depopulated in the war and now contained a hundred thousand square miles of wilderness.

He sat down at a table in an open-air tavern and ordered a cider. It proved to be both sour and tasteless but he nursed it along, keeping watch and listening. Port towns were easy to hide in, since they were used to strangers from far-off lands. Everyone wanted to know the news and people were glad to tell it, over and again. Then, for the first time, he heard some useful snippets of news.

Jal-Nish had not been seen for a week and his affairs had been managed by his deputy, Rudrigg, a cold-eyed warrior from "some outlandish place called Einunar". Then, two days ago, Rudrigg had also disappeared.

There were rumours that Jal-Nish had collapsed, rumours that he was dead, even rumours that he had entered a monastery to live as a barefoot monk in atonement for his wickedness. Flydd discounted the latter rumour and most of the others, though he was left with the persistent story that Jal-Nish was gravely unwell and undergoing treatment in secret.

It fitted what Flydd had seen when Jal-Nish had taken off his mask in Ashmode town square. His face, horribly scarred by a blow from a lyrinx's claws two years ago, had never healed, and even with the power of the tears he had not been able to do anything about the persistent infections.

The pustulent mess must have been exquisitely painful, and the burns from hundreds of globules of boiling quicksilver would have made it so much worse. It was a wonder he was still alive; no wonder at all that he had been taken away for treatment.

But where was he? If Flydd could discover that, he might be able to attack Jal-Nish where he was weakest. Once the twins were safely in hiding.

'You're not sending me to Borgistry!' said Liliwen.

'You can't stay with me,' Flydd said patiently, for it was an argument they'd had before, 'and you're not old enough to live by yourself. Besides, you don't have much money and I have little to give you.'

'I don't want your money! Mother made provision for us, years ago. She knew Father could be killed in the war.'

'Then where is it?'

'We don't know,' said Meriwen. 'They never talked about ... it was always assumed ...'

Meriwen still could not talk openly about her parents' deaths.

'Mother never imagined ...' said Liliwen.

Flydd could only think of one person who might know – Yara's sister in distant Borgistry.

'That's why you've got to go to your aunt, Mira,' he said.

'Lybing is two hundred leagues away,' Liliwen fretted. 'It'd take months to get there on foot. And who's to say the roads are safe?'

'Besides,' said Meriwen, 'Mira isn't there.'

'Where is she?'

Meriwen shrugged. 'Sometimes, when the grief takes her bad, she goes away and doesn't come back for months. She left Lybing the day we caught the air-dreadnought to Ashmode. Everyone thought the war was over; we wanted to celebrate.'

Flydd cursed under his breath. 'You could go to Mira's house. She has servants –'

'She sent them on holidays. Anyway, that's where Jal-Nish will look for us, as soon as he's better.'

'What other relatives do you have?' said Flydd.

'None,' said Liliwen. 'But even if we did, *I* wouldn't be going to them.'

'Where would you be going?'

'To avenge Mother and Father.'

He wanted to throttle her. 'You're fourteen! You're untrained, unskilled –'

'I'm nearly fifteen.' Liliwen met his eye. 'And I killed a man when I was twelve.'

The way she said it, he knew it was true. It was still shocking. 'Who? How?'

'It was when we lived in Nilkerrand. That's a city across the sea from Thurkad –'

'I know Nilkerrand.'

'The lyrinx set fire to the city,' said Meriwen in a little voice. 'It was burning and everyone had to flee ... but we got separated from Mother and Father. That's where we first met Nish, on the road, and we walked together for a while, for safety. But his leg was injured, and he was sick from bad oysters, and two ruffians grabbed us. They were going to ... ravage us, but Nish tracked us down. He killed one of the men ... but then ... then ...'

'The other man was strangling Nish and he was nearly dead,' said Liliwen. 'I whacked the brute over the head with Nish's mallet. Caved his head in and killed him stone dead,' she said with a look of horror. '*And – I'm – not – sorry!*'

'It's not wrong to take a life defending your own,' said Flydd. 'Or your friend.'

'Or to avenge your parents!' hissed Liliwen.

'Don't start that again,' Flydd said wearily. 'Jal-Nish is way beyond your power – or mine.'

'You liar!' cried Liliwen.

'Liliwen!' cried Meriwen, scandalised. 'Mister Flydd saved our lives.'

'The other day we heard you trying to convince Klarm to attack Jal-Nish,' said Liliwen. 'You said it had to be done now, while he's weak and ill. But Klarm wanted to run away like a coward.'

'How dare you slander my friend, you obnoxious little brat! Klarm is a good man. A brave man. I've a good mind to turn you over my knee –'

Flydd broke off, flushing. The twins were way too old for that kind of threat.

'If you dared, Father would have your hide stuffed and turned into a lampstand –' Liliwen's face cracked. She threw her arms around her sister, put her head in Meriwen's lap and wept.

After a long pause, Flydd said quietly. 'I did argue for attacking Jal-Nish, if Klarm and I could find him. Klarm is one of the most capable men I've ever met, yet the chances of the two of us succeeding were tiny. He was right to refuse.'

Liliwen raised her head and looked Flydd in the eye. 'We know where Jal-Nish is.'

'What are you talking about?'

'The best place for gossip and secrets is the women's bathing chamber. It's amazing what people say when you're all in the bath together.'

'Get on with it!'

'We met a rich old lady who used to be a healer on Healer's Isle, and she has a sister who still works there. They send messages back and forth by skeet.'

Also known as the Isle of Qwale, Healer's Isle was a large island seventy leagues north-west of Lugg.

'And?' said Flydd.

'An air-floater arrived at Healer's Isle seven days ago with a very important passenger, a one-armed man with terrible injuries to the face. Old injuries that won't heal, and fresh burns. He was so important that they cleaned out a special healery for him, underground. There are guards everywhere. It's got to be him.'

She was right. Given how scarce air-floaters were, and the power to make them fly these days, it could not be anyone else but Jal-Nish.

'Two days later the air-floater came back with another passenger, his deputy, Rudrigg,' Liliwen said triumphantly. 'Don't you see –?'

'Yes, I do see.'

'Well?'

'I'm thinking about it.'

'I suppose we'll have to catch a ferry to the isle – unless you know how to sail,' she said hopefully.

'I do know how to sail, but I'm not sailing a small boat that far out to sea – and I'm certainly not taking you.'

'Then we'll go by ourselves. Won't we, Meri?'

'No, we won't!' said Meriwen. 'Mother and Father would want us to look after each other, keep out of danger and not take any risks.'

'Then I'll go by *myself*. I'm not giving up.'

That was absolutely clear. Liliwen was one of the most determined girls he had ever met. Clearly, she believed that the way to succeed was to knock down every obstacle, one by one, through sheer, dogged persistence. But the idea of attacking Jal-Nish on Healer's Isle was absurd.

'I'm going to bed,' said Flydd.

He went to his room and lay on the flea-ridden straw mattress for the next three hours, turning plans over in his mind. Was this his chance to rid the world of Jal-Nish, and the tears as well? It was the only chance he would get. He had to take it – assuming he could get the girls to safety first.

Though no matter which way he looked at it, he did not see how he would survive.

~

In the morning Flydd went to a different open air tavern on the waterfront and ordered the local yellow wine. It came in a wooden mug whose rim looked as though a dog had chewed it, and tasted no better than the cider he'd had the previous day – he could feel the acidity stripping enamel off his teeth.

'But where is he?' Flydd said under his breath. He put a hand in his pocket to scratch his leg.

Healer's Isle, you cretinous little runt!

Flydd started and looked around hastily, thinking he had been overheard, but there was no one within yards of him. The voice was in his head. The possibility existed that he was going insane, though he did not think so.

'Who the hell are you?' he muttered.

You don't even know? The voice rose in pitch. *You utter bastard. I'll get you!*

13

F lydd tried to trace the voice but it was unfamiliar. Was it a *sending* or a *link*, both of which were forms of mental communication? It did not feel right. And it could not be a concealed farspeaker device, because they had all failed when the fields had been destroyed.

'Why Healer's Isle?' he said, to gain time.

They're the best healers in the west, everyone *knows that,* the voice sneered. *It's where he always goes.*

Flydd sat up. 'He's been there before?' Interesting, and unexpected. He sipped the dreadful cider.

Comprehension isn't your strong point, is it? No wonder Chief Scrutator Ghoor had your privates trimmed down to –

Wine went down the wrong way and Flydd choked, spraying a mouthful across the table next door. He went into a fit of coughing that had everyone in the bar staring at him. Wiping his eyes, he rose swiftly and went out into a chilly wind, blowing off the sea. He jammed his hands in his pockets and walked along the reeking waterfront.

The voice was sniggering now. Flydd went to the end of an empty jetty where he could not be overheard. 'Who are you, and how do you know about Jal-Nish's affairs?'

Was there with him, wasn't I? it said in a sulky voice, then, plaintively, *Where's my master?*

Then it hit him. Flydd took the little platinum-wrapped ball, in which the persona ejected from Gant's staff was trapped, from his pocket. Part of the platinum foil had bent back on itself to expose the pink persona, and when he'd put a hand in his pocket he had touched it.

It was not churning now; it was quite still, a lurid candy pink with small black flecks. Presumably it could only communicate with its master while he was in contact with the staff – and with Flydd when he touched the persona.

Took you long enough, the persona muttered. *Where's my master?* It was a cry of longing, almost of desperation.

'Being severed hurts, does it?' said Flydd. 'I wonder if you and I can come to some arrangement?'

Can't tell you anything about my master even if I want to, it snapped.

'What about Jal-Nish?'

It did not reply, though Flydd sensed a sudden expectancy. 'Treats your master well, does he?'

Jal-Nish made my master his deputy. One of only two.

Only two! It made Gant more important than Flydd had thought, and the loss of him far greater.

'And Jal-Nish trusts your master? Shares Gatherer and Reaper with him? Treats him with respect?'

Flydd felt a surge of fury; he'd put his finger on a nerve.

Jal-Nish doesn't trust anyone, *no matter how loyal.*

'Why did he go to Healer's Isle the first time?'

Surely it's obvious, even for a failed *scrutator.*

'Have you been there?'

So often that I know it like the prints on my master's fingers.

Ahh! 'But Healer's Isle is huge, and there are dozens of sanatoriums and healeries. Where does Jal-Nish go?'

The response came as a shriek. *Where's my master, you mongrel dog?*

'He's safe,' Flydd lied. 'Tell me where to find Jal-Nish ... and I'll reunite you with your master.'

The silence stretched out. Was it up to something? 'Assuming you want to be reunited,' Flydd added.

There's an ancient underground healery on the east side –

'The one built by Master Healer Habna after all the healeries were razed during the Clysm?' There was a well-known tale about the devastation of Healer's Isle.

Jal-Nish ordered the Habnarium cleaned out, for him alone.

'When?'

'The last message before you broke my master's staff.'

'Captain Yarb broke it, not me. How can I get in, secretly?'

Where's—my—master?

The persona was getting desperate; its agony of separation vibrated in every syllable. 'He's being held in a deep cave,' Flydd lied. 'But if you help me, I'll help you.'

To betray my master's master?

'If you won't help me to see Jal-Nish, why would I put myself out to give your master food and water?'

Flydd was taking a big risk here. If he antagonised the persona, and it was able to communicate with Gatherer, he would be walking into a trap.

After a long, fraught silence, it said coldly, *Get paper and a pen. There's a secret exit from the healery. I'll tell you a map.*

'If it's the best chance you'll ever have to finish Jal-Nish, why aren't you going?' said Liliwen.

'Surely that's obvious.'

'Not to me.'

'If I went, it's highly unlikely I'd survive. That would leave you and Meriwen stuck here, hundreds of miles from the only person who cares about you, with little coin and no hope. And Jal-Nish hunting you.'

'We can look after ourselves.'

'I promised your father that I'd get you to safety. It was his only comfort as he was dying. Would you have me break that promise?'

'I think you're scared,' sneered Liliwen.

'Lili!' cried Meriwen. 'That's an awful thing to say.'

'He's not denying it.'

'I am scared,' said Flydd, meeting Liliwen's eyes. 'Anyone who takes on Jal-Nish and claims not to be is either a fool or a liar. But I'm not abandoning you two to go off on a hair-brained attack, no matter how much you insult me.'

'If you were on your own,' said Meriwen, always the conciliator, 'how would you have done it?'

'By sailing to Qwale and sneaking in via the secret exit. With Jal-Nish gravely ill and in great pain, and the healers working on him, there must be long periods when he's not watching the tears.'

'He might give them to Rudrigg.'

'No, he's paranoid; he suspects even his oldest allies of treachery.'

'How would you get past the guards?' said Liliwen.

'By assuming Gant's identity. Wearing his clothes, and using his trident staff and its persona for verification.'

'Sounds dangerous,' said Liliwen.

'It would be.'

'You've got to attack him,' said Liliwen. 'And take me with you. It's my right.'

Flydd said nothing. The idea was monstrous.

'Isn't it, Meri?' said Liliwen.

Meriwen winced, then looked up at her sister, her eyes wide and shiny. 'If I said no, you'd go anyway, wouldn't you?'

For a moment Liliwen was a young, terrified girl again, but she defeated her fears and raised her pointed little chin. 'I have to stand up for my family and my world. Even if ... even if I'm going to die.'

'If Jal-Nish caught you, it would be a hundred times worse than the ruffians Nish saved us from.'

'I know,' whispered Liliwen. 'But I have to do it.'

'You're so brave,' said Meriwen.

Liliwen was trembling. 'I'm *not* brave. I'm terrified.'

'You ... you can't go alone. And Mother and Father wouldn't have wanted me to. So I have ... have to be just as brave.'

Flydd's eyes stung. Of all the people he had known, none had shown more quiet courage than these two girls. Now they were watching him with the penetrating brown eyes that laid bare all his frailties. They had to be protected at all costs.

'If you go without us,' said Liliwen, 'we'll take the next boat to Qwale and go after Jal-Nish ourselves.'

'I have no intention of leaving you. That would break my promise to your father.'

'If you try to take us to Borgistry we'll run away when you're asleep and get the next boat to Qwale.'

'Then I'll tie you both to a bloody tree every night before I go to sleep,' he snapped.

'There aren't any trees on the dry plains.'

Flydd read utter resolve in Liliwen's eyes, and her sister's too. They were clever and determined girls; no matter what he did, they would find a way to escape. They would go to Qwale, and they would be caught and killed.

Jal-Nish had murdered their parents and stolen their childhood. They had the right to do something about it. Dare he take them? Could he protect them?

If he took them in the secret way, there was a chance. A small chance. Tiny. He turned away and paced, grinding his knotted fists into one another until he took the skin off his knuckles.

'All right!' he said, making the most reckless decision of his career. One that, whatever happened, he was bound to regret. 'But you have to do exactly what I say. Is that clear?'

'Of course,' Liliwen said sweetly.

'I'd better find us a boat, then.'

They did not cheer, or even smile. They may have been hoping he would refuse them. Liliwen met his eyes and said, stiffly, 'Thank you.' Then the girls threw their arms around one another and burst into tears.

Flydd closed his eyes and prayed for forgiveness from his enemies. After this, even in the final days of eternity he would not gain forgiveness from Troist.

14

The waves were higher than the mast and breaking at their tips. The wind, which had been no more than a breeze when Flydd sailed the stolen boat through the heads of Lugg Haven two days ago, had strengthened steadily. They passed out the northern entrance of the Sea of Thurkad, hugging the coast of Meldorin Island to avoid the deadly currents now flooding through the Hornrace to fill the Dry Sea, and headed north-west toward Healer's Isle.

The little boat rolled sickeningly with every wave. Meriwen had vomited up everything she had eaten since they left, and Liliwen was currently spewing her guts into the bilge water. Even Flydd, seasoned sailor that he had once been, could taste porridge and pickled squid in the back of his throat.

Was this venture a criminal folly? The risk was staggering and, realistically, the hope of killing Jal-Nish and getting away was tiny.

Precisely where was he in the underground healery? How many guards did he have, and where were they? There was no way of knowing. In the past week Jal-Nish could have shipped in a hundred.

And then there was the map the persona had described to him. The more Flydd thought about it, the more problematic it seemed. Had he been set up? He did not think so – the persona's separation agony felt genuine. But just in case, he kept it carefully wrapped in platinum so there was no possibility of it contacting Gatherer.

He forced his mind back to the task. Time was short. Jal-Nish had been on Healer's Isle for ten days now, and the best healers in the west would be working on him. How much longer would they need? He had a world to take control of; he would not stay a minute longer than he had to.

Flydd felt utterly alone, abandoned by allies who could have made the difference. He was tempted to sail straight past Qwale and up the coast of Faranda all the way to the tropical Isle of Banthey, there to end his days under a coconut tree, watching the long green waves break over the coral reefs and dreaming about what might have been.

He closed his eyes for a moment, taking some small comfort from the silly daydream. Until a face filled his inner eye, a haggard, grey-faced man he recognised as Haddeus Nugit, one of General Troist's officers. Nugit's eyes were staring, his mouth gaping.

Flydd started. The viewpoint moved backwards to reveal a noose around Nugit's neck, but abruptly he fell away. The viewpoint moved back further and he reappeared, dangling from the rope, his legs kicking.

Meriwen screamed. The girls were on their feet, staring at Flydd but not seeing him. Another face appeared – another officer. Then another, a small woman, one of Flydd's pilots. And another. Each had a noose around their neck and, one by one, they fell. They were part of a long line of condemned, waiting to be hanged.

Flydd dived for the trident staff. He had to stop this before it showed the end of the line; he felt sure Yara would be part of it. He raised the staff high, slammed it down on the deck and cried words of power to banish the image.

But without the staff's persona it had little power and his banishment failed; the hangings were still as clear in his inner eye as a painting. Another male officer fell to his death, then a second woman, one of his battle mancers. Flydd cried the words of power a second time, then a third, shrieking the banishment into the wind, and the *sending* vanished.

Aftersickness hit him like a sledge hammer to the belly, doubling him over. He had not used power that way in a very long time. He clung to the staff with both hands, swaying back and forth with the rocking deck.

'Was that ...?' said Liliwen in a tiny voice. 'Was Mother ... there?'

'I didn't see her,' said Flydd. But there was no point trying to protect them from the truth. 'She might have been.'

'Jal-Nish sent it, didn't he?'

'I expect so.'

'Why would he do such a horrible thing?' said Meriwen.

'To show the world that resistance is pointless,' said Flydd. 'To drive home the message that all his enemies will die, along with their families. To terrify us and break our spirit.'

'He'll never break *our* spirit, will he, Meri?' Liliwen said unconvincingly.

Meriwen let out a whimper.

'The worse he gets, the stronger we have to be,' said Liliwen firmly. 'He's a mongrel dog and he's got to die.'

She lurched to the rail, spewed over the side and clung there for a minute or two, staring at the heaving water. Then she rinsed her mouth and her face from a bucket of salt water. She looked almost as green as the sea, but her jaw muscles were knotted. Flydd admired her for her utter determination, but something was terribly wrong with the world when a child had to live this way.

'How can we beat him, Xervish?' she said, using his first name for the first time. Since he was treating her as an adult, he supposed she was entitled to.

'We can either turn one of his strengths back on him,' said Flydd, 'or attack one of his weaknesses.'

'What are his strengths?' said Meriwen.

'Possession of the tears gives him unbeatable power.'

'Then we need to steal them,' said Liliwen.

'His other strength is utter, ruthless determination,' said Flydd. 'When he goes after something, he won't let anyone or anything stand in his way.'

Liliwen looked daunted, frightened, a little girl again. 'Um ... and his weaknesses?'

'What do you think?'

'He hides behind a mask; he doesn't like what he sees in the mirror.'

'Jal-Nish despises people who are maimed or disfigured in any way,' said Flydd, 'yet he's lost an arm and his face is grotesque. He hates himself, yet he hates whole people more, for having what he can never get back. Anything else?'

'He's in constant pain,' said Liliwen, 'and the infections must make him feel sick most of the time.'

'And with quicksilver poisoning, he may not in his right mind.'

'Mother ...' said Meriwen. Her face crumpled. 'Mother said he has a terrible fear of betrayal.'

'I knew Jal-Nish well, once,' said Flydd, 'when I was scrutator for Einunar and he was a perquisitor under me. He can't trust anyone. He only appoints deputies from people he's known since childhood, yet holds back real power even from them.'

'Can we destroy the tears?' Meriwen said after a long silence.

'I'd like to. But I don't know how.'

15

F lydd had been at the helm for most of the past three days and could not take much more; it was all he could do to keep his eyes open. The weather was wild and each wave carried the little boat up, up, up, then sent it down in a stomach-cramping descent.

The orange cliffs of Qwale, a series of ragged bluffs that ran for eighty miles along the east coast, towered above them for five hundred feet. Hundreds of rocky reefs lurked below the wild water, waiting to tear the boat's keel out and claim them. It would only take one mistake, or one lapse of concentration, and he was utterly exhausted.

Ahead was the sea cave they had to reach, for it was linked to the healery's secret exit, but the only way to get to it was via a long, narrow channel running between jagged rocks that were thickly coated with sharp oyster shells, to a tiny landing. A channel that it would be almost impossible to navigate in these seas.

'I know you're a good sailor, Mister Flydd,' Meriwen said carefully, 'but I don't see how we can land there. The boat will be smashed to bits.'

'Even in calm weather it'd be tricky,' said Flydd.

'There's no other way to get in,' said Liliwen. 'And Jal-Nish could leave any day now. We've got to take the risk.' She studied the cliffs, the waves, the brutal rocks. Her eyes were huge, staring, afraid. 'We're ... good swimmers.'

'So am I,' said Flydd, 'but if we end up in the water we'll be battered to pulp on the rocks.'

The danger was immediate, their bloody fate obvious, and even Liliwen was struggling with her resolve. 'Have we got a chance?'

It was the last opportunity to pull out, and he was tempted. He scanned the coastline. There were no lighthouses or other structures, no signs that anyone had ever been here, though that did not mean there were no watchers.

No, he had to focus on the job. Ridding the world of Jal-Nish was worth almost any risk.

'Yes,' he said, 'though there's only one way to do it and that's to go in fast. Leave your packs at the bow and take an oar each, so you can fend us off the rocks.'

Flydd put on the lurid clothes Klarm had taken from Gant: the yellow waistcoat, scarlet cape and pink knee britches, which he'd had cleaned of blood and repaired in Lugg. He looked down at his skinny legs, sighed, then used the staff to cast an illusion of the portly, big-thighed wizard upon himself. It was not an improvement.

'How do I look?'

Meriwen's shoulders were heaving and she was covering her mouth with her hand. 'Interesting,' she said brightly.

'Horrible!' sniggered Liliwen.

'I'm glad you've got a laugh out of it,' he said sourly.

He headed for the channel, slowing the boat to enter on the crest of a wave. All went well for the first thirty yards, but the closer they approached the cliff the wilder and more erratic the wind became. Without warning it swung through ninety degrees and slammed the port side against the rocks, splintering the end of Meriwen's oar and hurling her against the gunwale.

In vain, Flydd tried to steer away. The wind drove them against the rocks again before she managed to push the boat off with her broken oar, but by then two of the planks had sprung and water was running in. Flydd adjusted the sail and they made another twenty yards down the channel. Another gust flung them side-on against the rocks, *crash, crash, crash.*

Several planks had been smashed, one below the waterline, and water was flooding in. It was a foot deep on the floor of the boat and rising fast.

'We're not going to make it,' said Liliwen, eyeing the orange rocks of the channel, which rose for six or seven feet to either side. 'We're going to sink. Why did you listen to me?'

'Shut up and fend us off,' snapped Flydd.

The wind, treacherous as ever, now died. He adjusted the sail but the boat was moving sluggishly, bow down. Thirty yards to go. It seemed like a mile. Could he save the boat by running it up onto the landing on the crest of a wave? Not a hope; at this rate they would be lucky to get there at all.

The starboard side struck an out-jutting ledge and caught. Liliwen stared at it as if mesmerised. Water surged in.

'Push us off!' roared Flydd.

She shoved the boat away and they made another twenty yards down the narrowing channel. The boat kept crashing against the rocks on either side and there was nothing anyone could do to stop it. The water inside was two feet deep. Now two-feet-six.

'Up to the bow!' said Flydd. 'Grab your packs but don't put them on.'

The boat was bow-down now, only clearing the water by a foot. If a surge came over the sides it would go straight to the bottom.

'Chuck your packs onto the landing,' said Flydd. 'Don't jump till we get to within four feet.'

They threw their gear and waited, but the boat was no longer making headway and the gap to the landing was six feet. It was a dangerous jump with the deck heaving up and down, but they weren't going to get any closer.

'Jump! *Now!*' he bellowed.

They jumped. Liliwen landed on the broken edge of the landing and teetered there. Meriwen made a desperate grab for her, caught her arm and hauled her to safety.

Flydd hurled his own pack onto the landing, then the trident staff, which Meriwen caught. But the gap was eight feet now, more than he could jump from a standing start, and with the floor knee-deep in water he could not get a run up. He was standing at the bow, praying for a wave to close the distance, when a surge came over the sides and the boat sank beneath him.

Suddenly he was in the water and a huge wave was racing up the channel, breaking as it came. It would either smash him against the rocks or grind him between the landing and the bow. He swam as fast as he could but he wasn't going to make it.

'Grab this,' cried Liliwen, thrusting the three-pronged end of the staff at him.

He caught it on the third attempt, knowing she would never heave him up onto the landing – at the bottom of the trough it was four feet above him. But Meriwen took hold too and, with surprising strength, they lifted him straight up. His boots slipped on the vertical surface, gained a purchase, then he was up and gasping on the landing.

The monster wave lifted the stern, which was still afloat. The boat pivoted on its bow, which must have been on the bottom, and rose to the vertical, water pouring out of it. Meriwen let out a squawk; it looked as though the boat was going to slam down on top of them.

She ran backwards, dragging Flydd with her. The boat tumbled over, smashed on the edge of the landing and broke in half. Both halves disappeared in churning water as the wave burst on the landing and foaming water surged across it, three feet deep, with enough power to knock them over. They scrambled up out of the surge onto barnacle-covered rocks. The twins were staring at the wild water.

'That was close,' Flydd said laconically. 'Thanks; I'd be dead without you.' He bent his head to them.

'But how,' said Meriwen, who was white-faced and breathing hard, 'are we supposed to get away ... afterwards?'

Liliwen let out a hysterical peal of laughter.

Exactly, Flydd thought.

~

A passage ran from the rear of the cave, so low that they had to stoop. They followed the map for a long way through orange limestone with white hand stencils on the walls, and further in, paintings of fish, crab and whales. The rock graded to grey slate, bare of any paintings, then into iron-hard sandstone, and after that a yellow marble which became pink, then red. All was silent, all was still. Dust lay thick on the floor; there was no sign that anyone had walked this way in a hundred years.

Miles they walked, and hours, occasionally encountering another passage and doing as the map instructed. After some four hours they stopped for mouldy bread and the local specialty at Lugg, pickled meat. It was black as tar and blisteringly spicy.

'It feels like we're still on the boat,' said Meriwen, holding her head. 'As if it's still rocking under me.'

'Happens that way, sometimes.' Exhaustion crept over Flydd. 'I can't go any further.' He wrapped himself in Gant's red cloak, curled up on the floor and closed his eyes. 'Wake me after a couple of hours.'

The twins walked off a little way, 'We're going to die here, aren't we?' said Meriwen.

'Jal-Nish is going to die here,' Liliwen rasped. 'I'm going to throttle him with my bare hands.' She gave a little sob. 'I'm sorry, Meri. I got you into this, and –'

'Don't be ridiculous! You wouldn't really have gone by yourself, so don't pretend otherwise. We both got us into this situation, and we've got to find a way out.'

'Xervish is a clever man. He'll get us –'

'Mother was clever too, and so was father. Besides, Mister Flydd is really, *really* old.'

'He's really hideous,' said Liliwen softly. 'I think he's the ugliest man I've ever met ...' she lowered her voice further, 'yet they say women threw themselves at him, in the old days.'

'I heard Irisis was his lover, and she was beautiful.'

'Women don't swarm over him anymore. Not after what Chief Scrutator Ghoor's torturer did to him ... *down below*.'

'Lili!' hissed Meriwen in a scandalised voice. 'You can't talk about things like that. What if he heard you?'

They retreated. 'There's bad ugly and good ugly,' said Liliwen thoughtfully. 'Jal-Nish is bad ugly. The thought of him gives me the horrors. And Flydd is good ugly ...'

Flydd smiled to himself and drifted off to sleep.

16

'Once we pass through,' said Flydd quietly, indicating the round stone door at the end of the passage, 'we'll be in Habna's underground healery. But we're bound to face guards before we get to Jal-Nish. Are you ready?'

'I still don't see why our hands have to be tied,' said Liliwen.

'We've been over this.'

'Go over it again.'

'I haven't got the power to disguise you. I've barely enough to maintain the illusion that I'm Gant. The only way I can get you in is as my prisoners – the renegade daughters of the traitors Troist and Yara, because Jal-Nish will want to gloat over you. But if you'd prefer to wait here for me to come back ...'

Meriwen did; Flydd could see it in her eyes. Liliwen was harder to read. She ached to put Jal-Nish down but was terrified of being bound and helpless. And what if Flydd's rescue, and the attack on Jal-Nish, was part of a diabolical plan? What if Flydd was planning to betray her and Meriwen, so as to gain a high position under Jal-Nish's new regime?

'Your decision,' said Flydd.

'All ... all right.'

She held out her wrists and he bound them tightly with cord, then Meriwen's wrists.

'Try to look afraid,' said Flydd.

'Won't be hard.' Liliwen's voice was high with fear.

'I'll treat you harshly, to make it look convincing.'

'I bet you'll enjoy that!'

'Lili!' hissed Meriwen.

'We're helpless and he's taking us to the man who wants to kill us,' Liliwen snapped. 'I can't even pretend I'm happy about it.'

Flydd wasn't either. If he made the tiniest mistake, they would all die. He checked that the Gant illusion on himself was tight and the persona of the staff was fully enclosed in platinum. There was no room for error once they passed through the door.

'All right,' he said, opening it and checking for guards. He saw none.

They emerged from the concealed door into a broad passage cut into a magnificent deposit of red marble that would have enhanced the greatest palace in the land, yet here it was simply the stone that formed the walls, floor and roof of the underground healery. The proportions of the passage were grand, the carved decorations of medicinal herbs and flowers simple but elegant. Flydd's respect for the aeons-dead Habna rose.

Her healery, which was all on one level, was arranged like segments of an oval wheel with the individual passages being spokes radiating from a central hub. They circumnavigated the outside of the wheel without seeing anyone; the place seemed empty and there were signs that dust and cobwebs had been hastily, and imperfectly, cleaned away. A broad passage leading away from the wheel must go to the main entrance, which would be heavily guarded. There would be no getting out that way.

Flydd, peering down one of the spoke passages, noted a pair of sentries at a guard post. He headed that way.

The first of the sentries recognised Gant, and saluted. 'Your staff, surr.'

'Pardon?' said Flydd in a passable imitation of Gant's voice.

The sentry pointed to a plate on the floor, with a cup-sized depression in it. Flydd reversed Gant's staff and put its head in the socket. He slipped his free hand into his pocket, peeled away part of the platinum foil and touched the persona.

And held his breath. If the persona was going to betray him to Gatherer, it would happen now.

After a long pause, the guard nodded and said, 'Weapons, surr.'

Flydd folded the foil down again and handed the guard his sword and knife. The guard's eyes drifted to Liliwen and Meriwen, who looked suitably terrified. 'Who are they?'

'The daughters of the late General Troist. My troops killed him ten days ago, in a battle with –'

'That would be Jal-Nish's troops, surr.'

'Yes, of course,' said Flydd, cursing the slip. With Jal-Nish, every failure rested on his subordinates and every success was attributed to himself. 'He will be very pleased to see these girls.'

The guard started to say something but thought better of it. He waved to the second guard, who studied the twins, then a list, and checked them for weapons.

'Down the hall and around the corner to the right,' said the first guard.

Flydd gestured to the twins to go ahead. A series of emotions reshaped Liliwen's comely face: fury, a perverse anticipation, then the sickening dread that Flydd might be planning to betray them.

They continued, seeing no one on the way. It seemed wrong that the place should lie empty; even more wrong that this beautiful healery should have been opened for the sole use of such a monster. Liliwen turned to say something. Flydd curtly gestured her to silence. This close, Gatherer could be listening to every whisper.

They rounded the corner. Ahead, outside a large, sliding door of foot-thick red marble reinforced with rust-flecked iron, stood another guard, a tall, muscle-bound fellow with an angry look in his eye.

'Lurimon Gant,' said Flydd. 'And the daughters of the traitors Troist and Yara.'

'You mongrel!' cried Liliwen. 'How dare you call our parents traitors?'

The guard struck her across the side of the head with a weighted nightstick. 'Shut your mouth, girl! An insult to Jal-Nish's chief mancer is an insult to Jal-Nish himself.'

Liliwen was knocked to her knees. She swayed there for a few seconds, dazed, then the blood rushed to her face and she sprang to her feet, wresting with her bonds.

'Lili, stop!' cried Meriwen. 'You'll only make it worse.'

Flydd caught Liliwen's left shoulder and squeezed painfully hard. She went still. The guard, now glowering, slid the door open. Despite its weight and age, it moved easily and almost noiselessly.

'Go through!' Flydd said roughly.

He closed the door behind them and looked around. They were in a vast room shaped like a cut-off wedge. This end, the narrower third of the wedge, was empty apart from a polished silkwood table and two matching chairs, a pale green, two-person sofa and, on the far side, a huge, curtained-off bed.

Jal-Nish's bed! Fury surged in Flydd until it almost choked him. His heart was hurtling back and forth in his chest and little spots drifted before his eyes. He fought for control and checked all around him.

The other two-thirds of the room, divided off by folding wooden doors standing half open, was cluttered with furniture that appeared to have been hastily moved out of the way. Flydd saw a long table with surgical instruments – knives, saws, forceps, clamps, reamers, threaded needles of all sizes, a heavy mallet, and rolled bandages and folded pads – laid out on a white cloth, ready for use.

A smaller table held labelled jars containing lanolin and various balms and ointments, demijohns of oils and spirits, and bottles of tinctures and essences. A bookcase was full of leather-bound tomes on surgery, the setting of bones, a three-volume herbal and other topics. A series of tall cupboards, an empty dresser, another pair of sofas, blue, facing one another, and many more tables and chairs turned the rest of the room into a cramped maze.

No danger there – now to deal with Jal-Nish.

Flydd could not see the occupant of the bed, though he could smell the faint, foul odour that always hung about him, from the infections that no treatment had been able to eradicate.

He turned around the screen and there he was, the mass-murdering bastard. Flydd's heart combined three beats into a single leaden thud, then seemed to stop altogether.

Behind him, one of the girls sucked in a long breath. Meriwen, he guessed. Liliwen made a ferocious sound in her throat. Flydd whirled, signalling her to control herself. Her fists were clenched and the hatred on her face was searing. She extended her bound wrists towards Meriwen, who moved towards her.

Jal-Nish was a middle-aged man, a trifle shorter than the average, whose right arm had once been amputated at the shoulder. His left arm was covered in a red rash and had a tremor; both could be due to quicksilver poisoning. His hand, which lay on the white blanket, was pallid, with flaking skin that came from the caress of the tears, and fingernails stained a blotchy vermilion.

The left side and lower half of his face was covered by a burnished platinum mask that curved across below the right ear. From there, a thin band of metal ran around the back of his round head and another band across his forehead. The mouth opening of the mask was like a downwards-curving crescent moon. His exposed right eye was bloodshot and had an unfocused, mad-looking stare.

'Someone's coming,' whispered Meriwen.

A plump, red-gowned healer of some fifty years hurried in, carrying a cup with a straw in it. She gestured to Flydd and the twins to stand back, bent forwards with the cup and poked the straw in through the mouth hole. Jal-Nish made a revolting sucking sound as he drank.

'Foul!' he said in a thick, slurred voice. 'Disembowelled people for less.'

'If you want to get better you'll drink the lot,' said the healer, whose mass of silver-grey hair was woven around a globular shape at the back, the size of a pumpkin. 'Your next operation is in half an hour.'

'Incompetent fools! Why can't you do it in one go?'

'You're too sick. It'd kill you.'

'It'd be better than this.'

The healer turned to Flydd. 'Who are you?' she said briskly. Her rosy, oval face looked tired.

'Lurimon Gant, Chief Mancer,' said Flydd, imitating Gant's voice. 'What's your name?'

'Walis. I'm the Principal Healer.'

'What's the operation?'

'Many droplets of hot quicksilver have burned into his face. We have to get them all out ...'

'Or he'll die?' said Liliwen, eagerly.

Walis stared at her. 'Insomnia, headaches, memory loss, muscle weakness ... madness ... death. All are possible.' She went out.

An insane Jal-Nish did not bear thinking about. Flydd took out Gant's pink handkerchief, wiped his sweaty face and put it away. His eyes roved around the room. Where were Gatherer and Reaper? Being the size of grapefruit, the tears were not easily hidden.

Ah! A heavy steel plate, half an inch thick and a foot square, was fixed to the stone wall with four bolts. A chain ran from a ring in the centre of the plate, down to the floor and up under the covers to twin lumps in the bed beside Jal-Nish. On his other side, a small table held a large glass jug of water and a cup with a straw in it.

'Did you finish them?' said Jal-Nish, weakly.

'Flydd, Klarm and Troist are dead,' said Flydd. 'I sent you an image of the bodies.'

'Image be damned! Got to see severed, *recognisable* heads.'

'The other renegades set off a forest fire and the bodies burned.'

Jal-Nish made a seething sound. 'What about Yggur?'

Flydd put an apologetic and anxious tone into his voice. 'He got away.'

'You incompetent fool! He was the one I wanted most.'

'He's damaged. He won't be hard to find.'

'How damaged?' Jal-Nish said eagerly.

'I blasted him with a reversion curse. He went into uncontrollable convulsions, then reverted to a previous ailment of the mind. He barely knew himself.'

'Did he now?' said Jal-Nish. 'Yet he escaped; he *fooled* you.'

'He still had power,' said Flydd, in a defensive manner. 'And when pressed, he fought desperately. In the battle all my – your soldiers were killed, and I was struck down. I recovered but the sergeant, Fyn-Mah and the pilot got Yggur away. I'm sorry.'

Jal-Nish waved a frail hand, as if in dismissal. He coughed, a spasm wracked him from head to foot and he groaned.

Behind Flydd, Liliwen was making a sound like a kettle about to boil over; her hands were untied and Meriwen was struggling to control her. Liliwen broke free, slammed her shoulder into Flydd, knocking him aside, and went for Jal-Nish. Her fingers closed around his throat; she pressed her thumbs into his windpipe and began to squeeze.

'No!' cried Flydd, trying to hold her back.

Jal-Nish's platinum mask was knocked off, exposing the full horror of the two-year-old injuries that had never healed. Three jagged gouges ran from ear to mouth, under which the flesh had grown back in ugly lumps and depressions. The scars were spotted with pus-filled boils, his left eye was a purple socket filled with veins the size of earthworms, his nose a crusted hole linked by more scars to a twisted mouth that would not close. Overlying those old injuries were hundreds of little red lumps, charred on top, where the quicksilver droplets had burned deep into his flesh.

Liliwen froze, staring at the monster in his ruin. Her hands relaxed and Flydd dragged her backwards. Jal-Nish was gasping and choking, his bloodshot eye darting from her to Flydd. He looked confused, bewildered, a sick shadow of the man he had been. He tried to speak but could not.

'He killed my parents,' said Liliwen. 'It's my right!'

'Everyone has the right to kill in self-defence,' Flydd said quietly, 'and to protect their loved ones. But strangling Jal-Nish in cold blood is murder and you're still a child. It would utterly ruin you. I can't let you do it.'

'If we're still *children*,' she said with gut-punching logic, 'why did you bring us into such danger?'

Flydd had no answer. He was a fool.

'So,' she said softly, yet shaking with a rage so intense that blood was welling up under her fingernails, 'After coming all this way *you're going to let him get away with it?*'

'I'm not. Go down the other end of the room, both of you.'

Liliwen did not move.

'I can't do it until you do,' he added.

Jal-Nish was still gasping, his red eye flicking back and forth as he tried to understand. Meriwen, who clearly did *not* want to see the business done, dragged Liliwen back through the folding doors into the clutter of cupboards and book-cases. Flydd approached his enemy, not liking what he was about to do one bit.

He had killed many times during the war. As a scrutator he had even killed in cold blood when the need had been desperate. But never before had he murdered a helpless man and, monster though Jal-Nish was, it was not going to be as easy as Flydd had thought to put him down. Yet it had to be done.

Flydd flexed his fingers, took three steps and bent over Jal-Nish.

'Who is she?' Jal-Nish said plaintively.

He had always been the epitome of self-control; he had never given up despite taking injuries that would have destroyed most other men. He never lost sight of his goal, nor relaxed his utter determination to achieve it.

This pathetic, confused, shrivelled little man was not a shadow of the Jal-Nish who had swept into the celebrations at Ashmode eleven days ago and, within minutes, turned glorious victory into ruinous defeat. He was very ill. Again Flydd hesitated.

No! As a former scrutator, Jal-Nish was trained to shape every situation to his advantage. If he looked pathetic, ill and beaten, he was using it to turn the tables. He would never change.

'She's the daughter of Troist and Yara,' said Flydd.

'How – get here?'

Flydd released the illusion of Lurimon Gant and looked himself again. 'I brought her here, to avenge her parents.'

'You – *Flydd!*' Jal-Nish gasped. There was naked terror in his eye now.

Flydd slid his fingers around Jal-Nish's throat and squeezed. Jal-Nish convulsed and the covers slipped down. The steel chain Flydd had noted previously ran to the centre of the heavy gold chain linking the two grapefruit-sized tears, which were inside their black velvet bags. Before Flydd could stop him, Jal-Nish's red finger-nails slid into the left-hand bag. It must have been Gatherer, for Flydd heard the desperate cry for help.

Rudrigg – Flydd – HERE!

Flydd squeezed harder. How difficult could it be to kill a helpless man?

A concealed side door was flung open and Rudrigg, a big, florid-faced warrior with a lopsided jaw, bristly brown hair and upturned nostrils like twin mine tunnels, burst in. He took in the scene – Jal-Nish gasping, Flydd's hands around his throat – then drew a four-foot-long scimitar and raced to his master's defence.

Flydd hurled the heavy glass jug at his face. Rudrigg instinctively tried to block it with the scimitar but the jug smashed; water and shards of glass hit him in the face and blood welled from half a dozen cuts. Flydd grabbed the trident staff and raced down through the double doors into the maze of furniture.

'Get out of sight!' he hissed to Liliwen and Meriwen, who were peeping out from behind a cupboard. They ducked under a bed; he went the other way.

Rudrigg wiped away blood from a long cut on his forehead, snatched a bone saw from the table of surgical instruments and hurled it at Flydd. The handle cracked him painfully on the back of the head. Flydd tossed three chairs at Rudrigg, one after another; he hacked them out of his path with savage blows. He was driving Flydd into a corner, and he must not be trapped or he would die there, then Meriwen and Liliwen a minute later.

Flydd considered attacking with mancery but none of the little spells he had the power to do would stop Rudrigg. As he turned around another cupboard, he caught the movement from the corner of his eye and hurled himself backwards. The howling scimitar missed his forehead by the thickness of a fingernail and smashed the cupboard beside him to splinters, spraying them everywhere, including Flydd's left arm and cheek.

He scurried under a table and out behind a bookcase. He went to dive beneath a bed, realised that Meriwen and Liliwen were there and threw himself the other way. He was gasping; every breath tore at his throat and he could not keep it up much longer. Rudrigg was many years younger and a lot stronger.

Desperation gave Flydd an idea. He tore down a bed curtain, snapped the wooden rod in two and thrust the longer piece into a side pocket. Now, drawing on the staff, he cast the most reckless illusion of his life. An illusion of Jal-Nish himself, wearing the platinum mask.

The illusion was too good. Instantly he felt Jal-Nish's pain, so all-pervasive that it was impossible to focus on anything else, and a roiling nausea that made him want to throw up. He also sensed the corruption of the man, inside and out – and it was so foul that he froze for a second.

Flydd dropped the staff on the bed and, using every ounce of will he had left, forced himself to endure the horror of Jal-Nish's mind. It was necessary; it made his illusion more real. He emerged behind Rudrigg, and coughed.

Rudrigg whirled, swinging the scimitar up for a killing blow, then locked his arm. 'L-lord,' he choked. He wiped more blood out of his eyes. 'You're better?'

Flydd could see the confusion in him, and even a hint of doubt, but instant obedience was so ingrained in Jal-Nish's people that Rudrigg dared not show doubt. He lowered the blade.

'I am now,' said Flydd, and thrust his improvised skewer into Rudrigg's throat.

Flydd sprang backwards, reaching for the staff. Rudrigg's arm swung down, the scimitar hacking deep into the polished marble floor, then fell. Flydd turned and Meriwen was behind him, a look of utter horror on her young face.

'You just – you just –' She could not get it out. Could not come to terms with it.

'Kill or be killed,' said Flydd. 'Us, or him.'

'Yes,' she whispered. 'Yes, I suppose so.'

'Where's Liliwen?'

'Kill or be killed.'

17

F lydd ran back to Jal-Nish. Liliwen was by the bed looking down at him. He was scarlet in the face and sucking at the air but did not seem able to draw breath. She was gasping, her breast heaving, her face blanched. She raised her hands.

Before she could touch him Walis entered, followed by three assistants. She took one look at Jal-Nish, heaved the bedcovers off and gave him an almighty thump to the breastbone. He sucked in a breath that seemed to go in forever.

'Get out of the way!' she snapped. She worked Jal-Nish's arm up and down. His throat bubbled, then he breathed out explosively, spraying smelly green muck onto her apron.

Liliwen took a step backwards, but stopped. 'He's killed thousands of innocent people,' she said furiously. 'He murdered my mother and father.' Her voice went shrill. '*And you're healing him*! How can you live with yourself?'

'It's not a healer's job to judge,' said Walis.

Liliwen faced the bigger woman down. 'Jal-Nish owns the judges! He writes his own laws! You've got to let him die.'

'We all have our jobs to do, and mine is to heal.' But Walis avoided Liliwen's eye.

Walis turned, took in Flydd's true appearance and stopped dead. 'You're not Gant. Who are you?'

'He's Xervish Flydd,' said Meriwen, from behind him.

'The scrutator who led us to victory in the war?' said Walis, her eyes shining.

'I'm Flydd,' he said, 'but I relaxed my guard too soon.'

'You're a good man.' Her eyes searched his face, a trifle wistfully. She looked down at her patient and could not disguise a shudder.

Jal-Nish groaned and groped for the tears. Walis picked them up by the golden chain and slung them over the head of the bed, the steel chain rattling. As she did, an illusion was stripped from Jal-Nish's naked body and Liliwen let out a gasp of revulsion.

From the hips down, his skin resembled the hand he inserted into the tears – it was pallid, flaking and scribbled with bulging varicose veins, though they were grey rather than blue. His flesh had withered away; his legs were knobbly bones with so little muscle on them it was a wonder he could walk at all, while his organs of generation were shrivelled, flaking bumps.

Then Jal-Nish's eye opened and Flydd saw the rage there, undiminished. Whether it was keeping him alive, or the tears were, he was still deadly. If he recovered he would hunt them to the end. He would *never* give up.

He had to die. Flydd was considering how it might be done when Walis threw the blanket over Jal-Nish and the healers surrounded him. Flydd's fingers clenched on his staff. To get to him now, some of the healers would have to die. Perhaps all of them.

Many of the scrutators he'd known were capable of killing good people in order to destroy someone bad, but he could not. It was over and he had lost.

Walis, her professional self again, scooped Jal-Nish up in his blankets. 'No!' he croaked. 'Not again.'

'The quicksilver is slowly killing you,' she said. 'We've got to cut it all out.'

'I'd sooner die than suffer that again.'

'I'm giving you another dose of *gixil*. When you wake, it'll be done.'

'Gixil takes me out of my mind. I can't lose control; *I won't!*'

Walis nodded to the second healer, who thrust a green tablet into Jal-Nish's ruined mouth. He tried to spit it out but she put her palm over his mouth and Walis covered what was left of his nose until he was forced to swallow. Within seconds his eyes closed and his head slumped sideways.

Walis checked inside his mouth to make sure, then carried him away. But at the door she stopped. 'I'm very sorry,' she said to Liliwen, and went out. The other healers followed.

Liliwen spun on one foot. 'I had my hands on his throat!' she cried. 'I was ready to do it. Why did you stop me?'

'You would have regretted his murder for the rest of your life,' said Flydd.

'It wasn't murder, *it was justice*, and now it will never be done. Every evil thing Jal-Nish does from this moment – every innocent life he takes, every family he shatters, every child he orphans – will be *your fault*. I hate you, Flydd! *I hate you!*'

'I would have ended him,' he said lamely, 'had Rudrigg not attacked.'

'You had no right! *I* had the right.'

'Oh, I had the right,' said Flydd vehemently. 'As much right as anyone in this world.'

Gatherer and Reaper still hung over the head of the bed. For the first time since Jal-Nish had taken them two years ago, killing everyone with him to keep them secret, the tears were unprotected – or were they?

'Bolt the main door,' he said. 'Hurry!'

'What's wrong?' said Meriwen.

'Nothing, but I'm going to try the tears and I can't be caught doing it.'

'Do you know how?'

'No.'

'What if Gatherer calls the guards?'

'We'll be in a spot of bother,' he said laconically.

Liliwen looked as unconvinced as Flydd felt, but she and Meriwen heaved the two heavy door bolts into their sockets. Flydd checked the small room Rudrigg had come through, but it was empty and had no other exit. He edged towards the tears, his heart racing. Were they watching him now, or listening?

The steel plate was bolted into solid rock and the bolts and chain were protected by a charm he could not break. Could he use the tears to find a way out? He dared not touch Reaper, the killing tear, but it was worth the risk to probe Gatherer.

Liliwen and Meriwen came back. Liliwen had dried her tears but she was still so angry that she could barely speak. The passion of youth! It had withered in him long ago.

'I can't take the tears,' he said, breathing heavily.

'Can you destroy them?'

'No one knows how to destroy nihilium – or even if it *can* be destroyed.'

'I'll bet the tears know.'

'If Gatherer does, it would have hidden that secret very carefully, even from its master.'

'We came to kill Jal-Nish,' she said bitterly, 'and we failed. We came to steal the tears or destroy them and we failed at that too. We've risked our lives for nothing – and now we're going to die.'

'We're not dead yet.'

'If the guards don't already know we tried to kill Jal-Nish, they soon will.'

Meriwen was silent, staring at the tears. 'Is that one Gatherer?' She pointed to the left-hand tear, which was a pale, reflective silver.

'Yes.'

Reaper was darker, with ominous carmine plumes rising and falling in its depths, and a screechy whine came from it. Then, before Flydd could stop Meriwen, she reached out and touched Gatherer with a fingertip.

'Don't!' he yelled.

She drew back. 'I saw him!' she said wonderingly. 'His picture is burned into the left-hand tear.'

'What picture?'

'The true Jal-Nish we saw when Walis pulled the sheet off. What's a picture like that doing in the tears?'

'I'm not sure what you're saying.'

'If Jal-Nish controls the tears, why doesn't the picture show him dressed and masked, looking powerful and important?'

'That's a very good question,' said Flydd. 'A *brilliant* question.'

Why would Jal-Nish, who was obsessed with appearances, lay himself so bare at the very core of his power? He would not if he had any choice, so clearly he did not. Why not?

'Why does the image need to be there at all?' he mused. 'Can it be how Gatherer identifies its master?' He started. Now what did that suggest?

'What does he use Gatherer for?' said Meriwen.

The tantalising possibility slipped from Flydd's mind. 'It collects whatever information he's instructed it to get.'

'And he uses it to broadcast terror messages to the world. Like the hangings ... in the town square.' Meriwen's voice cracked; she rubbed her swollen eyes.

'Those too.'

'There's more than one way to destroy a man,' she said softly. 'Perhaps a better way than killing him.'

'Go on,' said Flydd.

'Do you know how Jal-Nish broadcasts those terror messages?'

'I'll have a look in a minute.'

'Can *you* use the tears?'

Flydd could feel their time running out. Hurry! 'I believe so, though it could expose all my weaknesses, *and all my lies*, to Gatherer.'

'Do you have to be a mancer to use the tears?' said Liliwen.

'Another good question. They're not magical, you know. Not the way a wizard's staff, or an enchanted ring, is.'

'What are they?'

'A phenomenal source of power.'

'Then why can't you use it to get rid of Jal-Nish?' said Meriwen.

'When the tears first formed, they were blank, but in the two years Jal-Nish has held them he's imprinted them with his own mancery, to make sure they do what he instructs them to. And,' Flydd realised, 'there lies his weakness.'

'How can you say that when he's the most powerful person alive?'

'A brilliant craftsman can create a masterpiece even if he only has poor tools, but a mediocre craftsman can't create a masterpiece with the best tools in the world.'

Meriwen frowned. 'What are you saying?'

'Jal-Nish is ruthless and determined, but he's always been a third-rate mancer. Therefore the way he's enchanted the tears must also be third-rate.'

'You still haven't answered the question,' said Liliwen.

'Using the tears is dangerous, both to the body and the soul, and they take their toll according to the way their master has shaped them. Because Jal-Nish uses them for domination and destruction, the tears are corrupting his mind and destroying his body. And anyone else who uses them also risks being corrupted and damaged.'

'What if someone were to use the tears to a noble end? Could that change them to the good?'

'If you're talking about yourself, the answer is no.'

'Why not?'

'Jal-Nish shaped them to his needs with *mancery*. Only a far greater mancer could reshape them to a better purpose.'

'One like you.'

'Perhaps, if I had weeks to work on them,' said Flydd. 'But in the minutes we've got left there's nothing I can do.'

'Suppose someone wanted to do a *single* good thing with them,' Liliwen persisted. 'Could they?'

'Possibly, though that person would need to be as strong-willed and determined as Jal-Nish himself.'

'I – am,' she said softly. '*I am.*'

'And she would need to be solely focused on doing the right and noble thing.'

'Not revenge,' said Meriwen.

'Not revenge,' echoed Flydd.

18

Flydd stood beside the empty bed, the clock ticking in his head, vainly trying to think of a way to get the girls out alive before the guards broke in. Meriwen appeared and gave him Rudrigg's scimitar and sheath. He went to buckle it on but the four-foot weapon was way too long. He slung it across his back.

The half-formed idea of ten minutes ago flashed back into his mind. The image of Jal-Nish, as he really was, must be how Gatherer identified him before it acted on his instructions. Could Flydd change the image – or displace it – while Jal-Nish was unconscious?

How long would it take for the healers to remove the remaining quicksilver from his wounds? Perhaps not long at all. There was no time to think things through; Flydd had to act now.

He slipped his left hand into Gatherer, very gingerly, and examined Jal-Nish's image – his *identity*. He expected to be attacked but nothing happened. Why not? Could it be because Jal-Nish, being obsessed with control, dared not hand over power to the tears he had shaped in his own image? Or was it because he had never imagined a situation where the tears would be out of his control? Or both?

Flydd laughed aloud. The twins stared at him in astonishment.

'Remember how we talked about his weaknesses, in the boat?' said Flydd.

Meriwen nodded.

'And his greatest weakness is his terror of being betrayed,' Flydd added.

'Yes?'

'The tears can't act of their own accord because Jal-Nish won't allow them *any* control. They only do what he tells them to and, since he's unconscious, they're not getting any orders. It's our way in!'

He went down behind the folding doors and cast the illusion of Lurimon Gant on himself again. Flydd returned, slipped his hand into Gatherer, then slowly moved Gant's image towards the place that Jal-Nish's identity currently occupied. It was incredibly hard work, equivalent to carrying a load of iron ingots up a ladder. After a minute, Flydd's heart was galloping and sweat was streaming down his back. After two minutes his back was bent under the strain and his knees were wobbly.

He had to stop and support himself on the side table. His mind seemed to be floating, as if he were slightly drunk; it was a struggle to concentrate. But scrutators were trained to overcome the frailties of their flesh. He worked through one of the self-control exercises he'd learned decades ago, and managed to regain focus.

Flydd went back into Gatherer but found a barrier he could not overcome; he needed more power and dared not take it from the tears. 'Pass – the – staff,' he panted. It was all he could do to say those three words; the tears were taking a heavy toll.

Liliwen handed Gant's staff to him. Flydd drew power but it was not enough and there was only one way to get more – a very dangerous way. Dare he?

There was no choice. With his free hand he peeled back the platinum foil from the persona, touched it and drew power, hard.

Ugh? it said dazedly, as if suddenly woken from a deep sleep.

He pressed the foil down, looked into Gatherer again, leapt the barrier and saw the images of Jal-Nish's most important enemies – himself, Klarm, Yggur and Troist, among others. What to do? Flydd dared not tamper with his own image; it might arouse suspicion.

Quick, quick! The bolted door could be discovered at any moment. He moved Jal-Nish's identity down among his other enemies, put Gant's identity in his place as the master of the tears, and slipped out of Gatherer.

'What was that all about?' said Liliwen, who had armed herself with a wickedly sharp surgical blade.

Flydd could barely stand up. He put both hands on the bed to support himself until his heart steadied, then led the twins away where he could not be overheard.

'When Jal-Nish regains consciousness after his operation and tries to use the tears, I'm hoping they'll reject him, or even attack him as an enemy. No, I mustn't expect too much; he might have a back door into the tears. He's bound to overcome what I've done, in time.'

'Hopefully, a very long time,' said Liliwen. 'Not that it'll help us –'

You killed him! the persona shrieked, so shrilly that Flydd could not think. *You murdered Master Gant. Guards, to Jal-Nish's room now!*

He wrenched out the platinum ball, pressed down a little gap he had inadvertently left in the foil, and the shrieking stopped.

'What was *that*?' whispered Meriwen.

'The persona. I took a risk and it went horribly wrong. It's called the guards.'

'And there's no way out.'

Pain speared up his right arm. The back of his neck throbbed, then a blistering agony churned through his head. 'None – I can think – of.'

'Then let's make our lives mean something.'

'Rudrigg?' a man called from outside. 'Are you there?' There was a thump on the door. 'Rudrigg?'

'Break it down!' said a second man. Shortly the stone door was attacked with hammers.

'What are we going to do?' said Liliwen. 'We can't just stand here, waiting to be killed.'

The crashing grew louder. The door, though massive, could be broken with enough force. The attack became furious; the foot-thick stone was shaking with every blow.

'There must be a lot of them,' said Meriwen.

'Jal-Nish's guards will get the blame for our attack,' said Flydd. 'Catching us means life or death to them.'

'And death to us,' said Liliwen.

'Unless I can think of a miracle.' His inexcusable folly, bringing the twins here, had brought them undone.

A tremendous crash formed a hairline crack in the door.

'They'll be through in ten minutes,' said Meriwen. 'Fifteen at the most.'

'Yes,' he said dully. He slumped into a chair, shaking. The throbbing in his head was clouding his mind and dimming his sight, and there were shooting pains in the hand he had put into Gatherer. The skin was as red as a bad sunburn, and his hand felt overheated and prickly. How on earth had Jal-Nish endured it all this time?

'And then they'll –'

'If we were to live –' Flydd dragged in a breath, '– after attacking Jal-Nish, his guards would die the foulest deaths anyone can imagine.'

'Are you all right, Xervish?'

'No. Gatherer – exhausting – painful.' His voice was slurred and he could do nothing to control it.

'Then there's no hope.'

'Fight to – last breath …' His head sank to his knees.

Liliwen and Meriwen conferred in low voices, then Liliwen called out, though he could not tell if it was a cry for help or a furious accusation. She seemed to be arguing but he could not hear, could not focus. Shortly afterwards he heard Meriwen's slightly lower voice. She was speaking slowly and carefully, enunciating each word, though he did not get the sense of what she was saying.

Time drifted; had a minute passed, or ten?

Liliwen was back, her brown eyes searching his face. 'I – I'm sorry for those terrible things I said. I know you acted for the best.'

'Sorry – too.'

Another mighty crash opened the crack across the door to the width of an inch. Jal-Nish's troops were visible through it now, swinging heavy hammers. They would soon break through but he could not summon the energy to care.

'Mister Flydd?' hissed Meriwen, beckoning from beyond the dividing doors. What was she doing down there?

Liliwen helped him up and he staggered down through the maze of furniture. Walis was in the far corner, her kindly face distressed, her fingers knotted together.

Flydd blinked at her. 'How – get in?'

'Habna built this place during the terrors of the Clysm; she made sure there was always a hidden escape route.' Walis reached out to him with both hands. 'Scrutator, you must understand, the healer's code is unyielding. We treat every patient, no matter who they are or what they may have done, to the very best of our abilities.'

'I ... understand.'

'Gossip isn't always true; the names of good people have often been blackened by lies. It's not our job to weigh truth or falsehood, nor judge right or wrong.'

'No, it's not.'

'But I *know* Jal-Nish is evil,' said Walis. 'I've treated many of his victims.'

'Umm?' Flydd had no idea where this was going.

'And I know about your ... troubles. Your pain.'

He assumed she meant from touching the tears.

'You came in the secret back way from Oystercatcher's Landing,' Walis said. 'Show me your map.'

Meriwen produced it. With a blue pencil, Walis traced a convoluted passage through the maze of tunnels.

'I have a boat, *here*.' She pointed to the end. 'It's small but sound. Take it.'

'We can't pay –'

Walis shook her silvery head. 'It's my amends. We must do our best, for *all* our patients. That's all that counts in the end. Take this.' She gave him a long, narrow white lozenge. 'Chew and swallow.'

He did so, and felt the pain and confusion lift a little.

'And these. One a week. They may assist ... lower down.'

She handed him a small, square black box. Flydd had no idea what she was talking about, but slipped the box into a pocket.

Finally she pressed a ring with three keys into his hand. 'Lock each door behind you, and when you're at sea, drop the keys in deep water. They must not know how you got away –'

'Or who helped us,' said Flydd. He clasped her hands in his own, anxious about the risk she was taking.

She pulled free as an almighty crash was followed by the thud of falling stone. 'This way.'

Walis slipped into the corner and behind a tall bookcase, where a small marble door, identical to the walls around it, stood ajar. Had it been closed it would have been indistinguishable from the wall. There was barely room enough to open it all the way. The twins grabbed their gear and passed through.

'Lock it!' Walis said. 'The green key.'

Flydd did so. Walis pointed left along a narrow corridor cut through mottled red and blue marble.

'Thank you,' said Flydd, overcome. 'You've saved our lives.'

'You're my patient,' she said, as if justifying her actions to herself.

They headed left, into darkness, going as fast as they could. Walis went right and was lost to sight.

'How did she know I was ill?' said Flydd.

'Not now,' said Liliwen.

A minute later he heard hammers attacking the marble door. A couple of minutes after that, a crash as it flew to pieces. They ran on, but Flydd was struggling again, his knees giving with each stride.

They stopped at a crossway and he made a glimmer of light to check the map. 'Memorise the next sequence of turns. Any light will give us away.'

They continued. Judging by the path Walis had drawn, the exit was at least an hour away. He would not make it.

'They've found our trail and they're gaining,' Liliwen said quietly, after they had been going for a quarter of an hour. They were at the top of a long, left-curving stair. The treads, cut from blue-black marble with round inclusions like red cherries, were steep, far apart and worn smooth in the centres. 'What are we going to do?'

'Help Mister Flydd down,' said Meriwen. 'I'll come in a minute.'

Liliwen took Flydd's left arm and helped him down one step, then another. On the third his knees buckled and he almost fell.

'Sorry.' He felt utterly useless. 'Leave me. Save yourselves.'

She sniffed, crouched, put her right shoulder under his left arm and, taking half his weight, got him down the next dozen steps without either of them falling. But he could hear their pursuers coming ever closer to the top of the steps.

'What's Meriwen doing? They'll catch her.'

'No, they won't,' said Liliwen, though he could hear the fear in her voice.

They continued, but Meriwen did not come. Liliwen stopped halfway, forty-five steps down, staring up into the darkness.

'I can get down the rest of the way,' said Flydd. 'If you want to go up –'

She gave another scornful sniff, heaved on him and they continued down. The thunder of soldiers' boots grew louder. Flydd's guts knotted themselves in guilt. Then Meriwen came running down the steps, light-footed. Her face was flushed and her eyes alight.

'Come on!' She squeezed past and took his other arm.

As they reached the bottom, lantern light appeared at the top. 'There they are!' The troops raced down.

The first man had only descended half a dozen steps when his feet slipped from under him and he fell, bouncing a third of the way before he came to rest, groaning. A second man fell, then a third, and Flydd heard bones break. The fourth soldier tried to stop; he teetered, arms waving, slipped and went skidding down feet-first, the back of his head thudding into the edge of every step until he crashed into his injured fellows.

The rest of the guards stopped. Someone shone a lantern down on the steps, and cursed.

'I greased a dozen steps with a jar of lanolin,' said Meriwen as they slipped away.

19

W ithin ten minutes Flydd could hear the enemy behind them again. They were slower this time, presumably checking for tricks and traps, but he had little hope of outrunning them. He felt sure Walis's boat was a long way off.

They reached the second door, a black marble one with veins of blue and white. Here the tunnel had a sour smell as if the contents of a drain was seeping in, and there were brown stains down the walls. After they had gone through, Liliwen began to fiddle with the latch.

'What are you up to now?' said her sister.

'Gumming needles underneath. When they grab it, *ow*!' Meriwen grinned, closed the door and locked it on the other side. 'Go ahead.'

'No, you go ahead.'

'Why?' Meriwen said suspiciously.

Liliwen produced a brown bottle from her bag and began to fix it above the door. 'Smelling salts. When they open the door, it smashes. Don't suppose it'll hinder them for long, but you never know ...'

Flydd chuckled. The girls were enjoying their little competition. It was good to see them smiling. 'There should be a prize for whoever holds the enemy off the longest.'

'There is,' said Liliwen. 'We survive!'

The smiles faded. Meriwen wedged the door with bits of rock. Flydd tentatively tried the staff, hoping to put a seal on the door, but it hurt so much he had to abandon the attempt.

On they went, and on, feeling their way in the dark. Meriwen greased a second stair with the last of the lanolin but caught no more prey. The floor had ankle-deep pools for the next quarter of a mile, and once the pursuit came close enough for a mancer to blast at them through the dark, spattering hot, muddy water on their backs.

They reached the third door and Flydd managed a glimmer from the staff, barely enough to illuminate the keyhole. Meriwen pushed the third key in but could not get it to turn. The mancer blasted again and orange light seared down the tunnel, dislodging loose rock from the roof with a clatter.

'What's wrong with the blasted thing?' Meriwen moaned.

'Give me a go.' Liliwen pushed harder and something gave. 'Keyhole's clogged.' She twisted and the door moved.

The three of them heaved and it opened a crack, enough to see. It was cut from a slab of white quartzite and hung on heavy brass hinges that gave a gritty squeak as they turned. The light outside, after an hour and a half in dark tunnels, was dazzling. A blast of cold air struck Flydd in the face; it smelled of the salt sea, rotting seaweed and fishy seagull poo.

The twins pushed through onto a doorstep only two feet across. A winding, rock-cut path ran down a steep bluff, though Flydd could not see where it ended. He tried to lock the door but his hands were shaking so badly he could not get the key in the hole. Liliwen snatched it from him, found the right key and jammed it in the keyhole. The lock would not turn.

'Leave the damn thing!' said Flydd, barely able to stand up.

'We promised to lock the doors.' Liliwen thumped the door with her shoulder again and again, and finally the key turned.

He wiped sweat from his brow, tottered a couple of steps down the track and his legs buckled. Liliwen grabbed the staff as it fell. Meriwen put her shoulder under his left arm, but his weight pulled her off balance and they nearly went over the side.

She had to support him all the way. It was a couple of hundred feet down, and frighteningly steep. If either of them stumbled they would crash down the bluff, breaking all their bones, and die when they hit bottom.

Liliwen was still where she had caught the staff, crouched down. 'What's she doing?' said Flydd.

Meriwen did not know.

After several desperate moments, and much gasping from Liliwen and grunting from himself, she got him down onto a small, crescent-shaped rock platform by the sea. A little skiff sat there, only twelve feet long, with a furled handkerchief for a sail. The water was protected by a long, finger-like headland, though out to sea the waves were menacingly big.

Liliwen picked her way down. They shoved the boat in and held it while Flydd toppled head-first onto the rear bench. Liliwen snorted. Meriwen hacked at the water with the oars, generating little forward motion. Flydd unfurled the sail and the boat moved slowly out.

Boom! The white door was shattered into pieces that came bouncing and clattering down the bluff. Fist-sized chunks plonked into the water beside them. The guards, now reduced to nine, burst out and came hurtling down the path. The leading man stumbled over something, caught the other foot in a crack, fell forwards and his trapped leg snapped like a dry stick. The other guards went around him and continued down.

'What happened there?' said Flydd.

'Trip line,' said Liliwen. 'I'd have thought they'd learned their lesson the first time.'

'If we get away, they're doomed,' said Flydd. 'And so are their families.'

Liliwen shivered. 'So whatever happens, Jal-Nish is going to put innocent people to death. *I should have strangled him!*'

The last guard, who carried a crossbow, went to his knees on the doorstep and fired over the heads of his fellows. The bolt went wide of the skiff by ten feet. The guards on the platform hurled rocks. The mancer cursed them out of the way and pointed a star-tipped staff at Flydd.

He tried vainly to block the blast but it struck the trident staff, jarring it out of his hand. He picked it up and tried to blast back but there was no power left that he could reach.

The mancer blasted again, slamming Flydd painfully against the mast. He had to do something. Dare he try the persona? He touched it gingerly. That was another mistake.

Die, you bastard, die!

Flydd felt a shearing pain in the centre of his skull, then scalding heat and a belly blow that drove him backwards, leaving him hanging half over the stern without the strength to pull himself back in.

Meriwen caught him by the collar and held him; Liliwen dragged him back onto his bench. He slumped there, head throbbing, barely able to see. The boat heeled over in a gust of wind. Liliwen cried out.

'Grab – helm!' gasped Flydd.

She did so. He could sense anxiety radiating from her but could do nothing about it. The boat was curving around, racing towards the long, jagged headland.

She swung the tiller but it made no difference – they were heeling over so far that it was out of the water.

'I don't know what to do,' she gasped. 'We're going to hit the rocks.'

The soldiers thought so too; he made out their blurred figures running towards the place where the boat would hit. Flydd heaved himself along the bench, caught the ropes and swung the sail with all his strength. The boat heeled over the other way, slinging gallons of cold water into their faces.

'Zorry,' he said thickly. 'Gan't zeem to ged id ride.'

Liliwen flung the tiller over hard, which made things worse. Flydd swung the sail again, managing it a bit better this time, and the boat curved away from the rocks in a hail of stones.

'Grouch down! Zmall dargets.'

The twins scrunched themselves up at the stern. A crossbow bolt embedded itself in the mast as the boat raced away. A parting blast from the mancer boiled water to their left. Flydd managed a sharp left turn around the headland and they shot out into the dubious safety of the open sea.

The archer kept firing but the range was long now and he made no more hits. Soon mist and flying spray obscured the bluff and the doomed guards. Flydd scooped cold water onto his face until he started to feel better, then turned south.

'Remind me to teach you how to sail,' he said, slumping against the stern.

'Where are we going?'

'Somewhere in Meldorin. Zile perhaps ...'

'Are we Jal-Nish's greatest enemies now?' said Liliwen.

'Oh yes. We'd better pray he doesn't have an air-floater on Qwale.'

'He could call one from anywhere,' said Meriwen.

'Not until he gets control of the tears. Before that happens we've got to disappear. Do you know where your aunty Mira is?'

'She went to Sith.'

'Why would she go all that way?' said Flydd. 'Sith is almost abandoned.'

'She lived there when she was little. It used to be a proud, free city, a place where law and justice mattered,' said Meriwen. 'Mira likes to think about what might have been.'

'Can we get to Sith in this?' said Liliwen.

'It's one hell of a sail in a glorified rowboat,' said Flydd. 'But –'

'Bigger miracles have happened,' said Meriwen. 'Thanks to you.'

'Thanks to our team. As good as any I've ever worked with ...'

'But?' said Liliwen.

Flydd was thinking about their future. Whatever happened, the twins' lives had been changed forever, and they would be forever scarred by the traumas they had endured and the terrible things they had seen and done. And it was far from over.

'When you find Mira, you'll have to go into exile, as far away as possible.'

'Home is where we're together,' said Meriwen, linking arms with her sister.

He laid the staff on the floor of the boat and put the wrapped persona beside it.

'What are you doing?' said Meriwen.

'I promised to reunite the persona with its master.'

'But Gant is dead.'

Flydd dropped the trident staff overboard and peeled the platinum foil off the persona.

No, no! it shrieked.

'A promise is a promise.' He sent it the same way.

'But now you're powerless,' said Meriwen.

'Better no power than one that wants me dead. And I've still got my wits.'

'Feeble though they are.' She laughed.

Flydd did too. Her cheerful insult established the new reality. In a way, the three of them were equals now, and he would not have had it any other way.

He let out a great sigh. He just wanted to sleep, but first he had to teach them the rudiments of sailing. And find out –

'One thing puzzles me,' he said. 'How Walis knew I was ill from using the tears.' His gaze fell on Liliwen's right hand, which was red and blistered. 'You didn't!'

She gave him a defiant stare. 'I called her through Gatherer.'

'How did you get her to change her mind?'

'I worked on her guilty feelings, then told her how ill you were. As a healer, it was her duty to save your life ... and so she came ... but the only way to save you was to help you escape.'

There was something else; something disturbing. 'Walis said something about my troubles. What was she talking about?'

Meriwen flushed the brightest crimson he had ever seen on a human face.

Liliwen could not look at Flydd. 'I had to gain her healer's sympathy,' she muttered.

'You didn't tell her about – *you wouldn't!*'

'About what Ghoor's torturer did to you, *lower down.*'

'You little cow!' he roared. 'What right have you got to gossip about my private business?'

She looked him full in the face. 'I learned my trade from a cunning and manipulative scrutator. One of the best, and I'm not sorry. I did what it took.'

After a long, considering pause, he said, 'So you did.' Flydd was quite disarmed. 'So you did.

'Well,' he went on, 'we didn't rid the world of Jal-Nish, and we didn't destroy the tears.'

'You did something to them though, didn't you?' said Meriwen.

He told them how he had replaced Jal-Nish's identity with Gant's, then moved Jal-Nish's identity to his list of enemies.

'Until he can find a way out of there, he won't be able to use the tears. And when he tries he'll get a nasty shock.' He laughed aloud. 'I wish I could see it.'

'There's something else you're going to wish you'd seen,' grinned Meriwen.

'Really?' said Flydd. 'What else did *you* get up to while I was indisposed?'

Her left hand was blistered. 'I found out how Jal-Nish broadcasts his terror messages.'

'And?'

'We did it together, each restraining the other so we never once thought about revenge – only justice, and protecting innocent people everywhere.'

'You're quite infuriating, you know. Just tell me what you did.'

'We broadcast that pathetic image of Jal-Nish, pale and flaking and withered below the waist, to the world. "It's no wonder Jal-Nish's wife abandoned him and his children despise him," we said. "He's no longer a man. He's a pathetic self-created monster and you need have no fear of him."'

A shiver passed through Flydd. 'He'll hunt you to the ends of the world for that.'

'With both his lieutenants dead,' said Meriwen, 'and the tears rejecting him, and a humiliation so deep that he won't dare show his face in public again, it's going to take him a long time to recover. We've done well, Xervish. Admit it!'

He smiled. 'I admit it freely. You've done exceedingly well, and I'll never forget it.'

Neither would Troist, had he still been alive. Despite the outcome, Flydd would have been a dead man for taking Troist's children into such a deadly situation.

They had failed, yet succeeded beyond his expectations. Even so, he wished he had managed to put Jal-Nish down. Had he been right to stop Liliwen killing him, or wrong? Where did childhood end and adulthood begin? Had she become an adult at twelve, when she'd killed that ruffian to save Nish's life? Or at fourteen, on learning that her parents were dead and she was the head of the family? Or beside Jal-Nish's bed when she decided that he had to die for the good of humanity?

Perhaps Flydd had been wrong to stop her. How could he know? Only the future would tell, if he lived to see it.

Oh well. We live, *and don't learn.*

This story details just one of Xervish Flydd's adventures in his long and desperate struggle with Jal-Nish. **The Song of the Tears** *quartet takes up the stories of Flydd, Nish, Yggur and others ten years later, when Jal-Nish has recovered and is the all-powerful, self-styled God-Emperor of Santhenar.*

There are some minor inconsistencies between this story and **The Song of the Tears,** *either due to Yggur's loss of memory or Shand's ongoing need to protect Liliwen and Meriwen.*

~

Chapter One of *The Summon Stone* follows.

CHAPTER ONE OF THE SUMMON STONE

'No!' the little girl sobbed. 'Look out! Run, *run!*'

Sulien!

Karan threw herself out of her bed, a high box of black-stained timber that occupied half the bedroom. She landed awkwardly and pain splintered through the left leg she had broken ten years ago. She clung to the side of the bed, trying not to cry out, then dragged a cloak around herself and careered through the dark to her daughter's room at the other end of the oval keep. Fear was an iron spike through her heart. What was the matter? Had someone broken in? What were they doing to her?

The wedge-shaped room, lit by a rectangle of moonlight coming through the narrow window, was empty apart from Sulien, who lay with her knees drawn up and her arms wrapped around them, rocking from side to side.

Her eyes were tightly closed, as if she could not bear to look, and she was moaning, 'No, no, *no!*'

Karan touched Sulien on the shoulder and her eyes sprang open. She threw her arms around Karan's waist, clinging desperately.

'Mummy, the evil man saw me. He *saw* me!'

Karan let out her breath. Just a nightmare, though a bad one. She put her hands around Sulien's head and, with a psychic wrench that she would pay for later, lifted the nightmare from her. But Sulien was safe; that was all that mattered. Karan's knees shook; she slumped on the bed. *It's all right!*

Sulien gave a little sigh and wriggled around under the covers. 'Thanks, Mummy.'

Karan kissed her on the forehead. 'Go to sleep now.'

'I can't; my mind's gone all squirmy. Can you tell me a story?'

'Why don't you tell me one, for a change?'

'All right.' Sulien thought for a moment. 'I'll tell you my favourite – the story of Karan and Llian, and the Mirror of Aachan.'

'I hope it has a happy ending,' said Karan, going along with her.

'You'll have to wait and see,' Sulien said, mock-sternly. 'This is how it begins.' She recited –

'*Once there were three worlds, Aachan, Tallallame and Santhenar, each with its own human species: Aachim, Faellem and us, old humans. Then, fleeing out of the terrible void between the worlds came a fourth people, the Charon, led by the mightiest hero in all the Histories, Rulke. The Charon were just a handful; they were desperate and on the edge of extinction, but Rulke saw a weakness in the Aachim and took Aachan from them ... and forever changed the balance between the Three Worlds.*'

'I'm sure I've heard that before, somewhere,' said Karan, smiling at the memories it raised.

'Of course you have, silly. All the Great Tales begin that way – it's the key to the Histories.' Sulien continued.

'*In ancient times the genius goldsmith, Shuthdar, a very wicked man, was paid by Rulke to make a gate-opening device in the form of a golden flute. Then Shuthdar stole the flute, opened a gate and fled to Santhenar ... but he broke open the Way between the Worlds, exposing the Three Worlds to the deadly void.*

'*This shocked Aachan, a strange world of sulphur-coloured snow, oily bogs and black, luminous flowers, to its core. Rulke raced after Shuthdar, taking with him a host of Aachim servants, including the mighty Tensor.*

'*The rain-drenched world of Tallallame was also threatened by the opening. The Faellem, a small, forest-dwelling people who were masters of illusion, sent a troop led by Faelamor to close the Way again. But they failed too.*

'*They all hunted Shuthdar across Santhenar as he fled through gate after gate, but finally he was driven into a trap. Unable to give the flute up, he destroyed it – and brought down the Forbidding that sealed the Three Worlds off from each other ... and trapped all his hunters here on Santhenar.*'

'Until ten years ago,' said Karan.

'When you and Daddy helped to reopen the Way between the Worlds ...'
Sulien frowned. 'How come Rulke was still alive after all that time?'

'The Aachim, Faellem and Charon aren't like us. They can live for thousands of
years.'

Sulien gave another little shiver, her eyelids fluttered, and she slept.

Karan pulled the covers up and stroked her daughter's hair, which was as wild
as her own, though a lighter shade of red. On the table next to the bed, moon-
beams touched a vase of yellow and brown bumblebee blossoms, and the half-
done wall-hanging of Sulien's floppy-eared puppy, Piffle.

Karan stroked Sulien's cheek and shed a tear, and sat there for a minute or two,
gazing at her nine-year-old daughter, her small miracle, the only child she could
ever have and the most perfect thing in her life.

She was limping back to bed when the import of Sulien's words struck her.
Mummy, the evil man saw me! What a disturbing thing to say. Should she wake
Llian? No, he had enough to worry about.

Karan's leg was really painful now. She went down the steep stairs of the old
keep in the dark, holding onto the rail and wincing, but the pain grew with every
step and so did her need for the one thing that could take it away – *hrux!*

She fought it. Hrux was for emergencies, for those times when the pain was
utterly unbearable. In the round chamber she called her thinking room, lit only by
five winking embers in the fireplace, she sat in a worn-out armchair, pulled the
cloak tightly around herself and closed her eyes.

What had Sulien meant by, *the evil man saw me*? And what had she seen?

Karan's gift for mancery, the Secret Art, had been blocked when she was a girl
but, being a *sensitive*, she still had some mind-powers. She knew how to replay the
nightmare, though she was reluctant to try; using her gift always came at a cost, the
headaches and nausea of *aftersickness*. But she had to know what Sulien had seen.
Very carefully, she lifted the lid on the beginning of the nightmare –

A pair of moons, one small and yellow spattered with black, the other huge and
jade green, lit a barren landscape. The green moon stood above a remarkable city,
unlike any place Karan had ever seen – a crisp white metropolis where the buildings were shaped like dishes, arches, globes and tall spikes, and enclosed in a
silvery dome. Where could it be? None of the Three Worlds had a green moon; the
city must be on some little planet in the void.

In the darkness outside the dome, silhouetted against it, a great army had gathered. Goose pimples crept down her arms. A lean, angular man wearing spiked
armour ran up a mound, raised his right fist and shook it at the city.

'Now!' he cried.

Crimson flames burst from the lower side of the dome and there came a cracking, a crashing, and a shrieking whistle. A long, ragged hole, the shape of a spiny caterpillar, had been blasted through the wall.

'Are – you – ready?' he roared.

'Yes,' yelled his captains.

It was too dark for Karan to see any faces, but there was a troubling familiarity about the way the soldiers stood and moved and spoke. What was it?

'Avenge our ancestors' betrayal!' bellowed the man in the spiked armour. 'Put every man, woman, child, dog and cat to the sword. Go!'

Karan's stomach churned. This seemed far too real to be a nightmare.

The troops stormed towards the hole in the dome, all except a cohort of eleven led by a round-faced woman whose yellow plaits were knotted into a loop on top of her head.

'Lord Gergrig?' she said timidly. 'I thought this attack was a dress rehearsal.'

'You need practice in killing,' he said chillingly.

'But the people of Cinnabar have done nothing to us.'

'Our betrayal was a stain on all humanity.' Gergrig's voice vibrated with pain and torment. 'All humanity must pay until the stain is gone.'

'Even so –'

'Soon we will face the greatest battle of all time, against the greatest foe – that's why we've practiced war for the past ten millennia.'

'Then why do we –?'

'To stay in practice, you fool! If fifteen thousand Merdrun can't clean out this small city, how can we hope to escape the awful void?' His voice ached with longing. 'How can we capture the jewel of worlds that is Santhenar?'

Karan clutched at her chest. This was no nightmare; it had to be a true *seeing*, but why had it come to Sulien? She was a gifted child, though Karan had never understood what Sulien's gift was. And who were the Merdrun? She had never heard the name before.

Abruptly, Gergrig swung around, staring. The left edge of his face, a series of hard angles, was outlined by light from a blazing tower. Like an echo, Karan heard Sulien's cry, 'Mummy, the evil man saw me. He *saw* me!'

Momentarily, Gergrig seemed afraid. He touched a green glass box, lights flickered inside it then his jaw hardened. 'Uzzey,' he said to the blonde warrior, 'we've been *seen*.'

'Who by?'

He bent his shaven head for a few seconds, peering into the glass box, then made a swirling movement with his left hand. 'A little red-haired girl. On Santhenar!'

Karan slid off the chair onto her knees, struggling to breathe. This was real; this bloodthirsty brute, whose troops *need practice in killing*, had seen her beautiful daughter. Ice crystallised all around her; there was no warmth left in the world. Her breath rushed in, in, in. She was going to scream. She fought to hold it back. Don't make a sound; don't do anything that could alert him.

'How can this be?' said Uzzey.

'I don't know,' said Gergrig. 'Where's the magiz?'

'Setting another blasting charge.'

'Fetch her. She's got to locate this girl, *urgently*.'

'What harm can a child do?'

'She can betray the invasion; she can reveal our plans and our numbers.'

Pain speared up Karan's left leg and it was getting worse. Black fog swirled in her head. She rocked forwards and back, her teeth chattering.

'Who would listen to a little kid?' said Uzzey.

'I can't take the risk,' said Gergrig. 'Run!'

Uzzey raced off, bounding high with each stride.

Karan's heart was thundering but her blood did not seem to be circulating; she felt faint, freezing, and so breathless that she was suffocating. She wanted to scoop Sulien up in her arms and run, but where could she go? How could Sulien *see* people on barren little Cinnabar, somewhere in the void, anyway? And how could Gergrig have seen her? Karan would not have thought it possible.

Shortly the magiz, who was tall and thin, with sparse white hair and colourless eyes bulging out of soot-black sockets, loped up. 'What's this about a girl *seeing* us?'

Gergrig explained, then said, 'I'm bringing the invasion forward. I'll have to wake the summon stone right away.'

'So soon? The cost in power will be ... extreme.'

'We'll have to pay it. The stone must be ready by *syzygy* – the night the triple moons line up – or we'll never be able to open the gate.'

The magiz licked her grey lips. 'To get more power, I'll need more deaths.'

'Then see to it!'

'Ah, to drink a life,' sighed the magiz. 'Especially the powerful lives of the gifted. This child's ending will be nectar.'

Gergrig took a step backwards. He looked repulsed.

Karan doubled over, gasping. In an flash of foreboding she saw three bloody bodies – Sulien, Llian and herself – flung like rubbish into a corner of her burning manor.

'What do you want me to do first?' said the magiz.

'Find the red-haired brat and put her down. And everyone in her household.'

A murderous fury overwhelmed Karan. No one threatened her daughter! *Whatever it took*, she would do it to protect her own.

The magiz, evidently untroubled by Gergrig's order, nodded. 'I'll look for the kid.'

Gergrig turned to Uzzey and her cohort, who were all staring at him. 'What are you waiting for? Get to the killing field!'

Ah, to drink a life! It was the end of Sulien's nightmare, and the beginning of Karan's.

～

Buy *The Summon Stone* in ebook or audiobook.

ABOUT THE AUTHOR

Ian Irvine, an Australian marine scientist, has also written 34 novels and an anthology of shorter stories. His novels include the Three Worlds fantasy sequence (**The View from the Mirror, The Well of Echoes** and **Song of the Tears**), which has been published in many countries and translations and has sold over sold over a million copies, a trilogy of eco-thrillers in a world of catastrophic climate change, **Human Rites,** now in its third edition, and 12 novels for younger readers.

BUY EBOOKS

BUY AUDIOBOOKS

OTHER BOOKS BY IAN IRVINE

OTHER EPIC FANTASY

THE TAINTED REALM TRILOGY

Vengeance

Rebellion

Justice

ECO-THRILLERS

THE HUMAN RITES TRILOGY

The Last Albatross

Terminator Gene

The Life Lottery

FOR YOUNGER READERS

THE RUNCIBLE JONES QUARTET

Runcible Jones, The Gate to Nowhere

Runcible Jones and The Buried City

Runcible Jones and the Frozen Compass

Runcible Jones and the Backwards Hourglass

THE GRIM AND GRIMMER QUARTET

The Headless Highwayman

The Grasping Goblin

The Desperate Dwarf

The Calamitous Queen

THE SORCERER'S TOWER QUARTET

Thorn Castle

Giant's Lair

Black Crypt

Wizardry Crag

ACKNOWLEDGMENTS

I would like to thank Simon Irvine for working so patiently with me on the cover. I would also like to thank all my Facebook fans who responded to my request for Three Worlds characters they would like to hear more about.